A Flock of Sparrows

Dec 19, 2017

With warmest wishes,

Helen L. Meyers

Enjoy *

God Bless, :)

Green

A Flock of Sparrows

A Novel

Helen Foster Reed

A FLOCK OF SPARROWS

ISBN: 978-1530851324

For more information, visit www.helenfosterreed.com

Cover Art: Stephen Marshall
Interior Layout: Vivian Freeman, *Yellow Rose Typesetting*

Printed in the United States of America by CreateSpace.

In loving memory of our husbands,

Robert Clinton Myers

Albert Wayne Foster

Dennis Michael Reed D.V.M.

Acknowledgments

WE HAVE BEEN blessed by a state of grace. This book is a journey that represents over one hundred years of marriage, and (none of your business) years of living. It has brought us to innumerable moments of insight and wisdom, and has rewarded us with countless friendships, along with being trusted with experiences of people who have walked the difficult road that we have walked. We respect—and within these pages—pay honor to you all.

In the most personal sense...

HELEN R. MYERS: After over fifty books, I've tried to keep up with my gratitude to those who have enriched my life and made my professional world so much easier to navigate. Since this unasked for fork in the road, I'd especially like to salute intrepid Leslie King for her diligent and resourceful handling of my online presence through the years. I treasure you and your friendship. And for being there 24/7 to dog sit, lend an ear, help me move, etc., since life turned upside down, special love to Dolores and "Dead Eye" James Dugger.

MADELEINE JUNE FOSTER: For four years, I have travelled a different and new road in life, navigating a journey I couldn't have managed without the support of my dear family and many friends. I can never name all of the ways you have helped me, but I pray that you grasp my sincere thanks and love. To my children and grandchildren—Kim and Bruce Gatlin, Jeff and Kristi Foster, Tucker, Caleb, Tyler, Madilynn, and Zachary—thank you all for the love and for holding my hand along this path that we've taken together.

MARY GAIL REED: I would like to thank my children: Robin and Steven Simmons, Laura and Clint Calvert, Keely and Bryan Sheets, and Michael and Meredith Reed. And I cannot forgo citing my sweet grandchildren: Blakeley and Brooks Briscoe, Sarah Grace Simmons, Evagail, Morris, and Reed Calvert, Thomas, Brylan, and Keegan Sheets, and Emmersyn and Easton Reed. You have not only been my ballast, you have been beyond encouraging. Know that you fill my heart with joy and laughter. I love you all so much.

A Flock of Sparrows

"Therefore I tell you, do not worry about your life, what you will eat or drink, or about your body, what you will wear. Is not life more than food, and the body, more than clothes? Look at the birds of the air; they do not sow or reap or store away in barns, and yet your heavenly Father feeds them. Are you not much more valuable than they?"

—Matthew 6:25-26

One

ONE INVALUABLE lesson I've learned in the last seven years is that things don't always fall perfectly into place, no matter how hard you work or will it. Life has its ebbs and flows just like the powerful ocean's tide, and come a riptide, the flow has a way of sweeping us off balance. It certainly did me. After thirty-six years of marriage, at the very moment I thought my feet had become buried deep enough into the sandy depths of stability to weather almost anything, my husband Charlie died.

I still remember the instant I found his lifeless body. I collapsed from the shock and abruptness of it, as if our land had incomprehensively turned into an ocean, and I had been sucked deep under water like bait grabbed by a single-minded predator starved to feed. I imagined that's what drowning must feel like, that inability to breathe, the sensation that my lungs were filling with water. Instincts and panic quickly took over; and, after using my cell phone to call 9-1-1, I went to work trying to save him. My eyes, my fifty-four-year-old mind that had absorbed years of experience, knew he was gone; yet my heart, suddenly flooded with almost teenage-like, unconditional love, wouldn't accept reality. That's the memory that continues to haunt me. I still miss him so. I'm missing him even more now at sixty-one, as the storm of the century is surging into Texas, bringing God only knew what trouble and danger with it.

It is strange, though, that I'm thinking as if I were a New Englander, a person of the sea. In my youth, I was a romantic and dreamer, an arm-chair adventurer thanks to voracious reading. I also fell in love with the dramatic art of the Wyeths, especially N.C.'s action-driven book illustrations, to the point that sometimes I yearn for the ocean. I guess my mother was right; she'd told me more than once when you're born under an astrological water sign—in our case, Cancer—you instinctively react and relate with metaphors about water, even if you're a native of land-locked Northeast Texas.

Full disclosure: We are barely five-hundred feet above sea level here, and the region is richly saturated with rivers, creeks, springs, ponds, and lakes, making this a perfect place to at least benefit from some of nature's subtler liquid vibrations. Interestingly, Mother and I came into this world with earth moons in our birth charts, therefore, we're also prone to love home and stability—and we married men born into the farming and ranching life, as we had been, which cinched the deal. We were and are East Texans for life.

Oddly enough, as much as I'm intrigued by such trivia, I almost never read my horoscope. However, like all of the old timers who have farmed land or raised livestock, I pay attention to lunar and planetary cycles, and know when it's a good time to plant, to dehorn animals, mate stock for the easiest birthing, and the rest. On this late November morning, the TV meteorologist's report served as confirmation a storm is coming and it is going to be bad. My favorite online website confirmed several of the planets are in water and air signs, indicating the atmosphere contained way too much liquid energy, and it was going to be propelled by a stronger wind than usual.

So far the breeze was from the west, light and mild, although I could tell that a shift was at hand. Soon there would be dramatic changes. Before noon a howling wind from the north would send temperatures plummeting over thirty degrees. Wind-driven snow, and perhaps ice, would be blasting through the trees, especially our more fragile pines, with the force of a hurricane making landfall. No one would go unscathed. As a widow still fending for herself on this big property, I had work to do.

When the phone rang, I had a gut hunch as to who the caller was even before the first jingle ended. Maggie Lamar and I had been friends for nearly six decades and seldom a morning went by that we didn't talk. Our agenda would be single-minded today.

Without wasting time on any greeting, she began, "Retta, have you seen the latest weather report on TV?"

"You know there's nothing else on our local channels. Do you have your bag packed?" I asked. "Considering how the power goes out on your side of town during the mildest thunderstorm, you'll be better off here."

My place was less than ten miles outside of the city limits of Martin's Mill, but I wasn't fully reliant on electricity the way the townspeople were. While the house was lit and warmed by electricity, the cook stove and hot-water heater used propane gas; plus, we had a lovely large fireplace designed in the old-fashioned way to cook a pot of beans or stew like the early pioneers would do it. There was also another fireplace upstairs in the master bedroom.

"I'm a step ahead of you. That's why I also invited Sybil," Maggie replied. "Since she lives only two streets over from me, she's bound to lose power, too. I knew you wouldn't mind."

"Of course not," I told her, glad she'd already thought of that. After changes in their lives, they'd moved into such a nice, new development; however, the city hadn't yet done the major upgrades in utilities to support the growing residential area. "The more the merrier. We'll have such a good time, we'll put adult slumber parties on everyone's bucket list."

After a slight pause, Maggie said, "Well, you might not say that when I tell you the rest."

My mind went on full alert, and my insides did an unnatural something that left me feeling queasy—an all-too-familiar reaction whenever Maggie allowed any pause in a conversation. I just knew she was about to drop a bombshell.

"Oh, Maggie, what have you done now?"

"Dana Bennett and Carly Kirkland are coming, too," she blurted out.

"You can't be serious?" My abrupt reaction had me instantly cringing. "Well, Dana, of course. The poor thing is nearly eight months pregnant. But *Carly?* You can't stand her."

"Things just sort of...evolved." Maggie sounded part apologetic and part disgusted. "With all of us being in the same neighborhood now, there's no way Sybil would leave Dana behind. If you ask me, she's still dealing with empty-nest syndrome—like she doesn't get her fill of kids at school. Problem is, in the last few months our sweet mother-to-be has befriended that blond alley cat, and Dana said she's not coming unless we invite Carly, as well. Thank goodness Dana agreed to extend the offer herself. I would have needed a shot of tequila to pull off sounding believable if I'd been forced to call Carly at eight o'clock in the morning."

Although I wasn't the least bit thrilled with this development, and had no time to figure out how it was supposed to work, I took a deep breath and said as agreeably as I could, "Then we'll have to make the best of it for Dana's sake. The question is, can *you* play nice for the duration of this storm?"

Between widowhood and aging, I was becoming too frank for my own good. On the other hand, Maggie had a lethal ability to turn simple conversation into a martial art. Under those circumstances, I would be concerned for the welfare of any guest under my roof, whether I'd intended to invite them or not.

"Why, Loretta Brown Cole—you know perfectly well that I can be the Southern version of Miss Manners if the situation seriously calls for it."

Even though she managed to sound convincingly wounded, I let my silence speak for itself.

"Whatever. We'll be there in a couple of hours."

I was still shaking my head when I replaced the receiver onto the phone's cradle. The five of us would make an unlikely group. Granted, we were all widows, part of that grimly singular club no one wants to join; however, we were from vastly divergent backgrounds, and our ages were equally different, ranging from the enviable thirties to the sixty-somethings. Maggie and I fall into that latter, depressing category. I don't care what aging actresses claim in magazine interviews, as publishers insist on air-brushed photos to suggest sixty is the new forty. And forget that fine-wine metaphor about how we're getting better every day. I say we're more like a couple of mature grapes that are moments away from withering on the vine.

Yes, we go back a long way, and she still refers to me by my maiden name, especially when making a pointed remark. I suspect Brown suits my appearance and personality at times. I'm simply not the peacock she is. While my dark-blond hair hasn't thinned, as it has for some my age, I do well to remember to use mascara and lipstick, if I'm expecting company or going somewhere. Then again, maybe Maggie is the one with the problem. She's been married so many times, she's finally admitting to occasionally having trouble remembering her latest surname. It could be my maiden name acts as some kind of psychological tether to keep connected to her inner core.

Maggie had been my matron of honor when I married Charlie. My given name is Loretta, but Charlie started calling me Retta in kindergarten. It was years before he shared that he'd done that because of a chipped upper tooth that cut his tongue whenever he tried to say my full name. Charlie was a character, and the hardest working man, but about as romantic as Valentine's candy on February 15. And so, repetition being the source of as many burdens as benefits, the nickname stuck, and that's how most who know me address me to this day.

Charlie and I had a good life here where we raised a son and daughter, along with several thousand beef cattle, and ten times that in hay bales. Hay and a few head of cattle are what I mostly limit myself to these days, since the kids are grown and have moved away to raise their families, and pursue careers and interests of their own.

Anyone involved with farming or ranching understands it's not an eight, or even ten hour-a-day job. We are the people who arrive late to weddings because of a calf's breech birth, and miss funerals for some other animal infirmity. Charlie and I had been looking forward to downsizing for a second time, and maybe taking a trip or two. Having never ventured more than a few hundred miles from Martin's Mill, I had always dreamed of going to Cape Cod. But before we could set our plans in motion, he died in a horrible accident.

He'd been hauling large, round bales of hay up an incline in a draw, when the tractor suddenly rolled over, killing him instantly. I don't know what possessed him to attempt the shortcut—he knew better than to gamble with an unwieldy load even on flat land. It triggered countless sleepless nights as I struggled with the *"why?"* of his abrupt loss, as so many had before me. What I've ultimately come to understand is how, in questioning the command in "Selah" we surrender to a demonic mockery of "amen."

Maggie had been great to lend emotional support, having been through sudden loss more than once. It was only last year when I found myself reciprocating again when her fourth husband, Hollis Lamar, died after an unusually short battle with prostate cancer. But then Hollis had been as stubborn about going to the doctor as Maggie was proactive. His death hit her hard, since their sixteen-year marriage had been her longest and happiest relationship.

At fifty, Sybil Sides is a little farther behind us in age. Three years ago, she and Elvin had just celebrated their thirtieth wedding anniversary when he passed from complications associated with emphysema. Charlie had met Elvin years ago following recommendations that Elvin was something of a shaman with anything mechanical. Upon learning that, Charlie had used his services routinely when finding himself out of his depth for one repair or another. I met Sybil one Sunday afternoon when Elvin brought her along, responding to Charlie's phone call for an emergency. While the men wrestled with the broken piece of equipment, Sybil and I got acquainted over one of our great, mutual loves—cooking—and we've been friends ever since.

The saddest story of all is that of forty-year-old Dana Bennett, who had replaced me as the pianist at our Methodist church. Her husband, Jesse, had committed suicide seven months ago upon learning the bank was about to foreclose on their restaurant. There were other complications—Jesse had been a veteran—but most important was that Dana had discovered she was pregnant only hours before his death. She'd been waiting to share the news until evening when they would be alone.

As for Carly Kirkland, I was fast concluding that her presence might well prove more threatening than the storm. At thirty-two, she was the youngest and most recent widow among us. Her husband, Walter, had died only three months ago. Walter and his first wife, Doris, had been lifelong friends with the Lamars and us. Doris was killed in a car accident early last year, which left Walter inconsolable. Or so we thought. What a shock we all experienced when, a mere six months later, he announced that he had married a woman more than thirty years his junior! There was another lesson in how life was nothing if not a graduate course in trying to make sense out of the inconceivable.

Walter had been the poster boy for logic, conservatism, and gravitas. Once a teller at First State Bank of Martin's Mill, he'd worked his way up to becoming president by learning the business inside and out, and eventually being invited to buy bank stock along the way. Having managed the rest of his money equally well, by the time of his death, he'd amassed what Webster might define as "honest wealth." That only added to the frenzy of small-town gossip that went as viral as any YouTube sensation—especially when it was discovered that he had died of a heart attack in bed with his youthful bride.

Maggie bore a particular disdain for "the little gold digger," despite her own somewhat blemished past. While she had suffered in relationships with men who proved dishonest with her, it could also be argued that Maggie had done some social climbing, and deserved what she got. How she and Carly—never mind the five of us—were going to survive this storm under one roof without causing our own environmental calamity was now my problem. Hardly what I'd envisioned when I first extended my invitation.

Accepting that I had much more prepping to do, I headed upstairs. Deep in thought, the ringing phone startled me. Backtracking to the table at the base of the stairs I reached for the remote. "Did you forget something else?"

"Retta?"

Not taking the time to check Caller ID, I thought Maggie wanted to say something more. Upon recognizing the attractive male voice, I smiled with delight.

"Sam! For a second, I thought you were Maggie again. How are you? Is it snowing there yet?" Although Sam Archer had been coming to Martin's Mill for almost a year now, he lived and conducted his business in Fort Worth.

"It's a photographer's dream, but the road conditions are deteriorating fast. I don't believe it's wise even at this stage to risk making the two-hour trip to East Texas. Will you be okay?"

"Not to worry," I said, relieved with his decision. Having lost Charlie the way I did, I wasn't up for another exercise in reckless bravado by someone I cared about. "It hasn't started to come down here yet, but as it turns out, I'll have a full house. Maggie is coming, and bringing a few others."

"Really? So why don't you sound as upbeat as you usually do when you two are about to visit?"

"One of my guests got invited in a round-about way. Carly. Sweet Walter's widow," I added after he failed to respond.

"Ah, now I remember. Are you girls ever going to give her a break?"

While I could hear the amusement in his voice, I couldn't deny it irked that his impulse was to defend Carly, not Maggie. Regardless of my own reservations about Maggie's ability to behave, women's logic allowed me to defend my friend—in as much as I could.

"Excuse me, you never met him, and I've known him longer than Carly's been on the planet." In fact, while Sam didn't need to know this, there were those who wagered that Walter would ask *me* out, although I was relieved that he never did. "All I'm saying is if the storm keeps us shut in for very long, tempers are bound to get hotter than last summer's prairie fires." Sam had become such a close friend that I'd shared most of the back story about who was who and what was what, in Martin's Mill—not that I expected him to remember all of it. But right now I needed a slight reassurance that he recalled at least fifty-percent.

With a sigh, he replied, "Then I don't envy you the predicament."

"Any words of wisdom?"

"Oh, I'm sure you don't want to hear it, but try to remember that Carly slept with the man. Maggie didn't, and neither did you."

"Sam!"

"You'll make the best of it, Retta. You always do."

Although I appreciated that he saw me as honest and resilient, I found myself wishing he was a bit more protective if not sympathetic. Another surprise, considering the push-pull of my feelings for him. Was my subconscious finally yielding to pull?

"We all have our limits," I said, doing my best not to grumble. Not sure I succeeded, I cleared my throat. "What are you going to do? I hope you'll play it safe and not even attempt to get to the gallery?"

Sam was also known as the artist Gray Archer and his home was close to KD Gallery located in the historic Stockyards District of Cowtown where most of his paintings were sold. Nevertheless, traveling even a few miles could be treacherous in icy conditions.

"I came downtown before this all started, but I've been able to book a room at the Stockyards Hotel, just across the street. They have a backup generator in case the area loses power. That said, I just can't believe my bad luck."

"You're calling a four-star hotel with room service 'bad luck?'"

"Not that. Missing the opportunity to be the one snowed in with you is the problem."

The caressing tone in his voice sent a lovely tingle through me, something I hadn't felt in so long, I hugged myself with my free arm to hold onto the sensation for as long as possible. "It is nice to be wanted."

"Would you mind saying that to my face when I finally make it over there again? I'd be more than grateful to prove it."

This was the most direct he'd been since he'd tried to do more than kiss me on the cheek. Unfortunately, his timing couldn't be worse. "Stop flirting with me, Archer. I have guests to prepare for."

"At least tell me that you'll be thinking of me once in a while?"

"You know I will," I said softly, then added a quick, "See you soon," and hung up before I had second thoughts over my divulgence. Things were building between us; however, this was not the time to dwell on whether or not I was ready for what he wanted.

As I went through the house, my thoughts stayed on the first time I met Sam. Since Charlie's death I had been managing the place by myself, and that often meant tedious repairs. I'd been struggling with replacing worn-out fence wire along the oil-top road when a red, vintage Dodge pickup pulled up beside me. Sam had since put it into storage, because it tended to get him far more attention than he wanted. These days he drove a much newer black Club Cab Dodge, which allowed him to blend in quite well with the locals.

On that morning, his tan-colored Stetson was also well-worn like a cattleman's, as was his denim shirt and jeans. I could tell from beneath the brim of his hat that his mustache and sideburns had once been a rich, dark brown, but everything was turning gray. He was tanned, which told me he spent a good deal of time outdoors. But his skin wasn't leathery, and he only had smile wrinkles around his eyes and firm mouth. If I'd never seen him again, I wouldn't have forgotten his eyes, how they could switch from being soul-searching to evoking mischief before you could blink. So mesmerized was I that it would be two visits before I would remember their color: a shade of rich mahogany, speckled with shards of flint.

Left feeling self-conscious in the presence of someone who seemed so comfortable in his own skin, I let him speak first.

"Mornin'," he'd said. "I'm Sam Archer. I'm staying at the Carter House Bed-and-Breakfast and I'm a painter. The owner there said that I should come see you."

"Because?"

In seconds, I'd mentally slam dunked owner-proprietor Lillian Carter into an imagined sludge pond. We were members of the same church and talked enough that she *had* to have known I would hire someone local if I'd needed a handyman, not some stranger, even if it appeared that he needed the work. Agitation made me even hotter, and I began fanning myself with my straw western hat, despite knowing it made me look even less attractive, what with my damp shoulder-length hair plastered to my head and neck.

"Because," Sam replied, as if he'd had all the time in the world, "she was impressively eloquent about how this is where I would find what I was looking for."

"Well, I'm sorry she wasted your time," I'd said, growing more impatient by the second. Forced to squint, which had to be doing wonders for the crepey skin around my blue eyes, I quickly replaced my hat knowing that without it I looked as worn as his old pickup truck. I hadn't even taken the time to put my hair in a ponytail that morning, let alone a braid. "As you can see, I do my own upkeep around here, and I've already completed my painting chores for the year."

To my amazement, he'd thrown back his head and laughed heartily. As vibrant as the sound had been, I immediately bristled, convinced that I was dealing with yet another man seeing me as a helpless woman. As the saying goes, Charlie had been hardly cold in the ground when several in town had approached me about buying or leasing our property, some even going so far as to ask, "What use will you have for it now that he's gone?" Incredible. They'd all seemed to have experienced some collective memory lapse forgetting that I'd been born on this land, and had worked alongside my father, and then with my husband our entire married life. What's more, I was as capable as most men when it came to maintenance and basic repairs.

Just as I'd opened my mouth to give this intruder a piece of my mind, he held up his hand in that universal gesture of requesting patience. I found some by reaching for the near-empty thermos at my feet. I hoped it had enough cool water left in it so when he did let me speak, my voice didn't sound like a crow's. I had read that in Europe they used to refer to an annoyed woman as, "Sounding like a fish wife."

"I'm not that kind of painter," Sam offered almost gently. "Although I'm not against such labor when it's needed back at my own place."

It was a miracle that I didn't choke on that last swallow of water. And, while it was still cool, my face burned with embarrassment. That must have showed even with my wide-brim straw hat casting my face in shadow because he abruptly leaned across the seat and extended his hand. From my vast readings, I knew he'd just committed a social error in that I clearly remembered by Emily Post standards, it was for a woman to decide whether to shake a man's hand or not. But I so wanted this moment over, I tore off my leather glove and reciprocated with my firm, if clammy, grasp.

"How about we start over?" he'd continued, his gaze searching. "I'm Sam and I was looking forward to meeting you, and seeing this beautiful countryside I'd heard so much about."

He was all easygoing charm and reassurance, and by evening we were sharing a bottle of cabernet on my recently repainted porch. Sam proved to be one of the most fascinating men I'd ever met. Soon, he even convinced me to rent him the guesthouse attached to the stables to use when he was in the area. He sweetened the temptation by giving me one of his first landscape paintings of my property. We kept our agreement as quiet as possible knowing what a surge of gossip would have spawned around town—something I didn't need any more than he wanted the celebrity ogling. It wasn't like me to consent to such an arrangement with someone I barely knew, but I am a person who trusts her instincts and believes she reads people fairly well, and those attributes told me it would be okay. My decision was soon supported by facts after I checked him out a bit.

A web search confirmed that Sam was far more than a painter. Yes, he was a renowned western artist whose work commanded incredible prices, but first he'd been a respected surgeon—a pediatric cardiologist. Not only that, he was equally famous for his philanthropy, including being responsible for a new wing at Cook Children's Hospital in Fort Worth, which I later learned is where he'd done most of his surgeries. That alone left me speechless and humbled for days afterward.

Fast forward from last spring, now we were rushing into an extra early winter given it wasn't even Thanksgiving yet. Sam had not only become a good and dear friend; he was fast becoming an important part of my life. I knew he would leave a huge emptiness if he stopped coming to East Texas. But he wanted more, so much more that I was growing overly warm again just thinking about our last conversation.

"Get out of my head for now," I pleaded, as I hurried to the main floor bathroom to be sure there were enough towels and toiletries for my guests. Otherwise, I knew when Maggie arrived, she would take one look at me and jump to the conclusion Sam and I had indulged in more than a little verbal flirtation.

When I was through with inside preparations, I pulled on my jacket to go to the stable. I'd already put extra hay out for the cattle, but my four horses needed to be fed and watered. Next I brought more dry wood inside, carrying some upstairs to the fireplace in the master bedroom. I'd almost returned to the bottom of the stairs when I heard the front door open.

"Yoo-hoo...Retta?" Maggie's first-soprano voice echoed throughout the house. "We're *here*."

"Perfect timing...now that the chores are all done," I sang back at her. Maggie would know I was teasing, just as she knew not to bother with knocking or ringing the doorbell before entering.

"Oh, thank goodness." Maggie pursed her lips to send a kiss my way as she limped toward the kitchen bearing what looked and sounded like quite the liquor supply. "This system has my bunions killing me. I can't wait to get out of these gorgeous but hideously tight boots."

There was only a few months difference in our ages; however, we were polar opposites when it came to fashion and style. Her hair—currently in a short, chic do—changed length and color more often than the seasons, and some of her clothing choices left me wondering if she sometimes dressed in the dark? Nevertheless, there was no denying Maggie still had whatever "it" was and, even at her age, managed to look sexy. Today, she was wearing a pair of snug-fitting jeans and some sort of orange sherbet-colored, shaggy-haired jacket over a navy blue wool tunic.

I raised my eyebrows at the jacket. "What had to die so you could wear that thing?"

"Nothing, smarty," she said over her shoulder. "Highland sheep are sheared."

"Sheep, huh? I would have put money on it being musk ox."

"Witch."

Fighting back a grin, I called after her, "I had no idea they came in that color!"

Behind her came Dana, her warm smile diluted by the sadness in her brown eyes. She was a pretty, petite woman, with dark hair cut gamin-short that framed an oval, photogenic face with an enviable complexion. Her pregnant belly protruded far beyond a well-worn suede jacket that perfectly matched her hair.

"Thank you, Retta. It's so good of you to let us come stay with you."

The way she carefully leaned over to set her canvas tote by the entryway table gave me concern. "None of us need to be alone during a storm, particularly one promising such unpredictable conditions. How are you feeling, dear? It looks like your back is giving you all kinds of trouble."

"Then I'm perfect for a woman who's six weeks away from delivery. The doctor claims we're both doing fine, although last week one of his repeat patients told me in the reception area that he doesn't always wait until closing time to start mixing martinis, so I'm not sure how much faith to put in his vision, let alone his medical prowess."

I hugged her gently. "Well, if it's any reassurance, you look as lovely as ever."

Carly entered with some hesitation. Her long hair resembled strands of golden wheat and appeared as naturally straight. Her hot-pink cashmere turtleneck sweater and skinny jeans perfectly accentuated a Hollywood starlet's figure. A black leather jacket with matching knee-high boots, and Chanel handbag with the iconic overlapping C emblem on the front completed the ensemble. Her outfit probably cost more than all of my living room furniture; however, I stopped speculating when I saw the white little dog she had tucked against her. It had to be a toy something or other, since it wasn't much bigger than the palm of her hand. I struggled to repress a wince as I thought of my cow dog, Rosie, who, since Charlie's death had been my only housemate. Even though she's been good to never actually kill one, Rosie's favorite pastime tends to be chasing after rabbits and squirrels. That had me hoping she wouldn't mistake the little fur ball for a cottontail.

"Carly," I said, with a more formal smile. "Welcome."

"Thank you for inviting me, Mrs. Cole," she said in a soft and melodious Marilyn Monroe-type voice. "Your house is beautiful and I loved driving up that tree-lined driveway."

"Thank you. But you'll have to call me Retta like everyone else. It's only fair given that we'll be sharing somewhat close quarters and all."

She looked at me as though I'd spoken to her in a foreign tongue, which left me wondering if she thought I meant for us to share the convertible couch? Barely able to suppress my sigh of exasperation at Maggie for getting us into this mess, I waved Carly in, eager to receive my last guest. Seeing the load that she carried, I quickly reached out to help.

"Sybil, good heavens! Are you planning to cook a church supper while you're here?"

Allowing me to only take the handled sack tilting dangerously, she continued to the kitchen bearing the other grocery bags. "Hardly, but I do intend to put some weight on you skinny white girls."

Back in the 1960s, Sybil Sides' mother had been one of the few blacks allowed inside the country club at Martin's Mill, and that was because she worked in the kitchen. Miss Imogene had been admired for many of her dishes, especially her delicious cornbread muffins. Sybil inherited her mother's culinary skills, as well as her recipes, and continued to love any opportunity to cook—especially in my sunny and welcoming cream-on-cream kitchen.

"Girl, I don't need any help packing on the pounds, but I sure won't refuse anything you prepare," I assured her.

"How about red beans and ham hocks with a side of cornbread for supper?" Sybil asked, immediately starting to unpack her bounty. "That new market out by the highway had some pretty strawberries shipped in fresh from the Rio Grande Valley. Since the berries are out of season, the price was as high as the fur on a wary feral cat's back, but look. Didn't they make a tempting pie?" She smiled proudly as she opened the lid on the plastic case.

I couldn't keep from groaning. "Sybil, that smells divine, but all I can see is three pounds heading for each of my thighs."

Grinning, Sybil added, "I also soaked the beans overnight because I'd planned to make them anyway, so it won't take them long to cook. If you'll let me use one of your big pots, I'll get them started. They'll be ready to eat in a couple of hours."

"The pots are right in this cabinet," I said, pointing to the island. "Use anything you need. As usual, *mi casa, su casa,* oh, talented one. Help yourself. Only I'd feel like a better hostess if you'd get out of your jacket first."

Laughing at her own eagerness, Sybil did unbutton her eggplant-purple, quilted jacket, leaving her in a comfy charcoal gray sweat suit. A pretty lavender knit scarf dressed it up, but I held my hand out for it and the coat.

"Give it here and I'll hang it up in the coat closet next to my office. Ladies, whenever you've warmed up and are ready, please feel free to do the same. There are plenty of hangers."

No one followed me, and I returned to find them praising my kitchen. One thing I'd insisted on when Charlie and I got around to our final renovating of this old farmhouse was vastly improving the place where I spent so much time. Back then I'd daydreamed of big family dinners, once the kids were grown and had their own children—or at least grand holidays with a house full of people. But my offspring had ideas of their own, which has taken Jamie, Mallory and daughter, Kimberly, to Houston, while Rachel, Paul and their children are in Virginia. The last time the house had this many people in it was for the reception that followed Charlie's funeral.

"Just looking at this abundance is making my stomach growl," Maggie said. She had put her jacket over the back of one of the bar stools, and had started to help Sybil unpack.

Carly ventured as far as the kitchen doorway and asked hesitantly, "Would you mind cooking a small portion of the beans without any meat?"

Most of us in the South had been taught to cook by our mothers, which meant we fried virtually everything in lard—unless it was smoked or barbecued. In time, we learned to make some healthier adjustments; however, the mere idea of not making beans with ham hocks had us all going still and staring at Carly in disbelief. Mercy, what next? Banana pudding without vanilla wafers?

It was Maggie who opened her mouth to challenge her, but Carly beat her to it, continuing with a slight shrug, "I'm a vegetarian."

One of those death-knell silences followed. The last time any of us had heard of a vegetarian in these parts had to be in our school history books. Deprivation had been a forced issue during the Civil War—after the Yankees ransacked every farm in their path, confiscating any and all livestock for their troops. The idea of a woman born and raised here being a willing vegetarian was...well, it just wasn't southern!

Two

SYBIL WAS the first to recover from Carly's unexpected comment. "Why, sure, hon."

She'd undoubtedly noticed Maggie's disapproving expression, as well as my own shock, and immediately reached for a smaller pot. Visually measuring a cupful of the plump beans, she said, "Carly, you and Dana don't know this about me, since neither of you were around then, but before I got my teaching degree, I worked in the cafeteria at Martin's Mill Elementary. Just like these girls remember it from their school days, everyone ate the same thing, or else they brought their lunches from home. Nowadays, things are way more complicated. So many people have food allergies. Even in the classroom we have to be very careful about making sure there's no cross contamination. Last year, a student in my second-grade class was extremely allergic to peanuts. That sweet little boy broke out even if he touched a crayon another child had been using, one who had eaten a peanut butter cookie. So believe me," she said, rinsing the beans then filling the pot with fresh water, "this is a small request and no problem at all."

Right then and there, I decided the S in Sybil also stood for *saint*. I was the hostess for pity's sake, and I hadn't recovered from my surprise fast enough to put my guest's comfort first. I'd focused only on the bizarreness of her request—and, okay, what I'd perceived as her rudeness. It was easy to see Carly's relief at Sybil's kindness. For a moment her remote, cool expression warmed under Sybil's caring nature.

"I can't imagine having to deal with such a condition," Carly replied, looking overwhelmed. "My decision not to eat meat has nothing to do with an allergy. It's more about a path toward a healthier lifestyle. Mostly, though, I simply don't like the idea of killing something so I can eat it."

Maggie uttered a skeptical grunt as she removed the cork from one of the bottles of wine she'd unpacked. "I gather those fine sensibilities don't extend to the poor critters that became your designer boots and handbag?"

"They're all street vendor imitations, but I'm flattered you think they look like the real thing." Carly's expression turned cool again as she met Maggie's sharp scrutiny. "So is the jacket. Excuse me. I believe the socially preferred term is faux."

What we needed at that moment was a bolt of lightning to rescue me from what I could foresee as the invitation I wish I'd never extended. But knowing I couldn't even hope for a three-foot icicle to impale me—since it hadn't even begun to snow yet—I stumbled out of my own tongue-tied state and said too enthusiastically, "Oh, what a good idea, Maggie, you know where the glasses are. Who else wants wine? Dana, I have water from our own well, which is wonderful, tea..."

"Pour me a glass of that potion." Sybil grinned at Maggie. "I want to feel like those chefs on those TV cooking shows that always have a glass of something on their work stations."

"It's Merlot," Maggie said. "If you prefer something else, there's Chardonnay, Cabernet, Pinot Grigio, Pinot Noir..."

"I'd love a glass, too," Carly told Maggie. "Thank you."

"I don't care what the wine snobs say, I like Merlot," Sybil replied. "Bring it on."

Although Maggie's raised eyebrows suggested what she thought of finding herself in the position of having to serve the leggy beauty, she efficiently collected enough glasses for us. I didn't know whether to kiss her for resisting the impulse to make some smart remark, or pinch her *Spanx*-covered butt for not hiding that she'd been tempted.

She poured the velvety-red wine into the first glass. Giving Carly a lethal smile, she all but purred, "No problem with grapes, I take it?"

Although it looked as though every drop of blood drained from her face, Carly managed a calm, "None whatsoever."

Patting Carly's back, Dana shifted sideways to ease her protruding belly past her. She gazed around the French-country cabinets with the top-tier glass doors, and the stainless-steel appliances with nothing short of awe and envy. "I'll take some water, Retta, thanks. I'm so envious of you having a well. You know how our city water reeks of chemicals. I keep a purifier in the bathroom, too, just to avoid having to brush my teeth with the awful stuff. Oh, my…this kitchen! It's exactly what I'd always dreamed of having. And everything is arranged so well. Where were you when we were trying to set up the restaurant kitchen?"

Before I could reply, my three-year-old Australian shepherd, Rosie, was at the back door giving me a soft, "Woof," to announce she had finished her business, or had her fill of exploring, and was ready to investigate what was happening inside. Rosie was as good a watchdog as she was company, and knew Maggie's platinum-silver Mercedes well. She hadn't been threatened by the vehicle's arrival. However, now we would find out how she would react to Carly's little fur ball.

"Carly, is your puppy intimidated by larger dogs?" I asked, hoping my tone exuded concern, not negativity. "Rosie is amiable, but I haven't had any other dogs inside to test her territorial instincts."

Carly's expression turned doubtful, and she gave Dana a see-I-told-you-I-shouldn't-be-here look. "I honestly don't know. But Wrigley likes me to hold him most of the time, so maybe that won't be a problem."

"Well, we can't leave sweet Rosie out in the cold, so we might as well put this to a test," Maggie said, abandoning the wine pouring to let my brown-and-black sweetie inside. "Hello, darling girl! Have you been telling the squirrels to leave your mommy's pecans alone? Missed me? Come see what we have for you to play with."

To be fair, Maggie enjoyed Rosie's company almost as much as I did, but she was laying on the saccharin-sweet tone a little thick. And I'm sure I wasn't the only one to catch the underlying dark humor when she made that last comment.

"Mags," I drawled, injecting only a hint of warning into my voice. "Do you need me to make you sit through back episodes of *Dog Whisperer* so you remember how to deal with canines unfamiliar with each other?"

My lifelong friend straightened from giving Rosie a two-handed rubbing to scoff, "Oh, where's your sense of humor?"

"I've always wanted a dog." Dana's confession matched her expression—sheer wistfulness. "What with Jesse having been at the restaurant at all hours, it would have been nice to have the company at night, but then he was concerned about an animal in the house and transferring dog hair to the restaurant."

Seeing Rosie had already noticed Wrigley and was venturing closer, I said in a conversational tone to Carly, "Just ignore her and act normal. What breed is he? I don't think I've ever seen one with a face so small yet framed by so much hair. Don't take this the wrong way, but he looks like a Christmas ornament."

"Or, a dashboard one," Maggie piped in.

Ignoring her, Carly directed her words to Sybil and me. "Wrigley is a Maltese. Walter got him for me last Christmas. Knowing we would never have a child together, I guess he thought Wrigley was as close as we could get. We spoiled him terribly."

In the next instant, the tiny dog leaped from her protective embrace and bounced toward Rosie, barking as though someone had flipped a switch on a battery-operated toy.

With the hair on the back of her neck bristling, and her tail rising high in alpha, pack-leader position, Rosie stood her ground with the yappy intruder. Her stare and body language said it all: *"My house. So you can just take your mouthy self elsewhere."*

Something must have reached through Wrigley's nerve-grating rant. Before our eyes, the Maltese suddenly went mute, did an impressive about face, and launched himself back toward his mistress. Carly bent to catch him just in time to save him from a belly flop on the hardwood floor.

Returning to fill the wine glasses Maggie noted, "Well, we know who won that territorial battle."

I couldn't have been more disappointed and embarrassed with Maggie's latest dig at Carly if she'd tried to high five Rosie. "No such thing, Mags. I thought Rosie handled that with her usual restraint. She's had to deal with far worse conduct from our cattle."

"I'm sorry, Retta," Carly offered quickly. "I'll do my best to keep him in control from now on."

I gave Rosie the hand signal to lie down beside me, before assuring Carly that I was comfortable with how things had turned out. "Given some time, they'll probably become friends."

Carly looked pleased and about to say something when a bright flash of light, followed almost instantly by a loud crack of thunder, had us all tucking into ourselves like turtles. The meteorological surprise was quickly followed by the lights flickering on and off a few times. Realizing that the storm had arrived, we all rushed to the wall of windows that ran the length, and half the width, of the kitchen and breakfast nook. I had yet to close the white plantation shutters I'd had installed to help against summer's heat and winter's cold, and the view was impressive.

"Oh, wow," Dana breathed in awe. "Thunder snow. Look at it coming down now. Minutes ago as we drove here, there was only an occasional flake hitting the windshield. Now it looks like an Alaskan blizzard out there."

"'Thunder snow?'" Carly looked as stunned as her pup that abruptly began burying himself deeper into the warmth and protection provided between her jacket and sweater. "That's a new one to me. Those flakes have to be the size of quarters. Do you think it will keep snowing as heavily the entire time?"

"I don't know," I admitted, awed myself. "But if the weather warnings are correct, we could see record-setting accumulations by this time tomorrow. Did anyone besides me hear the weather guy say they were studying several computer scenarios, and no two were agreeing on the same forecast?"

"I did," Dana replied. "Why do you think I didn't need Maggie to twist my arm to come out here?"

The others continued to stare outside as though mesmerized, until Sybil clapped her hands and headed back toward the stove. "Okay, beans are on and the bad weather is here," she said in her school teacher voice. Returning to the stove where she adjusted the flames under both pots, she continued, "Did we get everything we needed from the car? It'll get dark faster than usual with the skies so dense with moisture. The stairs and sidewalk will get slippery, too, and we'll trudge in all kinds of mess onto Retta's beautiful floors. We should go ahead and bring in whatever's left in the car that we need, and start putting our Girl Scout skills to use preparing our quarters."

Noticing the younger women exchanging concerned glances, I couldn't help but grin. "She's not suggesting that we need to stake tents." To Sybil, I said, "I think Dana and Carly have their things inside. Maggie, it has to already be getting slick out there. You're liable to break your neck in those high-heeled boots before you get halfway to your car. I'll get whatever else you need."

"You aren't going out there, either."

Another flash and ear-splitting thunder had Maggie putting down her glass to cover her head with her arms. By then I already had grabbed my red jacket with the hood from the mud room. It was what I used for quick town errands.

"I think it's mostly sheet lighting," I assured her. "The activity seems to be caught up in the higher level mix of warm and cold air. At any rate, we sure aren't going to dawdle."

"In that case, I want to catch a snowflake on my tongue." Before anyone realized what she was up to Dana hurried to the front door. She pressed her thumb onto the door latch, just when a frigid gust of wind pushed back at her from the outside, almost knocking the mother-to-be to the floor.

"Oh no, you don't!"

Carly and I protested in union, but Carly beat me to Dana. However, with Wrigley in one arm, she could only partially stabilize her friend. Fortunately, I was just a step behind and managed to put a bracing arm around the beautiful brunette, as well as slam the door shut with my foot.

"See there?" I gasped. The storm's power had surprised me as much as it did the others. "Even with a few extra pounds that wind is strong enough to knock you off your feet. Stay put, please."

"Click your trunk button again, Maggie," Sybil said, slipping back into her jacket. "I'll go with you, Retta. I think all that's left is my bag and Maggie's anyway."

"Wrigley's kennel is there, too, along with the tote containing his bowl and food," Carly informed us. "Oh, let me go with you. I hate to be such a bother."

"You just stick close to Little Mama," Sybil replied. "We've got this."

What Carly did was to stay by the door to open it the moment Sybil and I made it back to the porch. "The next trip to bring in wood is on me," she assured me.

"Brownnoser," Maggie muttered from the kitchen doorway, glass in hand.

Pretending that I hadn't heard the uncalled for comment, I handed over the bag to the young blonde. "I appreciate that. So far, though, it's all under control. Dana, dear, I think you would be more comfortable sleeping on the couch here on the first floor. That way, you don't have the challenge of climbing stairs. Actually, the couch converts into a bed and will put you close to the fireplace." Pointing to the right corner of the room, I said, "Another plus is that the bathroom is convenient. It opens on the other side directly to the mud-laundry room."

"You've really put a great deal of thought into this, Retta. Thanks."

"Believe me, it's my pleasure. I love that you're here. Between you needing to give up being the church pianist, and me trying to keep my head above water here, we've barely had a chance to visit." I turned to my youngest guest. "Carly, would you like to take the kennel upstairs to the first bedroom on your right? I suspect Wrigley will prefer to stay close to you during the night."

Her expression suggested that she would rather face the lightning and freezing temperatures. "Couldn't I stay down here with you?" she asked Dana. "Would you mind?"

"I'd love it. That way I won't feel like I'm missing all the pajama-party fun."

Their arrangement made better sense to me, too, and I nodded my approval. If Dana had any health problem arise, I was relieved that someone would be near. "Great. And Rosie will be upstairs standing guard over us old hens, so you don't have to worry about her. I'll just put the kennel next to your case, Carly, and you can decide where you want it."

After Sybil and I hung up our jackets again, I said to Sybil and Maggie, "Come on you two. Sacrifice the glass for a minute, Mags, and help me with your bags. I swear, did you pack the family jewels along with half of your wardrobe, or is all this extra weight your a.m. and p.m. beauty regimen?"

"Hilarious. No, smarty, it's my good jewelry. What's the use of an alarm system if there's no power? The larger suitcase is packed with my coats and boots. Shoes and slippers, as well, I guess. I didn't want to end up with cold, wet feet." She gave Sybil a mischievous grin. "If you're nice to me, I'll share my footwear."

Looking from Maggie's feet to her own, Sybil remained unimpressed. "Baby, in case you haven't noticed, my clodhoppers are the size of a basketball player's, so it'll have to be one of your furs or nothing."

Halfway up the stairs, Sybil's phone erupted with the sound of the '60s rock band The Troggs blasting their classic, *Wild Thing*. Maggie and I burst into laughter, which had us grappling not to lose our grip on the luggage. It was virtually impossible to merge the idea of such a song with sensible Sybil. Giggles from the younger two floated up from the main floor, too.

Muttering under her breath, Sybil reached into her pants pocket. "You don't know the half of it," she muttered. "Hang on. I have to take this. It's Debra—also known as my youngest child. She's the one who is going to have me lying beside Elvin before my next birthday if she keeps driving her mother crazy with worry. No telling when or *if* she'll check back in again."

She swiped her finger across the screen of her cell phone and soon began what to the rest of us was a fascinating one-sided conversation. There was never any question about giving her privacy. We were having too much fun.

"Of course, I'm okay. Tell me how you're doing, since you got this mess first. Uh-huh. Uh-huh. Oh, Debra. Don't change the subject. I'm with a few neighbor-friends at Retta Cole's farm where we will have heat and hot water, as well as a propane stove to cook on. What's that noise? You're doing what? Okay, I understand they cancelled classes, but you shouldn't be partying, you should be studying or looking into doing something for extra credit, since you almost flunked your last test. Well, hallelujah, you're staying off the roads, but Debra. *Debra.* You know my mantra. Make wise choices. Wait! Don't hang up! Keep your cell phone charged. Well, if I'm sounding like a broken record, it's because you never listen. Besides, I want to be able to stay in touch."

After a short silence, Sybil reared back her head, only to glare at the phone in her hand. "Well. Goodbye. I love you, too."

With a sigh, she glanced down at us. "This is why I wanted her to commute to a college nearer to home. That girl has developed an annoying habit of disconnecting in the middle of our conversations."

"Sybil," I crooned. "Take it from an expert, if the oldest child didn't succeed in making you believe in hair color products, the youngest will."

"You know full well that it was Elvin who gave me my first grays," she replied, finally smiling. "And I haven't been without an extra box of L'Oréal in Leather Black ever since." With a sideways tip of her head toward me, she asked Maggie, "Did she really have the nerve to say that to me with her Norman Rockwell family? My wild child is having a party at Tech because, although the worst of the storm has pushed east of them, the frigid temperatures are promising to keep the campus closed for several more days. Is it asking too much to just get that child some credentials and gainfully employed?"

We all knew she was referring to Texas Tech University at Lubbock where Debra was attending college. During our last visit, Sybil was fretting over Debra wavering on the decision to pursue a teaching degree, but I reminded her that the girl was only a freshman taking basic courses, and there was still time to explore options if she continued to have any doubts about her future.

Maggie waved away Sybil's concerns and went back to dragging her suitcase upstairs. "Retta's right. You worry too much. She's a good kid. Debra is just having a little fun like the rest of us did when we finally got beyond the city limits of Martin's Mill for the first time, instead of acting tied to our parents like horses tethered to a hitching post with a simple loop of the reins. She'll be fine."

Unable to resist, I teased, "Words of wisdom sanctioned by the woman who recently almost crashed the Division of Motor Vehicles computer system for having too many last names." It was good to feel that at least among the three of us, things were on a safer plane again.

After snickering, Sybil asked, "Retta, I know I don't even have to ask if you've heard from your kids?"

"Bless them. You are right. This storm won't affect Jamie much in Houston, except for a deeper plunge in temperatures than they anticipated, but it will probably hit Rachel in Virginia in a couple of days, as badly or worse than anything we'll get. Nevertheless, they keep tabs on me as though I'm a week away from needing to move to a senior living facility."

Once again, the lights dimmed. I also heard a suspicious pinging sound against the window up on the landing. Glancing outside, I saw the heavy downpour of snow was now mixing with sleet. I could barely see the stables. At the rate it was coming down, the precipitation would quickly pile up on roofs and trees. It was yet another reminder that there would be continuous work to be done to keep access into buildings, and to avoid areas where the weight of frozen matter could prove dangerous.

"Mags, Sybil, while I light the fire in the master bedroom, do me a favor and go from room to room and make sure I shuttered all of the windows. Also, in the bathrooms leave the cabinet doors open under the sinks. Let's keep all the bedroom doors open to the hallway, too. The fireplace heat is going to be welcome when we go to bed and I turn down the thermostat."

Sybil waved her agreement then turned into her room. In the master suite, Maggie dropped off her luggage and went to handle the other bedrooms at our end of the hallway.

Upon her return, her cell phone began to buzz. She wasn't as skilled yet with modern contraptions as Sybil, so all of her calls came in with the factory set sound. While I continued to work on the fire, she dropped onto my queen-size bed.

"Phil, darling," she crooned into the phone.

Although I mentally rolled my eyes at the theatrics, I was pleased to know who was checking on her. I'd also heard another sound to my right and realized that Sybil had joined us, and had a quizzical look on her face. Clearly, she was thrown by Maggie's come hither tone.

"It's not what you think," I said in a loud whisper. "That's Father Phil." Sybil's blank expression had me reminding her, "Monsignor Lamar in Dallas. Maggie's stepson."

With dawning recognition, Sybil whispered, "I'll get her for pretending she's got another man again. I've only heard her refer to him as 'Hollis' son, the Catholic.'"

That sounded about right. Yet, if Maggie didn't heard from Phil in more than three days, she'd get all anxious and call him regardless of the hour. "One and the same," I told Sybil. "No matter what she implies, she adores him."

"I'm sorry I worried you when I didn't answer the house phone," Maggie continued. "You remember my dear friend, Retta? She's invited a few of us to her place to ride out the storm. How are conditions there?"

Not bothering to put her hand over the phone, Maggie announced, "He says the garden Jesus is butt-deep in snow." A moment later she burst into giggles.

"Oh, I know that's not what you said, but we're five widow ladies here. Let us have our fun. Yes, and you check in whenever you have a minute. This rhinestone-crusted cutie is juiced. Not me, the phone, silly." With another laugh Maggie disconnected.

Forcing myself to overlook the "juiced" comment, I simply said, "He's always so considerate and tender with you."

"Hell, he's already halfway to becoming a saint. Why do you think they moved him up at such a young age?" With a bemused smile she added, "Who would have ever believed Hollis' only child would have converted to Catholicism let alone felt a calling to become a priest?" Her expression turned serious. "This is just between us, okay? The Pope has stopped a lot of the elevation process because he feels a good deal of it is excessive, but there's word that he's very pleased with Phil's work with the poor and ill, and may call him to the Vatican to expand his responsibilities."

Both Sybil and I landed on our bottoms—Sybil beside Maggie, and me on the hardwood floor grateful for the brick ledge to support my back. I said, "Why, Maggie, how exciting, and what an honor!"

Sybil added, "I'm Baptist. I don't know diddly about Catholic stuff, but I have to admit that every time they've picked a new Pope I've been as glued to the TV as anyone else. How proud you must be."

In a rare moment of humility, Maggie pressed the black-and-white rhinestone-encased phone to her chest and her eyes welled with tears. "There are no words. He's the son I never had."

I wanted to give my friend a hug for this moment of transparency, but knew her well enough to understand she would be embarrassed, so instead I teased. "How many candles will he have to light and Hail Marys will he have to recite for that 'butt-deep' comment you pulled on him?"

"Oh, believe me," she replied with a chuckle, "when he and his *compadres* get together tonight for an evening drink he'll share that and get a good laugh."

I could see the fire was going to be fine now. Replacing the screen, I stood and brushed off my hands, then my jeans and rust-colored tunic sweater that my style-savvy daughter sent me, insisting it would go well with my dark-blond coloring. From the admiration I'd seen in Sam's eyes when I last wore it I was convinced Rachel was right. Although I usually wore work clothes around here, I knew Maggie would be dressed Dallas chic, and guessed Carly would, as well. I'd had no desire to feel any frumpier than necessary.

"We should get back to the girls, unless you two want to unpack first?" I asked.

"My stuff is mostly wash and wear. These days, if it isn't easy-care,

I ain't buying it," Sybil intoned with carefree rebellion. "Besides, those beans need to be stirred."

"I'll come back up in a bit and do mine," Maggie said. "I'd like to finish my wine first."

As we neared the bottom of the stairway, we could hear hushed voices, that universal signal that secrets were being shared. It made me happy to think that Dana had found a confidant in Carly.

"We're back and headed to the kitchen," I called to them. "Can I get you two anything?" When both young women looked at me, something made me pause to correct myself. I stepped aside to allow Sybil to pass me. "I hope y'all know that I want you to feel at home here? Midnight raids to the fridge, or the bar, whatever. Have at it. If you've forgotten any toiletries, you'll probably find something you can use in the bathroom. If you don't find it down here, I'm sure I have it upstairs. As you can see I'm no glamour girl, but my Rachel is always sending me new products she's discovering, in the hopes of getting me interested in a semi-serious beauty regimen. She finds my soap-water-moisturizer routine positively archaic."

With a grateful smile, Dana said, "It works for you, Retta. And you can't deny that you were blessed with great genes. Thank you for the welcome. For everything. Being here is such a treat. I've never been this spoiled before. I feel like I'm at a ski lodge."

"Oh, she's right," Carly added. "Your house reminds me of our honeymoon in Aspen."

Not realizing that's where they'd gone, I asked, "Did you get to ski?"

Before she could reply, Maggie opined from behind me, "I can see it now: you, Walter, and the paramedics."

"Actually, we seldom left the hotel suite," Carly said.

"I need a drink." Maggie made a beeline for the kitchen.

Venturing closer to the younger women, I patted Carly on the shoulder. "Good for you. I'm glad you have some beautiful memories to hold close."

"I'm so envious," Sybil said, once I entered the kitchen. She had taken the alternate route there, but had heard our conversation. "Elvin and I spent our honeymoon at the Alps Motel in Mount Pleasant."

"We didn't get much farther," I told her. "Charlie and I ended up at the Excelsior House Hotel in Jefferson. Charlie was expected to be back helping at his family's place on Monday. As much as his father liked me, and approved of the idea of our properties eventually merging, Burnett reminded him that he and Miss Myra had been married on a Friday evening and that he was on the job at six-thirty Saturday morning."

"Y'all are just too depressing," Maggie said. "Sybil, did you know that I made it all the way to the Riviera?"

"Yeah, it just took you three weddings to get there." Of course, after reminding her of that, I half expected Maggie to smack my backside as I refilled Rosie's water dish. Instead, she offered a theatrical moan.

"No lie," she admitted to Sybil. "My first wedding night was spent under my in-laws' roof hoping that Scotty wouldn't shoot our bed's headboard straight through into his parents' room. Talk about being mortified. But I was just a baby then and most of Scotty's sex education was from watching farm animals go after it."

As our joking continued, I peeked around the corner to check with Carly about Wrigley's feeding schedule. When she said she had it under control—was in fact feeding him—I prepared my Rosie's dinner. By then, Maggie had perched herself on a bar stool and seemed to be enjoying her wine, while Sybil was collecting the ingredients for the cornbread.

After a minute, Carly entered the kitchen with Wrigley's dirty food bowl. "Retta, where would you prefer I wash this? In here or the bathroom?"

"This sink is fine, hon. It gets disinfected with bleach every night. Just do me a favor and throw any leftover food into the trash. The garbage disposal works, but I only use it in an emergency. Septic tanks don't respond well to too much diversity."

I couldn't see if the bowl was empty or not, nor did I hover over her shoulder to check. Rosie had finished her meal, and I intended to let her out the back door for a minute, as was her routine. This time, however, she took one look at the frozen commotion outside, and turned back into the kitchen to plant herself on her daytime doggy bed, which I kept for her by the huge palm plant at the entryway to the kitchen. The tropical greenery had been one of the gifts sent for Charlie's funeral, and Rosie loved to lie under the fronds as though she was an African lioness enjoying the privacy and protection while surveying her territory. She had other cat traits, as well, such as a predisposition to crouching in tall grass to keep an eye on the barn cats. What else could I have expected considering that she was born in July under the sign of Leo?

Noting Sybil was heating a little water in the microwave to add to Carly's beans, I could tell she had everything under control, so I looked around, ready to sit for a minute myself. "What did I do with my glass?"

"There," Maggie said, pointing to where it had been hidden by the case of wines.

After getting it, I finally enjoying a sip, then had a twinge of conscience. "Sybil, do you want any help making that cornbread?" Maggie was making me uneasy. She was watching Carly at the sink as though she wanted to take a serrated knife to all of that glorious hair.

"You just rest your feet for a few minutes and enjoy your drink," Sybil replied. "I know you've been preparing for us all day. You girls entertain me while I piddle. This is so nice not having to be on a schedule and all."

Having finished with cleaning Wrigley's dog bowl, Carly refilled her glass. Giving Sybil a shy smile, she quietly carried it and the bowl to the living room.

Noticing Maggie's snooty expression, as her eyes followed Carly's every step, I gave her a warning nudge with my elbow. In return she sent me a dismissive one-shoulder shrug.

"Please tell me that you're making your mother's renowned jalapeno and Vidalia onion version of corn bread?" Maggie all but cooed to Sybil.

"Is there any other? Why mess with perfection, although—" with a shake of her head, she looked up at the ceiling as though seeking Elvin's confirmation "—I did experiment once with a can of condensed milk and Elvin almost ate the whole pan by himself. They say for every slice of bacon you eat, you lose nine days off of your lifespan. I don't know what the ratio is for that sweet goo, but he was up all night eating what I call digestion candy, yet he still insisted, 'That cornbread was so good, honey.'"

Her reminiscing triggered some of my own. "Poor Charlie. I confess most of the time, he had to settle for the packaged mixes. As much as I like to cook, I'm just not as in love with cornbread as the rest of you. Now give me a good sturdy rye bread like my grandmother used to make and I'm in heaven. Only I almost never made it because Charlie's dentures couldn't handle anything that hard."

"I didn't realize Charlie wore dentures," Maggie said, looking sincerely taken aback.

"A partial. He admitted it was his own fault," I told her. "His family could afford for him to go to the dentist, but he just couldn't stand drills, let alone needles, so he usually found a way to avoid going."

"I've heard some people fear a dentist more than a medical doctor," Sybil replied. "But, girl, considering that you worked side by side with Charlie on this place, raised your family, *and* kept this splendid house, I don't think he ever complained—or had a right to—over whatever you did or didn't cook."

Maggie raised her hand as though requesting her time to speak. "If I could have found a house without a kitchen in it, I would have bought it on the spot. I did give it a good try in the new house, until my realtor convinced me that such a thing would be hell on the resale value."

Sybil snickered. "I can picture you trying to get away with that. Well, look at it this way—the person who buys your house will be tickled silly to get virtually all new appliances."

"They won't believe they are, unless the stickers are still all over the darned things, which is nothing I care to look at day in and day out—especially after the same realtor said, 'Sellers are liars, and buyers are worse.' I'm sure someone would accuse me of plastering them on things myself!"

"What an awful perspective of human nature," Sybil replied. "At any rate, I wouldn't know what to do with myself if I couldn't be in a kitchen at least a couple of times a week. I like to think that God lives in my kitchen. He's the executive chef and I'm the *sous* chef."

Laughing, Maggie slapped the counter. "Leave it to you Southern Baptists to figure out a way to be in church more than three days a week!"

Giving her a mild look, Sybil replied, "A little more church could do you good."

Without missing a beat, Maggie held up her glass. "Every time I pour myself one of these, honey, I'm having communion."

Sybil's lips still had a pinched look as she whipped together the cornmeal batter and poured it into the two muffin pans. Once they were in the oven, she set the timer.

"There, now," she said, wiping her hands in her apron. Untying it, she put it on an empty bar stool and reached for her drink. "Why don't we go socialize with the younger ones?"

Ignoring Maggie's muttered, "Party pooper," I picked up my glass. "Good idea."

We filed into the living room and Sybil declared, "No wonder y'all have been so quiet!"

Carly had unpacked her tote full of pedicure paraphernalia. She was in the process of giving Dana a foot massage. By now we all knew she used to work at a nail salon at a strip mall just off of the interstate in Sulphur Springs. That's where Walter met her. Self-conscious about how his diabetes demanded he take extra care of his feet, he'd preferred to go to a place out of town where he wouldn't be so easily recognized. Regardless of what the gossips charged, whenever I'd seen Walter in those last months, it struck me how happy he'd looked. I had to respect Carly for undoubtedly taking good care of him.

As for Dana, the poor expectant mother had the typical swollen lower limbs of a woman only weeks away from giving birth. But she also looked darling in her black yoga pants and turquoise tunic top. "You seem to be enjoying that," I said.

"I told her it was too much trouble," Dana replied. "But oh, my goodness, this is sheer ecstasy."

Although her answering glance spoke of modesty, Carly continued with her ministrations. "I had to do it. Just looking at your ankles makes mine hurt. Sit up now and put your feet over the side."

She washed off and dried whatever remaining oils were on Dana's feet. Recognizing my bowl and towel, I knew she had used the other entrance to the downstairs bathroom to avoid us. I didn't mind at all, but it told me if Maggie had gone viral in the kitchen, Carly wouldn't have missed a single one of her verbal stabs. I feared that was something I would have to guard against for the sake of everyone's harmony.

Draping herself on the other end of the L-shaped couch, Maggie eyed Carly's attentive care with half-hearted interest. "You know I treated Retta to a manicure once."

"Oh, here we go," I groaned. "Is it too much to hope that I would never have to listen to that story again?"

"Well, it was just so…unforgettable," Maggie mused, all innocence.

Sybil settled herself on the long ledge of the brick fireplace and stretched her legs before her. "What happened?" she demanded.

"Exactly what you'd expect from an ingrate. I was trying to convince her that a little pampering would do her a world of good. Her fingernails looked like something out of a horror movie from all the laboring around here. I can't imagine what condition her toes are in."

"It's not like I intentionally neglect myself," I protested.

Ignoring me, Maggie continued, "I booked an appointment for her with Shan Li at The Lotus Flower Day Spa in Tyler. He's an absolute magician when it comes to making your hands as soft and beautiful as the rose petals he puts in the soaking bowls. So we get in there and Retta goes immediately into panic mode. She doesn't have a clue as to what to do, and I have to point to the wall of nail polish samples and tell her to choose one."

Sybil gave me a sympathetic look. "I bet you started to hyperventilate."

"If a cop had come in and directed her to walk along the tile's grout line, she would have gotten arrested for pedestrian-under-the-influence," Maggie declared. "Then she went completely anal picking a shade that was practically clear. I mean in that case, why bother? Even Shan Li encouraged her to throw caution to the wind. Do you know what color she ended up with? Something a whisper beyond her naturally fair skin tone."

"Another exaggeration," I said with hard-won patience. "It had been summer and, as usual, I was both wind and sun tanned, not what Maggie calls, 'cloistered-nun nude,' which is how she refers to my winter coloring." I held out my work-hardened hands. "Seriously, can you see me in black, or with those cute little decals like the young people wear?"

"No one suggested that. Only for pity's sake, when you get a manicure for the first time, you should—upgrade a bit. But back to my story." Maggie pointed toward me. "Shan Li's eyes nearly popped out of his head when he first realized the condition of her hands."

Remembering all too well, I explained to the others, "He must have thought it his professional duty to show me every bit of dead skin he dug out and cut away from my cuticles. Excuse me? I'm busy, not blind. Bottom line? The man is a sadist, *and* has a fetish."

Puffing up like an indignant hen, Maggie offered a waspish, "You may not worry about your cuticle care, but he does."

Once again ignoring her, I all but snorted. "There were definite control issues. 'Sit still. No do dat!'"

"Admit it," Maggie replied, "you're a closet bigot and you were uncomfortable with his accent."

She might as well have slapped me. Me, who she well knew had spent almost all of my youth in the company of a Japanese family that I'd adored. Maggie also knew that I loved to watch international movies and learn as many words and phrases in new languages as I could.

I turned to Carly and Dana. "How would you feel if someone yelled— not asked—'Wah you haan!'" I turned back to challenge Maggie. "Honestly? The first time you walked into that place, you understood him?"

"He made hand gestures when you continued to just sit there and stare at him." Maggie said to the others, "I told her, 'Go wash your hands.'"

"So I did." Determined to take control of my own miserable experience once and for all, I continued, "When I finished I looked for something to wipe off with. There was nothing. But I caught sight of Maggie pointing to this microwave-like box. Inside, there were warm towels. Can you believe it?"

Looking sympathetic, Carly said, "It is simply a towel warming appliance. Didn't that feel wonderful, Retta? So soothing after his digging at you."

"All I remember was that I wanted to go home."

It could have ended there; I prayed it would. Unfortunately, Maggie wasn't getting the laughs she expected, which made her reluctant to leave well enough alone.

"That was just the beginning. When she gets back to her chair, she notices the lady at the end of her row getting a pedicure."

The woman had her pants rolled up over her knees and an attendant was rubbing small smooth rocks up and down her legs. I said, "Maggie, the woman was moaning and writhing. I didn't know whether to call 9-1-1 or ask them to continue what they were doing in one of the back rooms where they would have more privacy—if you catch my drift."

Already giddy with laughter, although she'd told the story at least a half dozen times to various people at my expense, Maggie wheezed, "She was *not* having the Big O, she was only sitting in a massage chair."

That earned a few chuckles from Dana and Sybil. Carly, bless her, sent Maggie an unamused glance, but otherwise kept her gaze on her work.

"It gets better," Maggie said. "See, what I love about Shan Li, is that when he's finished with the manicure, he always treats you to a nice, soothing neck massage. But you should have seen the look on Retta's face when he walked up behind her, lifted up her hair and started rubbing warm, lotion onto her neck."

"Never mind the neck. His hands were down in my shirt!" I resented her diminishing the episode as much as I'd been offended by the act.

"He was only trying to reach your shoulders. You were beyond tense."

"Oh, and being groped by a complete stranger was supposed to relax me? Excuse me if I've only been with one man in my life. I didn't know if what the guy was doing was foreplay or what!"

"Well, what did she want him to do—announce in front of the whole salon that he bats for the other team?" Maggie asked our audience. She added to me, "How was I to know that you weren't worldly enough to have watched his behavior and figured out that much?"

Dana sighed and leaned back against the pillows, all but lost in her pleasure. "Don't stress any more, Retta. It is a cute story. I'll also give this Shan Li the benefit of the doubt, but it does sound as though he has a bit of an ego thing going on. As far as I'm concerned, Carly gives the best massages and pedicures I've experienced. By the time she's finished, I feel as if I'm cocooned in a cloud of utter peace."

It was hardly what Maggie wanted to hear after giving her performance her all. I could tell she wouldn't resist having the last word, much like an impudent child seeking revenge by poking someone else's balloon with a pin.

"It's so good that you're keeping in practice, Carly," she crooned. "You never know when you might need to put those skills back to use."

Three

A BEEPING IN the kitchen proved well-timed. Sybil lurched to her feet, muttering under her breath, "Thank You, Lord."

From the expression on the younger women's faces, I had a feeling they wished they had an excuse to run, too. Hoping that I could ease the level of tension, I said to Carly, "I regret not having some skill to make me feel more secure when I was your age. Farming and ranching is all I've ever known."

"What are you talking about, Retta?" Dana asked, looking incredulous. "You're a wonderful pianist. That's why I hoped you would take back the position at church when I bowed out because of my condition."

Thanks to Maggie's deepening frown, it was difficult for me to take any pleasure from Dana's compliment. *What was going on with her now?* I wondered.

"Oh, playing for church and school while the kids were growing up wasn't exactly the accomplishments I once dreamed about." I hoped I sounded more casual about it than I felt. "They hardly compare to the success you had in California before you met Jesse. At any rate, as competent as Patsy Oliver is, people continue to say how much they miss *your* playing at services." The latter I added quickly, not to offend the quiet lady, who had jumped at the chance to take over the position and earn a little more money, after I had to decline the offer due to my obligations here. To be fair, Patsy's situation wasn't easy. While she'd had no formal training, she also had remained single to nurse an invalid mother, until the poor woman's death this year. It was my hunch that Patsy was struggling to make ends meet these days, so I was doubly relieved that the opportunity came her way.

"That's kind," Dana replied, although she looked away. "The truth is I fibbed a bit when claiming my health made me resign. I simply got to the point where I couldn't stand the staring from some who were gauging how fast my waistline was expanding. Their expressions were so transparent. I knew they were speculating how far along I was, and whether or not the baby was even Jesse's."

The bitter admission made me furious on her behalf. "I'm afraid we do have some people who should pay more attention as to *why* they're in church instead of focusing on other people's business. Though, please believe there aren't as many of those as you think. As for me," I added with a wry smile, "clearly God had other plans than letting me perform at Carnegie Hall. Don't get me wrong, I have loved my life and have no regrets. Only when you're alone at night—as you know well enough— the mind can play you for a fool. Mine can get too eager to wander into, 'What if...?' territory."

A sound from Maggie had me glancing her way. "Pardon?"

She got up with a huff. "I said, I think she burned the bread."

What on earth...? There wasn't the least hint of smoke or the smell of something burning. This had to be her way to escape instead of doing the right thing and apologizing.

I leaned closer to Dana and Carly in order to speak quietly. "Please, forgive her. Maggie can be a handful, but she's also been through a hard time losing Hollis."

"I don't know how you stand her, Retta," Carly replied. "She's mean."

As Dana put a soothing hand on her friend's knee, I said, "Maggie's complicated and conflicted."

"Aren't we all?" Dana asked without rancor.

I had to nod, giving her that. "I promise to explain when there's an opportunity, but right now I just want to thank you for being as tolerant as you are."

With the slightest shake of her head, Carly focused on finishing up with Dana's pedicure. "I'll try, Retta. For you. But I'm human, too."

Thanking her for her graciousness, I said, "I'll go set the table. Finish up and let's eat."

Once back in the kitchen, I couldn't help but sing-song to Maggie, "And how badly burned is the cornbread?"

Sybil did a double take as she topped off her glass of wine. "The devil, you say."

"Oh, I must have misunderstood." Setting down my glass, I started for the china cabinet to get the dishes. "Maggie, you want to stop drinking and help me set the table?"

"Only if I get to stick the forks where I want to."

"It *is* what you do best." I turned to Sybil, "My, what a mouth-watering aroma. Why is it that someone else's cooking always smells better than your own?"

"For the same reason that we say everything tastes better when cooked over an open campfire," she replied. "I guess it's the change of pace or novelty of it."

By the time the table was set—without any assistance from Maggie—Carly and Dana joined us. They stood back looking hesitant about where to sit.

"Please, choose a spot wherever you'd like," I said.

"Can we open the shutters and watch the snow?" Dana asked.

"Well, I thought to keep them closed to contain the heat," I told her, "but I guess it would be atmospheric. Rather like getting the window seats at a restaurant that has an atrium."

"Or at an ice skating rink like Rockefeller Center," Dana said, helping Carly with the shutters.

"Oh, I always wanted to go do that," Carly said. "Especially around Christmas to see all of the lights and the huge tree. When Walter asked me where I wanted to go for our honeymoon, it was my second choice—especially once he admitted it wouldn't be healthy for him to take long plane flights due to his circulation. He wasn't big on crowded places, either."

"Now I learned something new," I said. "I didn't realize either one of those things. Yet it makes sense. He was a true gentleman, always so quietly spoken and considerate."

Smiling her pleasure, Carly sat down in a corner seat beside Dana. They both gazed outside to observe the changes the weather was making to the landscape. It wasn't much so far, and yet the hint of what was to come, if things continued at this pace, was formidable.

Sybil and I carried the beans and muffins to the table. Once we collected our glasses and made sure everyone had what they wanted, we joined them. It was no surprise to me that Maggie had already seated herself at the other end of the table. Belatedly, I noted Carly in her direct line of fire; however, it was too late to do anything about that without making things too obvious.

Sybil turned to Dana, "Darlin', would you like to lead us in saying grace?"

Dana's expression looked as horrified as though we'd just told her we wanted to baptize her in a vat of ice water. "Oh, I'd rather not. God and I aren't exactly talking these days."

The silence in the room was suddenly so stark, the wind sounded as forlorn as a lone wolf's or coyote's howl. But before I could reply, she continued.

"Too much information, huh?" With a weary sigh, Dana bowed her head. "You didn't need to hear that."

I felt my heart threaten to tear at her jarring honesty and couldn't let her suffer a moment longer. "It's all right," I assured her. "Let's just bow our heads. Lord, thank You for bringing us together and giving us this opportunity to be each other's strength and support during a greater storm than we had imagined. Amen."

Sybil offered a resounding echo, while Dana and Carly's were barely audible. From Maggie, I heard nothing. So be it, I thought. I had said my own silent, brief prayer for her.

When our conversation resumed, it sounded a little too forced. At least it did until, gazing outside, Sybil observed, "Isn't it incredible how everything looks as though the world is being cleansed? If only we could figure out a way to do the same thing with our real and imagined imperfections. We could call it spiritual respite."

I loved her for her sensitive way of trying to send a message to each of us. This was a perfect example of why I'd long believed that she'd been born to be a teacher. "I don't know if we can manage that, but thankfully, your cooking is as good as a mother's embrace," I assured her.

Dana brightened and said with real relish, "Oh, yes, that's exactly the right description, Sybil. In fact, I don't know if there's going to be enough for all of us to have a second helping. How are your beans, Carly?"

"The peppers and spices Sybil added really give them a nice kick. Here, taste."

Dana took a delicate nibble from the offered spoon and made an appreciative sound. "Wow! I can't decide which I like better."

"Do you really believe the pilgrims ate this well?" Carly asked Sybil, her expression doubtful. "Considering how pitiful the holidays were at my house, I can't see that long table the size of half a football field that they showed us in schoolbooks when I was a kid. What fantasy are you selling to your students these days?"

Nodding her acceptance of the question posed as half-challenge, half-entreaty for truth, Sybil replied, "I believe my job is to simply make them think. It's not my place to put a yes or no in their minds. Reasoning is often not seen as valuable these days. So I tell them about the conditions the colonists were under, and what documentation through diaries shows.

"From my own research, I know it wasn't too bad at first. They had turkey, yes, but it was wild game, and those succulent breasts we relish were probably a bit thin and dry back then. Deer were plentiful, so they supplemented meals with venison and fowl like ducks and geese. White flour had to be rationed, meaning bread and pies wouldn't have been in abundance. No one knew when the next ship would arrive. However, things like nuts—walnuts, chestnuts, beechnuts—made up for that, as did berries of the season."

"The original party mix," Carly mused. "What about potatoes?"

"Also rationed at first. And there were no calorie-riddled green bean casseroles, either."

As everyone chuckled, Sybil pointed her spoon at Carly. "That's an extremely thoughtful question, young lady, even if it was spawned by cynicism. You also seem to be reading my mind. The way it's snowing, I'm wondering if we'll still be here for Thanksgiving?"

Maggie piped in with her usual irreverence. "Retta, do you have a bird in the freezer, or do we have to go out and chase down one of your laying hens?"

Although she knew good and well that the birds were penned and out of the rough weather in cozy laying houses filled with fresh hay, I was grateful for the opportunity to joke a bit. "You stay away from my girls. I do a head count every day."

The teasing helped moods to relax and conversation flowed. The muffin supply diminished rapidly as each of us reached for seconds. By the time spoons scraped the bottoms of bowls, Dana and Carly agreed that it was getting chilly in the corner and, as Sybil and I rose to clean up, they closed the shutters.

As I turned on more lights, Rosie roused from her bed under the palm. After stretching, she got herself a drink of water then wandered toward the living room. I knew she wanted to claim her other favorite place in cold weather—the thick, braided rug in front of the fireplace.

While Carly had been eating, Wrigley had been asleep on her lap. Now he made a soft sound of protest, as she repositioned him in her arms. He complained again as she came to me by the sink. "Retta, let me do the washing up."

"I'll help her." Dana brought the basket with the last of the muffins and set it on the island.

"Absolutely not," I said to both of them. "Carly, it won't take me five minutes to get this done. As for you," I told Dana, "it would be best if you stay off your feet. Don't undo Carly's efforts. I'll join you all in a minute. You can look through my DVD collection in the book shelves for a movie you'd like to watch, or we could play board games, cards, or dominoes."

"Oh, a movie sounds good to me," Sybil said.

She followed my pointing toward the pantry when I realized she had forgotten where I kept the plastic wrap. I had been in her house enough times to recall that she had a commercial size roller of the stuff hanging under a cabinet.

"I vote for anything other than *The Help* or *The Color Purple*," she informed us.

Maggie quipped, "Don't tell me, you're coming out of the closet? You're a racist?"

With a tolerant look, Sybil found the box of clear wrap and pointed it at her. "I just don't care to watch any movie I should have starred in." Over the younger girls' sputtering laughs, she told me, "You had your fantasies about a concert pianist career? I told myself more than a few times that Oprah and Whoopi didn't have any blessed thing that I didn't have—including brass and sass."

"Well, I'm game to watch anything but *Midway*," I said. "I swear, Charlie watched that one so often I think I can still recite most of the dialogue even after all these years. He had an uncle who served on the ship and I think he secretly wished that he'd enlisted in the Navy, too."

"Do you have *Body Heat?*" Maggie asked.

Sybil snorted. "Relive your youth on your own time." She then caught the pot holder Maggie sent flying her way.

"It's the holiday season," Carly reminded us. "Do you have something like *Holiday Inn* or *White Christmas?*"

My own surprise was mirrored by Sybil's shocked expression and Maggie's look of disbelief. Carly of all people—what did she know of such classics?

Once she realized she had everyone's attention, she shrugged. "Walter introduced them to me. They were wonderful. I had no idea some of my favorite carols come from movies."

"Well, I just happen to have both films," I told her. "Go dig them up, and decide which to play first. I'll be with you shortly."

While I worked, Maggie lingered to wipe down the table. Sybil put the minimal leftovers in smaller bowls, then she and Maggie followed the others to the living room.

When I came around the fireplace wall, my long-time friends were in the coat closet getting extra throws off of the top shelf. I was glad Maggie remembered where I stored them. Carly was already in bed under a blanket, remote in hand.

"Where's Dana?" I asked, realizing she wasn't there.

Pointing with the remote toward the bathroom, she smiled and said, "Again."

"I remember when I was pregnant with Jamie," I told her. "It was winter, and cold weather always makes me go more anyway. When I got closer to my due date, I was afraid to go too far out into the pasture for fear of having to find a bush to squat behind."

Muttering her agreement, Sybil said, "After all that child rearing, you get a short break—until menopause. But from then on, you'll be blessing your builder if he thought to locate a bathroom close to the kitchen. I sure hope I don't take after my mother in that department."

"There's always the exception to the rule. Look at Maggie," I said, nodding her way. "I swear I don't think I've ever seen her go more than twice a day. Ever."

For a moment, Maggie acted as though she'd let the comment pass, but she abruptly muttered, "Yeah, well, everything changes."

Something about those words and her manner—the way she avoided eye contact by taking her seat, and fussing too much as she adjusted her afghan—triggered a little quake inside me. It reminded me of what my mother used to say when we suddenly shivered for no reason: *"Someone just walked over your grave."*

Dana emerged from the bathroom and hurried to get under the blanket with Carly, which stopped me from asking Maggie about her cryptic comment. I made a mental note to bring up the subject later.

"It's a shock at how nice it is in this room, compared to how chilly it's already getting anywhere away from the fire," Dana said. "I don't want to think about how bad it will get if we do lose power. Then again, maybe it's just me. I've always been cold-natured."

"I did lower the thermostat," I told her, "to do our part in taking some of the pressure off the central grid. I'll lower it more when we go to bed. I thought a slow adjustment would be easier than going cold turkey. Be sure to grab more blankets or wear more layers if you need to."

"It's still sheer luxury," Sybil said. "You young ones should be glad you were born after the invention of indoor plumbing. Having your bare backside meet with a cold wooden board like I did when I was a kid? Woo-hoo! I don't miss that at all."

"You're not old enough to remember those days," Dana protested.

"I'm old enough to have had a grandma, who still had an outhouse. When she was scrubbing her floors, it didn't matter if there was snow on the ground or if it was a hundred-and-ten in the shade, we kids were exiled from the house, until those floors were dry. She lived on pure prairie land, so there was only the option of the outhouse or flashing the entire countryside."

Shuddering in rejection of such an idea, Dana told Carly, "Movie time."

That ended all conversation for a good while, as Carly pressed the play button and we all fell under the spell of Irving Berlin's *White Christmas*. It was a favorite of mine, as well, and our family had watched it every season as the kids grew up. Sadly, we had avoided it the last few

Christmases because Charlie had possessed quite a nice crooning voice, and we missed hearing him accompany Bing. Crosby had just started serenading Rosemary Clooney, who couldn't sleep. We were all anticipating the delightful song when, suddenly, everything went black. It was as if God had just yanked the big power breaker for the entire world—at least until we grew accustomed to the subtle amber glow from the fire.

Dana and Carly cried in unison, "*No!* That's not fair!"

Sitting beside me, I felt Maggie's warm breath hit my cheek, even before she spoke. "That's sooner than expected."

"Yeah, it is." Since I was the one who knew my house best, I relied on the firelight to get the cute LED flashlight I kept on the kitchen counter for emergencies. "Don't panic!" I called, although I wasn't feeling confident, either. Maggie was dead on: things were going to get more challenging than any of us had anticipated.

Opening the utility drawer, I collected the handful of mini-flashlights that matched mine, which I'd purchased from one of the TV shopping networks. Returning to the others, I handed them out. "These are great. They'll help you navigate through the house. Keep them close. Maggie, you know where I store the lighters and matches. Would you light the candles in the kitchen and breakfast nook? Sybil, upstairs in your room, the bathroom, and the master suite, there are battery-operated candles like these." I picked up the nearest one and flipped the switch on the bottom. "Would you take care of those? I'll feed this fire and then go upstairs to check on the other. We'll really need the fireplace heat now."

"You don't think the power will come back on?" Carly asked.

I didn't, but opted for a hedge. "I'm not sure."

"Do you suppose they've lost power in town, too?"

If they hadn't, perhaps the electric co-operative that provided our county's service might not yet be inundated with calls and would be able to make it out to this area and get us back online. However, the way the snow was coming down, the roads had to already be treacherous, which all but obliterated any glimmer of hope.

My delay in answering had Dana asking bravely, "I'll bet it went out there an hour ago, if not sooner. What can we do to help, Retta?"

I saw Carly was already hugging Wrigley, who was shivering in her arms, and said, "You two are perfect right where you are. This is central command for all of us." I could see that Rosie was glancing around with a wary look, too. "The dogs need reassurance and so do we. If you hear any popping outside, or smell something like smoke, holler. This black-out could be from a nearby blown transformer or downed line, as easily as a problem at one of the substations."

"I didn't know that," Carly said. "Could the house catch fire?"

"Hopefully, the problem isn't that close, but we're going to stay ob-servant," I replied. "I'll look out the side and back windows to make certain. Maggie, you check the front."

It wasn't my intention to sound melodramatic, but they needed to appreciate worst-case scenarios. With a parting wave, I moved on to do what sixty-one years of living on a ranch had taught me, while mentally doing a quick recap to recall what else I needed to check.

The refrigerator!

If we didn't get power restored in a few hours, I would have to peri-odically turn on the generator. Yesterday, I had filled a few gas containers, but I hadn't purchased enough to run the thing around the clock for more than two days or so. Eventually, we might have to bring out the ice chests from storage. There wasn't a huge supply of ice cubes, but I suspected that by then we would have plenty of snow to keep perishables safe.

For the next few minutes we were a strange combination of musicians and mechanics, eclectic in our dialogue with each other, which interest-ingly, created a reassuring melody of its own. Acoustics were provided by doors slamming, cabinets thumping, while footsteps kept an excited beat on the hardwood floors. Outside, the wind continued to howl as the Arctic Vortex kept blasting its way through Texas. It was quite intimidating, and a far cry from how we'd expected to spend the evening enjoying Bing Cros-by and company's gentle finale of *White Christmas*. From the continued wail of the wind, I could almost imagine that tomorrow, we would wake to radio reports about the concern for glaciers in the Gulf of Mexico.

When we reunited in the living room, I was a bit breathless from the adrenaline rush, as much as the racing about. Carly and Dana remained saucer-eyed, hunkering under their blankets with Wrigley all but hidden between them. In front of the fireplace, Rosie had tucked herself into a tighter ball, her nose buried under the denser fur of her tail.

"What happens now?" Carly asked.

I couldn't allow this setback, serious as it was, to depress us. "We do what the pioneers did," I told her. "Although we're still much better off."

"What do you mean?" Dana was looking increasingly uncertain. "Is this a bad time to tell you that I was never much for camping? Please tell me the toilets won't stop flushing?"

I chuckled. "They'll work fine. I'll have to periodically turn on the generator to trigger the pump for the reservoir to refill but, otherwise, we're good. You'll also continue to have hot water for a shower or bath, provided no one overindulges."

Seeing their unhappy expressions, I spread my arms, summoning an enthusiasm I hoped was contagious. "Come on, we're having an *adventure*! Carly, you voiced curiosity about the early colonists. Now we'll get a little taste of what it was like for our forefathers who first came to this land."

"Not quite," Maggie said, pulling her cell phone out of her pocket. She must have accidentally touched the screen enough that it lit, ready to perform.

"Put that away," I told her. "We don't know how long we're going to be under these conditions. Save the battery." Turning back to the younger two, I continued, "We're missing out on the best songs in the movie, so let's sing them ourselves."

Instead, Maggie began an off-key rendition to the melody of *The Twelve Days of Christmas*, "On the first day of the storm, the power went out..."

"A little more 'glass half full,' if you please." Sybil's dour tone made her sound as though she was reprimanding one of her students.

Catching on, Dana laughingly offered with perfect pitch, "I'm dreaming of a white Thanksgiving."

As much as I appreciated the return of their humor, I had to warn, "If you keep thinking about cold conditions, even a bonfire won't keep you warm. How about something livelier? Sybil, I've heard you sing Tina Turner at an Arts Alliance fundraiser. That would get anyone's blood flowing."

Dana thrust aside her blanket and wriggled off the couch. "I want to hear some of that."

As she waddled in her sock-clad feet to the piano, Sybil covered her face with her hands in what looked like a gesture of mortification, only to squeal like a teenager. In the next moment, she leaned over to roll up her pants legs. "I always said, God didn't give me and Tina these for nothing."

Carly hooted in pleasure and clapped her hands.

From her laid back seat at the far end of the couch, Maggie raised her wine glass in salute. "That's the spirit!"

Gingerly situating herself on the bench, Dana ran her fingers over the keyboard. Then she glanced over her shoulder at Sybil, and started playing the first notes of *Proud Mary*. "Do you know that one?"

"Indeed, I do," Sybil said, and began to croon.

I have witnessed Sybil bringing a church congregation to tears with her spiritual rendition of *Amazing Grace*, but within a few bars, she had us all on our feet, swaying and clapping with her sexy version of Tina's lusty song. We were all breathless at the end of that performance and Dana gave us an opportunity to recover by again getting whimsical at the keyboard. That's when I got another idea.

"Dana, do you know Rod Stewart's *Maggie May*? For years Maggie had my kids convinced he wrote those lyrics for her."

"You can't prove that he didn't." Maggie countered, sounding more like her old self.

Dana played several bars and asked Maggie, "Do you remember the words?"

"Only for a private audience, darling."

Dana gave Maggie an intrigued look. "So where was he in your line of conquests?"

"Oh…before von Horn to be sure. Andre, the Grand Prix racer," she said, clearly aware of Dana's open-mouthed stare. "Also the Pollack impersonator."

I choked at the inclusion of someone I didn't recall hearing of before. "You had an affair with a known fraud?"

"He was *very* good—and refreshingly honest," she replied with a shrug. "At that point, two of my three husbands had vowed to love and honor me, but neither did. It was as though Fate had offered an opportunity. There was a nor'easter blowing through during one of my return trips to the States, and part of the coast was shut down for two days."

Conversation for another day, I thought. I wasn't entirely convinced that she wasn't pulling all of our legs.

Blinking, Dana shook her head. "I have lived a sheltered life, and I'm from California—birthplace of hippies, Hollywood, and a great deal of other things hallucinogenic."

As she returned to experimenting with different melodies, I mused, "Think of how I feel. Maggie always says she lives vicariously through my kids, and I guess she does, but more than a little of my sexual education has come through anecdotes about her love life."

Groaning softly, Carly muttered, "As far as I'm concerned thinking about sex these days is a double-edged sword."

Although she looked repulsed at first, Maggie quickly pointed out, "I can guarantee you there will be gossip if you get back into the game too soon."

Dana paused, only to study Carly's profile. "Mercy, I get you. The one thing I'm grateful for is Jesse isn't here to experience what's going on in my mind because if there's one thing I know—he wouldn't be attracted to a wife turned land-whale."

Sybil made a throaty sound and purred, "It's all about the man, little girls. My Elvin was small built and I always outweighed him by a couple of slabs of bacon, but he called me his Brown Sugar from the day we met until the day he died. There wasn't a male rabbit born more ready for a romp than Elvin."

Lowering her head over the piano keys, Dana swayed from side to side as she began to play something bluesy. With as close to a baritone as her feminine vocal chords would allow, she offered a throaty, "I feel a Barry White song coming on."

Sybil purred her approval. "Bring it on, baby."

Dana laughed softly. "And here I used to think of you as Miss Church Lady."

I never expected to enjoy myself so much. My concerns that everyone would panic under these conditions were eased and we continued to chat and sing for almost two more hours, until it struck me that it was time for the dogs to go out again. Thinking that it would also be a good idea to bring in another armload or two of wood, I said as much to Carly, who reached for more sensible boots and a jacket, while I got into mine in the back room. I whistled for Rosie, intending to go out from that side of the house.

Then, up front, I heard Maggie declare with a little too much enthusiasm, "I want to check how deep the snow has gotten."

I suppose with her not being able to join in on the singing without embarrassing herself, she'd been feeling a little left out. That's the only excuse

I could think of when I heard her swinging the front door wide open. By the time I made it back to the living room, Rosie and Wrigley were halfway across the porch, flying like bottle rockets shot into the night.

Carly screamed in fear for her dog's safety which only had Maggie laughing. "Where's it going to go?" she chided. "The snow is already deeper than the squirt is tall."

"You…bitch." Seething, Carly could barely get the words out. "You did that on purpose."

"Oh calm down," Maggie replied. "I'll help you get it back. Here, Snow Bunny!" she called into the darkness.

I yanked the door shut behind me to protect Sybil and Dana, as well as to keep from losing any more heat. Then I followed Carly and Maggie to the edge of the porch, shining my flashlight out into the yard. It was easy to spot Rosie, dark against the snow, but of Wrigley we saw nothing.

Carly sobbed in despair, "The coyotes are going to get him."

"He couldn't have gone that far," I assured her, scanning the area again with my light.

"Not even that far," Maggie said, pointing not three feet off the end of the stairs to an indentation in the snow.

I found the target with the beam of my flashlight. Carly launched herself off the steps. In the midst of a small drift, Wrigley stood ear-deep and shaking in horror. As Carly lifted him up, we could see him relieving himself, the stream as powerful as if he'd ingested a gallon of apple cider.

Maggie burst into laughter. "See? He just needed to go. No damage done."

Anyone could have figured out that the tiny dog's reaction was a reflex of sheer terror. Wholly incensed, Carly didn't even bother to look at Maggie as she strode past her with her precious bundle to return back into the house.

As the door slammed, I said to Maggie, "Just for that, you can help me bring in more firewood. From out there." I pointed toward the edge of the porch and beyond into the storm.

Maggie began to sputter. "Are you nuts?" She pointed to her own genuine suede-leather boots. They weren't the high-heels she'd arrived in, but considering all of the buckles and chains, it was clear they were no less expensive. "Unlike some people's apparel, these aren't made from old tires or discarded snap-and-seal containers."

I knew that, just as I knew full well that Maggie had three more pair in other colors, and could afford dozens more. However, considering what she'd pulled on Carly and Wrigley, I wasn't in the mood to cut her any slack.

"The electricity is out, Maggie. Things are getting serious now. You can start bringing some of that dry firewood on the porch inside and pile it onto the hearth, or help me add to our supply from the stack out there. Both will have to be done because, between you and me, I don't think the electric company is going to get us back online anytime soon."

With a sigh Maggie said, "At least let me borrow a pair of your rubber boots. Besides, I left my flashlight inside. Who knows what all is out there."

If I'd really been concerned about wildlife in these conditions, I would have told her something more than a flashlight was needed. However, I was too angry to explain, and I wasn't about to put any ideas in her head, let alone tell her where she could find a gun.

"You know where the boots are," I said tersely.

Minutes later, we trudged silently through the storm toward the side of the barn where I had two more cords of wood stacked. Neither Maggie nor I had said a word since leaving the house. The storm made conversation a foolish endeavor anyway.

Just as we reached the wood piles, she suddenly exhaled in frustration. "Get it out of your system," she declared above the wind.

While I was glad she wasn't going to play me for a fool, I was exasperated that from her perspective I was the irrational one. "Just stop!" I exploded. "You've been acting like a shrew. Carly is here for the duration. Dana cares for her. They've become close. Where's the problem?"

"She's a fake." Maggie spat out the words like an angry cat. "So soft. So cuddly. She's as annoying as her idiotic dog. And just like him, she's nothing but hair and piss."

Unable to forget the image of the leaking dog I could barely stifle a laugh. In hindsight, it had been funny. "Mercy, Maggie. How you've stayed such an influence in this town, I don't know." Actually, I did. It was all about money. The more you had, the more you could abuse everything—people, laws, whatever was in your way, or irked. "When you dislike someone, you're about as subtle as a prostate exam."

That was a low blow considering what poor Hollis had endured, and Maggie drew herself up, resplendent in her indignation—at least as much as Charlie's old felt western hat allowed. "Hell, I should be an influence! The town's named after my ancestors. If I don't care about who and what goes on here, who will?"

I tried to soothe her with a gently reproving look. "Mags, I love you, but you're full of it. Carly is a burr in your butt. Now why is that?"

"More important, why are you siding with her over your oldest and dearest friend?"

"I'm not. But she's my guest, too. Try to remember that before your next impulse to cut another slice off her, or turn that little pooch into an ice sculpture."

"Poor Carly," Maggie sneered. "Missing old Walter so much, she's texting and grinning every time she thinks no one is looking. Haven't you seen that?"

I guess I hadn't. The only time I'd noticed a phone in her hand was when the rest of us had carried our things upstairs.

"I'll bet she's having *thumb* sex texting some boy toy she's keeping on the side," Maggie seethed.

My gaping mouth was too much invitation to the driving snow, and the combination of cold and tickling sent me into a spurt of choking, then laughter. "That's so blatantly jealous, you sound like a seventh grader!"

For a moment, I didn't know whether Maggie was going to push me down into the snow or what. It was obvious that she was fighting a battle within herself, and it didn't look good for me.

"Stuff it, Brown!"

If she thought I owed her allegiance regardless of her actions, I had news for her. She already knew we disagreed on the concept of unconditional love. As far as I was concerned, that extended only as far as newborn babies. Okay, maybe up to the age of five. Thereafter, conduct had repercussions. Whatever. I'd had enough of her theatrics for one day.

As she snatched up an armful of wood and marched awkwardly back toward the house in boots too large for her size-seven feet, I let her have it.

"You think living your life like a damned opera is fun to watch? It's not. It's exhausting. And for your information there was a Frenchman called Bizet, who pulled off with real panache what you can only play at, and it was called *Carmen!*"

Four

ESPITE THE driving wind that made the lashing snow sting my face as though I was being cut by tiny shards of glass, I took my time returning to the house. My best friend wasn't the only one who needed to calm down; in fact, I had to remind myself of her status in my life as I trudged through the deepening wintery mix.

I had no problem admitting that I'd never been as outwardly passionate as Maggie. My personality leaned more toward the slow-seethe type. I was the underwater volcano—the kind that only erupted every few hundred years, at best offering a few rumbles of warning, now and again, which was often overlooked by the negligent or the obtuse. I'm sure some would use the shortcut description and label me boring. I like to see myself as steady and reliable. If people took me for granted, that wasn't the end of the world. As far as I was concerned, too much emotional upheaval was draining and a waste of energy.

Maggie, however, had succeeded in pushing me to some abnormal breaking point. I didn't like feeling such negative reverberations. What was going on with her? Could she have just ended a short fling or found unexpected disappointment, perhaps even rejection, in what she'd hoped would be a deeper romance, and her ego wasn't allowing her to confess as much? To my knowledge, she had never been rejected by a man. She had always been blessed with that invisible something that attracted the opposite sex like metal to magnet. Contrary to what I yelled as she'd walked away, it could even be amusing to watch her when she was with "the chosen one" of the moment. Men always had this slightly glazed look in their eyes, and an undeniable satisfied smile on their faces after spending time in Maggie's company, rather like a male bee drunk on nectar.

Yes, I decided. All of this had to have something to do with man trouble. Anything financial or medical and she would have told me. Under different circumstances, I could respect that, even sympathize. However, the close quarters we were dealing with required greater adjustment and consideration, as with life in military barracks, where the welfare of the group was more important than the consideration of the individual. Now, how did I make that clear to her without adding embarrassment to her wounded ego?

The wind picked up and all but screeched to where I could barely hear the crunch of frozen particles under my boots. Everywhere I looked, trees rocked and shook under the assault. I could already see huge limbs scattered around, ripped from trunks by the storm's violence, or snapped off by the weight of other branches heavy with the density of this type of precipitation. What I didn't spot was the damage to explain our lost electricity. Whatever had happened it must have occurred somewhere up the road, more and more likely at the rural substation.

It was a relief to make it to the partial protection of the house's wrap-around porch. The wind had taken my breath away. I added my frozen load to the stack near the front door, only to trade it for several dry logs from the other end of the stand. Knowing the door was locked I called for Rosie. At the other door, I stomped my feet on the rubber mat, juggled the load to balance it in one arm, so I could remove my hat to knock off that snow, too, then stepped inside. My shoulder bumped against the door jamb as Rosie pushed by me in her eagerness to reach a more welcoming environment.

"Don't mind me," I muttered. "I'm here only to feed you and keep a roof over your head. I enjoy being treated like a traffic nuisance."

Closing and locking the door, I again wiped my feet on the inside rug. I could hear lively chatter in the kitchen, although the girls were out of my line of vision. However, Maggie was to my right, sitting on the bench as she undressed. Either she'd been too upset to remember, or didn't care, I don't know which; nevertheless, she hadn't bothered leaving any of the snow outside. Ice was already returning to its liquid form, and a towel or mop would be needed to clean up the puddles she was creating.

I started to remind her where I kept those supplies, but her stony expression stopped me. Better to do it myself, I thought, turning left to go through the bathroom to bring the wood to the diminished stack by the fireplace. I decided I would also keep what happened outside between us, if she would.

When I returned, Maggie had just finished hanging up her things and brushed by me without a look, let alone a word. With a heavy sigh, I sat down on the wooden church-style bench she'd vacated, accepting that whatever was bothering her it had a dually strong hold on her mood, as well as her manners.

"I've never had hot chocolate from scratch." Dana's voice was almost a moan of pleasure. "And it sounds like an awful lot of work—but too tempting to resist. Are you sure you don't mind, Sybil?"

Ah, I thought. So that's what they were doing. Silly as it might seem, I almost teared up at that sweet conversation. If anyone deserved spoiling, Dana did.

"It'll be worth it to see the look on your face when you taste it," Sybil replied. "Besides, when I saw Retta had the makings for it in her pantry, I knew she believed there's a time for comfort food, too."

"Do you think she has marshmallows?" Carly asked.

I smiled at how much her wistful tone reminded me of my grandchildren. Hanging up my things, I slipped back into my shin-high suede and sheepskin slippers, and joined them. "Pantry, left side, second shelf from the top. Some den mother you've turned out to be," I added to Sybil, pretending to scold. "Letting the kids have sweets before bedtime." But as we exchanged glances, my look expressed how I understood there was still too much upheaval in the air to turn in yet.

"Blame my sweet tooth," Sybil replied. "I've always had one, but since Elvin died, this is my way of feeling his goodnight kiss to his Brown Sugar."

Emerging from the pantry with a jar of marshmallow cream, Carly pressed her free hand to her chest and uttered a soft, "I so get that. He sounds like he was a special man."

"Oh he was...of course it took him some time to learn how to be,"

Sybil added with a pointed look. "He started to turn the all-important corner the day I had to give him an ultimatum. Was his life going to be about his moonshine business or me?"

I had already heard this story, but I liked how our California girl gasped. For all of her professional success, Dana had standards that matched our own: a woman in a marriage was an equal partner, and shouldn't be expected to put up with backsliding from her mate.

Sybil gave her a nod that spoke of her determination. "Yes, ma'am, I did. I wasn't about to get pregnant only to end up a single mother like so many others do. My mama didn't raise a fool. Let somebody else believe any man is better than no man."

"It's not only that," Dana said. "He was really into moonshine? Was there still such a thing then? I thought they quit making the stuff once prohibition ended?"

Carly snorted in disdain. "Was and is. My mother was born, baptized, and wedded to the stuff until the day she died. I remember being a senior in high school the last time I dragged her away from a bootlegger. Oh, yeah, the business is still alive and well. In fact, it's only an appetizer on the menu of addictive substances in rural America."

Tenderly stroking Carly's glossy hair, Dana said to her, "I knew you lost your parents young, but I didn't realize what else was going on."

For a moment it seemed as if Carly's whole being was about to fall in on itself. But drawing in a sustaining breath, she squared her shoulders and replied, "Mama died. The latest bastard that had been freeloading off of us left. Enough said."

Sybil shook her head at Carly's chilling words, but she continued to stand over the stove slowly stirring the milk and melting chocolate. "Too many folks act like their kids are of no more consequence to them than their so-called pets and livestock."

Her accurate perspective touched a nerve and I had to turn away. Over by the liquor cabinet, I spotted Maggie bringing out a bottle of cognac. "That looks good," I told her. "Would you mind pouring me one?"

Without comment, Maggie took two snifters from the china hutch, poured a generous dose in each, and walked away with hers. As Dana and Carly exchanged covert glances, I touched their shoulders to encourage them to let the slight pass before going to get my glass.

Before I could indulge in a sip, there was an ear-splitting crack, followed by the heaviest crash so far. It had us all jumping, and the girls couldn't quite muffle screams. However, the strongest reaction came from Wrigley, who acted like a squirrel fleeing a pack of dogs. He scrambled up over Carly's breast to her shoulder as though she was a tree. The pooch finally ended up under the blond cape of her hair, where he burrowed himself behind her neck until only his fluffy white tail stuck out, visibly trembling.

"Ow-ow-*ow*, Wrigley!" Carly worked to untangle him from her hair. "It's okay, baby. You're fine."

My Rosie came scurrying around the corner from the living room, and she pressed herself against my leg, only then offering a growl as she stared at the back door. I leaned over to stroke her reassuringly. "Yeah, that was a big one, pretty girl."

"What was *that?*" Dana kept looking around as though still trying to gauge which direction the sound had come from.

"My hunch? The seventy-plus-year-old pine on the far side of the orchard." If I'd craved the cognac before, it had become a necessity now, and I took a sustaining sip. That's when I realized that my hand was trembling, almost as much as Wrigley's tail.

Glancing up at the recessed ceiling, I said, "Well, Grandpa, you always said, 'Don't block the morning sun.'"

"Why?" Carly asked, her expression going from spooked to perplexed.

"It all began with my grandmother's rose garden. Roses need the early light of day to dry off the night's dew to avoid disease and insect infestation, which is why her rose garden was—and remains—farther out in the backyard, instead of by the orchard where my grandfather wanted it," I replied. "But she was partial to that tree and wouldn't let my grandfather cut it down, even though the shade did affect the crop yield on *his* fruit trees. Years later, my father concurred with Gramps, especially after he got advice from the Japanese couple, who once worked and lived here. But then there was my mother, who was just as partial to the majestic tree." With a shake of my head, I concluded, "It sounds as though Mother Nature has had enough of the female stubbornness in my family and took matters into her own hand—natural *Feng Shui* if you will."

"Oh, I've heard of that," Dana said. "It has to do with architecture, and designing rooms, too, doesn't it? Someone once came into the restaurant and told Jesse the *Feng Shui* was all wrong in the place and would bring him bad luck. Jesse was furious and threw him out." She rolled her eyes at the memory, only to tear up a moment later, forced to dab at her eyes. "Hindsight being what it is, I think Jesse should have listened to him."

As Carly hugged Dana with her free arm, Sybil uttered a deep, mournful sigh as she poured the hot chocolate into three mugs. Then she topped each with a generous dollop of the marshmallow cream.

"All I know is that I hate storms like this," she said with a shiver. "The fiercer they are, the smaller I feel. It's been that way ever since I was a kid—and no comment from anyone for how long that's been. Storms take total control of my mood and ability to function. It's only gotten worse since I lost Elvin. I guess it's because I feel life has already been sending me one storm after another, so weather trouble feels like overkill." She cast us a half-embarrassed, half-hopeful look. "If anyone understands, you all should."

I uttered a soft, "Amen."

Dana added a barely audible, "Yeah."

"Lately it's made me believe that happiness—the kind like I knew— might be over." As soon as she uttered those words, Sybil looked ashamed. "Don't get me wrong. I'm grateful. Things could be a lot worse. The kids are healthy, and I am comfortable in the financial sense, thanks to that developer paying top dollar for those thirty acres Elvin and I scrimped and saved to buy. And I do feel blessed to now live with the three of you in the subdivision his company created. But with the way the world is going, I can't help but wonder when the other shoe is going to drop, you know?" She glanced at the shuttered windows, as though focusing on what was beyond them. "I don't know how you manage out here, Retta."

"I love it," I replied, not knowing what else could be closer to the truth. "It would be far more upsetting if I'd been forced to give up all of this."

"You would have more time for yourself."

Dana's suggestion was offered gently and I smiled at her as she blew at her hot chocolate and took a tentative sip. "Oh, believe me, I'm with myself plenty." After a wry laugh, I gestured with my glass toward the outdoors. "Being part of nature, all of the work—hard though it can be—it's kept me sane and given me some sense of normalcy. Sure, there's the loneliness, that awful feeling that part of us is gone, as Sybil as much said." Suddenly, I frowned grasping how I'd short-changed myself. "No, half of me *is* gone. There's the ugly truth. I feel beyond decimated by Charlie's death. It's crippled me. I'm unable to function the way a whole human being should. It's the reason why I hate facing the bathroom mirror every morning. I've been at this the longest of all of us, and I see how my husband's loss has physically altered me." The impact of my acute accuracy triggered a harsh pain on several fronts and I grimaced. "Oh, I shouldn't add to the doom and gloom. I know you all feel the same way."

"I don't."

Maggie had been behind us, leaning against the end of the counter by the two-sided fireplace and staring through the glass doors, as though hypnotized by the flames. Finally winning my attention, she stared me down with a stubborn thrust of her chin. "Maggie," I began with a sigh.

"Yes, yes, I know what you're going to say," she snapped. "I *do* miss Hollis like hell, but I'm sure not ready to join him in his grave."

"But it's not just about him, is it?"

"Never mind. The point is, you could be happier if you let a certain someone do more than rent that guest house out back."

Once again, I had to agree with Carly. She was proving to be a nasty pill to endure, and with disturbing and increased ease. What on earth had possessed her to expose a confidence in front of the others when she knew I was inherently private? In fact, I came from stock that was equally reticent about laying all their business—personal and otherwise—out in public, unlike what was becoming the norm thanks to social media. It was only my equally strong respect of others' privacy that made it impossible for me to expose something personal about *her*, so she would realize what she had done. In the end, though, it was the excitement–dare I say hopefulness in the others' faces—that allowed me to be generous.

As I said, Sybil, Dana, and Carly were newer to this widowhood business, and I knew in their imaginations, my news represented a different possibility from what they saw for themselves at this stage. I saw no way out of the uncomfortable situation without giving them some explanation. I didn't want them to assume that I was convinced there was a happily ever after for any of us. A card-carrying optimist, I wasn't.

"He's Sam Archer." I forced the words through what felt like stiff lips, reluctant to do my bidding.

"*Doctor* Sam Archer," Maggie intoned. "A wildly successful pediatric cardiologist."

It would appear that having succeeded in getting me to acknowledge his existence, Maggie was determined that I make a full disclosure. I sent her one of my rare don't-push-your-luck looks.

"Sam doesn't practice anymore," I told the others. "He lives way over in Fort Worth, and has a full, fascinating life there. Meaning, Maggie is inferring too much."

"Ho-ho! I beg to differ." Likewise, Maggie addressed our rapt audience. "Like one fantastic career isn't enough? He's now an artist." She pointed toward the living room with a feline glint of satisfaction in her blue eyes. "The painting over the fireplace—that's how good he is."

There were gasps and coos as the women praised the work anew. They'd all commented upon it earlier, but I'd managed to direct their focus elsewhere.

"And would you believe," Maggie continued, "he just happens to have been last year's most eligible bachelor in *D Magazine?*"

"Well, aren't you the dark horse?" Sybil said, giving me a good-natured hip bump.

"It wasn't as though I was keeping him a secret," I said, suffering a pang of guilt over what was a blatant lie. "It's just that he has a difficult enough time keeping any privacy where he lives, so when he's here to paint, he tries to lay low. You know we have quite a few former residents from the Metroplex now retired in this region, and others have second homes by area lakes. A number of them are affluent, and interested in the arts. I've no doubt they would recognize him, or at least his name if their paths crossed."

"How on earth did you two meet?" Sybil demanded. "I would never have guessed you to be the one to have a secret affair—with a celebrity, no less."

"Gee, thanks a lot, friend," I muttered. "Are you suggesting I have the sex appeal of some nasty, overcooked turnip greens?"

Although she started chuckling, Sybil quickly protested. "No! No! No! You know me better than that. I've been right up there with Maggie, hoping for you to find somebody. Just don't berate turnip greens because you never like the taste of yours. You know good and well that *my* recipe has won county fair ribbons."

"Then don't go saying we're having an affair," I replied with equal good humor.

Leaning over the island, Dana rested her forearms on the counter. "Stop trying to skirt the issue. You have to tell us more. It's not like you can make us go home tonight."

I had to consciously keep myself from backing away from the beautiful brunette, who represented all of my reasons why Sam shouldn't be interested in me. Oh, I knew I had some assets still intact—Charlie had always liked my blue eyes, and several times someone had asked if my heritage was Scandinavian because of what one described as my milkmaid complexion. Otherwise, I guess I was doing pretty well compared to the national average for only being about ten pounds overweight. Nevertheless—and despite Dana being utterly charming—I was feeling as shy as I was selfish.

Sam was *my* personal joy, one that I had no expectations to keep. How could I when I thought his arrival was a miracle I didn't expect at this stage of my life? But even as I admitted as much to myself, I knew how utterly stingy I was being.

Wrapping my arms around myself, I responded first with an awkward shrug, "I don't know what to say. In logical moments, which control ninety-five percent of my day, he's a figment of an imagination I didn't believe I still possessed."

Dana abruptly hugged me. "Haven't we already had a form of this conversation? You're my goal if I survive this stage of my life, which added to your artistic and sensitive sides, makes you absolutely lovely. How perfect to discover Sam is a painter. He would immediately have seen beyond attractiveness and recognized your deeper qualities."

All but squirming because I had information she didn't, I said, "You wouldn't speak so glowingly if you'd been around the day we met. I'd been repairing fences all morning, sweating like a roofer in August. Even my hair was limp with my—what's the mid-life phrase? Radiance? He was in the area doing what artists do, searching for inspiration. Someone suggested Bc Ranch."

Carly asked, "That reminds me, how did you come up with the name for your place? I can't believe someone like you would settle for something as bland as the initials of your last names."

I was in danger of spilling all of my guts to these two angelic interrogators. "You have to take into consideration that we're both the third generation to have owned our properties. Originally, my grandparents called our place *Brown Ranch*. Charlie's people called theirs *Cole Ranch*. Can you tell there are no Pulitzer Award-winning writers in the family tree? Then when Charlie and I inherited the land and ultimately merged the properties…"

"I thought it was something different what with the odd lettering of the sign hanging off the front gate. So it really does stand for Brown-Cole?" Carly interjected, with some disappointment.

"If that's what you heard, then you didn't talk to anyone who knew Charlie," I replied, with a wry smile. "For ages, every time he went to the feed store or Farm and Ranch Bureau, or anywhere else, people would write receipts, or begin filling out forms for Brown Cole Ranch. He would crane his neck to look at what they were doing, and he would say, 'Nope.' So, they would start over. After wasting several forms, some started to accuse him of just being ornery. When they asked what he wanted the name to read, he would drawl, 'Bc,' and they'd write BC. Again he would say, 'Nope.' Finally, he relented and explained, 'Big B, little c.' More than a few were exasperated insisting that made no sense. 'It's misspelled,' they would insist. 'Why the devil do you want everyone to think you can't write proper?' And my Charlie would roll a toothpick between his lips and say, 'Be-cuz.'"

Carly kept frowning for a moment, until her face lit, and her eyes brightened with humor. "Be-cuz Ranch? That's so corny it's cute! And kind of romantic, too."

"How so?" I didn't follow at all, and thought she got it right with her first guess.

"The c is small not only for the 'cuz part. It was also for Cole. He wanted it to look like he was small potatoes compared to you."

I believed at best, he was pointing out Bc was reflective of our lives being joined and added a touch of his own wit, crazy as it could be. Again, this was a man who had been known to buy me chocolates on February 15. He followed his own logic, such as it was. Now I fell silent, needing to dwell a bit over the dear idea Carly had spawned in my mind.

"Stop frowning," Maggie chided. "You know he fell in love with you on the first day of school." She nodded to assure the others. "And there never was another girl on the planet, as far as he was concerned."

"Yet he could never remember my birthday." As much as I wanted to believe in what Carly had suggested, I had to point out another fact to keep this foolishness from spiraling into a fairy tale. "I would get a card a day early or supermarket flowers a day late, but never on the right day."

"Because to him, every day was *his* birthday," Maggie declared. "Charlie was an enigma, wrapped in a mystery, and…how did you re-phrase that saying?" she asked me, momentarily stumped.

"'Clothed in 197 pounds of *redneckedness.'*"

Nodding, Maggie murmured, "An honest-to-goodness cowboy."

At least my friend had shed her moodiness—and for the sake of someone we'd both loved. "Wasn't he just?"

Feeling too many eyes on me I forced myself to get back to Dana's question. "Anyway, I let Sam sketch and wander. Then he asked about seeing more of the place. When I discovered he could stay on the back of a horse, I gave him a real tour."

I couldn't have continued if I wanted to. I had come upon a revela-tion, and it was jarring, considering that we'd just been discussing my husband. The truth was, though, that I had begun falling in love with Sam, as he fell under the influence of everything he was seeing and hearing at Bc—including me. Overwhelmed by the moment to the point that my palms suddenly got clammy the way they did when I watched a high-wire act on TV, I drew in a deep breath and barely resisted pressing my hand to my flip-flopping stomach.

"And here we are," I managed, rasping, to the point of sore-throat painful.

"*Brava!*" Maggie purred, her lips all but caressing the edge of her snifter.

Dana's exhale echoed with wistfulness. "Oh, Retta. That is so roman-tic. If anyone deserves to find happiness again, it's you. I've been think-ing of you withering away out here like a character out of Steinbeck's *Grapes of Wrath*."

"When I run out of moisturizer and can't get to town for a day or two, I start to resemble them," I assured her. "The men, that is."

Cries of protest filled the room anew, until everyone sipped their in-dulgence of choice. I was relieved to have a break from being the focus of attention, partly due to Sybil giving motherly directives to Carly and Dana to not let their chocolate spill over onto the counter and make a mess. Raising my snifter to Sybil in salute, I turned, only to find Maggie watching me.

"Yes, if you can count on one thing, it's that life is full of the unexpected."

I thought those were Maggie's words, but it took me a second to realize that her lips hadn't moved. The observation had come from Sybil.

Maggie did jar me a moment later. Proving that the night was young as far as surprises were concerned, she offered a bombshell to make my news about Sam almost yawn worthy.

"You can say that again," she said. "I once had a one-niter with a complete stranger."

"I thought...I thought the Pollack impersonator was the complete stranger?" I asked, wishing she would take the awkward hint and quit while she could. She had already exposed plenty. What was she opening herself up for now?

"The technicality is the word 'complete.' The artistic Houdini and I had dinner over two bottles of wine first."

I concluded that she had to be suicidal—at least reputation-wise. "Oh, of course. That's practically a lifetime for some." Hoping that I was also telegraphing enough through eye contact, I continued, "You are the ideal when it comes to restraint."

Only when she took in the others' shocked expressions did she make a face. "*No*, not after losing Hollis. That would have been too much, even for me, although I recognized what I was feeling then, too. It was after discovering von Horn was a cheat," she clarified. "I was still on the eastern side of the Atlantic pond."

Which put the con artist later? No, it had to be earlier, since not long after von Horn there was Hollis. On the other hand, we *were* talking about Maggie, a law unto herself.

I didn't know whether to down my cognac in one gulp to finish numbing my brain, so I could quit trying to keep up with her, or yield to a stronger impulse to just walk away and go to bed. However, since this was my house, that last impulse wasn't an option.

"Europe, of course," I said, yielding to increased indifference. "Everything is so... *continental* there and you were in full bloom with just enough naiveté left to add to your allure. You couldn't have been more than what? Twenty-six?"

"Smart ass."

Slut.

I couldn't bring myself to speak the word, but I thought it. Heaven help me, after all these years, she'd finally driven me there.

"Who was von Horn again?" Dana asked, looking confused.

"The racecar driver," Sybil said, out of the corner of her mouth. "Grand Prix series. Quite the dish."

"And he enjoyed all of the attention that brought him, despite his claims that having found *me*, his roaming days were over. So I paid him back in kind. Not my finest hour."

Maggie had managed a tone between aloof, philosophical, and honeyed sarcasm. She was getting downright scary, and I put down my glass strategizing as to how to get hold of hers without her turning feral.

"Ah, well," she continued, turning philosophical again. "In the end it didn't matter because it turned out that racing jumpsuits, or coveralls, or whatever they call those outfits, are as useless against keeping you from burning to death in a bad crash, as they are dangerous to fidelity."

"How awful," Dana said, looking as though she might need to make a run for the bathroom at any second.

Sybil proved that she was the one who was keeping track of the conversation by asking, "So you had this spontaneous fling because you were angry or hurt that Andre cheated on you? Then you forgave him and his wayward Willy, only to lose him in the crash?"

"Forget the flings. That just muddied the water."

"You can say that again," Sybil drawled.

Maggie struck a senatorial pose, her right index finger in the air to demand control of the floor. "What I'm saying is that...regardless of the low odds our marriage had for survival, one of the first things a human being experiences in the loss of your sexual partner—if any of you will be honest—is this absolute ravenous hunger. You're at ground zero with your mortality, for pity's sake."

Sybil set her mug onto the cream-and-black speckled granite counter with a thud. "Do tell."

"So I may be more sexual than most people." Maggie's smile and shrug reflected her personal amusement. "Sue me."

"You're something, all right," Sybil muttered.

"Oh…" I moaned in total misery, as I pressed the slightly cooler snifter against my warm forehead. "Darn your hide, Maggie."

"Fine. Believe me or not, I don't care."

"Silly, I do. And I can't leave you hanging out in the wind on this one." Turning to the others, I said, "I felt the same thing. Right after the funeral."

Dana gulped. "Von Horn's?"

"No! Charlie's." Thank goodness, Dana sounded as though she'd been the one drinking cognac. With just an ounce of luck, this part of the conversation might be forgotten by tomorrow. "It was so…bizarre. Not to mention upsetting."

"What did you do?"

Unfortunately, now Carly was gazing at me as though I was the official spokesperson for *Good Housekeeping*, and kept their certification stamp under my pillow at night. I wanted to shake some sense into Maggie, until her eyes rolled like cherries in slot machine windows.

"Well, not what she did," I replied, with a toss of my head in her direction. Then I had to put down my glass to cover my face with both hands. "I'm sorry. I just had to confirm that the feelings have some basis of—authenticity."

"How long do they last?" Sybil asked, frowning. "I'm trying to figure out if I should be relieved that I'd missed out on that, or feel cheated?"

"Nowhere near as long as your preacher's sermons," Maggie offered.

The quip earned her snickers from the others, and "the look" from Sybil. As things quieted again, Dana voiced her perspective.

"I think I might have related—if I wasn't pregnant, and so angry with Jesse. I used to enjoy sex. Heck, I loved it. But after his deployment, everything was different. It was like being with a stranger. To be honest, I envy you girls your experiences."

Against my better judgement, I took another sip of my brandy, silently praying that the questions would end. Soon. In an attempt to make that happen, I pointed toward Maggie with my thumb. "Envy her. As I said, I had the urge. I didn't have the courage, or moral indifference, to follow through. And considering how guilty I felt for just the impulses, I'm sure Maggie felt worse for the, um, full experience."

"Well, you'd be wrong," Maggie replied without hesitation.

"Liar," Carly piped in, watching her closely.

Maggie's eyes narrowed, "Oh, look, the half-hatched chick thinks she knows something."

"I know what love is. *Now.*" Carly continued quietly, "I believe you ultimately found out, too. Don't assume that I'm judging you. We're all at the mercy of psychological and biological things we can't always explain, let alone control. But you should be like Retta and be honest about what you truly felt afterward." At Maggie's livid stare, she added, "If you didn't feel guilty, I'll bet anything you felt depressed. And it wasn't all about sex, it was about the empty bed, the loss of human contact, and the one person you knew you could trust."

Sensing things were about to go downhill again, I gulped down the last of my cognac, a sacrilege to the painstaking vintners, and announced, "Speaking of bed, I have to be up at the crack of dawn to tend to the livestock. If the electricity doesn't come back on, I'll need to get up even earlier to keep the fires going. I'm the one who'll deal with guilt for interrupting too much of your sleep. Carly, let's take our animals out for a last potty break."

"Oh, of course." Like me, she gulped the last of her drink, and let Sybil take the mug from her.

Following me to the mudroom, she accepted my coat I held out to her. I reached for Charlie's and quickly changed into boots. Finally, the four of us stepped outside to brave the elements.

"I don't know if I can make him go again," she admitted, once the door was shut and we were alone. "Not without carrying him way out there." She pointed to a pine, so dense with limbs that some of the fallen needles were still visible beneath it.

"I'll do it," I said, taking the unhappy morsel from her. I covered the distance as quickly as I could, certain the pooch would be stressed at being carried off to the point that he might wet me. I also didn't want to spend any more time than necessary under the snow-laden tree.

Fortunately, both Wrigley and Rosie cooperated, and I was able to hand the Maltese back to Carly without incident. "Go ahead inside," I told her. "I'll get an armload of wood from in back then exchange it for some of our dry stuff up here."

"I'll put Wrigley inside and do this side of things for you."

When I carried my last load into the house, I found Sybil finishing up in the kitchen, and—from the sound of things—Dana and Carly were sharing the bathroom as they got ready for bed. There was no sign of Maggie, as I carried the logs to the wrought iron stand in the living room. Maybe she had the sense to go upstairs and save me having to wait on her using the bathroom first?

Once I hung up my jacket, I quietly asked Sybil, "She didn't take the bottle with her, did she?"

"Not quite. She refreshed the drink in hand." Setting the damp towel on the edge of the sink to dry, Sybil patted my shoulder and headed for bed, too.

For the next few minutes, I rechecked things—made sure the doors were locked, the candles were blown out, and the battery operated ones were shut off. By the time I added another two logs to the fire, Dana was in bed, and Carly was sitting beside her, still drying off Wrigley.

"Good night, you two," I said, following Rosie to the stairs.

"Thank you, Retta," Dana said, her smile warm. "We love you. We couldn't think of anywhere else we could be and still feel so welcome and safe."

Touched, I struggled with a wave of emotion. "Dream of that strawberry pie we never got into."

"You shouldn't have put that idea in my head. Even if we eat most of it during the night, we'll be sure to leave a slice for you," Carly teased.

They both looked so young in their flannel sleepwear, and their faces scrubbed clean of makeup. Feeling overly sentimental, and missing my own children, I could only blow them a kiss and continue upstairs.

Rosie waited at the top, her tail barely wagging—unusual for her. She liked our rituals and addressed them all with enthusiasm, but I knew she was exhausted, too, ready to settle in her bed in the master suite. She might not have understood every word spoken today, but she grasped emotions well enough, and there had been a surplus of them percolating under this roof.

This house had not seen so much tension in years, if ever. Well, not without a funeral being part of the problem. It reinforced my belief of how utterly compatible in demeanor Charlie and I had been. Maybe that wasn't a recipe for a passionate life, the likes of which we'd discussed tonight. But it reminded me of how much I missed his calm and amicable nature.

Sam had a great deal of tenderness in him, but anyone who could paint raging storms wreaking havoc on the Great Plains, had to have a wide range of emotions inside him. I had yet to experience all of them, and I wasn't sure I wanted to. He had given me a hint of how deep and complex he was when he told me he was a New Year's baby—a Capricorn. Maybe that's why I was still denying the depth of my feelings in front of the others. Forget his leading-man good looks and wealth. Could I really sustain the interest of someone so creative and intelligent? What gave me a glimmer of hope was that Capricorn was an earth sign, like my moon, so we did share one bottom line—the love of stability.

As I started down the hall, I could feel the churn of cooler air like a ghostly caress. It didn't spook me; if there were lingering spirits in this old house, they didn't have a problem with me. No, the change in temperature was proof the fireplace heat downstairs wasn't enough to warm such a big place, and what was emanating from the master suite wasn't reaching this far down the hall. That triggered my concern for Sybil. I couldn't bring myself to leave her in the guest room.

Peeking inside the dimly lit room, I said to the still form hunkered under the comforter and blankets, "Considering how we have to rely on the fireplaces for warmth, you'll need more than that down comforter if you stay in here. Come join us."

Sybil bolted upright, destroying the illusion that she'd fallen asleep in record speed. Eagerly grabbing her things, she dashed out of the room like an eloping bride. "Thank You, Jesus."

Upon entering the master bedroom with the fire crackling in welcome, she pointed to the camel-colored, leather recliner nearby. "You won't even know I'm here, girls. I was of a mind to claim the end of the bed, but that chair looks mighty fine. Did I ever tell you that I slept in a closet for a while as a child? Daddy had been in the service and housing was cramped, at best. That little bungalow had only two bedrooms, and I was the only girl in a gaggle of five kids, so the folks put me in their room."

"There's a unique form of birth control," Maggie said.

"Nah," Sybil replied, although she did grin. "I wasn't more than four or five, so if anything went on, I was too young to understand it. What I'm saying is, those were the happiest days of my life being tucked in beside Daddy's footlocker with his uniforms hanging over my head. I would be asleep in seconds–uniforms instead of a moon and stars. I never felt safer before or since."

Maggie had been lying on her back gazing at the ceiling, and rose on one elbow to watch Sybil get resettled. "He was Army, wasn't he? He must have been in Korea?"

"That's right," Sybil replied, spreading the comforter over the recliner. "He often spoke of the cold winters, and the mud when the thaw came. I have pictures of him in the snow standing beside cannons. I overheard him tell Mama once that his one fear was of dying in the cold, and some-one taking his boots. A few years later when Vietnam started, he said how glad he was to know he wouldn't die in a jungle, where sometimes a body started rotting before it was found. Or was never found at all." With a throaty murmur of compassion, she concluded, "Nobody wants to die anywhere but in their own bed."

"I hear that."

Sybil froze then looked over her shoulder, her expression full of re-morse. "*Maggie*. I meant no disrespect to Scotty's memory."

"I know." Adjusting her pillows, Maggie continued, "Keeping up with all the wars is widows' and orphans' business. Poor, sweet Scotty. My first husband. We were such innocents. It's been so many years, I'm ashamed to confess how sometimes I almost forget what he looked like."

"I don't believe you."

Giving Sybil a grateful smile, she amended, "Well, there are those moments when I face myself in the mirror every morning, like Retta said, and wonder what he would think if he was stuck with me today?"

"I heard an interview on the radio a while back," Sybil replied. "A man was celebrating his fiftieth anniversary with his wife and told the reporter that a happily married man doesn't see the hand of time on her, he sees the girl he fell in love with. I asked Elvin about the accuracy of that, and he said, 'Give me our Bible, baby, and I'll put my hand on it to swear that's the truth.'" Laughing softly, she then gasped upon reaching the bottom of the case she was rummaging through. "I forgot my body cream at home. Shoot. All I need is for y'all to start seeing my ashy skin taking over me."

"There are a few bottles on the vanity in the bathroom," I told her. "Some aren't even opened yet. Help yourself. Take a bottle or two with you if anything strikes your fancy."

As Sybil retreated into the master bathroom, Rosie circled in her bed next to my night table three times before dropping with the canine ver-sion of "Ah!" I sat down on the edge of the bed and looked at Maggie.

"I didn't mean to offend you," I said, cutting to the important stuff. Sybil had shut the bathroom door and, while I didn't feel a need to be secretive around her, I wanted Maggie to know I was first and foremost protective of *her.* "Downstairs? It's just that I couldn't agree with you without adding my own complicated and surprising reactions after losing Charlie."

A bit of fire reignited in eyes a shade or two darker blue than mine. For a moment, I thought I'd made a mistake to bring up the subject again. Then she gestured toward the hallway, only to let her arm fall to the slate blue comforter.

"Oh, I know it. It was just that leggy mental midget's comment. Like she knows one iota of what I'm all about. I swear, before this is over, I'm going to get me a handful of that blond hair. Maybe half of it isn't extensions, as I first suspected, but at the least I'll find out the real color of her roots."

From beyond the closed bathroom door, Sybil offered, "Thank goodness you're not rabidly envious that your legs don't go up to your armpits, too."

I couldn't help laughing, only it earned me a whack on the head via Maggie slinging one of her pillows at me. I didn't care. The gentle mockery was exactly what Maggie deserved. But she quickly snatched back the pillow, and with a huff, turned out her light and buried herself under the blankets. We didn't get another peep out of our indignant friend for the rest of the night.

Five

THE NEXT morning, programmed by years of routine, I woke before the alarm went off. Switching off the clock, I let my eyes adjust to the dark. This was what I liked least about this time of year—the knowledge of how there wasn't enough daylight for all that needed to be done.

Easing out of bed, and being as quiet as possible, I added a few logs to the red coals in the fireplace. Then, avoiding as many of the squeaky boards as I could remember, I picked up my clothes from where I'd set them on the chest by the door. Last night, I'd already decided to dress in one of the bathrooms down the hall. There was toothpaste and mouthwash always available, so I could feel somewhat refreshed, since it was my routine to hold off showering until after my laborious outside chores were completed. Farming and ranching is dirty work, making it both foolish and a waste of time to get all cleaned up, only to have to do it again in a few hours.

As Rosie followed me, I couldn't help grimacing at the click of her toenails against the hardwood floor. When living alone, you grew ultra-sensitive to sounds, and I wanted my friends to sleep on if possible; however, I'd forgotten that Rosie would challenge that.

"Sit. Stay," I whispered outside the bathroom door farthest down the hall.

I changed out of my black, long-sleeved sleep-shirt and leggings that was my uniform from the first freeze in fall, until the hint of spring in late February, or early March. But I kept on the white, men's socks I wore to bed to help with my year-round cold-feet challenge. My ensemble this morning consisted of jeans, one of Charlie's newer undershirts, and his red-and-black plaid flannel shirt—one of the few left that hadn't yet been washed see-through thin. Fashion was the farthest thing from my mind for what I had to do. I would also appreciate how the long tails would offer a bit of warmth as it covered my backside, even as I bent to rake, and lift hay and feed sacks.

Afterward, carrying my slippers to change into later, I motioned to Rosie to follow. It was time to stoke and feed the other fire.

Despite Rosie's eager race down the stairs, Dana and Carly barely stirred. On the other hand, Wrigley did raise his head from his perch on Carly's pillow and stared with his usual combination of indignation and suspicion. Thankfully, Rosie ignored the little interloper, and detoured through the bathroom to take her post by the back door. She knew sooner or later, I would be heading out that way.

Once I had the fire revived, I continued to the kitchen to get the coffee maker going. There was enough glow coming from the fireplace to make lighting any candles—real or the battery type—unnecessary. The coffeemaker sat on the counter beside the stove. It was one of those models that had the timer where you can set it to come on by itself, only I never used that option. Being from the school of thought which put safety ahead of convenience, along with respecting Charlie's lifelong warning, "Those contraptions aren't engineered worth a damn," I was only now about to plug it in. Then my caffeine-craving mind sent me a cruel reality check.

There's no electricity, dummy.

Considering all of the adjusting we would have to do, this was small potatoes; even so, I hated the extra time it seemed to take to pour water into a saucepan, and wait on it to boil. As I grabbed the jar of instant coffee in the pantry, I made a mental note.

Get the generator fueled and running before the others wake up, and this place starts to resemble a psycho ward.

While I knew there were studies about people's plunge into bad behavior when deprived of caffeine, I also worried how the girls would react to my mundane offerings. I'm no coffee connoisseur. All I care about is that mine is almost tongue-stinging hot, and black. At least there was fresh whole milk, and if they craved other doctoring, they would find sugar and cinnamon in the pantry.

I managed to ingest the contents of most of one mug, before Rosie—still sitting watchfully at the back door—offered a breathy, "Ha!" to get my attention. Glancing over, I saw she'd added a toothy grin to make her anxious plea all the more appealing. Either her bladder needed relief, or she was simply eager to get outside and start our daily routine.

"Okay, I'm ready," I whispered.

The first hint of daylight was creeping around the edges of the shutters, so I drew on my boots, jacket, red crocheted scarf, and black felt hat. Finally tugging on my leather work gloves, Rosie and I went out to see what Mother Nature had produced overnight.

The view took my breath away. Yesterday's world of autumnal rusts and ambers was almost totally hidden, blanketed with every variation of silver and white, as the sky continued to deliver an early winter in all of its frozen, yet majestic glory. There was at least a foot of snow—mixed with some ice. I could see by the pellets at the edges of the sidewalk, and against the base of the patio, that it had either hailed, or we'd had sleet at some point. The landscape was in pristine condition for the moment, thanks to our night indoors. I couldn't see any evidence of nocturnal animal traffic, either. The evergreens—pines and cedars—had been transformed into creatures out of a fairy tale. All but covered in snow now, their trunks and limbs were bent toward the ground like giants bowing before some great unseen authority.

Finally, I saw I'd been correct about the old pine yielding to the weather's assault. It had broken from about twenty feet up the trunk, indicating the tree had developed a weak spot due to its age or some beetle damage. The wind had carried the upper part onto three or four plum trees. At least they were the oldest in the orchard and near the end of their lifespan. Nevertheless, it was a sad sight.

Rosie lingered on the porch as I did, equally transfixed. Leaning over, I patted her dense coat. "What do you think, pretty girl? This makes last year's flurries seem like nothing, huh? Come on. I'll bet you'll be playing snowplow in seconds."

I'd never had a dog, who didn't love to stick his or her nose into the snow, then run, and toss the fluffy flakes into the air, like sweltering city kids in the summer using their hands to capture water from a ruptured fire hydrant and flinging it over themselves. Rosie proved no different. After a few clumsy steps due to the slippery stairs, and an abrupt, if short, pause in surprise upon realizing how deep the accumulation was, she began prancing in circles, then darting in one direction, only to spin around to go in the other. The world had become a new playground, and she was a puppy again, not a business-first cow dog. She romped for nearly a full minute before it struck her that she did need to empty her bladder.

Chuckling to myself, I started for the stables, marveling at how the world had become mysteriously silent from what the norm was around here. Of course, people in the country know silence is relative. The world is never really quiet, regardless of the weather, not with every breeze, no matter how slight, creating music from whatever is in its path—leaves, a bough of evergreen needles, a windmill, or loose piece of tin somewhere. My favorite nature sounds were the trickling of springs, and bubbling from flowing creeks, the patter of downspouts releasing a night of heavy dew or melting frost. Not to be outdone, there were birds chirping, and livestock rousing.

Today, though, those sounds were more hushed, as if I had cotton in my ears. Contrasting that, I could hear the groaning of trees protesting their frozen burden. I knew for every hour we dealt with below freezing temperatures, the sap inside those trees would get closer to congealing, and would add to the threat of sudden fracturing under the force of wind. As with people living where there was the threat of rockslides and mudslides, we, who adored our piney woods, and country roads framed by nature's version of pergolas, knew there was a price to pay for such visual beauty.

Occasionally, there was a sudden thump when the weight of an unwieldy clump of snow on a branch—assisted by a wayward wind—lost its tricky balancing act, and fell to the ground. Despite common sense telling me what had happened, I would glance over my shoulder in precaution, in case a stealthy bobcat, or something larger was trying to make a fast retreat—or worse, come after me and my sweet companion.

I created my own sound effects, and smiled at the crunch of snow under my feet. Each step sounded like a child enjoying the first few bites of a favorite cereal before the milk soaks in, turning it to mush. Raising my face to the heavenly onslaught I thought how, despite the damage and inconvenience, it was wondrous to experience something outside of the norm for this time of year, and so farther south than such things usually occurred.

My presence stirred the birds into activity. They began leaving their night's protective sanctuaries, knowing that I would soon be providing them with food. First, feeders would need to be cleared of snow. I could already see where one had fallen and shattered, due to a broken branch. Repairs, replacement, or relocation was one more thing to deal with, since my winged friends would be more reliant than usual on me for sustenance, until the melt. It wasn't all bad news. There were still some berries to harvest; some on dogwoods, many more on cedars and scrub brush, but we had always kept wild vegetation to a minimum on the place, except for around the outer perimeters because in the end, ranching was all about pasture.

The four-legged inhabitants that I didn't worry about were the squirrels. Even if the acorn crop didn't yield enough to get them through winter, there were enough pecans left in my orchard to keep them happy before they started to raid the bird feeders.

The cattle spotted me and began complaining about being unable to reach their pasture grass—all the more reason to compel me to make haste with their pellets and hay. Apparently, the stabled horses heard something was going on, too, and added their whinnies. In the tricky hierarchy of livestock these days, unless you were raising race horses, equines were low on the value meter, but you could never convince a good saddle horse owner. Never mind the condescending remarks about horses having brains the size of chestnuts, a well-trained quarter horse would face off and outmaneuver a bull twice its size, trample a coyote or snake threatening it, or its rider and, if need be, stand like a half ton-guard dog over a beloved, injured master. No, as far as I was concerned, there was no debate.

The cattle could wait. I was going to tend to the horses first. Charlie would have agreed. He would also be pumped by this weather. That turned the pleasing moment bittersweet, as I thought again of how we used to do all of these chores together, as I'd indicated during our conversations last night. But one detail I would never share was there was nothing Charlie liked more than morning sex, especially in inclement weather. It made me realize we would still be in bed, if he were alive—until the complaints from the livestock drove us groaning and laughing outside to deal with the day's needs. Later, what a hearty breakfast we would enjoy.

As I arrived at the stable doors, and found the metal latch frozen in place, I was forced to push those nostalgic thoughts aside. Grunting, at my first and second efforts to free it, I finally had to get a log from the wood rack, and smack the bottom of the bar several times before the metal braces surrendered their hold.

Setting the log and bar against the stable wall, I heard a slight commotion behind me. Looking over my shoulder, I saw that Carly had emerged from the house with Wrigley. Hugging Charlie's coat tightly against the wind, she tried to lead the little dog down the stairs. The spoiled animal was having none of that, and refused to go farther than one of the flower pots. With an indignant bark, he lifted his leg. Before she could stop him, he peed against it.

I would have sworn I heard a guttural sound of disgust from Rosie. Even when she was healing up from her spaying surgery, she had been a lady, and knew what was expected of her. Porch wetting was not remotely on that list.

We watched as Carly scolded him, then hurried him back inside. By the time I had succeeded in getting one stable door shoved open, Rosie uttered another throaty sound, and I looked back to see Carly returning with a bucket of soapy water. She flung the liquid at the planter to flush away the small offense.

"She's growing on me," I said to Rosie. "She's trying to be thoughtful, and helpful."

My Australian shepherd shook her whole body, as though rejecting the idea, her left yellow eye, and the right blue one staring at me with something akin to incredulity.

"I said *her.* I haven't warmed to that canine version of Napoleon, either." However, it struck me that Wrigley might be struggling with acceptance the same as Carly.

Spending any more time on such musing had to wait. Upon seeing the stable doors open, and feeling the colder air rush in, my horses surged to life. They pressed against their pen doors to see where I was, whinnied to win my attention before it was extended to others and, from the sounds of the ruckus, one even wanted an apology for being subjected to cabin fever.

"I hear you, Blackjack," I said. He preferred the outdoors, even if it was pouring rain.

Actually, nothing would surprise me with this bunch of four-legged friends. They were as sensitive and social as any of God's creatures. No one was going to convince me that it was only humans who suffered from idiosyncrasies.

"Good morning, my darlings," I called in a soothing alto, as I headed for the feed room.

Despite the economic foolishness of the idea, I still kept four horses: Dolly, my palomino-and-white paint mare, Charlie's Blackjack, an onyx beauty if there ever was one, Jamie's Geronimo, a black-and-white paint that horse people said had a lot of "chrome," referencing his gorgeous coloring and sheen, and Pickles, Rachel's bay gelding with the sultry dark mane. My CPA and a few rancher friends advised me repeatedly to lighten my load by reducing my horse inventory, but how could I? Which should I deport to heaven knows what future—likely a slaughterhouse considering the international market for horsemeat? That wasn't happening. They were as much family as Rosie was, and she wasn't going to end up on some international chef's menu, either.

This morning I could cut a few corners in cleaning because I'd worked ahead in anticipation of the storm. However, everyone got some grain to go along with their usual alfalfa. That and their blankets would help to keep them warm enough to fight off illness. During the feeding, Rosie followed me pen to pen to keep an eye on things, and offer a soft growl of warning if any of the horses got a bit temperamental. Frankly, all of my sweeties loved the outdoors, the way fish relished water, and this necessary quarantine wasn't the happiest turn of events—one they continued to want to discuss.

By the time I'd finished, I was a bit winded and sat down on a stack of sacked feed. It was a good time to check my cell phone for messages, before continuing on to the cattle. I smiled as I noticed there was one only a few minutes old from Sam, who was also an early riser. But motherly duty made me respond to Rachel's text first.

Power out already, but we're OK. In the stables. Heading for the cattle. Love.

I sent a duplicate to Jamie to save him concern when he took in his first weather report of the day. Only then did I allow myself the indulgence of calling Sam.

"I'd hoped you could squeeze in a call to me," he said, instead of any formal or casual greeting.

I smiled, realizing we were on the same wavelength. "It is a bit hectic, but I'm out here in the stable. I have a house full of sleeping women and no electricity, so I have a limited idea of what the forecast is at this point. Is it still snowing there?" I asked him.

"It is," he said, not sounding too happy. "No power, huh? How are you holding up?"

"Environmentally, not bad. As for the human side of things, let's just say it was a mercurial day and night, and we barely avoided a full-fledged cat fight right before bedtime."

I shared enough in the hope Sam would give me his two-cents' worth as a professional with some background in psychology.

"I'm not surprised about Maggie saying what she did," he replied. "It's a challenge to keep things harmonious in constrained conditions even when the willingness to get along is unanimous."

I don't believe we ever got close, I thought, remembering Maggie's conduct throughout the day. Waiting for more perspective, and advice, Sam startled me by changing the subject.

"Forget that. We need to talk. About us," he said.

After a slight hesitation, I admitted softly, "I know, and I want to."

Clearly heartened, Sam said quickly, "I'm falling in love, Retta. Undoubtedly, for the last time in my life. I meant to say this in person, to say it to your..."

Overwhelmed, I dropped the phone into my lap, as though experiencing an electrical shock. Torn between the thrill of hearing words I had actually fanaticized about in the secrecy of my solitary bed, only to dread having to explain my feelings to family who worshipped Charlie and believed no one could ever replace him, I panicked. Not at all proud of myself, as I picked up the phone, I hit the End-Call button.

My cowardice shamed me. What had I done? A most beautiful, brilliant man had told me he'd fallen in love. With me. What kind of idiot thought such a moment was apt to happen every Friday at 6:22 A.M.?

As some inner voice screamed at me to call him back, I could feel the words he wanted, expected, to hear stuck in my throat like a coffin lodged in the doorway of a burial vault.

There's an appropriate analogy.

Did I really feel as though I was betraying Charlie? There was no going back; that much I understood. On the other hand, something was keeping me from going forward.

Yes, in the end, that was the black-and-white truth for this long-married woman. I wasn't one to judge other people who found happiness after the loss of a spouse. In fact, for several acquaintances I was most tenderly pleased when they did find new companionship or even deeper love. My psychological quandary was separate and personal.

Sam didn't ring me back—no surprise there—which triggered a new tidal wave of emotion, namely regret and dread. Nevertheless, I left the situation as it was.

Fully understanding what I was risking, I convinced myself I had enough on my plate without being pressured into a complicated discussion about our future. We were not teenagers, or even newlyweds needing constant and multiple reassurances. Surely he would recall my agreement for the need to talk? What's more, he was right: this was something we should discuss face to face. It was too big and important to handle over the phone during what I'd warned had to be a quick check-in call.

Despite feeling a tad better, it was all I could do to focus on the rest of my chores—the cattle, the hens in the chicken house, the birds. My weighted-with-guilt heart would thud with doubt one moment, only to skip into an almost giddy thrum the next, as I thought, "He loves me!"

It was the top of the hour before I returned to the house. It made me wish I'd left Sybil a note to go ahead and make breakfast as soon as she was ready, and not wait on me.

I set the straw-lined basket with today's fresh eggs on the stairs, then gassed up the generator stored under the porch, plugged it into the outlet connected to the breaker box, and turned it on. The noise wasn't much easier on the ears than that of a welding machine, but it would give the refrigerator the boost it needed, as well as provide us with some TV time, lights—although not needed as much at this hour—and use of the freaking coffee machine.

Still half lost in the world of Sam, and dying for another mug of something hot to thaw my frozen limbs, I whistled for Rosie. When we stepped indoors, it was to a single cheer. Sybil hopped up and down, punching her arms toward the ceiling.

"You got the power back on! Woman, you are amazing."

"It's only the generator." As she approached me, I handed her the basket. "Hear it? We have two hours of power max, unless I refill the tank, which I won't. Not yet. We still don't know if we're looking at days of this before the power company can get to us or what, but if you need to charge your phone, now's the time. Just help me remind everyone not to turn on their blow dryers at the same time. That tends to flip breaker switches."

"We can all go a day without salon-perfect hair. My, these eggs look fine. I miss having a few chickens around. Let me get you coffee," she said, quickly setting the basket on the counter. She stuck my rinsed out mug under the machine's spout. "You look frozen solid."

Backing into the mud room to carefully lower myself onto the bench, I closed my eyes. For a moment, I absorbed the warmth and the initial, promising scents from Sybil quickly putting bacon and ham on the griddle. Right then and there, I knew I was going to humiliate myself by gorging on breakfast. But I was fairly certain I'd burned as many calories as if I'd run at least half of a 5K race. Not bad for a junior senior citizen in the twenty-first century.

"Here you go, sweetheart." Sybil arrived with the mug. "Take off your gloves."

I did, even as I opened my eyes tempted by the scent of coffee. It was only at that moment I realized she was wearing Charlie's favorite gray cardigan sweater over the lighter-gray sweats that she'd slept in. She'd probably spotted it as she came in here to check on where I was, and grabbed it, belatedly realizing she wasn't dressed warmly enough. I liked seeing that she'd chosen it. Charlie's sweater had brought me many an hour of comfort, too.

"Ah...bless you, Sybil." I eagerly accepted the steaming mug. "You're the gift that keeps giving."

"Girl, you're one to talk. I felt terrible you went out to work by yourself. I was of a mind to join you when I realized you were gone. You looked so small and alone surrounded by all those bellyaching cattle. Problem is those things scare the lady out of me, and I decided I would be of more use getting some hot food ready for you and the others. I was about to make biscuits in the Dutch oven in the fire, and heat the ham, there, too, 'cuz it's a wonder you don't weigh as little as a rib and a hambone for how you go on and on out there."

I wasn't in the mood to laugh, but I exhaled with gratitude as the coffee's steam caressed and thawed my numbed face. "Your students should hug you every day for the rich visuals you give them with every word out of your mouth. I've got the boots, dear friend," I added, as I realized she had begun to kneel. "Get back to that magic you're creating in the kitchen. I've worked up a serious appetite."

Patting my thigh, she took off and, after two greedy sips of coffee, I set down the mug to start peeling off my frozen-stiff outerwear. Lying beside me on the mat, Rosie was licking at the ice caked between her toes. Knowing how painful that was for her—as unbearable as a person trying to walk with corns—I slid off the bench to help her.

"It will be better in a minute," I said destroying what fingernails I had left, by slicing at the hard balls of ice with my thumbs. When she licked at my fingers, I knew she understood I was providing relief faster than she could achieve it herself. "You are welcome, pretty girl. One more, one more..."

When I was done, she gave me a soft "Woof," before heading for her bed under the palm. I knew she was ready for a snack whenever I could get it to her, and then a well-deserved nap.

"The TV satellite is trying to boot up," Dana announced, entering the kitchen to pour a mug of coffee. "I took out the DVD. Considering the time, I'm not expecting much reception-wise. I doubt anyone in Texarkana or Tyler gives a fig whether or not to report about those of us in the boonies anyway. If we can get the news, I'm sure they'll be focused on conditions in the downtown areas."

"Well, if it's bad in town, they'll know it's worse beyond the city limits," I replied upon entering the room. Confident that we would find out soon enough, I enjoyed studying her instead. She looked like a Christmas tree bag in her pine-green, flannel gown, and I couldn't resist telling her, "You look adorable in that get-up."

With good humor, Dana also showed off her thick socks and leg warmers underneath her ensemble.

All three of us were laughing as Maggie arrived in gorgeous, cheetah-print silk, designer pajamas, looking like something out of a 1940s film. But from the way she was clutching an ivory cashmere shawl around herself, I could tell she had yet to make fashion take a back seat to practicality.

"Oh, for pity's sake," I scolded, shivering all over again from just looking at her. "Grab one of those dry jackets in the mud room and give the fashionista addiction a rest."

Surprisingly, she did exactly that, only to gasp when the last member of our group trudged out of the bathroom wearing a pair of men's blue-striped pajamas that all but swallowed her. In fact, there was no missing the purple belt from some other outfit tied around her waist to keep up the bottoms.

Of course, I'd briefly had a partial glimpse of her last night, but now seeing her standing there, the amount of excessive material triggered a suspicion in me. "Are those Walter's?" I asked gently.

With a shy smile, Carly nodded. "At first, I wore them because they smelled like him. Now, I wear them because it makes me feel like I'm still in his arms."

I saw Maggie turn away to meet Sybil's gaze, only to stick a finger in her mouth as though to gag. The insensitive exhibition lasted only a second before she proceeded to get her own coffee, fortunately, not long enough for Carly to notice.

With pursed lips and a quick shake of her head to Maggie, Sybil said to Carly, "That is mighty sweet, darlin'. And isn't that the truth about missing our men's particular scents? Lord, I cried and cried the day I re-alized I couldn't smell Elvin anymore."

"I think I'll turn on the radio to listen for updates," I said, crossing over to the counter where it was set. "Chances are the cloud cover is too thick to get TV reception anyway."

The real reason I was changing the subject was to avoid opening the can of worms that would come from discussing relationships again. With my luck, Maggie would ask if Sam had called yet. There was no way I wanted to deal with an inquisition, particularly after the way I'd left things with him.

The radio turned out to be helpful. We learned that power outages were at a record high for our region. The forecast was for precipitation to turn to ice before this system pushed out of the area sometime tonight or early tomorrow. I confirmed that when I brought up the radar screen on my cell phone, and shared the image with everyone. The huge swath of white and blue representing snow and ice still covered most of our state.

It was Carly who spoke first and her thoughtfulness was endearing. "It looks like you're stuck with us for another day."

"Terrific," I said, mostly meaning it. "The next chapter of our adventure lies ahead. How boring, or scary, would it be if we were each fending for ourselves at our own homes? Now, I don't know about you, but I intend to stuff my face like my livestock are doing. Someone set the table, while I dash upstairs to wash up and change so that I don't offend everyone with my barn and pasture smells."

In record time, I returned having made do with a sponge bath. The table was set, and we sat down to Sybil's banquet of ham, bacon, cheese grits, scrambled eggs, fresh biscuits and gravy. It was several minutes before anyone uttered more than a moan of pleasure, as we satisfied the first pangs of our hunger. Even though I was the only one who had been outside there was undeniably something about frigid conditions that triggered appetites.

"We'll need to help Retta in the barn or shovel the sidewalk to work off these calories," Dana said minutes later, as she spooned a second helping of scrambled eggs onto her plate.

"Not *you*," I replied, horrified at the thought of her injuring herself or the baby. "Besides, everything is under control."

"Until she checks the critters at noon," Maggie added, "just in case they need a tissue for a runny nose or a snack. The reason we don't see Retta at more socials, is because her four-legged friends mean more to her than her two-legged ones."

Hoping Maggie would take my reply with the humor intended, I drawled, "Well, of course, I do. They're tax deductible."

Her expression wholly amused, Sybil added, "We all need to come back as one of Retta's animals."

"Seriously, though, I need to do something," Dana declared, with almost genteel Southern desperation. "If I sit all day, my back will be killing me more than it already is. Retta, I noticed you don't have any decorations up yet. Don't you start this early?"

Immediately grasping what she was driving at, I could only hope I was wrong. It was my pleasure to house and entertain them—but to a point. What she was suggesting would literally turn my house upside down.

"As you can see," I began, trying to sound apologetic, "I haven't even gotten around to doing anything for Thanksgiving. To answer your question, though, I usually start the Christmas part on what they used to call Black Friday–that is before those wizards of internet marketing strategy changed everything."

Sybil leaned forward with enthusiasm. "If it wasn't for online shopping, my family would still be waiting for Christmas by the time summer break rolled around."

"Well, my dilemma is that Jamie's family and Rachel's all have tough schedules this year." I hoped that would squash my guests' growing enthusiasm. "They've told me that a visit probably isn't going to be possible, at least not before spring. I guess that just killed any incentive I had to get excited about doing much."

"If Sam hears your news, he'll want to come for sure," Maggie replied. "Or does he have his own family obligations?"

Although her tone sounded conversational, my heart thudded sharply against my breast. I'd never disclosed anything else Sam had told me about his past, but one only had to type his name into a computer search box to gain enough information to put together a fairly accurate hunch about him. Had Maggie already done so? I'd been sincere in my apology last night, so why was she acting as though she was determined to find an exposed nerve and dig at it?

"No," I replied quietly. "To my knowledge he has none."

"There you are then," she replied, brightening. "You have to spruce up the place for him. Retta used to do the holidays in grand style. She decorated every room," she explained to the others. "The kids had their own trees in each bedroom. Every bathroom had a winter wonderland scene on the vanity. She also routinely makes her own wreaths and swags. Me, I buy a dozen poinsettias, and turn the stereo to holiday music."

As relieved as I was for the reprieve from being cross-examined, her audacious understatement about her lack of traditions had me choking on the last of my coffee. *"What?"*

With a snooty sniff, Maggie replied, "You don't know that I didn't keep things minimal chic. Last year, you chose not to attend even one of my parties."

"Excuse me—I caught the hideous intestinal bug going around, remember? Would you have been happier if I showed up and shared it with all of your A-list guests?"

"They sure seem to like to write about your parties in the local paper," Sybil told Maggie.

"Correction, they used to." Maggie all but pouted. "Until someone started a rumor that a big Nashville star was to perform at my Christmas Eve open house. Only the entertainment had actually been provided by my hairdresser's brother-in-law, who did actually sell a song to I forget who, but that's hardly the same thing, is it? And as is often the case with songwriters, his talent is greater than his voice. So now our paper's editor-in-chief thinks I serve hallucinogenic hors d' oeuvres, and he won't return my calls even though elected officials and potential candidates count on me to host gatherings and get them exposure."

"The point is," I said, "she usually hires someone from Dallas to handle everything, and entertains practically every night from Christmas Eve to New Year's Day. There's no comparison to my novice impulses."

Instead of the mischievous grin I was expecting, Maggie kept her eyes on her plate. Nothing in her expression gave away any inner thoughts.

"I might just keep things a little more low-key this year," she finally said.

At the other end of the table, Dana leaned forward, clearly focused on one thing. "Retta, let us do it for you!"

Carly piped in, "Yes!"

"Adult decorations would be a nice change of pace from the colored paper garlands and snowflake cut-outs we do at school," Sybil mused.

"Besides, we would feel like we're contributing something for all of your hospitality," Dana added.

"You will be if you promise to come back on New Year's Day and help me take it all down." Despite my droll reply, I couldn't deny their enthusiasm was breaking through my resolve. "You're serious?" I asked. How different I sounded from the young wife and mother I had been, eager to share the joy of the holidays with my new and growing family. I'd also been proud to see the appreciation on our parents' faces when, growing tired, they saw the traditions of family holidays were being successfully passed on to the next generation.

Oddly enough, my kids hadn't mentioned lifting me of any, let alone all of that. Maybe they didn't see me as old enough to worry about it yet? Right. I knew better than to look for that compliment. My suspicion was that those classic family gatherings were heading the way of dinosaurs, proving too much trouble at this stage of their lives, especially considering everyone's geographic challenges.

"It's either that," Sybil warned, "or emptying your propane tank by baking cookies."

Her teasing threat snapped me out of my gloomy thoughts so fast, I felt as though I'd been struck with a boomerang across the bridge of the nose. "Oh, now wait a minute."

"Oh, please, no," Dana entreated. "The way I'm going, I'll end up gaining six pounds on top of the eight we're *alleged* to gain for Thanksgiving." She puffed out her cheeks like a blowfish to suggest what the results would look like on her.

Already feeling breakfast challenging the waistband on my jeans, I relented. "Let me show you where I store all of the decorations. Then, while I clean up these dishes, you all can get dressed." I gave Maggie a special warning. "No high heeled boots today. Be nice to those bunions for a change. Besides, there's no way to get anybody medical help."

"I'll bet Dr. Sam would find a sled and team of huskies to get here if he knew you needed him," she crooned.

Maybe not at this point, even if he was still practicing, I thought, my heart suddenly too heavy a weight in my chest. "Don't test your fate—or my luck."

Although I pretended that I didn't notice, out of the corner of my eye, I spotted Maggie raising both eyebrows. Disgusted with myself for exposing that much, I rose to follow an animated Dana and Carly, who were already on their way into the living room.

Six

WHEN WE regrouped at the coat-storage closet almost a half hour later, Carly and I grabbed both ends of the bag with the seven-foot tree, and navigated around Sybil. She chose one of the big plastic containers, the one bearing the label "Lighted Garlands."

"Oh, I love this angel!"

Although we'd exited the closet, the exclamation nearly gave me whiplash. Sure enough, as I looked over my shoulder, Dana was holding a two-foot-tall, crystal figurine, and my breath caught in my throat. I knew exactly how heavy it was—too weighty for someone of her size and condition.

"Maggie, help her with that," I blurted out before I could stop myself.

In the midst of reaching for her own box, Maggie managed an impressive pivot, soon embracing Dana and the cherished piece from behind. "Darling, we don't need you to go into labor from carrying anything this unwieldy."

Not remotely "slow" by anyone's standards, Dana bit softly at her lower lip. She'd stopped wearing lipstick once she'd learned she was pregnant, but her lips were already a deep pink, as though she'd grown into the habit of worrying the tender skin quite a bit.

"It's very old and expensive, isn't it?" she asked, gazing at it with new respect.

"We haven't figured out its age," Maggie replied, almost as softly. "But the kids found it at an antique shop, and gave it to Retta the first year they had to endure the holidays without Charlie."

As Dana followed Maggie out of the closet, she moaned, "Oh, Retta, I'm sorry to have upset you. It is exquisite."

"Thank you. And I'm sorry for overreacting," I added quickly. "I know it's foolish for possessions to trigger such strong emotions."

"She's not a possession. She's a piece of art. It was so thoughtful of your children to get her for you, and what a touching tribute to a husband and father. If someone had done that for me, my reaction to seeing it snatched up would probably have been hysterical."

Dana had changed into a plaid flannel shirt, not unlike the one I'd worn earlier, only she wore hers over a tunic. The shades of her ensemble were blue and green. Was the shirt Jesse's? I suspected so, and that made me think that regardless of the anger she had voiced, she ached for him, too. Or was her financial quandary forcing her to make do with what was in the closet to get through these last weeks of her pregnancy? Whatever the reason, it struck me again what a tall and broad-shouldered man Jesse had been. Much like Sam, I thought belatedly, which explained why the shirt all but swallowed Dana. When she launched herself at me, everything billowed out making me think of sails on a small craft catching the wind, and I instinctively spread my arms to welcome her.

"I wish you were my mother."

The unexpected statement and almost fierce hug humbled me, even as it triggered a dozen questions. As I held her and the precious gift she was carrying against me, I could sense her raw emotions. They unleashed my own, as well as my maternal instincts. "That's one of the dearest things a woman can hear after 'I love you.' I feel that baby kicking you like a punching bag, too. Come sit down here at the dining room table, and let us bring the work to you."

"That hardly sounds fair," she began. However, she obediently lowered herself onto the chair I pulled out for her at the end of the table nearest to where we would be working.

"You may take that back, once I show you what I want to do. Back in a second."

On my way to the closet, I paused. Maggie was placing the angel in its traditional spot on the Bombay chest by the front door.

Sybil was watching, and I said to her, "Help me move this small end table and chair away from the window, please? That's where we always put the tree."

Carly had come over and was crouching beside the green canvas bag. Unzipping it, she asked, "This is one of those self-locking, instantly lit designs, isn't it?" When I nodded she continued. "Can I have a try at this? Walter and I thought about getting one, but he talked me into traveling over the holidays instead."

"By all means, see how you like this model, and I'll tell you who usually carries it at a reasonable price."

Continuing to the closet, I brought out another plastic storage box marked "Kids' Art," and set it on the floor beside Dana. "These are all of the ornaments my children made through their school years. You'll find each one is wrapped in tissue paper. If you like, you can spread out everything on the table to help you determine what should go where on the tree."

Dana's expression reflected gentle reprimand. "Understanding you more with every hour, I would bet everything is already packed in order of where it belongs on the tree."

The comment had me grimacing. "Do I really look that anal to you?"

"No, just organized. Efficient."

"Well, I assure you that I'm open to change, so improvise to your heart's content."

Once Dana lifted the lid, she uttered a soft "Wow. You did keep them all. How darling...and different than at our house. My mother would buy me one ornament each Christmas from some collection or other depending on what she'd heard children of my age should be interested in. Would you believe the year I went off to college she donated everything to a charity?"

I couldn't suppress a huff of agitation. "How...thoughtless! She didn't think you'd like them for your children?"

"It was so in keeping with the rest of her and my father's behavior, I didn't think to ask. In all honesty, it wasn't really too hurtful. I suppose by that point I was inured."

I couldn't believe we'd never discussed this before, but I had to ask, "Am I correct in guessing you were an only child?"

Dana nodded. "My parents were in the sciences. They still are despite being in their seventies. Very intelligent. Unapologetically different. I was as difficult for them to comprehend with my right-brained, creative mind, as they were for me with their prove-it, minutiae focus."

With my heart aching for the lonely child she'd been, I said, "Well, now you can start your own traditions…for you and your baby." I stopped in mid-step and turned back to her. "By the way, you haven't said—are you having a boy or girl?"

"When I had the sonogram, they offered to tell me—correction, let me see—but I turned my head away. I mean I wanted it to be a surprise."

"Now that's restraint. The curiosity would have driven me crazy."

I left her looking a little dazed—or was it guilty? I shook off that illogical thought and checked on Carly, who had no problem with the tree. But we all had a good laugh when Sybil plugged the cord into the electrical outlet and uttered an uncharacteristic oath. Nothing was happening.

"What gives? I still hear the generator," she muttered. "We have power everywhere else."

"That sure puts a wrench in things." Maggie looked equally miffed. "What's the point of doing all this work if the lights aren't any good?"

"The tree is only two years old. It's fine." I went over to the wall by the door and pushed in the dimmer button controlling the outlet.

The girls let out a cheer and applauded when the room was suddenly transformed from the glow of tiny white lights. For my part, I nodded my pleasure upon accepting it would have been a mistake not to do a tree. The ambiance it added to the room was immediate.

With a youthful whoop, Carly hopped over the canvas bag to get another box. Then she all but ripped off the lid. "This is so much fun."

Having heard enough yesterday to know Carly's childhood had been anything but happy, I was delighted that she, too, was enjoying the moment. "Did you manage to have any kind of decorations at your home?"

Without looking up, she shook her head. "There was no money. At first all I could think to do was sneak into the library and rip out a holiday picture from a magazine. I'd fasten it to the wall by Willow's bed with a piece of gum I saw Mama spit out." As she heard our collective gasp, she smiled with chagrin. "I know. Gross, huh? Anyway, then I would tell her, 'One day we'll have this.'"

"Who's Willow?" I asked, confused.

"You don't know?" Carly checked herself. "No, why should you? She's my half-sister. She was born when I was ten. Now she's a senior at Texas A&M-Commerce. She wants to be a writer."

Since Carly was thirty or close to it, I assumed she remained more mother figure than sister to her younger sibling. However, sensing a bit of reserve returning to her demeanor as she cast a wary glance Maggie's way, I resisted the latest rush of questions that flooded my mind. "You must be very proud."

"There are no words," she replied, emotion turning her voice husky. "Unlike me, she's a natural when it comes to learning. All of it. I'm okay with general math, but algebra might as well have been hieroglyphics when I was in school. I so wanted things to be better, at least easier for her, but until Walter, it took just about every ounce of willpower I had to get her to believe college was possible. I worked as many shifts and odd jobs that I could to save money for her to go. Yet it was Walter who made her feel that she had something to contribute and to take her future seriously. She practically devoured every word out of his mouth, and worked doubly hard to impress him, as she did me. I guess he became the defining male figure in both of our lives."

"You couldn't have found anyone better," Sybil murmured.

"No, especially since I wasn't looking for a relationship, let alone love." With an impish look, Carly said, "Do you know what one of the stylists at our salon said? This will tell you what a character she is. When a client asked her opinion of the perfect man, she said, 'A guy who's sterile and an orphan.'"

We all laughed, and I agreed, "It certainly would cut down on the bulk of domestic conflict for a greater part of the world population."

"God bless both you and Willow," Sybil said. "I can see you can achieve whatever you need, or want to accomplish. As much as I fret over Debra, it wasn't a picnic with the rest of the children, either. What with working in the school cafeteria, attending night school, and waiting on Elvin to get his big boy pants on, there were times when I fell into bed at night and didn't know if I would have the strength to get out of it in the morning. I don't know if it was stubbornness or pride, but I do know I prayed to God continually to give me the courage to keep going. The thought finally struck me—why would the good Lord give you some brains and strength, then not help you do all you could for yourself, and your family?"

Carly nodded. "I'm beginning to understand that. I mean about how it refers to me. Putting all of my faith and energy into Willow was easier. But when it came to having it in myself, I struggled with fear and anger. Oh!" she declared, all but blooming with pride. "Do you know that Willow's now a mentor to troubled girls at a junior high school?"

"What a compliment," Sybil replied. "There's your reward, darlin'."

On a hunch, I glanced Maggie's way before asking, "Is she who you've been texting? I saw you a minute ago checking your cell phone and grinning."

Carly rolled her eyes. "I don't know how she gets anything done, let alone concentrates. She's constantly seeing or hearing the most incredible things. I think she likes to share with me because she knows I didn't have the opportunities she's having. She really is a great kid. I'd like you to meet her."

Before I could assure her that I'd love to, there was a crash... only this time the sound came from inside the house. I knew Rosie had been curled up on her bed in the kitchen, but glancing around, I couldn't see any sign of Wrigley. Uh-oh, I thought.

A second later, Wrigley raced from the bathroom with Rosie in fast pursuit. As the little dog tried to climb up Carly's leg, she scooped him up into her arms.

"What on earth...?" she gasped, immediately inspecting the pup for any injury.

Right on the little dog's heels, Rosie had to brake hard not to crash into Carly. She glared up at Wrigley, and began barking. Her tone was a clear scolding if I'd ever heard one. However, I knew my dog well enough to trust she had no intention of taking it out on the offensive rascal's owner.

Spotting Rosie's saliva-soaked ear, I said, "I think I see what happened. Wrigley must have been trying to get her attention and has been tugging or gnawing on her. I suspect when she'd had enough, Rosie tried to hide behind the ironing board in the laundry room, and subsequently knocked it over. Rosie used to hide there during the worst storms when she was a baby. Maybe you could kennel Wrigley for a while?" I asked Carly.

"He's shaking as though he's given himself a good scare. I'm sure he'll behave now."

"Maybe. But he could have been injured. He needs to recognize wrong behavior. Like a mischievous child, he needs a time out." Retta thought of a teaching analogy she could share. "All animals have their own techniques, but take horses for example. A mare has to be extremely strict with her foals and you can catch her giving them a bump with her head or a sharp nip with her teeth when they aren't learning acceptable conduct. I believe puppies need disciplining, too."

"I hadn't thought of it that way. Goodness, little man," Carly said to the dog as she brought him to his carrier. "Don't you realize we wouldn't be able to get you to a vet clinic?"

On the other side of the room, Maggie abandoned her box containing figurines, and my manger scene that was three generations old. "I need a break," she said, heading for the shortcut to the laundry room. "I'll check for damage, then turn on the weather radio for the latest report."

As soon as she was out of sight, Sybil leaned toward me, and said out of the side of her mouth, "She actually managed to avoid sounding tacky. What's taken possession of her, and where's our feisty Maggie?"

I had the exact same thought. "Maybe these decorations reminded her that this is the season for peace on earth?" With a shrug, I added, "Just don't voluntarily put any sharp objects within her reach—at least not until we can be sure this isn't some kind of feint."

Chuckling softly, Sybil turned back to the box of garlands she was laying out on the other end of the dining room table. "You know, this is giving me a pang of guilt, Retta. My kids aren't coming home, either, and the idea of skipping the decorating didn't bother me one bit. Even without my family, pleasing a second grade class full of kids will take every ounce of energy I have. Yet the way you have everything packed to perfection all ready to go along with being a full-time ranching woman, makes me feel like I don't know diddly squat about hard work and commitment."

"Oh please," I said, although I secretly basked in the compliment. "I have a decade on you, practice-wise. I should hope some of it stuck. Charlie once teased I would have made a good Army supply sergeant."

Sybil grinned. "Not all compliments sound poetic."

"One of my mother's favorite English novels from the Victorian era about staff at a mansion had a good line: 'Everything has a place and everything is in its place.'"

"Pride in one's work, no matter how simple or tedious," Sybil murmured. "There's a lost virtue. Too many don't have a sense of work ethic anymore."

About to agree with her, I saw Maggie come striding back into the room. She was holding the weather radio out before her, as though it was ticking suspiciously.

"You know how you wanted us to come out here because you expected the worst?" she began. "The way this guy is talking, even you don't have enough firewood."

What now? I pointed toward the back. "I have half of Noah's ark out there. Exactly what did you hear?"

"Two to four inches."

I was ready to shrug off her concern. "That's not much different than what we heard earlier."

"Two to four inches of *ice*, once the switch happens."

My mind didn't want to accept what she'd reported. Snow was one thing. Ice was an entirely different story. Ice was heavy. Many more trees would snap, and there were older houses in our area where the roofs probably wouldn't be able to take such a weight. What's more, we could forget about getting power back anytime soon. Every available utility crew member would be working around the clock. Chances were, personnel from states not touched by this storm would need to offer their personnel, and still it would be a drawn out and daunting challenge to recover from all of this.

"Oh, Retta, what are we going to do?" Dana asked. "At the risk of sounding selfish and petty, I have at best one more change of clothes left."

With an affirmative nod, Carly said, "I didn't plan much better than she did."

That much I could handle. "While I can't keep you all looking ready for a magazine layout, I can assure you there are plenty of clothes in this house for people of all ages and sizes," I told them. "What's more, we can always turn on the generator for the hour or two that's needed to run the washer."

"You are *not* putting any of my fine lingerie in a machine that handled Charlie's manure-stained overalls," Maggie huffed, all indignation.

So much for thinking that she had gone phlegmatic on us. She knew perfectly well that if Charlie ever got that dirty, he would first soak his clothes using the old machine in the guesthouse. It had finally given up the good fight shortly after he passed. I'd also had to replace the one in this house last year, so there was no threat to her dainties.

Not about to explain what she should have remembered, I mimicked her cranky tone. "Then go without and chafe your skin raw on denim and wool."

"No need. I'm perfectly capable of hand washing them—provided we don't run out of water, too."

I was getting tired of this game or whatever she was doing. "We're not going to run out of hot water," I chided, reminding everyone of how the water heater was fueled by propane. "As for the well pump, the generator is going to keep it functioning. And in the unlikely event we do run low on firewood, which means we'd used about a winter's worth of wood in a week, let me assure you I'm as handy as any man with a chain saw."

"You know this place inside and out, Retta, and the exact right thing to say for any crisis," Dana said.

She sounded so young. I wondered if I had ever been so inexperienced? Of course not, I thought, with undeniable pride for having been in this field of work all my life. What I wasn't about to admit, though, was if Sam could somehow snap his fingers and transport me to his four-star hotel room, I'd happily vanish.

"Why don't we take a break, so you all can bring me what clothes you want washed while the generator is still going?" I told them.

They complied with eagerness, and a few minutes later, we had the washer humming away. As for Maggie, she remained upstairs, undoubtedly doing exactly what she'd insisted was her preference.

"I was wondering, Retta," Carly said, as we returned to decorating. "Do you visit Charlie's grave routinely?"

Glancing at her perfect profile, I knew she was still thinking about Walter. "If you're looking for advice or comparison, I'm not sure I'm the right person to ask. From the perspective of my faith...his body is there, but not his soul. In fact, sometimes I've felt him more here than at the cemetery. So I go about twice a year. I put small wreaths on all of our relations' graves for the holidays, and take them away after Twelfth Night. If there's a storm, I'll stop by to check on things and put everything back in order. In the end, I think it's a personal choice you have to make for yourself."

"I go talk things over with Walter," Carly said. "I'd like to leave something, but he made me promise not to do any artificial stuff."

"Oh, Charlie was that way, too. Occasionally, I see a single stem, some gaudy-colored silk flower lying at the base of the headstone, and I know it's from an old friend of his that had come by and left it just to tick him off."

Carly checked my expression before she let herself grin. "That's funny. But I like your wreath idea. I might try that."

"I think if the bank takes the house, they can have Jesse's ashes, too," Dana muttered. "It's not enough to leave me with that last vision of him, he also didn't tell me what to do with his remains. I mean—he didn't want to stay with me, but I get to keep his ashes in the bedroom closet for the rest of my life?"

"Baby," Sybil said, coming over to stroke her back. "You know he wasn't in his right mind. You have to do what's right for you. I'm with Retta. I don't have a second home at the cemetery. I go on Elvin's birthday, and our anniversary, and Christmas." A twinkle lit her eyes. "You know Maggie would need a whole new wardrobe to visit all of her husbands."

It was exactly what we needed to hear to lift our spirits back to their former lightheartedness. After a few hoots and giggles, we got back to work with new enthusiasm.

IT WAS NEARLY noon when Rosie uttered a soft, "Woof" and stood facing the front door. I knew it was time for her to go out, and told Carly she should probably release Wrigley from his confinement, so he could join us. She was faster than me in getting ready, and I was only rising from pulling on my boots when I heard her scream. It took me a moment to drag on my coat and get outside. That's when I spotted her standing under the ancient cedar tree where I had carried Wrigley the night before.

She was pointing farther out toward a small wooded area. "Those black things," she called to me. "What are they? They look dead."

It had been decades since I had experienced something like this, but it was a scene one never forgets. Following an excited Rosie through the calf-deep snow, I joined her under the semi-protection of the tree. The location also gave me a confirmation of what I thought I was seeing.

"Buzzards," I said. "They were probably killed by the initial hail storm or by all of the falling branches we've been hearing. During colder months, they come up at dusk from ponds and lakes to roost on dead trees amid a grove of evergreens to protect themselves from frigid winds, clueless as to what a heavy frozen branch will do to them."

"Gross. And scary. What should we do?" Carly asked.

I could have teased her about fighting the rock-hard earth to dig a mass grave and holding a funeral for them, but the weather conditions made drawing this out so unappealing, I just shrugged. "We let them be for now. At least we can rely on nature's own refrigerator to keep them from stinking up the place, and creating a health hazard. No doubt there'll be more of them before this is all over. We'll eventually burn them along with all of this brush. In the meantime, let's get out from under here, so you and Wrigley don't end up in the same condition."

"Oh, my God!"

Shushing her for fear a loud noise could help the vibrations create an avalanche from the limbs above; I drew her from under the tree and pointed to the wood pile. "Grab an armful of logs."

"I meant to tell you," she said, as we worked side by side, "when I first headed outside, I spooked a whole line of little birds pressed against the storm door, their wings spread over each other. They looked like a mini-chorus line. I felt terrible for disturbing them."

"Sparrows," I told her. "They're trying to absorb any warmth leaking under the door sweep. They recognize there's safety in numbers, too. One for all and all for one like in *The Three Musketeers*. Not to worry. They'll be back as soon as we're inside."

Once we returned to the others, Carly reported all of the excitement with the birds. When she shared the startling news about the buzzards, she said, "I grew up here. I can't believe I've never seen such a sight."

"That sounds like something out of a horror movie," Dana said, looking as though her morning sickness wanted to make a strong comeback.

"It usually doesn't happen but once in a person's lifetime," I assured them. "There's no denying these conditions are having a terrible effect on wildlife, just as it is the land."

"Oh, wait! Before I saw the buzzards, the most darling thing happened," Carly said. "When I first opened the door, I saw fifteen or twenty sparrows pressed against the base of the storm door. They had banded together and were hugging each other. Retta says they were trying to absorb the little bit of heat leaking from the house. Doesn't that remind you all of us in a way? All huddled here helping each other to survive?"

"We're hardly in dire straits yet."

While we'd been outside, Maggie had returned downstairs. She was now working with Sybil to get the garland just so on the mantle, and her censorious remark dripped with mockery.

"I get what you mean, Carly." Dana leaned back in her chair and wrapped her arms around her belly. "I wonder if they stay with their own families, or is it a haphazard thing? How awful for the youngest ones, last spring's hatchlings."

When Dana and Carly exchanged glances again, my heart ached anew. They were seeing themselves as far more vulnerable than the rest of us. After all, their families were small to nonexistent.

Looking almost as mournful, Sybil said, "All your beautiful trees, Retta."

"I know. The entire region will be effected," I replied. "Between the commercial timbering going on over the last ten years and now this weather, we won't be known as the East Texas Piney Woods anymore."

"Everything changes."

It was the second time Maggie had said that, and it was getting on my nerves. I knew she wasn't a tree hugger, and her ancestors had owned the first lumber mill in these parts, but she used to claim she loved the pines here as much as I did.

I decided to count my blessings. At least she hadn't had anything to drink yet.

As though reading my mind, she abruptly headed for the kitchen. "I need a glass of wine."

Sybil eased over to me and whispered, "I wondered how long it would take."

As we listened to the sounds of a cabinet opening and then the refrigerator, a pensive atmosphere took over the room. Dana and Carly had glanced after Maggie, too.

Sybil asked in a normal voice, "Why don't I get lunch started?"

Although she gave her an appreciative look, Dana said, "You know I'm gaining all of my weight in these last weeks, and I haven't worked off breakfast yet. Please don't do too much, since I have no willpower?"

"As long as it's something warm," Carly said, hugging her dog. "I'm still cold from that trip outside."

"How about some soup?" Sybil asked.

"That sounds perfect," I told her.

It couldn't have been more than twenty minutes later when she called us to come eat. Dana headed for the bathroom. Carly washed her hands in the kitchen sink. I saw Maggie had finished setting the table and was carrying a platter of cheese and crackers in one hand and what had to be a refilled wine glass in the other.

Once the four of us sat down, Sybil came bearing a big pot of tomato basil soup and placed it on the mosaic trivet in the middle of the table. Simple enough fare, yet I felt a slow tightening around my throat and tears burn in my eyes. Lowering my head, I tried to blink away the spillover that threatened.

"What's wrong?" Ever observant, Sybil gripped my shoulder in concern.

I tried to dismiss the question with a shake of my head, and struggled for a brave smile. "That's the last soup I made for Charlie."

"Oh, honey. I should have asked you first what you'd prefer."

"No, no. It's okay. I'm being way too emotional today," I replied. "Some people's arthritis acts up with these low pressure systems. I guess my tear ducts get overactive." It was a pitiful attempt at humor, yet my friend was full of support.

"There's no okay about it. We live half of our lives building these memories with our loved ones, only to have to spend the rest of our time without them getting knocked on our butts by those very same recollections. And there's never any warning. It's always sudden."

"'Sudden'…" I took a deep breath to force a subtle quavering out of my voice. "There's a word that seems to mock people like us. It reminds me of the time…only a few months after Charlie passed, when our pastor asked me to speak to the Stephen Ministers."

"The loss counseling group," Dana said. "You know, he asked if *I* would like a caregiver. There was no way I could understand what was happening, let alone verbalize that to someone else. How on earth did you manage, Retta?"

"I couldn't—not for a few years. You're looking at someone, who started to do grocery shopping at six in the morning when the only people in the store were the night shift stocking shelves. That's how desperate I was to avoid running into anyone I knew, regardless of their good intentions and kindness. It took nothing to turn me into a broken water faucet, which only heaped embarrassment onto misery. Plus, I was endlessly exhausted. There was too much to deal with here, and our children were struggling with their own grief, and needed to lean on me. The irony in that is once they got over their first shock and grief, they had plenty of opinions of how I should be coping better, too."

"Lord, bless them," Sybil said. "You give birth to them, you raise them to be as smart as they can be, and one day they decide they know everything, while you must've been napping inside an incubator since you hatched the little darlings."

I nodded my agreement. "There've been moments when I was tempted to suggest mine go psychoanalyze someone else, but then came the day...my son was visiting and he was keeping up with a golf tournament on his iPad while we talked. He abruptly blurted out, 'Sudden death!' Once he explained to me what was going on, it struck me how what he'd described paralleled what I'd experienced in losing Charlie. It was then I knew I could do what our pastor had asked of me."

"Say *what?*" Sybil's expression reflected utter confusion.

"Think about it," I said. "Charlie and I were like two lifelong friends on a golf course, both aiming for the same goal, the eighteenth hole. Then suddenly something goes catastrophically wrong—and only one of us makes it.

"I know in some ways the metaphor weakens," I continued, "but try to understand the loser's devastation—and *mine* for him. Charlie was dead out of luck. There I was the so-called winner, but, I was really just the survivor, because everything was on my shoulders now–every decision, every debt, and every problem. And I'd *won?* That's what sudden death means to me—and in a way I think it must give a golfer pause—at least if he's playing with someone he truly cares about."

I shared a wry smile with the small group. "Well, if it wasn't for my faith, children, and grandchildren, along with some great friends, I would have had a time finding any peace, let alone state of grace." I reached over to squeeze Sybil's hand, "Thank you for the wonderful soup and memory I clearly needed to revisit."

I took a deep breath. I still didn't want the soup, but I would eat it with gratitude, just as I would move forward with a thankful heart, if not complete understanding of why life had turned out as it did.

Dana seemed to be lost in her own world, only to ask, "So, did you do it? Did you give the talk?"

"Yes. It didn't go quite as well as the motion picture in my mind, but I felt a strange push to do it. Carly, you may not know this but Stephen Ministers are lay caregivers to 160 Christian denominations. The impetus was born from the book of *Acts*. It explains Saint Stephen ministering to those who are hurting. It's also referenced in Saint Paul's letter to the Ephesians. Need means different things to everyone whether it's triggered by death, divorce, illness, or job loss, to name a few, and Stephen Ministers offer a tether to those who need a sign to grasp they're not alone."

In that instant, Carly became the image of a proud wife. "Walter was a Stephen Minister."

New tears welled in my eyes. "Yes, he was. I'm glad he shared that with you."

"He said you helped him get through losing Doris. One more thing I have to thank you for, besides inviting me here."

I sat back in my chair awed by this latest example of the universe taking its own sweet time to put together the pieces of our shattered-life puzzles. How wondrous that when it does, we can come across small pockets of bliss containing the seeds and potential to spawn unanticipated greatness.

"Well, where was your gilded tongue when Daddy decided I should marry *The Schmuck?*"

I gasped at Maggie's timing, not to mention the challenge. Then I saw she wasn't as in control as she wanted to appear: she needed a bolstering sip of wine.

"You can't be serious? I was still a kid, the same as you—and, by the way, your father was a bully, albeit with Southern manners."

"Who's the schmuck?" Dana asked.

"Stanley Dickens. My second husband," Maggie replied. "Handsome and charismatic in his own way, although nowhere close to being as smooth as Andre had been. Still, he somehow convinced Daddy he should be the one to carry on the timber business, since all I'd done for the family was to become a widow while still in high school. Only it turned out Stanley loved the country club life and schmoozing with the town's elite much more than tending to business at the mill. And heaven knows, he wasn't interested in *me*. My confusion and wounded pride ended the day I came home and found him wearing one of my prettiest negligees and stilettos."

"Lord have mercy," Sybil drawled, using a little Southern drama herself by fanning her neckline, as though suffering a hot flash. "I remember when that revelation was the talk of the town. What amazes me is he left Martin's Mill a *whole* man. Your Daddy wasn't known for his tolerance any more than he felt obliged by any devotion to fairness, even with his flesh and blood."

"Yeah, it's a tossup as to which of them I miss more," Maggie said, her voice oozing with sarcasm.

After mouthing a silent, "Wow," Dana asked, "So your ex agreed to a divorce?"

"A quiet one without any financial demands," Maggie replied, with a nod of satisfaction.

I waited for her to meet my gaze, but she took her sweet time. I didn't begin to try to understand why. "Well, you paid your father back for forcing him on you, didn't you? You married von Horn, proving the old mule wasn't the only one capable of bad judgment."

"You say. It got me my own money to where I could come back to Martin's Mill as Daddy lay dying without having to fear being brow beaten into some last grand plan of his."

I told the others, "Ultimately, Andre's family paid her to stay on this side of the pond."

"The race car driver! Husband number three."

Maggie rewarded Dana's good memory with a regal nod. "The esteemed member of the broken zipper brigade. But what a beautiful male specimen. Did I mention he was Austrian? Of noble birth—that's what the von denotes. He and the rest of the clan hated the PC police deciding you shouldn't spell it with a capital V anymore."

"Why? Did he worry women wouldn't fall into his arms as fast without it?" Sybil asked.

"Exactement."

One other thing Maggie had come home with was the ability to at least sound legit as she uttered a declaration here and there in society

French. It was a waste in Martin's Mill, but she didn't seem to care. If she needed to dye her hair purple to stand out among the masses, Maggie would die her hair purple.

Trying to keep a straight face, I did my own reminiscing. "The day after your father's funeral, Charlie and I reintroduced you to Hollis." It was he who had the best influence on her life and kept her relatively grounded in what the rest of us called "reality."

Maggie straightened in her chair, her shoulders as straight as any young military officer. "You did nothing of the sort. I happened to stop by for a visit and he was here. It would have been impolite of you not to make the obvious gesture and invite me to stay for dinner, given my sad circumstances."

"I could have had a moment of conscience and chosen to protect Hollis," I countered, waiting for her to see the laughter in my eyes.

Lifting her glass to her lips, Maggie purred, "You may kiss my couture-clad ass."

We all fell back in our chairs and over our bowls laughing. Maggie rose to refuel herself with wine, but at least her expression held more amusement than annoyance.

As the giggles died down, Dana said, "I was Jesse's rebound."

Nodding sagely, Sybil replied, "The Eleventh Commandment should be: Thou shalt not be the rebound woman. My brother thought he would be doing a friend a favor once by fixing me up with a guy, when he broke up with his wife. Some brother. In between trying to get his hand up my dress, all the dude wanted to do was cry about the Jezebel who'd locked him out of the house. What was your Jesse's story?" she added to Dana.

"He was a marine and she didn't have the patience for his long deployments."

"And you did?" Sybil asked.

Dana looked a little surprised at the question, a testament to her maturity. "We weren't kids. I was doing well with my career, and he wanted to stay in the service for the pension."

"Did you know she was doing background vocals for major performers and getting commercial jingles?" Carly asked us, all but gushing.

"One of thousands," Dana reminded her. "In any case, our plans took a nosedive when Jesse came back early from his last deployment. Nothing was the same again."

"I get that," Maggie said, resuming her seat. "Post traumatic what-chamacallit. Only it's the first part of what you said that keeps my head spinning. Why the hell did you leave a thriving career in a big city, only to end up in Martin's Mill? I had to come back because this was home, and the family business was here."

Dana took a deep breath. "The doctors said with his PTSD symptoms, it would be best to be close to family. You're right, his family isn't around here anymore, but they are living down in Tyler, which is nothing really if things had been different. But our personalities didn't mesh."

"Oh, honey, I can't imagine someone not loving you to death," Sybil said.

"It wasn't just me. Their beliefs remain vastly different from what medical personnel recommended would be a good atmosphere for Jesse. He was supposed to put his trust in God and suck up whatever symptoms he was dealing with." Dana gestured helplessly. "How do you work around such rigidity? Without more support between VA appointments, it was difficult for me to keep Jesse on his medication."

"Yet you still opened a restaurant?" I asked, although I almost anticipated what she would say in response.

"I loved him, and he thought staying busy would help. 'For better or worse,' isn't that what the vows say?" she asked with a sad smile. "But you're right, the restaurant was the worst thing we could have done. He didn't have the temperament, or the psychological stability to start a business. Heck, the failure rate for perfectly healthy people is off the charts. We were fools."

"I went there for takeout several times," Sybil said. "I'd been too tired to cook and had an armload of papers to grade. Everything I ordered was wonderful."

"You must have caught him in one of those first weeks when he was having some good moments." Dana looked off into some private torment, where the images were still painful and embarrassing to recall. "There were plenty of customers who left because they were offended by his attitude. Some found their meals suddenly becoming wall art. The day I realized it was too late for the business was the day he killed himself—the same day the foreclosure letter from the bank was in the mailbox. The same day I planned to tell him I was pregnant."

A heavy silence descended upon the room, and an equally heavy sadness. "I can't imagine how devastated you must have been," I said. "We're trained in our faith to always consider there are worse situations out there than what we're dealing with, but this so yanked you out of the life you were built for. In your own way, you could be dealing with your own PTSD."

"You might be right. It's also probably why I didn't have a service," Dana said. "Would you believe when I notified them of what had happened, Jesse's parents announced to me he was in Hell for what he'd done to himself? I knew they were different, but I didn't know they were crazy!"

"Some people..." Sybil whispered.

"Unfortunately, there are plenty more like them out there," Dana continued. "On my return to church the following Sunday, one old biddy patted my hand as she assured me Jesse blowing his head off was part of God's plan. But the one that made me unable to listen any longer was when some asked me if I was sure I should continue with the pregnancy, given how flawed I already knew the father had been?"

Sybil covered her ears with her hands and groaned. "Awful. That's just awful."

"But what can you say to someone as clueless as that? It's not like I could offend our pastor and tell the fools what I really thought of them," Dana replied.

"Next time you run up against one of those sweethearts, call me," Maggie told her. "I have no problem telling people to go to hell."

Thinking I could easily have become a hermit if I'd had to listen to such vulgar talk, I couldn't help but ask Dana the question that loomed in my mind. "Why on earth are you still here? Why haven't you gone back to California where you were happy and successful? Surely you would have more than a foot in the door with your talents?"

"It doesn't take people long to forget you. I told you I was one of thousands. In any case, I do have a few options here." As she saw our interest, she demurred. "I'd really prefer not to say anything more yet."

Carly leaned over and kissed Dana's cheek, then pushed back her chair, preparing to stand. "I don't know about y'all, but I'm ready to get back to decorating."

I couldn't have been more proud of Carly if she'd been one of my own. She was showing again what a good friend she was to Dana. I gave her a covert wink of approval. As curious as I was about Dana's hint at opportunities, I had to respect her right to privacy, and started to put my silverware into my empty dish. "I'm right behind you. Let's find some holiday music on the radio. My ears are aching for something uplifting."

"I'm so tired of this cold already, I want to hear a samba or rumba," Maggie countered, swaying her hips to some Latin beat in her mind. "Heck, I want to move where I could hear it every hour of every day."

"Send me a postcard," Sybil replied, rising. "I'm not moving anywhere that the snakes grow as long as cruise ships."

Seven

FTER WE all helped clean up the kitchen, we drifted back into the living room. Sybil fretted over her beautiful strawberry pie, still intact in the refrigerator. Despite their teasing last night, Dana and Carly hadn't touched it.

"Why don't we have a real high tea around three o'clock," I suggested. "We can eat the pie then. My poor, neglected china could use the attention. Having a hot drink will also bolster me before I head out to do the evening chores."

Sybil's face lit with excitement. "What a good idea. I've admired that Royal Albert set every time I've been here. And I've never been to a proper tea."

"I don't know about getting the 'proper' part right," I said, "but I agree with the entertainment divas who say if you have nice things, you should use them. My daughter already told me I might as well sell the set on EBay or Craig's List because she has no interest in them."

Sybil gasped, her expression reflecting disappointment. "Times are just changing too fast. I hate seeing the younger generation abandoning traditions. Their indifference sure seems to carry over to other parts of their lives."

"You're not the only one who believes that." Before adding a log or two to the fire, I paused to admire the tree, even though there was still more work to do on it. "I do have to admit, though, they've made impressive progress in technology. Just look at all of this gorgeousness— and remember the embarrassing things that were produced when we were younger? Strings of lights with bulbs so big, the tree didn't look pretty until you were standing out on the street."

Sybil gave me a sheepish look. "I know this is showing my age, but my first artificial tree was my idea of being a successful, *modern* woman. It was one of those aluminum models with the rotating color wheel."

"Oh, I remember those. That's so 1960s," I said, as the younger girls eyed us with disbelief. "My brother wanted one, but Dad said there was no way one of those monstrosities was coming into this house. It was going to be a real tree or nothing while he was still head of our family."

Glancing Maggie's way, I expected her to nod her agreement or add some comment, but she just continued to decorate the tree with robotic efficiency.

"No offense, Maggie. I know you had no say so about things back then, but the worst example had to be at the bank," Sybil said. "I remember the ugly thing they put up because it was the last year Debra agreed to sit on Santa's lap and his sleigh was right beside it. Lloyd Crum had the honor of wearing the suit longer than he deserved, since he was usually so polluted he could barely keep from sliding off the seat. It was late by the time I got off work, and we were one of the last in line. When it was finally Debra's turn, she made some of the strangest faces you ever saw. The minute she came back to me she tugged on my sleeve and announced loud enough for everyone, even someone back in the vault to hear, 'Mama, Santa stinks! He smells worse than Daddy did 'fore you made him go to church.'"

I groaned imagining the embarrassing moment, then saw Sybil's gaze linger on Carly. The younger woman did look momentarily haunted.

"I'm sorry, darlin'," she said. "I know you had too many worries to laugh over our nonsense."

"Well, I do admire how you were able to change Elvin. When I got older to where I could go farther from the house without getting in trouble with my mother, I started collecting aluminum cans to save money for Willow's Christmas. I had three bags saved when her boyfriend turned them in and spent the money on hooch."

With a wince, Dana said, "Now you make me feel ashamed. I was just thinking how clueless my parents were the time they gave me a microscope. Expensive though it was, I didn't want it. All I'd asked for was a little transistor radio."

Sending her a sympathetic glance, Carly turned her attention back to the tree. Almost immediately, she squinted to scrutinize something more closely. "I didn't realize you have a brother, Retta," she said, pointing to a photo ornament that was of two children visiting a store Santa and labeled, *Danny and Loretta.* "I mean, you just said as much a minute ago, but it didn't sink in until I saw this."

"Had," I said softly. Out of the corner of my eye, I saw Maggie quietly leave the room. "Daniel died in Vietnam."

"I'm so sorry," Dana and Carly said in unison.

"Thanks." It was so far back I could usually talk about it without getting emotional. It had been so much more difficult for my parents. "He was four years older than me. Mother called him Danny Boy, after the Irish ballad," I added. When they nodded with recognition, I continued, "She had a lovely voice, and would sing him to sleep with that melody. He was a rascal, but he could do no wrong in her eyes. Then came Nam, and the draft. When he learned he had a low number, he didn't wait for it to come up. He thought he would get the matter done with. His dream was to come back and prepare to take over things here—only he was a chopper gunner, and they were shot down during his last month of duty. Mother never sang again, not *Danny Boy* or anything else. Dad went virtually gray overnight."

"How awful for all of you," Carly said. "I can't imagine something happening to Willow." She shivered, as though almost sickened by the thought.

"That's one more thing that bonded you and Maggie," Sybil noted. She glanced over her shoulder into the kitchen where Maggie was pouring herself another glass of wine. "You lost Danny when you were barely out of junior high, and she lost her Scotty before she could graduate from high school."

She was right, and with both of our loved ones, we'd lived in fear, always dreading the worst. Then, for one moment, I'd believed Danny would get out and be safe, and so did Maggie, upon reading in the newspaper that President Nixon had reached an accord to end the war. We'd been so wrong.

"That's the end of it."

It was Dana who spoke, and I realized, she'd stood up to put the last of the children's ornaments on the tree. But I had the sneaking suspicion she wanted to change the subject, and I couldn't blame her.

"Wonderful," I said, admiring everyone's handiwork. "I don't think it's ever looked better."

Her expression pleased, Dana went to the other end of the table to pick up one of the bare vine wreaths. "We need to go and collect some pine cones and branches with berries."

With a frown of concern, Carly said, "You can't risk it. I'll go. Wrigley probably needs a potty break anyway. I saw him at the water bowl twice since we were last out."

"I'll join you, and show you where the best places are for the cones and branches," I told her. "Those pine boughs should be hanging so low by now, we can pluck the cones right off the tree and not worry about digging them out from under the snow."

WE FOUND THE snowfall had eased considerably, and the wind had gentled to where flurries literally danced like white-gowned ladies at a Southern cotillion ball, flakes rising and falling in the way chiffon and satin gowns do when sweeping around a ballroom floor during an elegant waltz. If we hadn't had Maggie to report earlier how the worst was yet to come, we might have been lulled into the false belief the storm was giving out.

I waited on Carly to let Wrigley do his business and return the little dog inside. Afterward, with Rosie still keeping us company, we waded through the snow along the east tree line, carrying the baskets we had brought to collect nature's treasures. I had accumulated a good selection of pine cones in various sizes, and gave Carly my garden clippers as we approached a massive holly tree lush with crimson berries and sharp, green leaves.

"This is the largest holly tree I've ever seen," Carly said. "The berries and leaves look like wax, they're so perfect and shiny. I used to break off a branch or two wherever I could find them to stick in one of Mother's beer bottles. I'd put it by Willow's bed. On Christmas Eve, I would tell her to look out the window and watch for Santa Claus. She was young enough at the time to think a jetliner moving across the night sky was Santa's sleigh."

Carly's sensitivity was quickly winning a special place in my heart. "I'm so glad your sister has you."

As we walked toward the pines the stables and guest house caught her attention. "What's that painted on the building? I didn't notice it until now. It looks like Asian writing, I think."

"Japanese to be exact. *Kachou Fuugetsu*," I said, hoping I remembered the pronunciation correctly, since the words were in my soul, but I rarely spoke them aloud enough to feel confident. "It literally means flower, bird, wind, and moon. They're symbols to remind us that by experiencing the beauty nature provides, we learn about ourselves."

"That's lovely," Carly said. "Who thought to paint it there?"

It was a long story, but I could see she was fascinated, so I shared an abbreviated version. "After World War II, but a few years before I was born, my grandparents were still running the farm when a young Japanese couple came by. They had been released from the internment camps in California, and were trying to start over. They were looking for work in the hopes of someday saving enough to buy their own bit of land. Even with the help of my mother and father, my grandparents needed reliable labor. Our ranch was much larger then, and finding skilled and dependable people was difficult, so they gladly took them in. Katashi—Watanabe was his surname—worked with my grandfather and father while his young wife, Amaya, cleaned house, and cooked in order for my grandmother and mother to spend more time with the bookkeeping, sewing, gardening, and canning—any and all of the other myriad of things a woman does on a place like this. When I came along, Amaya helped tend to me, too."

"What interesting names. I'm always intrigued and curious about what international names could mean," Carly replied.

"I remember being told Watanabe means firmness. When I was old enough to look up things for myself, I learned it's rather common today, but those who first bore it were strictly court nobles.

"Katashi means plowed field and scarecrow," I continued. "To my young mind, it meant something like scarecrow in the field, which made me laugh, because he really was wiry."

"So in a way he could be seen as a durable worker of the land?" Carly asked.

"Very good. At least that makes as much sense as anything else we thought of. It certainly described him perfectly."

"And Amaya?"

"Ah," I said with a smile. "Amaya means night rain."

Carly gasped softly. "How romantic. Tell me she looked the part?"

"Well, I hadn't met too many people from their side of the world, but she was dark and exotic, yes. And it was obvious to me they adored each other. They were both the kindest, most gentle people we ever had the pleasure of knowing. Mother and Gran said so repeatedly in the years after they left."

"What happened to them?"

"They broke my heart." The ache I still felt was every bit as real as what I experienced with Daniel's awful loss. "The year I turned thirteen, Amaya sat me down and quietly told me they had family who had found land in Mississippi, and they were moving to buy adjoining acreage."

"Did you ever hear from them again?"

"For some years, but you know how those things go. The last time I received a letter was after I notified them that Mother had died. They were of an age themselves by then."

Still gazing at the unusual characters, Carly said, "But they meant a lot to you. It looks like you've taken pains to keep those symbols vivid."

I nodded. "That's because I would no sooner paint over them any more than I would willingly slice the memory of the Watanabes from my mind."

Carly worked quietly for almost a full minute before speaking again. "The best foster home Willow and I ever had was with Fredric Lazicki and his wife, Fannie. We called him Mr. Fred. He got me my first job at the Dairy Queen, and they were very good with Willow, which allowed me to get through cosmetology school. He wanted me to go to junior college, but I didn't have the confidence yet."

I could tell by her secretive, sidelong look that she wondered if I would see her decision as a weakness. I didn't.

"You're plenty young to continue your education now. You have the time and financial ability. It's not as though you would have to go routinely to a campus. There are plenty of online classes you can take. Is there something you're interested in pursuing?"

She pressed her lips together as though trying to contain herself, only to blurt out, "I have an accountant, an investment banker, and I have a lawyer. But I can't help feeling as though I need to know as much, if not more, than they do."

She had focused on the blinding white ground the whole time she spoke. Was she anticipating I would laugh at her? Nothing could be further from my mind.

"Carly, you've just drawn one the most intelligent conclusions I've ever heard—including from Maggie, who—despite the impression she's been giving—has developed quite the business mind."

Carly turned away, and from the sudden shift of her shoulders I could tell she was struggling not to embarrass herself by getting emotional. I so wanted to drop my basket and wrap my arms around her, the way I would my own child or grandchild if they were navigating through a difficult crisis.

"I think *you* have business school in your future," I said, hoping I sounded as reassuring as I wanted to be. "Walter would be so proud. If there's anything I can do to help, a letter of recommendation, being a sounding board, whatever, I want you to know I'm here for you."

She still couldn't bring herself to look at me, and when she spoke her voice was strained.

"Thank you, Retta. I can't tell you what that means to me."

WE FINISHED OUR collecting and returned inside. Dana and Sybil immediately pounced upon our baskets, praising the quality of what we'd chosen. While I'd unplugged the generator for now—which left the tree dark again—we lit candles, as well as the battery-operated garland lights. It all added up to retaining the festive atmosphere.

Noticing Maggie wasn't around, she surprised me by emerging from the closet carrying Charlie's dressier western boots. That's when I looked over my shoulder and realized mine and the kids' were already set on the fireplace. It had long been my family's tradition to use them instead of knit or felt Christmas stockings; I could only imagine Sam's reaction upon seeing them.

"Maggie, maybe we'll skip the boots this year," I began. "Particularly not that pair."

"Trust me."

While she seemed a little unsteady on her feet—which strongly hint-
ed at what she'd been doing while we'd been outside—she also sounded
way too sure of herself, even given our close relationship. "Please listen
to me."

"Sam won't hesitate telling you how he really feels about you if he
sees you still have these stashed away like an old prom corsage. When
all else fails, you can rely on the male competition gene to kick in."

She snapped her fingers together so crisply that I expected her man-
icured nails to trigger sparks. Added to her audacity, I could feel my
hackles rising, and I had to press a soothing hand at my nape to subdue
the sensation and my annoyance.

"Not all men approach life as though it was a competitive sport, Maggie." I spoke slowly, and quietly, letting my pointed look do the work of
transmitting the displeasure I was feeling.

"Oh, fiddle-dee-dee, as my idol Scarlett would say. I've known a few
more men than you have, my girl."

"For pity's sake, Maggie," Carly snapped. "Does everything have to
be a contest of wills and manipulation with you? Retta knows what is
comfortable for her, and what isn't."

I was thinking, *Oh God, oh God, oh God,* when I saw lasers shoot
from Maggie's blue eyes and the tendons in her neck tighten, as she
drew herself erect. Before I could think of something calming to say, the
beast was unleashed.

"I have known *my* best friend for almost sixty years, and I will talk
to her any damned way I please."

Hoping that Maggie was still lucid enough to recognize what I was
about to sacrifice, maybe even risk, I abandoned my own counsel and
admitted, "Actually, I spoke to Sam while out at the barn this morning. He is coming, as soon as the storm passes and the roads are clear
enough for travel, so we can have Thanksgiving together. Knowing that,
I wouldn't feel right with keeping to the family's old traditions. Charlie's
boots would be a third presence under this roof, and having everyone
else's there but his would be equally glaring. Do you hear me, Maggie?
Ultimately I have to stop doing things that invite Charlie's spirit to not
only reside, but to control what happens in this house."

I could see she understood the wisdom in that, but my staging was
all wrong. I should have taken her to the next room and quietly said

those things, not share them in front of everyone. As far as Maggie was concerned, I had just betrayed her.

Sure enough, with a stiff nod and a rigid back, Maggie pivoted and returned every pair to the closet. Maybe World War III had been avoided, but at what cost and for how long?

None of the others seemed too worried. They were more interested in my news and inched closer, gushing and clapping as though we were sorority sisters celebrating that I'd just been pinned by a fraternity heart-throb. Everyone started asking questions at the same time.

"When do we get to meet him?"

"If I promise to bring dessert, can I accidentally on purpose drop by?"

"You said that so calmly. How are you really feeling, Retta?"

The latter was Carly's question. I could see she was getting quite good at discerning my feelings.

"I feel...nineteen trying not to act like a thirteen-year-old," I admitted. It was that true and that ridiculous, which made me shrug, further exposing my dubious control of my emotions. I'd never felt this way in my life, leaving me to wonder if anything so intense could last?

"Sounds like you should be preparing for Fourth of July fireworks," mused Sybil, "more than a calorie-rich dinner."

"Now, I really want to meet him," Dana said. "I have to see the man who can reduce Retta Brown Cole to tongue-tied girlishness."

"Don't tease her," Carly said. "In another second she'll be writhing. You're not a careless woman, Retta," she added. "Trust your instincts."

Oddly enough, her comment had me burying my face in my hands. Advice from someone half my age. She had known sadness, to be sure, but she didn't have a clue as to what else was coming down the transom for her, let alone me. I sure wasn't ready to make an idyllic leap into something which asked me to ignore the last six decades of my life. I couldn't help but think of my mother repeating a remark by a friend, who'd worked at a senior-care facility. She'd said, "They may be old over there, but there's just as much romance and shenanigans than when they were in high school." If I was due any grace at all in the rest of my life, I would pray to avoid making myself look ridiculous.

Someone's arm came around me. It was Sybil's and she was gazing at me with complete seriousness.

"Love is love at any age, my friend. We can't help where our hearts take us."

True enough, I thought. However, for the immediate future, the only person I wanted to discuss this with was Sam. I was handed a reprieve by Dana's sudden shift of focus.

"Does talking burn calories?" she asked, looking hopeful. "I need some excuse to explain why I'm already hungry again. Isn't it almost time for our tea? I'm in the mood for a little ritual to go with this romantic atmosphere. Candles and beautiful china—we can let our pinkie fingers lift as we sip, even though we *are* dressed more for helping you clean the stables."

"You get the tea going," I told Sybil. "We'll set the table."

For the next hour, the four of us enjoyed our little soiree and Sybil's wonderful pie. Earlier, I'd looked for Maggie and found her still in the closet putting up the empty containers.

"That can wait," I'd told her. "Come join us."

"No, thanks. I need to move a bit, or I'll fall asleep from boredom, and then I won't sleep tonight."

As insults went, hers was mild, so I found it easy to ignore. Besides her judgment was clearly effected by the amount of wine she'd ingested. "Suit yourself," I said quietly.

TWO-THIRDS OF THE pie was devoured with relish when Dana asked, "What's for dinner?"

Sybil burst into laughter. "You poor baby, that child must be in there gnawing on your rib bones. What do you have a hankering for?"

"Just more Southern cooking. I can't seem to get enough."

"How about chicken and dumplings to help keep us warm through the night?"

As soon as she made the suggestion, I saw her grimace, giving Carly a guilty look. However, before she could apologize and amend her suggestion, Carly took the issue out of her hands.

"There's still a bit of tomato basil soup left," Carly said. "That will work for this vegetarian. Please don't deprive the others."

Dana must have had a sudden mischievous thought. Stifling a giggle, she pressed her hand over her mouth.

"At this moment, I feel as though I could eat an entire pot of those dumplings. If this baby comes out in a sea of chicken broth with Carrie Fisher's Princess Leia's hairdo in *Star Wars,* you can explain it to the hospital staff."

"I've never heard anyone worry so much about their weight," Sybil replied. "I'm a mother of three, none of which reached daylight weighing less than eight pounds. Believe me when I say you have nothing to worry about."

As Sybil rose, and began gathering our dishes, Dana asked, "Retta, by chance do you have a glue gun?"

"It's in the same closet as the decorations. The container is labeled Crafting Tools. By the way, I love how you girls wove the garland around my antique wooden thread spools-turned candleholders."

"Is that what they are? I love it! Where did you find them?" Carly asked.

"They were my paternal grandmother's. All of the women back then could sew, but *she* was a seamstress." I got the box of plastic wrap and covered the remains of the pie. "I know they're rustic looking, but I like to have old things from our past, and remember the stories behind them."

"Oh, I think a house full of nothing but beautiful and expensive things would be a bit off-putting and cold." As soon as Sybil spoke, she clapped her hand over her mouth.

I knew she was worried Maggie had overheard her, and I quickly reassured her. "Well, you sure don't have the risk of that here," I said with self-deprecating humor. "My challenge has always been to recognize when it's time to throw things out."

"I like your decorating style," Carly said. "It's so elegant without being pretentious, and yet it's welcoming, too. I'm taking mental notes because I still feel like an imposter in my own house."

"Listen to that," Dana replied, adding to her friend, "Your house is beautiful—if slightly empty. As for personal style," she directed at me, "if I didn't love her so much, I could easily hate her for the ability to look good in anything she wears."

"It's natural for us to live in a state of horror at the end of our pregnancies," I said, remembering how I cried and cried at my widening butt and protruding belly, which I knew would never be flat again after

Jamie's birth. "And you should have seen my mother's face the day I went against Southern dictum and threw away my panty girdle."

Looking bemused, Dana said, "I haven't a clue whether my mother wore one or not. I never even saw her in a bathing suit, let alone her lingerie."

Carly uttered a delicate snort. "I was happy if my mother got dressed."

I couldn't help but reach out to stroke her beautiful hair as I'd seen Dana do, and as I did with my daughter in tender moments. "All the more reason to be proud of your accomplishments. You've quietly and gracefully been watching, learning and making a life of your own."

"Quit," Carly groaned, "before I have to crawl onto your lap."

From the other side of the room, Sybil said, "Would you believe on opening day of school this year the principal had to send our newest teacher home to put on a bra? Talk about being educated and still clueless."

"What grade does she teach?" I asked. "I'll start worrying about what my grandson is being exposed to."

"Oh, this will really thrill you—fifth grade."

I gasped so fast that it almost sent me into a coughing fit. "Good grief. That's even worse than I thought—although pulling such a stunt while teaching any grade level is troubling."

"Why do you think there's such a momentum for home schooling? If folks aren't worrying about what's not being taught, they're upset about inappropriate behavior."

As Sybil returned to her prep work, a sad-eyed Dana offered a mournful, "Yet another reason not to be thrilled about bringing a child into this world."

"You're due a change, and I believe you're going to get it," I told her. "Now, I need to check the fires before I head outside."

After removing ashes from the downstairs fireplace, and placing the bucket in the snow to dispense with when I came back out, I went upstairs to find Maggie lounging on the bed playing solitaire on her cell phone. An empty mini-bottle of scotch was on the night table. I had to guess she'd had it in her purse or luggage just in case the supply downstairs ran out.

Hoping the indulgence was only because she wanted to avoid the rest of us, I said, "Why don't you give that phone a rest, before you wear down the battery?"

"Well, I have a car, don't I? I can easily give it a boost out there." Not even bothering to look up, Maggie muttered. "Run along and play with your new friend."

Her attitude confounded me. She'd always been able to hold her liquor, or at least refuse to let anyone see her in less than total control. Why did my few minutes with Carly turn her into someone I didn't want to be around?

"Do you mind if I clean out some of those ashes that are building up, and stoke the fire? It doesn't look like you intended to."

I spoke with only mild censure; however, it was getting cool up here. It surprised me that she hadn't noticed—but then she'd imbibed plenty of antifreeze.

"I'm totally comfortable," Maggie said, without looking up.

Mentally sighing, I gave my attention to the work at hand. Midway through, I heard something outside that chilled me to the bone. One of my pregnant cows sounded like she was in the midst of labor. It was said calves born in the worst conditions of winter tended to end up being the heartiest. That might be true, yet all I could think of was how miserable it was to come into the world under cruel conditions like this. What's more, there was a tone in the cow's calls that told me something was amiss.

I went to the window to look outside, but the closed inner shutters had allowed frost to build up on the window pane which thwarted my ability to see anything. Since Maggie seemed determined to pretend she hadn't heard that either, I didn't bother sharing my concern with her. I just grabbed the bucket with the ashes, and hurried downstairs.

Sybil noted my rush immediately. When I came back inside from setting out the other pail, she asked, "What's wrong?"

"I think one of my pregnant cows is having trouble birthing," I said, dragging on my coat. I'd already changed into my boots to get the buckets outside.

Slapping my hat on my head, I all but ran out the door and down the steps, Rosie right behind me. Conditions were pretty much the same as when we were last outside, and I paused in the middle of the yard to determine where the cries were coming from. Alone from the herd by a stand of cedar trees to the northeast of the stables, I saw her. I should have known it was Freckles, my Angus heifer with the unusual mix of spots on her nose. She had been a big baby in more ways than one from the day she was born, rejected by her mother, and devouring the bottles I hand-fed her, until she could start eating hay and pellets. Nothing had changed in the last year, as I dealt with her separation anxiety issues with me. As soon as she spotted me, she let out an even louder bellow. If spoken in words, they would surely have been, *"Do something!"*

Fortunately, I didn't have to run across the pasture to where the other cattle were, and I fell to my knees at her side to stroke her with heartfelt sympathy. "Oh, my poor girl. It's not going easy for you, is it? Let me see what the problem seems to be."

Leaning over, I gauged things were progressing and there didn't appear to be any noticeable problems which told me this might be typical Freckles. She didn't want to do this alone.

"All right then," I said, shifting so she could put her head in my lap. "I'm here. Let's get this done."

Freckles' big brown eyes locked on mine and she moaned in painful agreement. Sucking in a deep breath her belly swelled and then she expelled the calf. I knew immediately this wasn't going to be a happy situation. The calf was small by any standards and looked more jellyfish than bovine. I quickly tore open the intact amniotic sack then wiped away the mucus from the nostrils and mouth—all to no effect. Increasingly distressed, I pumped on the chest to encourage the heart to beat on its own.

Breathe.

Despite my mental entreaty, Freckles already knew it was all in vain. She turned her face deeper into the snow and refused to look at her baby.

"Oh, sweetheart," I said, stroking the length of her body in sympathy and comfort. "I'm so sorry."

I was late in realizing that I was no longer alone. Carly had dressed and run out to join me. She stopped a few yards away, realizing what had happened.

"What can I do?" she asked, her expression stricken, but her tone determined.

"Come sit by her head and talk to her. Stroke her. Her name is Freckles, and she really does think she's part of the family. I'll take the calf away and bury it in as much snow as I can to buy us some time, until I can get it in a deep enough grave to keep varmints away."

When I returned Carly said, "She's pretty special. I've been chased across pastures by cattle before, but she seems more like a big lap dog."

"She would follow Rosie and me into the house if she could."

"What do we do now?" Carly asked.

"Give her time to regroup. Since you're here—and thank you for coming out—we'll go take care of the horses and check back when we're done. She should be on her feet by then. If not…well, no need to worry yet." I patted Freckles one more time and urged, "You catch your breath, girl. I'll be back with something special for you."

As we walked to the barn, Carly said, "I'm sorry about Maggie. I don't want to make trouble between the two of you, but I couldn't stand how she put you in the position she did, either."

"I honestly don't get what's going on with her," I admitted. "On the other hand, she's a big girl, and there's never been anything wrong with her mouth. I have to trust she'll tell me what her real problem is when she's ready."

I looked toward Carly, again admiring her surprisingly Patrician profile. "You keep forcing me to re-evaluate my analysis of you. You're certainly quieter than I expected, yet when you do speak, it's for a reason."

"You're judging my looks again, but I'm used to that," she said. "The truth is, if someone asks me a question, I'm trying to remember the correct grammar to use before I answer. When *I* have a question, I'm worried about people's reaction to any assumed motives. I turn myself into such a big knot that most of the time silence is my way of avoiding embarrassment."

"Ah." I nodded in understanding. "You've eloquently stated what my Charlie used as a motto throughout his life, 'Better to remain silent and let people think you're a fool, than to speak and remove all doubt.'"

Carly looked unconvinced. "Really? Why would Charlie feel that way? I would have thought him to be like you, having it all pulled together."

"Honey, *no* one has it all pulled together. We're all born with strengths and weaknesses, often more of the latter. Sadly, you and my Charlie have had the misfortune to run into that certain class of people who enjoy pointing out your flaws, in order to ignore their own."

As I got the log to free the metal latch on the stable door, I sighed remembering how we were all so relieved when Charlie actually made it to our high school graduation. "Charlie wasn't much for books or regimen, and with him what you saw, you got. But any time word was out that Bc Ranch was taking stock to a sale, our cattle triggered a bidding war, because Charlie knew his business, and we raised quality beef. I've kept up the tradition, and although my trips to sale barns are far from what they used to be, I'm still grateful and proud to see the turnout when word gets around I'm there."

"That's reassuring to hear. Stigmas are difficult to face down."

"Well, I've yet to sense one in you," I told her.

"Only due to my angst—Walter taught me the word—that Willow would turn out like me," Carly admitted. "He was the one who convinced me how in breaking the pattern of poverty and ignorance in myself, I would free her."

"Thank you, Walter," I sang to the gray sky.

It took both of us to pull open the door and push back a day's worth of piling snow. By then, the horses were greeting us.

As she walked down the center of the stable, Carly's expression was one of sheer rapture, as the horses stretched their necks over the stable doors to sniff at her.

"They're definitely curious about you," I said. "Feel free to ease up to them, and let them get to know you. Keep your movements calm, your voice as soothing as when you're pampering Dana."

She gave me a grin at that last part. I should have known she would turn immediately to Dolly, my palomino paint mare. Carly giggled as the horse soon tried to nibble at her collar. With a snort, Dolly then spread Carly's blond hair over her face like an extra mane.

"I think she likes me," Carly said.

"I think she's jealous that your hair is prettier than hers, and I'm miffed my horse is the one who ignored me to get at you. But then she's a woman's horse. She's never reacted that way to a man."

"I've always dreamed of learning how to ride, Retta, ever since I went to the Gladewater rodeo the year George Strait was the concert headliner. It was one of my indulgences to show Willow more of the world. I loved watching the girls' barrel racing event in their sequined and embroidered outfits. All but hugging their horses' necks as they charged around the ring, fighting what seems to me to be an unforgiving clock."

Had she heard herself? I wondered. And she worried about correct speech? That was utterly poetic.

Giving Dolly's white-and-cream neck a last stroke, Carly sighed and turned back to me. "What can I do to help? Can I feed them?"

"Absolutely, but feeding horses is very precise. Not like cattle."

"Why?"

"Too much or too little and they're susceptible to colic, or they can founder, causing foot problems." I pointed to the feed room. "In there is a fifty-gallon drum of grain with a scoop sitting on top. Give each horse a single scoop and a block of hay from the square alfalfa bales. Once you cut the line binding the whole bale together, they tend to separate into fairly solid blocks resembling couch pillows. I think there's still one bale cut, so you shouldn't need the clippers, but if I'm wrong, they're hanging in the storage cabinet next to the refrigerator where I keep medication.

"While you're doing that," I continued, "I'll clean the water pails and refill them. Then as a safety precaution, I'll detach the hose again, so we don't have a pipe break from the freeze tonight. If we had electricity, I could turn on the heat lamps. We have a generator out here for long-term outages, but I don't think I have enough gas for both the house and here. At least I don't have to worry about anything in the fridge getting warm."

As I worked around her, I kept an eye on her progress, admiring her perseverance, even with stubborn Geronimo, and frisky Blackjack. She didn't show any intimidation when the former bumped her back with his head to urge her out of his stall, and the latter nibbled on her jacket and gloves almost nipping a finger.

Upon closing the stables for the evening, a plan formed in my mind. "I have a proposition," I began. "After the thaw, or the holidays—if you need the time to think about things—why don't you come out here and help me with these big old emotion sponges? In exchange, I'll give you riding lessons. My hunch is that you'll get the hang of it in no time. What?" I asked upon catching her uncertain look. "Don't I look serious?"

"No. I mean, *yes*, I believe you. It's the 'emotion sponges' thing. That's a strange description for a horse—at least I've never heard it before."

Relieved, I exhaled loudly, my breath clouding the air between us. "Didn't you notice how they're much like children? Each wants one-hundred percent of your attention, especially as you're trying to groom another one in the next stall. Patience isn't always their strong suit, nor is diplomacy. They'll try to get hold of your hat or sleeve through the bars in their eagerness to draw you to them. It was less of a challenge when

Charlie was around. We could split chores. These days it takes me hours to do what we used to do in one, and what compounds the situation is that none of these critters are getting the exercise they need, even when Sam makes it out this way." I paused to gauge her mindset. "Well? What do you say?" I asked.

Eight

ITH A laugh Carly spread her arms as though ready to embrace the world. "I would *love* that, Retta. Yes, definitely!"

"Great. And don't worry that I'll leave you on your own too soon." Thinking of another selling point, I added, "You know there's nothing like brushing a grateful horse for a half hour to put the worries of the day behind you."

"I'm ready to know what that feels like. I've been trying yoga and it's good, too, but sometimes you like the company of another living being." She checked herself. "I do see Dana every day, but most of the time I have to worry about keeping her positive, and don't do enough for myself."

"Well, one thing I'll tell you—because I've also grasped how weighed down you've been with responsibility for most of your three decades— once you get on the back of a horse, and give him or her their head, there's nothing that'll clean the pipes faster than a good run."

Looking less confident, Carly replied, "That may take some time, but I want to get there. I can't remember a day when I didn't feel tight bands around my chest from dealing with one thing or another, or just trying to make it through the next twenty-four hours."

I put my arm around her, as we headed toward the barn. It was time to give the cats some fresh milk from my one goat, Elsa, and feed her. Then we would check on Freckles.

"That's what I thought. You're young and durable, but that won't last forever—especially if you keep draining your spirit. As you said, Walter helped you a great deal, yet I can see how losing him made you take some steps backward to keep company with the more doubtful Carly. You need to remember there's supposed to be fun in life and, until you can embrace that, friends like me should direct you toward projects or hobbies to inspire you."

By the time we'd finished, dusk had descended. Without the security lights by the stable and barn to illuminate our way, we felt more than saw the snow was intensifying again. The flakes were still small, but they crowded each other to where our jackets were soon dusted white. Rosie shook a light covering off her coat before giving me a soft "Woof," urging me to return to Freckles. After all, I'm the one who had picked up the promised treat for the cow.

Thankfully, my sad-faced mother had collected herself enough to get to her feet, and had even ventured a few yards toward the rest of the herd. She sniffed the air when she realized I was carrying a brick of the horse's alfalfa. I figured she deserved that, considering what she'd been through. Hopefully, it would bolster her even more, and encourage her to rejoin the group before true darkness set in. I still didn't think we had to worry about coyotes, but once in a while there was word of a big cat in the area. As vulnerable as she was, I would feel better if she stayed close to the others.

"You look better," I told her as she munched. Both Carly and I stroked her. "I'm sorry about your baby, but you'll have another."

As though she understood, she shifted to where she pressed her bulk against me. I was prepared for that and was ready to push back, but I did rub her all the more as emotion rose in my throat.

"Big baby," I whispered. "Eat up and get over to the others."

BEFORE CARLY AND I headed back to the house, we each collected an armful of wood. Her help would allow me to avoid needing a second trip out here. I had to admit, this evening's added work—on top of Maggie's conduct—had worn me out, so I thanked her again for joining me.

"I learned so much in this brief time," she said. "I'm the one who should be thanking you."

I paused to refuel the generator. Carly stopped, too, wanting to see how that was done.

"We can catch up on the news now, and enjoy the tree lights," I said. "Maybe watch the rest of the movie, or another one, if you'd like."

As we entered the house it looked as though Sybil and Dana had been keeping up with our progress from the kitchen window. They met us at the door, eager to help us with the wood.

"How did it go? Did she have her calf?" Dana asked. "We couldn't see you half the time due to the buildings and trees. We were starting to worry considering how dark it's getting."

I wished I could have avoided the truth. At least Dana's comments told me they hadn't seen me drag off the calf.

"The calf was stillborn. But the good news is that Freckles is going to be all right. And Carly was wonderful help. I wish you could have watched her working with the horses." I could see Sybil's studious look and responded to her sigh with a sad smile. She and Elvin had raised a few animals in their time, and she understood it was often as emotional a loss, as it was financial.

"What?" Dana stepped back, abruptly coming up against the kitchen island. "The calf is dead?"

It didn't take a psychic to know what she was thinking, considering her own pregnancy. "It was probably for the best, dear," I told her. "The little heifer was too small. Freckles is quite young . I'm sure her next calf will be fine."

Carly tried to change the subject. "But the horses started talking to us the moment we opened the stable doors. Retta let me feed them. She said I can come back. She said I was a natural, and she would give me riding lessons in exchange for helping her."

Maggie appeared from around the corner by the fireplace, her cell phone still in hand. "Awesome. Can adoption be far behind?"

While I was mortified by Maggie's juvenile mimicry, it was Dana's sickly expression that had me snapping, "Maggie!"

For an instant, she looked as though she might apologize; however, stubbornness took control again. With a shrug, she poured herself a glass of wine before retreating to the living room. Moments later, I heard the TV come on.

"Get out of the rest of your wet things," Sybil said, returning from depositing the wood on the living room rack. "You're not going to fix that piece of work anytime soon."

"You're right," I said. "By the way, dinner smells great. Carly and I sure worked up an appetite."

"What can we get you to drink? You both look frozen through and through. Wine? Brandy?"

"Oh, not for me, thanks," Carly said. "As soon as I get out of these frozen things, I think I'll make myself another cup of hot tea with honey. That sure hit the spot before."

"I think I'd like to defrost with something warm myself," I told Sybil.

"Then I'll just put some water on," she replied.

Once Carly got out of her outerwear and slipped back into pretty, mauve moccasins she continued to share her excitement with Dana. "Some of the horses are so big I feel like a kid next to them."

"I would be terrified," Dana told her. "Are you sure this isn't too much for you?"

"No way. Okay, Geronimo—Jamie's horse—is a bit intimidating, but I think he was simply testing me. This is the best I've felt since—I can't remember. Dana, you should have seen Dolly play with my hair."

"Who's Dolly?"

"Retta's horse."

Dana nodded and finally summoned a smile, albeit a weak one. "Then I'm happy for you."

But she didn't look happy. As I crouched to work on Rosie's snow-packed paws, I wondered if she was still rattled by the calf's death, or was it something else? I hoped nothing had happened with Maggie while we'd been gone.

By the time Rosie was in good shape, and I'd set out her dinner, the water was boiling. Sybil had put away the china already, and had our mugs, tea bags, and honey on the island. As she poured the steaming water, I washed my hands

"We noticed the snowfall is getting heavier again," Dana said.

Although I kept my tone casual, I took note of how vague or pre-occupied she sounded. "True, but they're miniscule flakes compared to when this system started. As far as I'm concerned, that's a positive."

While Carly and I warmed our hands with the mugs and savored the soothing tea, Sybil set the table and urged us to sit. We did; however,

Maggie didn't join us until Sybil placed my heirloom *Spode* blue tureen in the center of the table.

This time, I didn't ask anyone else to say grace. I needed to do it myself. In the process, I silently asked forgiveness for my burgeoning impatience with my friend—*and* for help in snapping her out of her irrational jealousy.

As Sybil rose to start ladling the chicken and dumplings into our bowls, she slid a watchful look at Maggie, but said to me, "Shortly after you girls went outside, you had a call on your cell phone, Retta."

My thoughts went immediately to Sam, which sent my insides quaking. I fought the sensation by focusing on the kids. "Oh, no. I promised my brood I would never leave the house without it. The way Charlie died had them all but ordering me to sign an oath, grandchildren included. Which one was it?"

"Rachel," Sybil replied, a smile finally playing around her mouth.

"Of course. She's always the first to read me the riot act about one thing or another—proof she's in the perfect line of work. Darn it, now she'll accuse me of only paying her lip service. Who took the call? Maggie?" Although I glanced her way, Maggie refused to look up from her bowl. In fact, her fascination with the contents made me wonder if she had spotted the Shroud of Turin in it.

"I did," Sybil said. "I assured her all was well and Carly was with you."

"Thank you," I moaned. "I can point out that Carly had her phone." I glanced over to my youngest guest. "Don't tell me if you didn't."

"She also used the opportunity to ask if you were really eating like you claim?" Sybil continued. "She thinks you've been losing weight."

Although I was touched at her concern, I had to roll my eyes. "I'm more physically fit, that's all. The extra pounds are there, believe me." I explained to Carly and Dana, "I think I told you my daughter is a principal at a private East Coast school, plus has three children of her own to keep track of, but she still thinks it's part of her responsibility to keep tabs on old mom. I'm only half-joking when I say she's considering drone monitoring so she can keep tabs on her feeble parent."

"She can't think of you that way, Retta," Dana replied. "I'm sure she simply hates being half a continent away."

"My Joseph is right up there with her," Sybil said. "Although in his case, part of the reason is that he's crazy about any and all gadgetry."

Carly paused, about to taste a spoonful of her tomato basil soup. "He's your eldest, right? I like the way you say 'my Joseph.'"

"That's the one—and since Elvin passed he tends to think he now wears the pants in the family. Don't think I'm not proud of him. Plenty of mothers in our church only see their sons at holidays, and too many come with their hands out. Joseph and Tamera come up from Tyler as often as they can. Where she gets her energy, I don't know. She teaches special needs kids, in addition to chasing after their four-year-old, Joe, Jr."

"I don't know what I would have done," Dana said, putting down her spoon, only to place her hand over her womb, "if they had told me during my ultrasound there was something wrong with this child."

"There's no denying it would be a hard life," Sybil replied.

While I nodded in agreement, what troubled me more was how Dana said, "this child," instead of "my child." Surely I was just being extra sensitive due to my concerns over Maggie.

"There could still be," Dana continued, sounding almost insistent. "Retta's perfectly healthy cow lost her calf."

"You're going to have a healthy and beautiful baby," Carly assured her. "Stop torturing yourself."

It was only when Maggie stood that I realized she had gobbled down her food in record time. As soon as she set her bowl in the sink, she grabbed up her phone and keys. *Why* had she brought down her keys?

"I'm going to recharge my phone," she said to no one in particular, and headed for the front door. I didn't see her get a jacket, but knowing Maggie, she believed the car's heater would warm her in no time. I couldn't even remember which shoes she was wearing; however, the sharp tapping that came with her departure told me she was in heels—and gone.

What the devil...?

Sybil looked at me as if I'd spoken out loud. "Where's a straitjacket when you need one?"

"I do have a bottle of horse tranquilizer in the stables," I mused, not entirely joking.

Dana and Carly exchanged impish glances, and I knew they wished I would go get the sedative. Frankly, I couldn't blame them. Maggie's behavior was getting increasingly disturbing.

"Maybe she really does need to charge the thing." I looked around the table compelled to say more. "None of us should feel obligated to stay together. If anyone is craving time alone, go for it. Only please, stay inside. There are plenty of nooks and crannies to cure the strongest urge for privacy."

"I'm not going anywhere," Carly replied. "I love having this opportunity to get to know you all better. But I did notice that Dana's feet are in need of some TLC, so I think we're going to go to the living room where I can give her another massage."

"Great," I said, "and I'll text my daughter that all is well. Right after, Sybil, I'll help you with the dishes."

"You know, Retta, she's probably watching the news and saw the report of over six hundred traffic accidents in Dallas alone," Dana said. "Someone with her intelligence would naturally shudder as she estimated how many more there's been in the entire region."

"Yet she doesn't credit her mother with having the smarts to stay put and not become a statistic." I shook my head. "The South is made the laughingstock, considering the feet and yards of snow other areas receive annually, I get it. But that's the point," I replied. "This isn't the norm for us, and not only do we not have the equipment to deal with frozen stuff, most people have no experience in driving in it."

"People also forget that plenty of folks don't have the luxury of staying home," Sybil added. "While I was waiting on dinner to cook, I saw online where a Tyler hospital's generator wasn't acting reliably. They were preparing to move their critical cases to Longview, Shreveport and Houston. Never mind driving, we're talking Care Flight evacuation. Their temperatures can't be but a degree or two warmer than ours, if that, so icing is a danger." She made a throaty, mournful sound. "You couldn't get me on a helicopter right now if you stuck me with a cattle prod."

The sobering remark had us all agreeing with her. It also turned us introspective and we finished our meal in silence.

With soft-spoken thanks for the meal, Carly and Dana carried their dishes to the sink and relocated to the living room. Sybil and I tended to the leftovers and cleaning up. Once she had the wash pan full of hot, soapy water, Sybil turned off the faucet and leaned closer to me in order to keep her voice low.

"You know I've been helping my minister with his wife, and how she's been bedridden since her last stroke?"

I had met Thomas More Tidwell and Naomi, and remembered her declining health. The most severe setback to date had occurred over the summer. "I'm sorry I haven't asked sooner. How's she doing?"

"Not well. I'm afraid this is going to be one of those slow slides into the grave," Sybil replied. "And that's so sad, because Naomi and Thomas More used to be a real team. You have to be when you're serving a con-gregation. I can tell the toll the situation is taking on him, and I've tried to do as much as I can to help out, since we also used to be neighbors. The thing is…Retta, I hope you won't think poorly of me. Something is happening between us, and I don't know what to think, let alone have a clue as to how to handle it."

I was both startled and intrigued. "He made a pass at you?" I whis-pered.

"It didn't get that far. I don't believe he ever would, at least not while Naomi is alive. Believe me, I've been part of congregations where minis-ters and deacons are of the opinion that 'taking care of the ladies of the church' means way too much physical contact. No, Thomas isn't turned that way."

I nodded, understanding the old Southern phrasing. However, if any-thing more was going to be shared, I was leaving the choice up to Sybil.

Instead, she continued, "Besides, he and Naomi have shared an abid-ing love." Her sigh reflected her humanity. "About two weeks ago, she suffered another stroke. It's come to the point where she can barely swal-low food. Thomas discovered that the hard way. I arrived in time to help him out with her. Of course, I set to work cleaning her up right away, so he could gather himself."

Sybil explained that when she carried the soiled clothing and bed-ding to the washroom, she came upon him sobbing.

"You know I'm strong, Retta, but that gut-wrenching sound broke my heart. I'm not hard enough to be able to walk away from someone so tired and breaking under the weight of despair. Long story short, that sweet man hugged me almost like a child would. I knew exactly what he was feeling, having been there myself, only he didn't have any family to hold onto like I did. You might not know that they never could have children."

"Now that's tragic," I murmured.

Sybil drew a sustaining breath. "Suddenly, we were just looking at each other. It was so strange, yet familiar. I knew he was about to kiss me, and…Retta, I'm sorry. I wanted him to. It was all I could do to pull away and mumble stupidly that I needed to get the laundry done."

"You don't have to explain, let alone apologize, Sybil," I began. "I may tease Maggie about her relationships, but I'm not about to judge…"

"No, you don't understand. Before, I was pretending that I didn't have the sexual feelings you and Maggie had discussed. Okay, it's been a few years since Elvin's been gone, so I thought this wasn't the same thing. But what if it is?"

I quickly reassured her. "I didn't look for Sam, either, but I can't deny I'm happy he's in my life. There hasn't been anything consummated between us, yet there's the promise there could be."

Sybil all but collapsed in relief, her suds-covered hands gripping the edge of the sink. "I was right in reaching out to you. I see that we're of similar minds. It's not like I would be willing to take things any further," she assured me. "Not in Naomi's home, or mine, for that matter. He's not free. It's that simple, and that final."

"Have you two talked since—the incident?" I asked gently.

"Just a little. At first we worried about what the other might be thinking. Eventually we could agree it was a natural thing to occur, given the circumstances. Even so, you could have knocked me over with that towel you're holding when he declared he'd never experienced anything similar with anyone else, and respected me too much to make me uncomfortable. He gave me an out, Retta, only to confess he hoped I wouldn't take it because losing the two most important people in his life would finish him."

"That's very noble—of both of you," I assured her.

Sybil abruptly clutched my hands as I wrung the towel with worry. "No, don't think what you're thinking," she said. "Except for me, Thomas doesn't allow anyone but married couples to come to the house. I've heard it confirmed by others. He's no rooster."

"Oh, Sybil, it was the fleetest of thoughts."

"A knee-jerk reaction." She nodded in understanding. "Believe me, I've had plenty of my own concerns."

"All I can add is my hope and prayers for you to be happy again. You deserve to be."

"Treasured words coming from you, my friend."

"Who's helping out during this storm?"

"Charles and Melba Brooks. They're the neighbors on the other side of my old place. It'll be my turn again next week." She sent me a grateful look. "I can't tell you how badly I've needed to talk this out. With your news about Sam, I thought it was a God moment—He was giving me direction that I should seek your input." She shook her head, bemused. "For all the fussing and muttering about this storm, I for one, am grateful for it."

Breaking into a relieved smile, I hugged her. "I'm glad. Isn't it interesting how our emotions evolve as we go through life? When we were kids experiencing the first inklings of attraction for the first time, we were just giddy with pleasure, even relief that someone cared about us. Yet time and experience makes us see all of the potholes and obstacles to where something that should be a joy can seem like a burden, if not a nightmare."

"Isn't that the truth!" With a last squeeze, Sybil pushed me to arm's length. "Enough about me. You need to go check on Maggie."

"Heavens, yes." Thanking her for finishing up, I slid on my coat and hurried to stuff my feet into boots. "I should never have let her go in the first place—at least not without insisting she put on a jacket. Her car is probably frozen solid, and I have no doubt she's on her way to catching pneumonia."

About to head toward the front door, I checked myself. The girls didn't need to suffer that horrible cold.

"On second thought, I'll go out this way," I told Sybil. In the last second, I grabbed Charlie's jacket in case my stubborn friend refused to come in yet. "Come on, Rosie. Let's give this to crazy Maggie."

Upon shutting the door behind me, I could hear the elegant purr of Maggie's Mercedes beneath the workhorse rumble of the generator. Rosie snorted at the sound of expensive engineering, and trotted around the porch to the front. I followed and soon saw the snow-and-ice-encased vehicle. Only the door handle area was cleaned off, and barely any of the windshield had melted. Vapor was pouring out of the muffler and, due to the heavy air, it looked like we were dealing with fog as well as snow.

Goodness, I thought. It seemed to be taking an extraordinary amount of time for the heater to do its job. To be fair, though, there was plenty of the frozen stuff caked on the vehicle. If I didn't already know it was Maggie's car parked there, I couldn't have guessed what model it was at this stage. How long had my irascible friend been out here? Twenty minutes? A half hour?

I went up to where I gauged the window to be and then brushed away what I could. After tapping on the glass, I pulled on the door handle. "I can't bear the thought of you out here without a..."

I stood open-mouthed in disbelief. The car was empty.

The lights had come on the moment I opened the door and I could see Maggie's phone on the console plugged into the charger, but both front leather seats were empty. So was the back, although why I looked there, I couldn't have explained. She had no reason to be there. Nevertheless, where else would she be, dressed—or rather *under*dressed—as she was?

Straightening, I glanced around the indigo-blue world, squinting as fine flakes struck me in the eye and pricked my skin. I should have put on a hat, but I'd only planned to be outside for a moment.

"Maggie?"

Scanning the area, I saw that what was happening to the pines and cedars on the sides and out back, was also turning the pine and pecan trees that lined the driveway into a mess. Piles and piles of snapped limbs were everywhere, some already resembling beaver dams the way they'd landed in complex, nearly engineered mounds, while others looked like skeletal fingers reaching up from the snow in some final desperate appeal toward heaven. But of Maggie there was no sign.

"Maggie?" I shouted.

There had to be footprints still visible. I looked down for a sign of hers. Apparently, Rosie had the same idea, and stuck her nose into one of the depressions, moved on to another, then another at the back of the car and, suddenly, she took off in a running leap through the snow. It was at that point that I noticed there were prints heading down the driveway.

"You can't be serious?" I muttered to myself. Surely she hadn't decided to go for a walk? Not without being properly dressed. And in her current frame of mind, she wouldn't have thought to check the mailbox. Surely she understood that as the roads became impassable, the Martin's Mill Post Office would have suspended service? The days of the noble and dogged pony express were over.

Midway down the driveway, I heard Rosie's urgent bark. It compelled me to break into my own awkward run. Several yards farther, my breath caught in my throat at the sight of the darker mass marring the eerie blue-on-blue landscape. Some of what I saw was branches for sure, but inside their finger-like clutch...

"Dear God, Maggie..."

I hadn't run so hard since I spotted Charlie under the tractor. Back then, I was surprised the effort hadn't killed me, even though I had been a star on the cross country and track teams in high school. Now, much older, and with the air frigid enough to flash-freeze everything, my lungs were searing by the time I reached my friend.

There was a ten-foot limb lying across her back with smaller branches extending over her head as though she were being held down by some ponderous creature trying to decide what to do with her. I saw enough splinters of bark and wood scattered around like an ungodly halo to as-sume she'd taken a hit to several parts of her body, including the head.

I couldn't immediately get close enough to tell if there was any blood. Considering the size of the limb across her back, my second dread was a fear of what could be broken.

Ordering Rosie to get out of the way, I tugged and pushed to ma-neuver the ungainly weight off of her. The burden of the offending thing was enough to have shoved Maggie's face through snow to frozen ground and suffocated her. That made me yank and pull all the harder.

Finally, I managed enough of a clearing and dropped to my knees. Breathless, I gasped, "Can you hear me?"

"I used to like these damn pecan trees."

She sounded as tipsy as a cheap drunk, which told me, the limb had knocked her senseless. The good news was she could talk.

"Me, too. We'll discuss taking a chain saw to them later. Are you bleeding? How badly are you hurt?"

"How the hell do I know?" Maggie cautiously lifted her head, and glanced around warily. "I guess my neck and back aren't broken. It's true then—it's only those whom the gods love that die young. The rest of us will get to turn into gargoyles with body parts missing."

Dear heaven, I thought, she was about to freeze or bleed to death and she still had the wherewithal to be vain. "Didn't I tell you not to test Fate? What possessed you to come out here without the proper clothes?"

"I saw a puppy."

Concussion, I thought. She was delusional. "A puppy couldn't last any longer than you could out here."

"I thought it was a puppy. I guess it was a fox. It was the loveliest thing." Maggie looked down at the snow. "There's no blood, so I'm not half-knocked out of my mind."

"One doesn't necessarily have anything to do with the other. Are you having vision problems?"

"No, it's perfectly clear now. I can see I should have kept my ass at home. And I don't mean inside *your* house."

I let the subtle jab pass, relieved her sense of humor had returned to a degree. If it had taken a blow and a scare to excavate it, so be it. Of course, I wasn't about to voice my opinion; I didn't have enough medical knowledge to know if a concussion could trigger violence. "Do you think you can stand?"

"I don't know." What she did do was roll over onto her back. That drew an awful groan from her. "Uh…how about you just bring me a blanket, and I'll sleep out here?"

"Sure," I replied, not even pretending to be accommodating. "There's nothing I want more than to deal with second degree manslaughter charges." I eased a supportive arm around her back. "Sit up and put on this jacket. Then I'll get Sybil to help me get you to the house. If necessary, I'll bring up the tractor. We can set a wooden skid or something across the hay forks, and lay you across it."

"You'd dare."

The look she sent me had me gesturing in frustration. "I'm being practical, Mags. If you can't walk…"

"You're not scooping me up like I was some foundering cow or a feral hog you shot for tearing up your pasture. Just give me a second."

Maggie took a stabilizing breath, sat up, and let me help her slip on the jacket. It seemed like a small eternity before she extended her hand.

I tried to be as gentle as possible as I pulled her shivering self to her feet, yet she moaned and shuddered hard when bruised muscles and bones protested. I couldn't help it; I hugged her, reassured when those skinny legs somehow held her weight. "You scared me to death," I all but growled.

She actually patted me weakly. "Thanks for coming out to check on me. The way my luck has been going, if I had been left out here much longer, the whole damn tree might have come down on me."

"Don't even think such a thing," I said, shifting to better support her with my body. "Come on, let's start with baby steps, until we can gauge your balance, and determine if trying this is a stupid idea."

After only the first small step, she moaned. "You know I'm an advocate of early voting. Put me down for 'stupid idea.'"

I adjusted my hold and eased her arm around my shoulders. "We're running out of options, Mags. Let's try again."

She leaned heavily against me for the first few yards, but soon stopped again. "I'm a little...woozy." Touching her hand to her forehead, she then looked at her fingers, and uttered a guttural, "Good God. Is that me?"

We both stared at the dark glistening across three fingertips. Blood. Apparently, her hair had been hiding the wound. Leaning forward to see for myself, I carefully lifted her bangs away. Despite the lack of light, my eyes had adjusted to the darkness enough to where I could see a two-inch gash on the right side of her forehead near her scalp.

"I can't tell if that's going to need stitches, but my guess is it will." Reaching into my pocket I pulled out a handful of folded tissues I always carry with me and put them in her hand. "Here, press this against the wound to stem the flow of blood, and to keep the swelling down. "I'll focus on getting us to the house. Just keep leaning on me."

"It wouldn't surprise me if you have a roll of toilet paper in the other pocket, too," Maggie drawled. "I wish you were more genie than Girl Scout and had thought to pack a little bottle of *Courvoisier.*"

"You have a head wound. The last thing you need is more alcohol, even though the cold is apparently slowing down your heartbeat and blood flow. Do you need to stop and rest?"

"I *need* my hot tub."

I'd forgotten she had one at her house. "Considering that the power is probably out there, too, I suspect it's no longer hot. Whereas I can offer you a steamy soak in my claw-footed tub if you can keep moving forward."

With a throaty sound, she purred, "I knew it. You do still love me best."

Rosie, sweetheart that she was, chose that minute to leap up the stairs and bark at the front door. We'd been gone long enough to where the others must have been worrying, and it opened almost immediately.

Sybil and Carly burst from the house to meet us, and we met at the back of Maggie's car.

"Lord, Maggie! You *have* been hurt," Sybil cried. "What happened?"

"Carly," I said, since she was on the side nearest the driver's door. "Shut that thing off and bring in Maggie's phone. I'm sure it has enough juice in it to at least last through the night."

With Sybil's help, we managed to assist Maggie inside, although she groaned and muttered under her breath the whole way. It might have been from pain, but my hunch was she resented Carly touching anything of hers, never mind having access to her phone.

Upon seeing Maggie's condition, Dana quickly moved Carly's pedicure supplies off the bed and onto the coffee table. The others carried Maggie to the end of the pulled out sofa and laid her across the foot of the bed, which put her closer to the warmth of the fireplace.

"Does she need a pillow to keep her head up?" Dana asked, turning her head away from the sight of blood. "Here's a towel to protect it."

"Probably the one being used to dry off that platinum rat," Maggie said to me.

"Shut up, please," I told her, and folded the towel before putting it under her head. To the others, I said, "No pillow yet. Let me get her cleaned up first. I'll get the first aid kit, and extra peroxide and cotton balls."

"I'll get a wash cloth and a bowl of warm water," Sybil added.

When I returned, I could see Maggie continuing to shiver, despite the benefits of the blazing fire and Charlie's jacket, which she wrapped as tightly around herself as she could. As I sat down on the edge of the bed, Sybil came with her things. After a quick glance around she caught Carly's eye.

"Hon, bring one of the breakfast table chairs so I can set this down within reach for Retta to use." Sybil craned her head to give Maggie a sympathetic look. "How are you holding up?"

"Retta's trees ambushed me."

"Say what? I thought you went to charge your phone and fell. What were you doing way out there?"

Before she could reply, I said drolly, "What made Alice take a nose-dive into Wonderland?"

Sybil's expression exposed her struggle to make sense of things. "You went after a rabbit? Dressed like that?"

"Stop yelling. And it was a fox."

"She told *me* it was a puppy," I said, as I went to work.

"Uh-huh," Sybil murmured. "I'll start praying we don't have to ex-plain any of this to the l-a-w."

Maggie lifted one foot to mournfully inspect her soaked designer boots. "Crap. These were the most comfortable pair, too. Now they'll be water stained."

"I'll get them off as soon as I set down this bowl," Sybil assured her.

"Bless you," Maggie crooned. "And afterward, would you be a dar-ling and bring me a brandy?"

"Nice try, slick, but I think that's what got you into this mess in the first place," I pointed out.

Carly brought the chair. Once Sybil put down the bowl of water, she worked on removing Maggie's boots. As I brushed back my friend's hair, I removed the cushion of tissues from the wound and handed it to Carly to throw away. It was a relief to see the flow of blood had eased, and a bulge was forming instead of a concave wound. As I flushed the area with hydrogen peroxide to cleanse the cut, I heard Dana moan.

"Carly, grab her and make her sit before she loses her dinner or faints. I think all this blood has triggered too many memories."

"I should have thought of that myself." Carly urged Dana to the other side of the bed. She used her body as the other barrier to block the ex-pectant mother's view of what had to be an ugly reminder of when she'd found Jesse's body.

Taking the soiled cotton balls from me, Sybil asked, "Do you think she needs stitches?"

Maggie's eyes widened. "Don't you even think about coming near me with a needle threaded with horse hair."

"You spend hundreds every year on wrinkle removers. Now you're willing to live with a scar?" I scoffed, albeit gently.

"Up yours. Do you still have any of the Valium your doctor slipped you when Charlie passed? I definitely remember you refused to take them."

"I do not," I told her. "And even if I hadn't disposed of them, they would be expired by now." I leaned closer to inspect the wound. "We'll try for a pressure bandage. The scar won't be as impressive as an eye patch, but it should get you some attention at your next cocktail party."

"A pressure bandage *and* a drink. My back is killing me. It feels as though two elephants and a water buffalo are digging their knees into my spine."

Aware the offer of Tylenol would be rejected in a way none of us needed to hear, I bought some time by telling her, "Let me finish up and I'll get you something."

Once I was through, Sybil took the soiled material away. I could hear her working diligently to clean up in the kitchen. Although it seemed like it should be time for bed, the six o'clock news was on TV. We heard a limb from a century oak had broken off and literally cut a house in half.

"I'd say you were really lucky," I told Maggie, while nodding at the images on the screen. When she made a face at me, only to wince because her wound protested the use of too many facial muscles, I said, "Sit up and let me check your eyes for dilation."

I reached over to the coffee table for one of the LED flashlights I'd passed out and clicked it on. Then I directed Maggie, "Look over my shoulder."

The bright light had her swearing like two sailors and a roughneck oil-rig worker combined. "What are you trying to do, see the registration number printed on back of my skull?"

Unable to resist, I replied, "Actually, there seems to be two. It looks like you're a refurbished model."

I anticipated learning a few new words to add to a vocabulary I would never use. Instead she stared at me as though I'd just poured acid on her soul. Someone may as well have yanked a chair out from under me; I was so taken aback by that look.

"Mags, I was only trying to get a smile or spirited comeback out of you," I said quietly.

She turned her head away and whispered, "I hope so."

Nine

AS FAR AS I could tell, Maggie didn't have a concussion, at least not a bad one; however, something was wrong. Yet wrack my brain as I did, I couldn't put my finger on it. My suspicion haunted me throughout the night, to where I barely slept thirty minutes at a time. It also sent me downstairs by four o'clock the next morning to sip instant coffee while sitting in my office by the light of my favorite kerosene lantern, which had been part of this house since my grandparents' time. I needed the comfort of old things carrying loving vibrations around me this morning.

At first, Rosie had looked confused at the change in our schedule, but she'd finally curled on the carpet under my desk with her favorite chew toy as a pacifier. Every now and then, she would shift and either rest her snout on the suede of my slippers, or stretch out and just put one leg across my feet. They were signals of love, the need for physical contact, and a deterrent against me leaving without taking her with me.

"Not to worry," I crooned to her as she effected the latter position. "I need you as much as you think you need me."

Enjoying the lazy waft of steam rising up from my big mug of black coffee, I shifted my gaze to the photograph on the edge of my desk. It was of Charlie and me, with Maggie and Hollis, the last time we'd gone to The Futurity in Fort Worth. That was the National Cutting Horse Association's gathering for contests, stock sales, and the opportunity to size-up the competition at other ranches. It had always been a big deal for us.

There are trade professionals like master electricians, plumbers, and sheet metal fabricators, and anyone who has had a need for their services understands the years of schooling and internship required to be good at what they do, just as there are teaching schools for a surgeon to become a cardiac or neurologist specialist. It turned out Charlie's expertise was in cutting. The United States might have fought a war to rid itself of royalty, but few achievers like Charlie could return to the Will Rogers Coliseum in Fort Worth without spending a good portion of his time being surrounded by fans, answering a myriad of questions from red-cheeked youngsters fantasizing about a career in the arena, or posing for photographs with fans from around the world. There was an honor wall for those special few who had retained their titles for three successive years or better, and Charlie's plaque stood at the top of his class.

I studied the photo with new understanding. The fact was, he never looked more alive than when November rolled around and we were back in Fort Worth. And he hadn't competed in years! The reason had to be that he no longer had to live up to anyone's standards. It was the younger generation's challenge to live up to his—and what a relief it had been for him.

Charlie had never been a bragger. For all of his teasing and joking, he was a self-conscious man; however, sitting here I realized he was all too human and needed the adoration his talent and hard work had brought him. How less fulfilled his life would have been had he not achieved what he did. In fact, his riding gifts probably allowed him to become a better cattleman.

I felt as though someone had turned a floodlight onto what I'd thought was a serene time capsule photo—my life with Charlie. But in the last few years, I had done a dangerous thing in painting it, and the rest of my memories, with colors that were unfaithful to the whole man. I seem to have passed some unwritten test, or grown in philosophical acumen to deal with reality and accept the truth.

As good a man as Charlie had been, he also had been extremely human. Yes, he had been a good and patient father and supportive husband, but in business too many tried to take him for granted because they recognized that he wanted to be liked more than he wanted to make the best deal. That sometimes forced him to compromise himself—or us.

Weren't those actually qualities he had in common with Maggie? An effortless ability to charm, combined with the frustrating tendency to leave a stressful situation for someone else to resolve. In Charlie's case that person was me. I'd fired people for Charlie because I knew they'd idolized him, and he hated to be seen as the bad guy. I cancelled orders for Charlie because he'd changed his mind about a product and didn't want the supplier to think some other company had offered a larger discount, even if such had been the case. The most difficult times were having to explain him to his children when he'd gone hypocritical on his own values, or otherwise disappointed them because there was an opportunity elsewhere to shine.

I drew in a long, deep breath and slowly exhaled, and with it expelled any residual disappointment or resentment I might have been ignoring. "Is that what you were thinking when I caught you watching me with some secret worry in your eyes?" I asked him as he smiled at me in the photo. "Didn't you know I loved you anyway because the good in you so outweighed the bad?"

Blinking away tears, I felt a spasm of frustration. If I could figure this out, why couldn't I grasp what I was dealing with regarding Maggie? I remembered her expression only hours ago when I made that crack about a serial number in the back of her skull. It was one of several moments that preyed on my mind; however, with so much going on, I couldn't sort them into a cohesive picture yet. What I did know was a husband and wife, lovers, can't survive secrets above a certain magnitude. Best friends can't, either.

What could possibly be the mystery? Had someone talked her into a financial investment that had turned out to be a scam? It would have to be a whopper for Maggie not to concede such a misstep, not when plenty of celebrities and so-called business geniuses get taken every day. Or, had a lover she'd trusted committed the unforgivable? What made a woman so edgy and angry that she would test her own alcohol limits, when she wasn't verbally, and repeatedly stabbing someone she barely knew?

"Good grief," I whispered to the Maggie in the photograph, clenching both hands around my mug. "You're losing a lover to Carly?"

As soon as the thought materialized, I knew I was off track. Carly didn't strike me as someone ready to be intimate again. On the other hand, there were all variations of intimacy. Maybe Carly had gained some support from a bank board member to the point Maggie felt threatened? Carly also didn't seem ready to pressure anyone for a seat on the board of directors. She'd admitted her feelings of inadequacy only hours ago. Besides, Maggie had been a cornerstone in the foundation of the bank since her father died. A small faction of ideologues would successfully campaign to add a face to Mount Rushmore, before Maggie lost leverage to Carly in this town.

Frustrated, I leaned back in the chair, put my feet up on the corner of the desk, and closed my eyes. It was all exhausting, and I needed a less cluttered mind if I was going to cope with whatever today would bring.

My last thought was of Sam and the hope that he was able to sleep better than me tonight.

SOMEONE NUDGED ME hard enough for my feet to come off the desk. I sat up and automatically replied, "I'm here." But as I glanced around the room, I saw I was speaking to a ghost at best.

A soft grunt soon explained what had happened. Rosie was sitting beside me with an expectant look on her face. That had me glancing at the battery operated clock awarded to Charlie during his last year as President of Franklin County Cattlemen's Association.

"No!" It was after six o'clock. I'd not only napped, I'd slept a good half hour longer than my usual time to get outside. Stroking Rosie's head, I whispered, "I'm right behind you, darlin'."

Although I detoured to tend to the living room fire, I decided not to go upstairs to take care of that one, or to change out of my sleepwear. Instead, I put on my jacket and boots, and we went out the back door.

The wind had eased, and the snow was another deceptive waltz of light flurries. There didn't seem to have been much accumulation overnight, and Rosie trotted around to check for signs of night visitors. Finding none, she caught up with me, and beat me to the stable.

The cold and quiet must have made the horses more lethargic because I had the doors opened before they realized I was there. I knew Carly would be disappointed to miss another opportunity to join me, but I would happily return with her after breakfast. The oversized lapdogs would appreciate the added attention. For now, I would tend to immediate needs, and also get milking Elsa out of the way, so the cats would have their fresh milk. The rest could wait until I was in warmer clothes.

Cats were all but essential to farms and ranches. Lately there were two mousers, both strays. Buzz Saw was a gray-tiger striped male with the widest head I've ever seen on a domestic cat, and fur so bristly it refused to stay down. It was just as well; his personality indicated he was born to wear a Mohawk, which is why his name had come so easily to me. Getting him neutered had been a story all its own, but he'd eventually forgiven me—most likely attributable to the good treatment he received here. Cats had long memories and held grudges, but they weren't fools.

I'd always believed there was plenty enough good hunting around the barn to even keep a male from venturing too far. Then came the day Buzz dragged the King Kong of all gophers across the pasture. The thing was half his size, yet with a flip of his massive head, the monster cat flung it into his stainless milk bowl the way a WWW wrestler would toss an opponent to the mat. Then he proceeded to devour the thing head to toe. Although the vision left me bug-eyed, and queasy as I listened to the crunching of bones, I couldn't stop watching. When finished, he drank an entire bowl of fresh milk. Afterward, he climbed up to the top of the stacked feed to sleep it all off. Sometimes, like a snake, it would be several days before he was interested in solid food again. The exhibition I'd witnessed explained why.

Holly was named after Holly Golightly, Truman Capote's famous character from *Breakfast at Tiffany's*. Sleek and elegant-looking, her personality more reflected the book's version of the character than quirky, darling Audrey Hepburn created in the film. But our Holly G did enjoy sitting with our Elsa for hours at a time, the way you would sometimes see a sole goat sitting in a pasture with a horse. Since Elsa was white and black, too, I wondered if Holly just assumed her a homely cousin with a serious eating disorder?

From time to time, we've had other cats, and visiting cats, but since Buzz's arrival, the population has stayed what it is. Holly G did have one semi-regular visitor, whom I called Denny after Karen Blixen's great love-torment, Denys Finch Hatton, told memorably in *Out of Africa*. Our tom version of Denny managed to figure out when Buzz wasn't around, and wooed Holly, as though he didn't have a clue she couldn't give him what he wanted. Thwarted, he would vanish for weeks at a time, much like his namesake. Since I've never seen or heard any evidence of alter-cations, I have concluded it's working out for all parties involved. I would find out if that continued to be true as soon as I got next door.

The horses blew through their nostrils in greeting, as I went to the storage room for their grain. Everyone looked as though they'd had a comfortable night, so as they ate, I mucked each stall. The brushing could wait until I returned with Carly, which helped me regain some time. Nevertheless, as I checked my watch, my stomach muscles sponta-neously clenched. I knew I had to make a call.

"I wondered how long you'd need to hide," Sam said, as soon as we were connected.

There was no question of protesting, let alone attempting an excuse. "I was overwhelmed," I admitted.

"Tell me something I don't know."

"You weren't going to call me back, were you?"

"I would try not to," he began. "But I would have lost the battle eventually." After a slight pause, he added, "Unless you don't feel the way I do?"

That told me he needed some reassurance from me. Fortunately, having watched Maggie, and having talked to Sybil in the last few days, I had a better perspective of life and second chances. "Sam…I *do.*"

Exhaling in relief, he said, "I keep forgetting that you have your shy moments. But that's all I needed to hear. For the rest I want to be with you when you tell me."

"The way things are going it could be a long wait," I said, glancing at the conditions outside. Now that I'd stopped working, I was starting to feel foolish for coming out here without more clothes. My legs and backside were starting to go numb. "What does the latest weather report say? Everyone is still sleeping, and I honestly didn't think to check the radar before calling you."

Sam uttered a sound of disgust. "The meteorologists insist the frozen stuff should quit sometime today for us, so probably this evening for you."

"No wonder it looks like a repeat of yesterday. Well, I hope we can last. I have some bad news. One of my pecan trees halfway down the driveway tried to do in Maggie last night."

"Whoa! How badly is she hurt?"

"I haven't talked to her since 2:00 a.m. when I thought it was safe for her to sleep. She suffered a two-inch gash on her forehead."

"And you sacrificed your rest to watch for signs of a concussion."

"My house, my friend. Don't try to turn me into one of the Sisters of Mercy," I added. I couldn't sleep anyway due to frustration and confusion as to why she's acting the way she is."

"This isn't exactly weather for an evening stroll."

"She was in one of her moods. I thought she went to recharge her phone in her car." I quickly filled him in on the rest.

"Sweetheart, you should have called me. At the least I would have walked you through a list of symptoms to look for that could mean trouble, and then while you steadied your nerves with a glass of wine, maybe I could have charmed Maggie into confiding in me."

I didn't want to think about him charming anyone, including my best friend but he needed an answer, which had me confessing the second most painful truth. "I wasn't convinced you'd take the call considering how I left things between us."

"But you had to know I understood? You *do* know I understand, don't you?"

I loved how his voice grew gruff as it deepened. "You're too good to me. I'm already on my way to turning you into the icon of overly romantic widows. In any case, I would have had three other women competing to hear you breathe, thanks to Maggie blabbing about you earlier. Now they all want to meet you."

"The only one I want to get close to is you."

That husky-voiced assurance had me confessing, "You almost make me forget that I'm standing out here in my PJs."

"Out where? Damn it, Retta. You couldn't find privacy in another room? You had to go outside?"

"I finally fell asleep in my office and the next thing I knew it was a half hour later than we usually talk. I'll head back inside as soon as I close the stables." *And milk Elsa*, I added to myself. "Don't be annoyed."

"I'm not. I'm ticked off that I'm not there to help you, and feeling pretty damned useless." He sighed. "Go ahead. You wanted to talk about Maggie's behavior."

Grateful that the tension had eased in his voice, I said, "She sounds like Ingrid Bergman and Humphrey Bogart in *Casablanca*. All fatalism, evasion, and enigmatic comments."

"It sounds to me like she's trying to tell you something."

"That much I get. And I've asked her, more than once, given her plenty of opportunities to open up. It's crazy. I can't believe that jealousy over a younger woman can turn a person into someone I barely recognize."

"Why not? There've been murders committed for less passionate reasons," he replied.

"Sam when did I ever suggest Maggie was that far gone?"

"You haven't, but I've learned enough about her character in this last year to gauge Hollis was a steadying force in her life that she sorely needed. Maybe that knock to her head will make her slip up, and expose what's really going on. In the meantime, watch her for sudden headaches, or loss of balance, that kind of thing. And no heavy lifting. There's always the danger of blood clots."

"Now I'm glad I didn't call last night. With that kind of worry, none of us would have gotten a wink of sleep." Between the falling snowflakes, I saw Carly bringing Wrigley outside. "The girls are rousing, Sam. I have to get back and fuel up the generator."

He uttered another bitter oath under his breath. "Take care please?"

"I promise."

"And call anytime. I'm here. For you."

He had a talent for putting a lot of meaning into a few fragmented assertions, and I felt a tickle on the side of my neck as though his lips had just brushed against my skin. I also knew exactly what he was telling me: he saw me as an equal and my putting him on a pedestal was as uncomfortable for him, as his celebrity and talent were for me.

"Thank you. You might as well know, though...I'm still feeling like a fraud for believing I can handle this. Us."

"I know. I have my work cut out for me until I stop triggering your flight instincts. But I'm putting you on notice," he added, with some new emotion entering his voice. "When I get there, woman, you'd better be prepared, because I'm coming to prove a point—and don't you even think about dropping that damned phone again."

"Oh, Sam. I can't wait to see you, too."

"Babe, that's the best thing you've said to me yet."

After a few seconds of silence, I let my hand drop to my knee and stared at the screen. "You hung up." I smiled, understanding why, as wave after wave of warmth and love swept through me.

What he'd done wasn't payback. Nothing so juvenile or petty was in Sam's character. But his voice had grown thick with passion, and desire and he hadn't trusted himself to keep his intent not to say too much, until we were together. If I'd needed an extra push to fall head over heels, he'd just given it to me.

Minutes later, I was back at the house and had the generator filled. There was enough adrenaline pumping through my blood not to be craving caffeine, but I was cold, and knew the others were in need of their share of something hot.

Carly opened the door for me when she heard my footsteps on the porch. I handed her the fresh milk and said, "Don't be disappointed that I went out without you. We can go work with the horses later."

"I figured as much. Oh, gosh, you look frozen through and through."

"Just from the waist down," I said barely able to keep my teeth from chattering. "How's it going?"

"Maggie's still not up, but when Sybil came down, she said she seemed to be resting comfortably."

"The generator will wake her," I said. "I'll have to go up and warn her to keep the bandage dry if she gets into the shower."

"Sybil said none of you got much rest. Dana didn't sleep well, either, but I don't mind. I'm guessing it's what you would expect for a woman close to term."

Remembering those days, I nodded. "It can be a challenge to find a comfortable position. At least she doesn't have to suffer the misery of enduring a summer pregnancy."

"I guess I'll never know."

Realizing what she was telling me, I mused, "Fate has a lot to do with that. None of us should ever say never. And you shouldn't put up barriers that might keep opportunity away. You're too young."

As I shut the door, and Carly brought the milk to the kitchen, Sybil called a cheery welcome. "Get ready for Canadian bacon, flapjacks, and my own blackberry syrup from the spring crop. Carly, if the pancakes aren't okay, I can get some oatmeal going for you? I do use Retta's goat milk and butter in the batter."

"You know what? I'll pretend I didn't hear a word," Carly said. "Willow and I liked to pick blackberries on our way to school, even though they stained our fingers, and the kids usually teased us, which ruined some of the fun. We couldn't let it matter too much, though. The berries were our only breakfast. Pouring your syrup over pancakes will feel like an early Thanksgiving."

"Poor babies," Sybil replied. "I wish I'd known you then. I don't stand for a child in my class going hungry. I bring extra food to school all the time. I'm so glad Walter could make a difference for you. Now, as soon as you put down that milk, you can set the table for me. Mama Sybil is going to spoil you a little bit. You've never had syrup like mine."

I got out of my things and focused on getting Rosie fixed up. "That's as true as the gospel. Charlie never liked messing with anything with thorns, but when he learned that Sybil would share her syrup if he would help provide the berries, he would stop along the roadside if he saw a big bush of them."

Since we didn't spend as much time in the deeper snow, Rosie's paws weren't as packed as usual, so I finished quickly, patted her, and rose. The maneuver brought me directly into Sybil's line of vision and she stared at my sleepwear.

I held up my hand to entreat her not to voice her opinion about my foolishness. "I'm heading upstairs to have a hot bath, right after I check on Maggie."

"Please do because we'll founder along with you if you come down with pneumonia."

I blew her a kiss and hurried upstairs. As I entered the master suite, I saw the bed was empty. "Good morning, sunshine," I called. When she remained quiet, I ventured closer to the bathroom door. "You're being awful quiet in there."

"I have fifteen hundred dollars of makeup in my suitcase, and it's not going to be enough."

Leaning my head against the door jamb, I said with as much reassurance as possible, "Bruising is inevitable, Mags. You took an awful blow. At least you're among friends."

"One friend. Maybe two if I haven't yet offended Sybil thoroughly. Hey! Confiscate all cell phones downstairs," Maggie demanded. "I don't trust that leggy bimbo not to put me on one or all of those internet sites."

Even when she felt miserable, her mouth refused to stop spewing venom. Not good news. "Did you end up with a black eye on top of everything else?"

As the silence on the other side of the door lengthened, I thought she planned to ignore me. Then I heard the lock give.

The door creaked open. Living alone as I did, I preferred noisy hinges and squeaky floors. However, my reasoning was swept away as I found myself face-to-face with Maggie, posed hand on hip as she leaned against the door jamb. Her expression was an understandable mixture of disgust and humiliation.

She didn't only have one black eye—impressive though it was—both eyes were bona fide shiners. Her nose also had suffered, looking as though she'd lost a layer or two of skin over the bridge, an injury I hadn't noticed last night what with her whole face being red from near frostbite. I suspected one of the smaller tree branches had whipped her hard.

"Poor Mags." I started to reach toward her, only to draw back. I knew she had to be too sore to want to be touched. "It's a miracle you didn't suffer a cornea scratch or worse. Any residual headache, or vision problems?" As I spoke, I tried to check her pupils for even dilation, but her lids were too swollen to tell.

"My sinuses are messed up, which isn't helping the throbbing. I'm a freaking mess! Be a dear and bring me some coffee? I can't possibly go downstairs."

I'd been too concerned with her wounds to notice she did sound congested. "You can put on your loosest and largest pair of sunglasses." I knew she had brought several of those, too.

"Forget it. I already feel like an ass. Why would I want to invite a unanimous vote? Besides," she muttered, "I'm the one who mocks other people for wearing their sunglasses indoors, as though they're trying to look like celebrities hiding from the *paparazzi*."

"Okay, but at least you have a legitimate reason for wearing them. I'll back you. They sure would offset the need for makeup. Frankly, Mags, it can't be smart to put anything but medication on your face for a few days."

"Sure because getting blood poisoning and dying would be such a bad thing," she drawled. "Worse would be to let your darling Carly see me like this."

I could have hit my head against the wall in exasperation. "Maggie, I cannot believe she thinks of you a fraction as much as you dwell on her. Right now Dana has her full attention."

"When she isn't sucking up to you. I think she's trying to hoodwink all of us."

Crossing my arms over my chest, I raised my eyebrows and stared at her in challenge. "To what end? Nothing I have a vested interest in. Besides, she's been working too hard to make a life for her and her sister to hone the talents needed for the kind of cunning you're suggesting. Give it a rest, please."

With a haughty look, Maggie wiggled her fingers at me in dismissal. "Weren't you going to get me some coffee? I'm going to take a shower."

I slipped past her and got out one of the shower caps I kept in a vanity drawer, and set it on the counter. "Put this over the bandage, so it doesn't get wet."

"I have to wash my hair! It looks like it belongs on a crime scene corpse."

"Not today." My tone was adamant. "Give the wound time to close. Shampoos are full of perfume and chemicals. After you're done showering, sponge the blood out of your bangs at the sink if you must. I'll help you if you like. First though, let me get a quick bath."

Without waiting for her to slam the door in my face, I collected the clothes I intended to change into, and left the room. I hadn't even messed with the fireplace yet; however, there were enough hot coals to last a bit longer. The fact was if Maggie was so banged up to where she couldn't stand, let alone talk, I would gladly have gotten coffee and more for her; I would have brought up a tray with breakfast. But under the circumstances, she had yet to count her blessings over last night's close call, so as far as I was concerned, it was time for tough love.

Despite good intentions, it was half an hour before I made it back to the kitchen, well worth it, though. The hot bath rejuvenated me, and I felt refreshed in my clean jeans and wine-red cable-knit sweater over a matching long-sleeved knit top.

Sybil and Carly stood on opposite sides of the island looking like politicians in the midst of a debate. Sybil was insisting how it wasn't fair to compare cooked okra to slimy raw oysters. I did my best not to burst out laughing.

"I'll eat it fried or not at all." Carly waved her hands before her face, as though warding off bad images.

"Here's Retta," Sybil said. "Tell her that my okra gumbo is every bit as good as my turnip greens."

How much easier would this be to what I'd dealt with upstairs. "Her secret weapon is bacon," I told Carly in a loud whisper.

"Retta!" Sybil cried.

"And you don't just throw in bacon because that defeats half the purpose," I continued. "You bake or fry it first, and only add it moments before serving. The sneaky woman deduced if you're tasting and crunching on bacon, you can't possibly dwell on slime."

Hands on her ample hips, Sybil muttered, "I didn't tell you to give away my secret."

I winked at her. "I think it's safe with Carly. Now, don't let us ruin your breakfast. When Dana finally emerges from the bathroom, you three eat. It may take me a while to get Maggie down here."

Sybil looked doubtful. "You think she's able to come down?"

"Able, yes, willing is another story."

"She looks bad, huh?"

"Oh, she's a vision." Collecting two mugs, I started to pour the coffee. "Look—if I manage to get her here—and so far sunshine and balmy seventy-degree temperatures are more likely—please try not to stare. The bruising is significant, worse than I anticipated."

"Poor thing." Sybil gestured toward the browned Canadian bacon plated on the stove, and the griddle and bowl of pancake batter waiting beside it. "I can make her a plate for you to take up. It won't take me but a minute to fix."

I shook my head. "How does the saying go? 'Feed a cold, starve a fever?' Maggie's determination to avoid coming down here is at fever pitch. My bitter pill will be reminding her of the conduct that brought on all of this. We're not going to baby her."

Looking less than convinced about the plan, Sybil said, "Good luck with that strategy."

"You think I'm being tough on her? People undergo major surgery these days, and mere hours later, they're being made to get out of bed and walk. Maggie's injuries are nowhere near as severe." I finished doctoring her brew the way she liked it. "Her ego might not be too happy about it, but she can do this."

"Well, make sure you let her go ahead of you when you start down the stairs," Sybil replied. "Just in case she decides she's acquired some Turrets-like tick and accidentally-on-purpose gives you a push."

I lifted one mug in salute and returned upstairs.

The bathroom door was shut again, so I set down Maggie's mug at the door and sipped my coffee before tending to the fire. I made plenty of noise to signal that I was back. Once I had the ashes in the pail ready to go outside, I reloaded logs over the coals, and took another drink.

"Come on, girlfriend, before your panacea gets cold!" I called as I moved to the bed.

She made no reply, so once I was finished, I straightened Sybil's blankets on the recliner. I caught myself humming a melody from a silly jingle getting way too much playtime on TV these days. What was it that kids called them?

"Earworms," I murmured. "Gross."

Finally, I heard a click and the door opened. Prepared for the worst, I turned to see her posing again. This time she'd dressed in vampy elegance reminiscent of a movie star from the golden age of Hollywood. Despite my warnings, she'd muted the bruising with an over-generous application of cosmetics, and had wrapped one of her favorite navy, gold, and white Hermes scarves low over her forehead to hide her bandage. Had she tended to the wound herself? My concern over that was quickly replaced by hope upon seeing the pair of sunglasses she held in the hand on her hip. Could she actually be ready to make an appearance downstairs without me having to wheedle, cajole, or plead?

"You don't deserve to look as good as you do."

"A back-handed compliment is better than none."

I indicated the coffee to her left. "Down that before it's so tepid it's disgusting."

Spotting it, she made a mewing sound of an infant or kitten. "Bless you," she murmured before gulping with relish.

Maggie's version of coffee meant tainting it with two envelopes of artificial sweetener, and further poisoning it with a generous dollop of those artificially-flavored creamers. Intestinal suicide, although in my house she had to settle for the real thing—milk a la Elsa, blended with cinnamon. Anyone who'd imbibed as much alcohol as she did had no business counting calories.

"Good?" I asked, once she finally paused to breathe."

"Sublime."

"Why didn't you wait for me to help you with your bandage?"

"Despite the blow to my head, I'm not so dimwitted that I've overlooked how busy you are without having to nurse me."

"But I would have, and gladly, because I love you." I gestured toward the hallway. "Do you think you can make it downstairs with me now?"

"I'm starving, so I will. I'm also aware they'll be nicer to me if you're around."

Relieved, I collected my mug and the bucket of ashes, and nodded for her to lead the way. Noting how she walked with marked stiffness, I stayed close, especially while going downstairs, in case she had injuries she was keeping to herself.

Sybil was the first to spot us. "Praise the Lord," she said, rising.

Her declaration had Dana and Carly turning in their seats. I felt a twinge of pity for Maggie having to endure the intense scrutiny.

"Look at you," Dana said.

"It's good to see you're able to come downstairs," Carly added, politely.

With sunglasses secured, Maggie offered a royal wave. "It was only a little bump to the head. No need to call for an emergency meeting of the bank board to ask for a medical competency review."

As polite smiles withered, so did my sympathy. "Sit down, Mags. I think the hours spent in the higher altitude upstairs has caused a momentary oxygen shortage to your brain." Ignoring what I knew was a glare behind those sunglasses, I added, "I'm going to set these ashes outside to cool off and be right back."

"Let me get you a refill." Sybil stepped forward to take Maggie's mug. "I watched Retta. I know how to do it."

Upon my return, I washed my hands, poured myself more coffee and joined the others. That's when I noticed by the scraped-clean plates the others had eaten, but they were lingering over coffee.

Sybil brought our plates before returning to the microwave to rewarm her blackberry syrup. As good as it looked, I asked, "We're out of eggs?" I hadn't yet checked the hen house, but I was certain we still had some from yesterday.

"I decided to skip them, once I realized I'd made too much pancake batter. Did I do wrong?"

"Not if it means we can have omelets tomorrow?"

"Works for me." Her grin said she knew exactly what I was doing. "I saw you had bell peppers from your garden in the freezer."

"I'll bring you in onions I have hanging in the barn, too."

"How is Freckles?" Carly asked, leaning forward.

"I only saw her from a distance, but she seems okay. She was nibbling on one of the big round bales. I'll bring them all pellets later and get a closer look." I allowed myself a chance to really study her and had to smile. "You're looking particularly pretty this morning. I love that teal on you," I added, referring to her sweater-vest ensemble.

The compliment left her all but glowing. "Thanks. I suspect, though, that it's mostly due to yesterday's fresh air and honest labor."

Maggie all but drowned her pancakes in syrup. "Doesn't this look wonderful?" she gushed.

"Yes, it does," I murmured, with a covert glance. "I'm going to miss this spoiling once the weather clears." I know I sounded more cautious than convincing, but I sensed a change in Maggie. Tiny warning bells went off in my mind. "Too often my breakfast tends to be cereal or oatmeal."

"It doesn't have to be." With every word, Maggie almost brutally sliced up her food, as though she was intent on her own version of Death by a Thousand Cuts. "If you didn't insist on maintaining this place as you do, you could take the time to enjoy some creature comforts."

Having just reclaimed her seat, Sybil popped up again. "Let me refill that syrup pitcher. It soaks in fast."

"Thank you, dear."

Watching Maggie begin eating, using her silverware in the elegant European manner, I couldn't resist asking, "What am I depriving myself of?" I realized her annoyance had been triggered by my compliment to Carly, and I couldn't allow her to control me.

"The point is about ending up old before your time." She paused, waiting until she had the attention of the entire table. "I read—and experienced for myself—that in France, a widow is a hallowed person. That's the way it should be here."

"So when are you moving, Marie Antoinette?" I drawled.

"Believe me, it's increasingly tempting."

Suddenly Dana covered her ears with both hands. "Stop! I can't stand this any longer."

Immediately contrite, I tried to soothe her. "I'm sorry, Dana. It's my fault."

"It's not, and you know it. Don't make excuses for her."

"No, I succumbed to exactly what I promised myself I wouldn't do."

"How can you help it? No matter what the conversation is about, she'll figure a way how to ruin things or make it about *her*." Dana looked down the table at Maggie. "If a blow to the head can't jar you into having a real and intelligent conversation, let's try this. While you're acting like the silliest and most selfish diva on TV? I'm facing the decision of giving up the baby."

Ten

THE SILENCE that followed Dana's outburst was as profound as her announcement. No one hearing such news could remain unresponsive for long, and we were no different. There quickly came the aftershocks, the high-pitched clatter of silverware tumbling—Maggie and I dropping our forks, Sybil the handful she had begun to collect at the other end of the table. I suppose, short of the propane tank exploding, or a transformer blowing, we couldn't have been more appalled, or shaken.

Carly snapped out of her stupor first. Her cheeks, then her entire face filled with the color of passionate emotions.

"You can't! Your own flesh and blood?"

Dana reached over trying to take hold of her friend's hand. "I can if it means…"

"No!" Carly pulled away, as though recoiling from the affront of a stranger. As though that was inadequate, she shoved her chair back to put more space between them. "You're better than that. You won't be able to do it."

"Please hear me out. The child deserves opportunities."

"You'll see it happens."

"How? With what?" Dana shook her head frantically, struggling to make herself understood. "Don't you understand? It's not just that. I want to spare it from having to endure an embittered, half-crazy mother."

"You're not crazy, you're going through a terrible time. Things will change. They'll get better."

"Dear friend, I know you can't help but remember your childhood. Instead, try to think of people who can't have children, who are aching to be parents and have the wherewithal to give them the best. Who am I to deprive this baby of not only a loving home, but a thriving one?"

"Money can't replace your own flesh and blood."

Considering what we were already trying to take in, Carly's pain and anger was almost too much to witness. I felt my throat and chest tighten in my grief for what Dana's announcement was putting her through. Sybil must have noticed I was struggling and stepped behind me to gently kneed my shoulders. I realized she was doing it for herself, as well; it was like someone seeking relief from stress by reaching into a pocket to finger a worry stone.

"Darlin', Carly's right," she began. "Sometimes things look as bad as they can get, but there's no replacing family. And you would be a wonderful mother. I can see it. You just have to give yourself the chance."

"I've watched you," Carly continued. "Don't tell me you feel nothing for your baby."

"I do," Dana assured her, her expression as tortured as her breaking voice. "That's why I'm willing myself to find the strength to do what is best for it."

Out of the corner of my eye, I noticed Maggie shaking her head over her plate. "What?" I croaked, not sure I wanted to know. I silently prayed she wouldn't spout something that would send Carly lurching across the table and reaching for her throat.

"Don't you get it?" Maggie asked softly. "That's why she didn't want to know if she was having a boy or a girl. This isn't a recent decision."

"No, it isn't." Yet Dana's voice was as raw as a fresh wound. She gestured helplessly, only to collapse onto the table to hide her face in the well of her folded arms.

Sybil circled around to offer comfort. "Oh, sweetheart, don't cry. Please. You'll have us all bawling our eyes out, too. Just because we disagree, doesn't mean our hearts aren't breaking along with yours."

Yet one of us remained stoic in her anger. Carly turned her face away from Dana, as though she couldn't bear to look at her a moment longer. I'd never seen anyone so strong in her conviction, but I suspect she'd earned it by fighting for her sister. What an advocate young Willow had growing up. How many examples of love and devotion had she been shown by her older sister. If she didn't adore her with every ounce of her being, there was no justice in this world.

"I'm not crying," Dana finally replied, straightening in her chair. "I don't have any tears left. I'm so dry, I feel like I've been wandering aimlessly in a desert just waiting for it all to end. I'm exhausted, which is why I have to do this while I can."

I had to ask the question no one else had voiced yet. "What about Jesse's parents, dear? I remember what you said earlier, and I understand, I do, but the news about becoming grandparents could change things. And shouldn't you have a talk with your family?"

She offered an indelicate snort. "I told you, my folks found parenting awkward. Can you imagine them having to deal with a newborn at this stage of their lives? No, as long as I tell them something that parallels physiological stability, it's all good. Then they can shelve me in some back room of their minds and focus on what they really value. As for Jesse's people, why would I expect them to treat their grandchild any better than they did their son? Besides, there's no way I would tolerate filling the child's mind with prejudice and stupidity."

"But Retta is right—a baby changes everything," Sybil insisted.

"It sure does," Dana said, nodding adamantly. She started to tick things off each finger. "Hospital bills, doctor bills, clothes, daycare, groceries...you name it. I'm already starting this situation in a deficit, and it's about to get much worse. You think I want it to suffer the way Carly and Willow did? Endure ridicule in school, whispers in church? What do I say when some playmate repeats an overheard comment from home, and announces before I can explain, 'Your daddy killed himself'?"

"We were called 'bastards,'" Carly replied, with quiet dignity. "As bad as it felt at the time, it didn't kill us."

"Because God sent you Walter. Me? I get the IRS."

That could have been a Maggie line, funny even in its grim accuracy. Dana's despair made laughing impossible.

She abruptly raised her hands to plead with us not to say another word. "I need to change the subject."

"But Dana," I began, my mind spinning. "You have to give us a chance. We're your friends, and we want to help. We're all in a position to be here for you to various degrees. Before you make a final decision, you have to give us the opportunity to think and discuss options."

"Bless you, Retta. No," she replied. "I've made my decision, and now all I want is fresh air. Let's all go outside. I want to make a snowman. No, I want to make a snow*woman,* to celebrate this time with you all."

Even though I understood what our conversation was costing her, I didn't feel good about her choices, including this latest idea. "Dana, really, what you're suggesting is too physical for you at this stage."

Sybil echoed the concern. "And it's slippery out there, hon. Why take unnecessary risks?"

"Because I may never experience anything like this again," Dana replied. "I want to feel the kiss of snowflakes on my cheek, to learn what snow smells like. I *have* to get rid of that stomach-roiling, metallic stench of death that's still in my nostrils!" With a whole-body shudder, she cried, "Oh, I just—I *need* to get away from myself for a little while. Please. Don't treat me as though I was as fragile as an egg shell. I'll be careful."

I could easily have stopped this by informing her that I'd only done half of the outside chores that needed to be done, but her desperation wore me down, and I could see it had a similar effect on the others. As I reached into my pocket for my cell phone and brought up the screen I wanted, I said, "Well, if we're going to do this, we'd better head outside now." Confirming what I suspected, I showed the radar to the others. "The icing has started in the DFW area. Once it gets here, the crust will make the snow too hard to build anything, except an igloo."

"In that case, let's leave the dishes for later," Sybil said.

As Maggie rose with the rest of us, Carly looked doubtful. "Maybe you shouldn't risk physical exertion, any more than Dana should."

Maggie stared at her from behind her sunglasses. "You can't get rid of me that easily. I'm not ready to be the old bag sitting by the window wrapped in a shawl with drool running down my chin."

"Knock it off, Mags," I demanded. "Carly's right. It will be unsafe for both of you to wrestle with heavy objects, not to mention bending. You could easily open that wound, trigger a blood clot—anything."

"I'll be fine. I'll just change into something warmer. Meet you outside."

Knowing she wouldn't be back too quickly due to her diminished condition, I began to clear the table. Despite her suggestion, Sybil started to help me, as Dana had detoured to the bathroom, and Carly to the living room. Carly had said something about putting a little sweater and boots on Wrigley.

"What do you think?" Sybil whispered, as I ran hot water into the wash pan.

I didn't pretend not to follow. Dana's predicament remained in the forefront of her thoughts, too. "It will be yet another tragedy if she goes through with it. But I'm grateful she got upset enough to finally share her thoughts with us. What if she'd kept the decision a secret until she was at the hospital? By then things could already be in motion, commitments made. At least now we have six weeks to try to come up with a plan."

"It was so good of you to reach out the way you did. I want to help, too. Just let me know whatever you need."

"You have your hands full with your commitment to Naomi and keeping Debra focused on her studies, not to mention your school responsibilities, which is no more an eight-hour-a-day job than mine is. I didn't mean to suggest—"

"I know you didn't," Sybil assured me. "Only I can't stand what's happening here. We could arrange a shower for her, if not a fundraiser. She doesn't have as much as a crib yet."

"She wasn't planning on needing one."

"Don't remind me." Sybil shuddered. "But now listen—I could hold one party for her in the neighborhood. You could have one here for people from your church."

"At the very least."

Sybil's expression grew worried again. "Do you really think the government will take her house?"

"Texas is a homestead state, so they shouldn't, but we're talking federal law and business debt? Who knows? Only, if the feds don't, the bank probably will due to the mortgage. We need to put Maggie to work on that side of things. She may not know the law, either, but she does have access to the best attorneys, who might be willing to help, considering that Jesse was a veteran. Preferably one who would take Dana's case pro bono. No matter what though, if she does lose her home, there's plenty of room here. She's welcome to stay, until she gets back on her feet."

"When Carly gets over being upset with her, she'll realize she has more house than she needs, too."

I heard the bathroom door open and touched Sybil's shoulder. "We'll figure it out. As I said, thank goodness there's time."

We dispersed to change into boots, jackets, and whatever else needed to protect us from the challenging conditions. Thinking we would be returning out back, Rosie sat in the mud room waiting on me, until I tugged on my wide-brimmed hat and said, "Front door."

She zipped through the house to bark her version of the announcement at Wrigley, as though the small dog's red sweater and matching booties didn't give him enough of a clue as to where they were headed. By the time I reached Carly, she had changed her footwear and had on her jacket.

"If you don't mind, I'm going to go borrow a hat from your collection?" she asked.

"Help yourself."

Sybil descended the stairs, in the process of tying a maroon scarf around the upturned collar of her jacket. "The last time I played in the snow, it was to help Debra make her first snowman. The thing turned out to be only knee high to me, and we used most of the snow in the front yard to achieve that much."

The scarf matched her hat, which was adored with a crocheted, mauve-pink flower. She tugged the knit cap lower over her close, curly do, which salons were calling a Short Big Chop cut these days. Even though the hat was cute, it wasn't her usual ladylike style. I asked, "That's Debra's, isn't it? No wonder she's on your mind."

"She left it behind, meaning she'll never miss it, and I'm not about to subject one of my Sunday church hats to this weather."

Outside, we surveyed the windfall we would have to work with. "You're right about timing," I told her. "Why couldn't this have happened back when the kids were younger? I once watched my bunch try to sculpt a longhorn with similar results to yours. The tree branches were a good attempt at horns, and I showed them how to mix cocoa and cinnamon for splotches on the so-called hide, but there wasn't enough snow, and they ended up with a steer the size of Elsa."

Dana and Carly joined us, then Maggie brought up the rear. She'd traded the satin caftan for skinny jeans, a cashmere sweater, and her wild-colored jacket. I figured she would be freezing in minutes, but at least she'd kept the scarf on.

For a moment, we stood on the porch and discussed ideas about the placement of our not-so-merry band of snowwomen. Rosie sniffed around Maggie's Mercedes, and Wrigley comically tested her booties on the bottom stair.

"For pity's sake," Maggie snapped. "If we have to vote on every blessed thing, Dana will have to pee again before she's made a snowball, never mind the base." Launching herself down the steps, she declared, "It's every gal for herself. I'm already warning you that I'll win for Best Use of Bling!"

Realizing she was serious, a competitive spirit took over. We looked like busy ants all but bumping into each other to get at the prime snow.

Sybil was puffing when she finally brought her thigh-high base to a stop where she wanted it. Only seconds later, Maggie rolled her slightly smaller specimen in front of it. Sybil huffed in indignation.

"Hey!" She stomped over to karate chop some snow off of the back-side of Maggie's work in progress. "Take that! You needed to get that flat-butt proportional, anyway." If it wasn't for the mischievous glint in her eye, she would have seemed serious.

With a shriek, Maggie threw a handful of snow at her back, only her aim was off. Most of it hit the back of her head, almost pushing off her hat.

"Why you—" Adjusting her hat, Sybil rolled her base several feet away, and proceeded to ignore Maggie.

"And that's what you call the end justifying the means," Maggie called after her. "I think I'll take a picture when we're done and send it to the local TV station and our newspaper. On the radio, they said they were looking for photos to put on their websites, too."

No one responded to her blathering, signaling that they were siding with Sybil. Carly also seemed to have put Dana's decision aside for now and was helping her with the first part of her snowwoman. I rolled my snowball safely away from Maggie, but protested when Dana directed Carly to situated hers behind mine.

"Don't do that."

"You heard her," Dana replied, as though Maggie was invisible. "She's going to take pictures, while I'm donating my—what did you call it?—Christmas-tree-bag nightgown to my gal here. It wasn't my intention to share the results with anyone other than my friends."

The way she emphasized "friends" made it evident that Maggie was not included. For her part, Maggie gave no indication that she'd heard, let alone caught the innuendo.

"Don't worry, baby," Sybil called, heading for the house again. "Mine will be more embarrassing. I'm going for a pair of my sweats and fill the baggy butt part with snow to remind myself never to dress for comfort again."

Liking her inspiration, I said, "Then I'd better donate my ragged straw western hat to mine. It will finally force me to buy something new. My Christmas present to myself."

"I think you'd look stunning in an Aussie-style one," Dana suggested.

"Are you trying to get me thrown out of Texas?" I teased her because as much as she tried to show that she was glad she'd suggested this project, the enthusiasm didn't reach her eyes.

Carly finally focused on her own creation and soon showed her individuality. She didn't roll an increasingly larger snowball, she sculpted legs.

Even though I was concerned that she'd chosen to work between Maggie and Dana, I applauded. "Very creative!"

Maggie eyed the shapely legs and scowled, only to start molding boobs on her statue. They were voluptuous and hardly a true representation compared to Carly's depiction of herself. It was all I could do not to groan out loud.

We worked for several minutes in studious silence. Every once in a while a small ice pellet fell amid the intensifying snow. To the northwest, I could see the sky darkening. It made me doubt the odds of us finishing our frozen renditions of ourselves.

Sybil returned and, as promised, started filling the lower half of her gray sweat suit with the snow. Then she sat the thing on top of her base, so the fullest part of the hips spread even more. Standing back to inspect it, she scowled.

"You know what's scary?" she muttered. "From the back, this is actually starting to resemble me."

"You'll still end up smaller than I am," Dana assured her, as she kept packing more snow onto her figure's belly.

In minutes, the wind started to pick up and, when a branch broke from a nearby tree, Dana shuffled over, seeming to be enthralled with it.

She stuck it in the side of her figurine so it looked like the snowwoman was pressing the back of her hand to her forehead. The amusing result had the desired effect; it stirred memories of the divas from *Gone with the Wind*.

"Can't you just hear her?" Dana chuckled. "I have the vapors."

"Retta, do you still own any cotton-and-lace hankies?" Sybil asked. "You have to let Dana attach one to the hand."

"You bet," I assured her. "I have packages unopened yet. I still use them in my linen and lingerie drawers. I dab them with perfume so everything will smell pretty. After a long day with animals, it's rather nice to remind myself I have a feminine side."

Carly paused from her own work. "You're more than feminine, Retta. You're a four-dimensional woman."

The compliment startled me, particularly coming from someone so clueless about her naturally beauty and warrior-princess strength. "Why…thanks," I said, feeling a too-familiar sting in my eyes. Needing to get the attention off of myself, I asked, "What are you going to use to represent your wonderful hair?"

At the moment, it was all hidden under Charlie's fur-trimmed trapper's hat. I had grinned when I saw she'd chosen it. The only times when I used it was when the winter wind forced me to protect myself against an earache. Carly had apparently chosen it to keep her hair from getting drenched.

"Would you be willing to donate a package of spaghetti?" she asked.

It was a clever idea. "I think you should go with the angel hair variety?" I replied. "You may need two boxes. Pantry, right side, third shelf."

As Carly scrambled up the steps and disappeared inside, Maggie muttered, "Good grief. The BS is getting thick around here." At the sound of a whine, she lowered her sunglasses and narrowed her eyes at Wrigley, who cried and pawed at the front door, wanting to get to his mistress. "I think it would be funny to carve a hole into her snowwoman and stick that little yapper in it the way it hides inside her jacket."

"Just stay away from there," Dana warned. "And stop being so nasty."

"Who's being nasty?" Arms akimbo, she affected an image of pure innocence. "I thought we were aiming for realism? Oh, I've got it—we're making *snow totems*."

"She must be suffering residual effects from last night," I told Dana and

Sybil, grateful that Carly had missed her mean-spirited suggestion. Then I addressed a question to Maggie. "You aren't fighting a headache, are you?"

"I'm a little sore, thank you for asking, but that has nothing to do with my artistic eye."

Sybil huffed at her overstatement. "'Artistic eye,' my petunias. Just because you once slept with a painter, doesn't mean talent rubs off like wet paint."

"Y'all quit ganging up on me!"

"As soon as you quit forcing every issue as though you're itching for a fight," Sybil countered.

"I don't have to do a damn thing except pay taxes and die."

The familiar phrase triggered a memory, and I groaned. "Now she's quoting her father. There's proof that it's likely you did suffer a concussion after all. The last time you agreed with him about anything was when he died."

"Which saved me from any more fantasies about loading one of his pistols, and leaving it within his reach."

I think I stopped breathing. For her part, Sybil just bowed her head. Neither one of us dared look at Dana.

I couldn't argue that Angus Martin had been one tough customer. He had used his daughter as a commodity, no doubt about it. However, for her sake it would have been healthier for Maggie to put the past to rest. Thankfully, Carly emerged from the house waving the boxes of pasta in the air.

"I found it!"

Looking annoyed with her excitement, Maggie announced, "I know what I'm going to do." She began to slip off her sherbet orange Highland sheep jacket and fit it around her snowwoman.

"Maggie!" I cried. "Really? Your designer jacket?"

"It's a bigger statement than pasta."

It was a ridiculous comment, but I let it pass for something more important. "Go put on one of the jackets in the mudroom. You'll catch your death if you don't stay dressed." She was only wearing the cashmere sweater set and jeans now.

Not only did she ignore me, I noticed a set to her mouth and chin that had the pulse at my temples starting to throb. My concern deepened when Carly started rolling snow for the head of her snowwoman, only to be cut off by Maggie blocking her as she scooped up two handfuls of snow in Carly's path.

"My girl needs bigger boobs," she declared. "The jacket is hiding my cleavage."

"Whatever."

I had to give Carly credit for her restraint, but although she turned away and started rolling in a different direction, Maggie managed a hip bump, which knocked Carly to her knees. Looking all too pleased with herself, Maggie scooped up another handful of snow to further augment her sculpture's measurements.

Still on her knees, Carly glared. I'd never seen her so provoked.

"Seriously, Maggie?"

Maggie continued packing snow. "It's not my fault if you're rolling when you should be rocking. But then with Walter, you didn't even have to worry about the rhythm method, did you?" She snickered, pleased with her own off-color humor.

"That's it." Carly rose to her feet and planted her hands on her hips. "You've been an obnoxious bitch for three days now and—"

When she suddenly burst into uncontrollable giggles, I didn't know what to think. I glanced over to Sybil, then Dana, to see if they were grasping what was going on, but they were startled, as well. It was only when we stepped around to see where she was pointing that we realized what had triggered her reaction.

The red lining in Maggie's expensive jacket had begun to bleed. Dye was streaming all over her snowwoman's cleavage. The results looked like the climax in a low-budget slasher movie.

"Oh, gee, Maggie, you sure got your money's worth out of that thing," Carly taunted. "Are you sure *you* didn't buy it out of the trunk of somebody's car?"

Three of us backed away when we saw Maggie narrow her eyes. I don't know if it was wise or not, but Carly held her ground.

Taking a step forward, Maggie smacked her in the shoulder with the flat of her hand. "I know where I bought this, and I can guarantee you I will be returning it for a full refund."

Although Carly wobbled for a moment, this time she stayed on her feet. "I think you're as big a liar as you are a bully, and I've had it with you."

"Whine, whine. You can dish it out, but you can't take it."

"What do you want from me? I've tried to be decent to you. But I don't believe you can stand it if everyone isn't as miserable and angry as you are," she said, giving Maggie the same kind of push as she'd received.

Petite, older, and not in prime condition at the moment, the shove caused Maggie to stumble backwards a few steps before she could regain her balance. Then, with a feral growl, she launched herself forward, using her outstretched arms as a battering ram to hit Carly in the chest.

We watched in horror as Carly was knocked off her feet, flying straight into Dana's snowwoman. Standing behind it, Dana never had a chance. She vanished under the assault of packed snow.

"Maggie—no!" Sybil cried.

We rushed to the aid of our petite friend, and frantically dug her out from under the weight and density of the packed snow. For an instant, even her face had been covered.

"Dana, dear," I cried. "Are you all right?"

She moaned first then seemed to collect her wits. "I'm okay...I think." But then she looked over my shoulder, and anger blossomed. "Only...damn it, Maggie! Carly's right."

"I didn't mean—I wasn't aiming for you."

"You weren't thinking at all, that's the problem. You were just purging all the junk going on inside you," Dana snapped.

"No."

"You're turning into a mean, old drunk," Carly muttered. Regaining her bearings, she rolled over and helped us finish brushing the heavy snow off of Dana.

The dogs shared their opinion of the stressful situation. On the porch, Wrigley hopped up and down, as though he was standing on springs, all the while barking frantically. Rosie's behavior wasn't much better; she raced around us, sharing her own displeasure and directives. She kept looking at me for a signal of what to do next.

"Rosie, heel," I commanded. As soon as she dropped down beside me, I turned to Maggie, "And that goes for you, too. We're not having one more minute of this. I'm embarrassed for you. And ashamed."

Looking as if she'd just taken a hit to the heart, Maggie crumbled to the ground. Her lips moved for a moment, but no sound came out. After several more breaths, she managed, "I'm so sorry, Dana. I honestly didn't see you. I was just...oh, hell."

Breaking down completely, she buried her face in her hands and burst into sobs. She cried as I've never heard her, not when she lost Scotty, and not even when she lost Hollis. Despite the fact she'd earned all of the negative emotions she'd churned up in us, my heart twisted upon hearing the ragged sounds. But when I started to reach out, she put up her hands to ward me off.

"Maggie, I know what I said, but let me help you."

"You can't. No one can. They think I have cancer."

Eleven

IT WAS THE second life-changing blow of the morning. As a result, we were once again jettisoned into shocked silence. In that vacuum, everything hinting toward this moment came back to me the way people say it happens when their life flashes before their eyes—the foreshadowing, the hints Maggie dropped as though begging one of us to guess her crisis... suddenly it illuminated the mystery like floodlights exposing a straight highway to one's destination. There was still no excuse for her conduct; however, I knew I could forgive her for her weakness.

"Oh, Mags," I groaned, still frozen in place by her rejection, as much as for her unbelievable news. "Are you sure? How long have you known this?"

"The first hint... about six months. I had a bit of abdominal pain. I blamed it on a new workout video someone recommended to me. But even after quitting the exercise, the pain stayed. Last month I started spotting." She finally raised her gaze to mine. "You know if it happens at our age, it's time to quit playing the denial game."

Sooner would have been better. I'd bled a little for twenty-four hours a few weeks after Charlie died. I figured it made sense considering the stress and workload. I'd also been in the middle of menopause. Had it gone on any longer, I would have made an appointment, but it quickly stopped when I recognized I was going to kill myself if I didn't pace myself better.

"So what did the doctor say?" I asked, hoping to get some specifics out of her.

"He did a sonogram and found two cysts on my right ovary. He also drew blood. One of the tests they do is the CA-125."

"I don't know what that is," I admitted. Charlie and I had been fortunate to avoid any type of health crisis during our marriage, the result being that I remained unfamiliar with many of the acronyms that were becoming almost commonplace to others.

"It's primarily the test they do on women that gauges cancer cells. Anything under thirty-five is normal. Mine was thirty-nine. Today, I was supposed to have an ovariectomy, but they phoned just before I called you, and rescheduled to next week."

"You mean you were ready to have a major procedure done and didn't intend to tell me?"

She had the grace to look away, but she didn't deny my question. That hurt almost as much as everything else she'd pulled in the last few days.

Sybil looked confused, as much as troubled. "Why aren't they planning on a full hysterectomy?"

"Because that's not necessary. They did a partial almost thirty years ago when I was showing signs of endometriosis, but back then they had started to understand the benefits of leaving the ovaries to try to deter other health problems."

A delay in removing a cancerous tumor was dangerous so despite my personal feelings on how she was handling all of this, I had to ask, "Have the doctors given you a preliminary prognosis about its malignancy?"

"Dr. Novak, my OB-GYN, said usually these cysts are benign. However, considering my age, elevated number, and the fact Mother died from ovarian cancer, he was more concerned."

Maggie had been fifteen when Mrs. Martin—no one dared call her Helga except her husband—became ill. Every bit as willful as Maggie, she'd been the only one able to keep her husband in some kind of control. However, she'd been less diligent about her own needs, and delayed going to a doctor until there was little anyone could do for her. She died the day before Maggie was supposed to have her sweet sixteen party.

"The good news is you didn't keep the bleeding a secret like your mother did and you're being proactive."

Maggie was having none of that. "Oh please. My life is over. I might as well forget about sex. They'll do chemo, radiation...I'll lose my hair and puke my guts out, until I don't even have the energy to do that. And don't you know, I'll bloat so much I'll be able to be my own spectacle over at the Longview Hot Air Balloon Race."

I was too involved in her plight not to take her literally. "But they just had that back in August. By next year's event, you'll be done with your treatment and back to being your svelte self again."

Her answering look reflected fear as much as bitterness. "That's easy for you to say. Because that's what I deserve, right? After all, I've been such an example of humanity."

At least she was recognizing the error of her ways. "From what you've told us, you don't know they'll need to do any chemo or radiation at all," I said. "The tumors could be benign. That's what you should be focusing on and praying for."

"What I need to pray for is that no one offers to bury me for free," she muttered. "There are people in this town who—once they get this news—are apt to express ship me a voodoo doll in order to hurry my demise. We're close enough to New Orleans to know those aren't hard to come by."

Sybil made the ceremonial spit into the snow and ordered, "Maggie, that's enough of that evil talk. We're not going to buy into mumbo-jumbo. You know good and well God's power overrules any and all of black magic nonsense. Besides, anyone with half a brain knows such thoughts tend to go back on them. Now get up, girl."

As Maggie started sobbing all over again, Sybil took hold of one side of her and I supported the other. Although we succeeded in getting her to her feet, she wasn't yet ready to rely on her own power.

"I'm sorry. I'm so sorry." Maggie finally raised her head to look pointedly at Carly. "All I've been seeing since we've been here is you...your youth...your sexiness. It was just too easy to hate you."

"What?" Carly gasped.

"Oh, don't you get it? It's what you represent," Maggie snapped. "You're what I'll never be again."

Carly had been standing several feet away from us, and Maggie's latest pronouncement had her gripping the hat she wore as though she was about to tear it off and scream. "Are you for real?"

"Yes, damn it, I am! I don't expect someone of your age to grasp what I mean."

"Hold it." Carly held up a hand. "I'm sorry for this health scare you're going through, but Retta and Sybil are right. That's no excuse for the way you've been behaving." She pointed her finger at Maggie's nose. "Lady, over the last few days you've heard enough to know there's been nothing easy about my life. You want to know something funny? This time together has been an amazing reality check. Up until recently I would have changed places with you in a heartbeat. I've *never* been comfortable in my own skin–except for those few precious months with Walter—and you seem to have known all too well what to do with yours."

I felt Maggie reel. Shifting, I put a supportive arm around her back, and exchanged uncertain glances with Sybil. Were we going to have to continue holding her up, or restrain her from another outright attack on Carly?

"I see I have underestimated you," Maggie replied slowly.

It was all I could do—even with Maggie's news challenging my perspective—not to let her drop back onto her butt. Here was the perfect opportunity for her to make things right, and what was she doing?

All but seething, I said, "How dare you go all regal and uppity, Margaret Martin. In your rabid need to punish her, you could have sent Dana into early labor."

As though she'd been given a stage direction, Dana came out of her trance-like stance and started for the steps. "I think I'll get my monster nightgown to put on my snowwoman."

"Let me get it for you," Carly said, following her.

"Sweet thought, but can you also pee for me?"

The attempt at humor was welcome, but our weak laughter ended the moment the front door shut behind her. Once again we were left with too many strained feelings.

"If you would hear me out," Maggie began, her tone that of a broken woman, "I was about to apologize. To Carly. It's become abundantly clear that she has far more character and depth than I'd allowed myself to believe."

"That's...a good start," I said, looking hopefully at Carly.

"I appreciate that," Carly said, although her gaze remained wary.

As Maggie nodded at the nominal crack in the hostilities she alone had created, her gaze fell on the sad remains of Dana's sculpture. With a sound of dismay, she said, "I have to put this back together. No matter how silly this idea was to me, it seemed of value to Dana."

"I'll give you a hand," Sybil said.

Initially, it had been my impulse to make Maggie struggle through the repairs herself, but with the injury last night, and her news just now, I knew I couldn't be so cold hearted—especially when Sybil was watching me for guidance. "All right, let's get this done. Have you noticed the snowflakes are turning into ice pellets?"

"I've been hoping it would be temporary and would switch back and forth for a while yet," Carly said. "If they get any larger, they're going to hurt."

"Exactly," I said with a nod. "Let's hurry."

For the next few minutes, we worked feverishly, until we reclaimed the broken mass, bringing it back to its previous potential. As Carly had feared, the size of the ice drops started to get larger, which created an intimidating sound all round us, as the lentil-size balls struck the roof, gutters, windows, and everything else in the way.

With the snow figure ready for Dana's gown, I urged everyone to stop, and get to cover. I hoped my friends were as done with this endeavor as I was. At this point, I didn't have any interest in finishing my creation, never mind dressing it.

Stomping the snow off of her boots, Sybil said "What on earth is keeping Dana? I'm game to slip on the gown if it will make her happy, but she's been gone a good while."

"I'll check," Carly said. But just as she reached for the door, it opened.

Dana stood there, her arm under her belly, an anxious look on her face. "Okay, nobody panic—except me. I think I'm in trouble."

We all stared at her wet sweat pants; however, she'd just been lying in the snow. Of course they would be wet. Right? *Right?* I thought.

Sybil drew in a sharp breath. "Your water broke."

"No. Maybe, yes." Dana moaned, "Oh, I don't know. Something came out."

I ushered everyone inside so we could shut the door. "The mucus plug," I guessed. I could see Dana was embarrassed. "Kind of a jelly-like substance with a bit of blood?"

"Yes." She didn't sound totally convinced. "What does that mean?"

"Didn't your doctor explain? Or your trainer?" The questions blurted out of me before I could check myself. "I'm sorry. It could be they didn't feel you were close enough to your due date yet to tell you."

"They did give me pamphlets and booklets to read," she began, only to worry her lower lip again. "I haven't been able to make myself read any of them."

I understood. She hadn't done any reading because of her mindset. It would all be too emotionally painful, so she ignored what was going to happen. But such thinking had health risks—like now.

Although she looked like she might collapse, I said with as much reassurance as I could, "It's probably not anything to panic about, just a result of the jolt you took from the fall. The mucus plug is in the cervix. When the cervix starts to widen, it comes out. It can happen even a week before your labor starts."

Instead of looking reassured, Dana's expression turned worried again.

"Okay, but even with an extra week, I'd be giving birth over a month early."

Yes, but at least by then she could get to a hospital. Keeping that thought to myself, I stroked her mussed hair back from her face. "Not to worry, sweetheart, we're all here for you. Carly, let's get her off of her feet. The way she's holding her belly, it may be the lightening has occurred, too."

"Lightning?" Carly shook her head, clearly not understanding. "Sorry, I'm not following."

"Lightening." I enunciated more carefully. "As in easing the weight of something. In her case, it means that the baby is sliding toward the birth canal."

Having locked up behind us, Sybil asked Dana, "Hon, do you feel any contractions at all?"

"I don't think so. Just rattled, I guess."

That was understandable. Her lovely skin was also too pale. Add that she was standing awkwardly, her body tilted forward, it all seemed to confirm a shift had occurred.

The controversy over finishing the snowwomen had become moot. We all drew closer to Dana. It seemed like we were of the same mind-set—touch her, stroke and reassure her. Keep her from getting anxious.

One thing was for certain—we had to get her horizontal to stop the pull of gravity on the baby. As soon as we got Dana by the bed, Sybil and I took off her jacket then eased her down. Carly removed her boots.

"Is there anything you need or want before we start changing you out of your wet things?" I asked, hoping I sounded convincingly sooth-ing. "What if I make you a mug of hot tea with honey and lemon? That should warm you."

"I'd much rather have another hot chocolate like Sybil made the oth-er night," she replied. "If it's not too much trouble? That's a joke. I feel like I've already turned your life upside down."

"Don't even think such a thing," I said. "Hot chocolate it is." Turning, I crooked my finger at Maggie. "You can come help me."

She looked as though I'd asked her to take on preparing Thanksgiv-ing dinner for fifty, and hung back. "I wouldn't know how to make hot chocolate from scratch if my life depended on it."

"I know. But you are capable of getting a mug out of the cabinet and the marshmallow crème from the pantry while I shave the chocolate."

"Retta, you have a lot of things you're going to have to do what with this weather changing again," Sybil said. "Let me make the drink for her. Carly, should I make enough for you, too?"

"That would be wonderful, but only if there's enough." Carly went to Dana's suitcase. "Retta's right. Let's get you into dry clothes so you'll feel more comfortable. Go ahead, Retta. I can manage here."

As we left them to the task, I led the way to the kitchen, where I immediately put an arm around each of my longtime friends. It was as much to talk softly, as to thank them for accommodating me. "Are any of you thinking what I am?"

"Why do you think I insisted on coming into the kitchen with y'all?" Sybil whispered back.

"Obviously, I'm not on the same page you two are," Maggie said, looking doubtful. "Did you just want me out of the room? In that case, why don't I go upstairs and stay out of everyone's way? Believe me, it wouldn't hurt my feelings. If I cause any more damage or hurt, I don't think I'll be able to stand myself."

I shook my head rejecting the idea. "You stay here. Anything could come up where we may need another pair of hands."

"I get it," Maggie said. "You need me to be moral support for Sybil so you can finish what you never got to with the animals before the deteriorating conditions make it too bad to get anything done."

That was certainly on my mind. I would have a revolt on my hands soon if the cattle didn't get their feed replenished. However, I didn't think it could be risked yet.

"No, we need to stay close to Dana for a bit and see if anything else happens. What I'm going to do is call Sam. We could use some expert input."

I let myself and Rosie out the back door, knowing better than to order her to stay inside. She wouldn't move off the porch if I didn't. The dull roar of ice pellets pounding everything in their way was the other inhibitor to her getting adventurous. The ice would also make hearing Sam a challenge, but I would just have to cope. Privacy was crucial.

"This is a nice surprise," he said, as soon as we were connected. "I thought you girls would be deep into a game of Texas Hold 'Em."

His gently teasing voice made me wish he was here. He would have handled this whole mess so much better. Of course, I knew if he *was* here, none of this would have happened.

"Retta? Are you all right?"

I forced myself to take a deep breath, and, exhaling shakily, I blurted out, "Dana suffered a fall. The mucus plug came out."

"How bad a fall? What happened?"

His voice had dropped an octave, and his concern was evident. I just wanted him to keep talking and picture his dear, handsome face for a minute. Then, perhaps, this spinning-out-of-control sensation would stop.

"Retta?"

Groaning inwardly, I pressed my free hand to my forehead. Realizing that I'd left out something vital, I ordered myself to get a grip. "Yes, wait. There's Maggie, too. She may have cancer."

To his credit, Sam stayed calm and patient. "Sweetheart, you've had a couple of big shocks. Take another breath. Start over."

His soothing tone helped more than I could say. Doing as he directed, I tried again.

"Maggie has been unbelievable since she arrived, I told you as much, and how none of us understood what was going on. A few minutes ago we finally found out why she's been having such strange mood swings. She got into a shoving match outside with Carly, only it was Dana who ended up on the ground."

"You were outside?"

What else did "outside" mean? "The snowwoman crushed her."

"The what?"

"Aren't you listening to me?"

"I'm trying. But there's a lot of background noise, too."

"I'm on the porch. The icing has started."

He uttered an undecipherable epithet. "It sounds like it's coming down worse than it did here. Well, you need to get out of the cold, so who do you want to talk about first, Maggie or Dana?"

"The mucus plug came out." It was all I could do not to have shouted at him.

"Yes," he said, drawing out the word. "That is important. However, you'll remember that's not necessarily an immediate concern. She could have several more days left yet."

"I *know* that, Sam. I told her so myself."

"So, there's something else significant in her status?"

"I'm pretty sure the baby has dropped."

"Has she shown any sign of contractions?"

"She said no."

"That's good. From here on be sure to make her stay in bed with her feet elevated. She needs to remain as calm as possible. Your goal is to get her back into town in order for her doctor to check her out thoroughly. That means slowing the process the purged plug can create."

"We're doing that. She's in bed and Sybil's making her hot chocolate. She asked for it. I wanted to make her lemon tea with honey."

"That would have been the better idea. However, it's one way to find out if she's going into labor," he continued dryly. "The combination of the pain and milk could have her upchucking in no time."

"Oh, great," I said, not recalling any of that from my own pregnancies. I made a mental note to put an empty trash container beside the bed. "I was just trying to pacify her."

"You did nothing wrong. I may be acting overcautious."

And I wanted him to be proud of me.

"Have you taken a blood-pressure reading?"

"Not yet. I'll do it as soon as I get back inside. At the moment, she's changing clothes."

"Let me know if the numbers are significantly elevated from her norm. Hopefully, she'll be forthcoming with what that is. I'm assuming you haven't reached out to 9-1-1 yet?"

"Since she insists she's not having contractions, I thought a call wouldn't be welcomed."

He made a sound of agreement. "Everyone is reporting all systems are overwhelmed. So," he continued, his tone growing tender again, "you have everything under control that you possibly can. Do you want to tell me about Maggie now?"

Heartened by his reassurances regarding Dana, I felt better, and I most definitely wanted his input regarding my old friend's situation. "She was due to have surgery today. She called it an ovariectomy?" I drew out the pronunciation hoping I'd memorized it properly.

"Uh-huh. Well, that's usually the scientific term for removing the ovaries of animals. Our term is Laparoscopic Salpingo-oophorectomy—much less invasive as in the old days, but a challenge for anyone outside of the medical field to remember, let alone say."

"You've got that right." I wondered if I would be able to recall half of that to share with Maggie and Sybil?

"What's her CA-125?"

"Thirty-nine," I said, pleased I could provide that information. "Also, there's the technicality that her mother died from ovarian cancer."

"I'm sorry to hear that, but you've given me enough information to reassure you to a degree," he said. "It sounds as though this is still a manageable situation. What's more, the success rate with the procedure is high."

His words were like a hand lifting me out of a chilling and murky sea. It was good to hear such positive feedback from a doctor. "Thank you, Sam. That's wonderful news, and I know Maggie will be reassured, too."

"Good. Then let's talk a little more about Dana," he suggested. "What's her lifestyle? Is she active?"

"She used to take a yoga class, but I don't think she's been able to bring herself to participate in anything since her husband's suicide.

There's been too much stress in her life, and too many fires to put out. Financial as much as psychological. Sam, she even admitted she wants to give up the baby for adoption." Considering his own story, I knew he would find such news disturbing.

"Ah…now, we're talking about depression, and that can manifest itself in many ways from insomnia, to eating disorders, anger issues—what did you say about the altercation with Maggie?"

"Actually, it was between Maggie and Carly. Dana was the innocent bystander. She admitted she is angry with Jesse, her late husband, but that's about the extent of it. She's the sweetest person, Sam. I can't believe she would ever do anything to harm anyone."

"Desperate and deeply dejected people are a danger to themselves, and others," he said, his tone grim. "She's not taking any medications, is she?"

"No, absolutely not. Just her pre-natal vitamins. I saw them in the bathroom."

"Okay. And how's Maggie's head?"

"The swelling is down, but the bruising is hideous. She has two black eyes."

"Hmm," he murmured. "Impress upon her to see her MD when she gets back to town. She'll need to be in better shape to have surgery. They won't risk the procedure otherwise."

"Thank you for that information. She might listen, since it's coming from you," I told him. "I so appreciate your help—and your patience."

"You're dealing with more than you should have to." His voice grew tender again. "Call anytime."

"I will. But I do have to get back inside."

"Consider yourself already missed. And kissed."

I was smiling as I disconnected. In fact, my lips tingled as though he had actually kissed me, and I wanted to hold onto the sensation a bit longer. Sticking as close to the protection of the eaves and gutters as possible, I went to refill the generator. In all of the day's drama, it had run out of fuel a good while ago.

Once that was done, I braved the punishing ice to bring up as large a load of wood as I could carry. With any luck, we would now have enough left on the porch to get us through to the end of the storm, which was a good thing, since the crust on the snow was growing thicker by the minute.

Out in the pasture, my cattle spotted me and began calling in excitement and displeasure. Sadly, I couldn't pacify them yet. Wracked by guilt, I trudged toward the house. Each of my steps created sudden, awkward cave-ins and challenged my balance. Even Rosie was intimidated, and mostly slid on her belly to return to the safety of the porch.

Not far behind me I heard two sharp cracks and crashes in quick succession. My insides quaked, and I thought if these conditions lasted throughout the night, none of us would get any rest, regardless of Dana's condition.

Exchanging my snow-covered logs for dry, I went inside. Maggie and Sybil were immediately in my face. Poor Rosie had to squeeze her way through the barrier of their legs.

Sybil grabbed the wood, but rather than carry it into the living room, she set the load on the kitchen side of the hearth. In the meantime, Maggie took my hat and gloves and set them on a towel on the dryer. When I turned back from hanging up my jacket, Sybil had returned and stooped to address my boots.

"Oh, jeez, please quit," I told her. "You're embarrassing me."

Rising, she explained. "I'm trying to hurry you into talking."

"I will, but—" I yanked off the first boot "—how's Dana?"

"Pensive. How concerned is Sam about her fall?"

"Let's just hope she stabilizes and this is the end of the excitement for today. Is she keeping down the hot chocolate?"

"Why wouldn't she?" Maggie asked.

Ignoring the question, Sybil said, "I peeked. Mostly, she's been holding the mug against her chest like a heating pad. I'm not sure she really wanted it as much she said. Could be she's savoring every drop."

Pulling off the other boot, I tugged on my slippers. Sybil's news wasn't reassuring. "Okay, or it could be what we don't want to hear. I'd forgotten, but Sam pointed out how a bad reaction to milk is another sign things are going downhill."

"Speak English would you?" Maggie entreated.

Sybil closed her eyes. "If she was heading into labor, the milk would make her sick. Retta, I should have remembered that."

"Did he say anything else?" Maggie asked.

"We need to take her blood pressure," I said. "Probably her temperature, too, but unless she shows signs of having a fever, let's hold off on the latter, so as not to make her more anxious than necessary. While I check Rosie's paws and feed her, you all go in there and make small talk. Turn on the tree lights and garlands to make things look more festive."

"Holiday atmosphere, upbeat attitude, got it," Sybil replied and with Maggie in tow, she took off.

The ice proved to be somewhat of an ally after all—at least in one way; freezing into a sheet, there was little impact on Rosie's paws. Grateful, I fixed her bowl, and refilled her water dish. Once I saw that she was content, I went in search of the blood-pressure machine.

As I hoped, I located it in the bottom drawer of the bathroom Dana and Carly were using. Since Charlie's death, I rarely thought of it, since I wasn't on any medication. His doctor had only put him on a prescription for his rising numbers a short time before his death. He would never have bothered filling it, let alone monitoring himself, so I'd taken over that for him. It had become part of our morning routine before having our first cup of coffee to take a reading.

Given how long ago it had been since it was last used, I changed the batteries, before joining the others. "Sorry for the delay, ladies," I said, trying to sound warm and upbeat. I was challenged by the steady drumming of the ice on the roof. "Oh, how pretty everything looks. Dana, how's it going?"

"Okay." She swallowed and shifted her hold on the mug she held against her. "I guess I'm a little too shaken up for the hot chocolate after all."

Before I took a seat beside her, I exchanged a fleeting glance with Sybil. "Not a problem, dear. We can reheat it later if you want."

Her gaze lowered to the monitor now resting on my lap. "Why did you bring that?"

"To reassure myself. After all, I am a mother and grandmother," I teased. "Be glad I don't want to feel your nose the way I do Rosie's, and half the critters on this place if one of them seems to be a bit under the weather."

Dana tilted her head as she studied me, seeing right through my act. "You called Sam."

"What's the benefit of dating a doctor if you can't call him in the odd moment?" Maggie asked wryly.

While Maggie meant well, Dana pretty much ignored her, which told me not to insult her with further prevarications. "He thinks if you've stabilized, you should be fine until we can get you checked out in town. But he is a white coat and asked me what your blood pressure numbers were, and I didn't know."

Sitting on her other side, Carly said to her, "That sounds completely logical to me."

"I guess."

Putting down the mug on the end table, she extended her arm, as though expecting me to give her an injection. I took the reading, and it turned out that her blood pressure was slightly elevated from what she told me was usual for her; however, not to where the change disturbed me. I planned to jot down the information in the kitchen, as soon as I could get back in there.

"Did Sam offer any advice?" Dana asked.

"He pretty much confirmed what we've been addressing—keeping you relaxed and comfortable. Do you feel like taking a nap? It could help bring your numbers down a bit more."

"Who could sleep with such a scary racket going on?"

As she glanced up at the ceiling, I nodded my reluctant agreement, although I knew the generator intensified the noise. "The way it's coming down, our snowwomen may become so well encased, they'll still be there for us to dress in Easter bonnets."

That won a weak smile from Dana. "I'm actually glad you called Sam."

"Great. Positive thoughts in, negative ones out," I recited, as I had to my children and grandchildren. Putting the blood pressure monitor on the table, I picked up the mug. "Carly, if you're done with yours...?"

She handed me her empty one, and I passed both to Sybil, who carried them to the kitchen. Apparently, Maggie saw that as an opportunity to make her presence scarce, and followed. The image of a dutiful handmaiden came to mind; a thought I wouldn't share with her. She wouldn't like it in the slightest.

"Thank you for turning on the generator again," Carly said. "Are you going to keep it running? If so, maybe we could watch TV? That might help get our minds off of the storm noise."

Timing being what it is, her suggestion was followed by several more dramatic sounds from outside. Inevitably, I thought fleetingly of tomorrow, and the days to come. Like so many, I would have to hire a crew to clean up the place once the thaw came; it was ridiculous to believe that I could manage the mess on my own. However, with everyone suffering the same problem, reliable help would be hard to find. Then we would be praying for a break in the seasonal winds, in order to burn all of the brush piles that would be showing up everywhere. The whole thing was too overwhelming for now.

With an apologetic look, I said, "You're welcome to try, but I don't think you'll be able to get a satellite signal. The cloud cover is too dense. You might have to settle for a DVD. Now I'd better get moving, starting with fireplace maintenance. I never did clean out the excess ashes down here."

"Because of me and my stupid snowwoman idea," Dana said with no small chagrin.

"Oh, I think there was a little matter of tending to Maggie's needs, too." Giving her a pat on the thigh, I first detoured to the kitchen.

I stopped at the bar by the phone where I picked up the steno pad and pen I kept for messages, shopping lists, and impromptu thoughts I didn't want to forget. Flipping to a fresh page, I started a log with the date and time and wrote down the monitor reading.

Across the room, Sybil opened the refrigerator. "I think I'll get out some ground chuck to defrost for lunch." She glanced at the clock, then back at me and shrugged. "Well, early supper."

"Sounds good to me." Circling the bar to where Maggie leaned against the island, I said, "Sam sent you a message, too."

"Head down Death Alley again," she asked, nodding toward the driveway, "and do a thorough job this time?"

Although I smiled at her self-directed sarcasm, my look communicated gentle rebuke. "He said you'd better see Dr. Wilcox when you get back to town."

"What the devil for? My appointment is with..."

I cut her off by tapping my temple to indicate her most severe injury. "Your surgeon won't operate if you're not cleared by your GP."

Groaning, Maggie said, "Tell him I'm fed up with doctor visits."

"Share your complaint about people who are trying to keep you well? I don't think so."

Needing a few moments for myself, I decided to first pick up the wood on the hearth and deal with the upstairs fireplace. Aside from the extra work, I had grown unused to having around-the-clock company, and I could feel the drain on my energy and psyche.

Once I was in my bedroom performing the routine task I had done hundreds of times, I let thoughts return to Sam. His words replayed in my mind. I felt guilty for having to cut him short knowing he wanted what Charlie used to call, "honey time." There was no doubt he was missing our longer conversations as much as I did. It had become our habit to talk for an hour before bedtime. Yet all I'd been doing these last few days was focus on others. Although the reasons were more than justified, the pattern needed to end soon. To a point of pride, I had never been a neglectful wife; nevertheless, after several years of living a relatively monastic life, the awareness of someone else's needs or desires being a priority had ceased to be an issue. However, I had no intention of short-changing the man who wanted to be my lover and soul mate for the rest of our lives.

"Retta! Where are you?"

Carly's cry allowed no reflexive query on my part. I quickly added new logs to the fireplace, and closed the doors. Thinking, *"What on earth now?"* I grabbed the dangerously full bucket of ashes and hurried downstairs.

"What's happened?" I called, as I descended.

"Dana's in pain."

I was far enough down to see Carly. I also saw Maggie and Sybil had come to the foot of the empty bed looking as anxious as I felt. "Describe it."

"Here," Carly said, rubbing her hand over her abdomen.

"She's in there?" I asked, my gaze shifting to the bathroom. I already knew the answer to that. Giving her a what-were-you-thinking look, I automatically headed for the half-opened door.

It was Sybil that stopped me. "Let me take that."

Realizing what I'd been about to do, I released my hold to hers. "Thanks. Just set it in the snow, and hurry back. I have a feeling she needs both of us."

To Carly, I whispered, "You were supposed to keep her off her feet."

"She threw me a curve. She said she was thirsty and wanted some-water."

In the bathroom, I found Dana exactly as Carly had described. She was rocking back and forth as she sat on the commode, clutching her hands between her bare thighs. Her lovely features were contorted by pain.

"Talk to me, dear. What's going on?"

"I don't know. Menstrual cramps? Oh, God, that can't be," she ground out between clenched teeth.

I couldn't help but glance down at the hand-woven, brown-and-cream rug looking for a sign of what I hoped wasn't there. Although there was no evidence of anything, I still asked Carly, "Is she bleeding?"

"No."

"Dana," I said, "could your water have broken?"

She shook her head, resolute. "I just had this need to pee. The moment I sat down the pain came." With a sigh, she began to relax. "Thank goodness, it's going away."

Her excellent summary left me feeling a wave of dizziness. Cramps passing. In her case, that could mean only one thing.

"We have to get you back to bed," I told her. "Let me call the others."

"Oh, no, I'll walk."

She didn't even make an attempt to stand, which told me the poor dear couldn't summon the strength yet. "Right," I said as mildly as I could. "And halfway there your water will break, and then your labor clock will have been set in motion." I called over my shoulder, "Sybil! Maggie! I need you."

They were undoubtedly hovering nearby because they appeared in seconds. I kept my directives succinct as to what I wanted everyone to do. They responded with nods and positioned themselves, and we carefully got Dana to her feet.

"No need to look mortified, darlin'," Sybil drawled, draping Dana's right arm over her shoulders, while Maggie did the same on Dana's left side. "Just pretend that you're Cleopatra."

"Even if I wasn't headed for bankruptcy, I couldn't manage that," she muttered. "This is totally humiliating."

Nevertheless, she obeyed directions. When Carly and I clasped hands, creating a seat for her, she sat.

"All right everyone, take it slow," I said. "Especially through the doorway."

It was awkward; however, we made it without anyone so much as cracking an elbow on the door jamb. Once we gently placed her onto the bed, Sybil fixed the covers, and I sat down by her side. Leaning over, I smoothed her furrowed brow with the backs of my fingers to check her temperature as well as to soothe some of the fear I suspected was building inside her.

"Now, my girl, you'll have to be specific. When did this all start? I wasn't upstairs ten minutes."

"I know. But the hot chocolate made me feel queasy."

"Good grief, why didn't you say something?" Sam had been right.

"I thought I could make it pass. I believed I did. Only when I got to the bathroom, this pain in my back started, and it moved like fingers crawling toward my abdomen."

"Could it be Braxton Hicks?" Carly asked me hopefully, only to add to Dana, "Remember, like they told us in class? False labor?"

I remembered that a few glasses of water, or a warm bath might relieve those symptoms, but I didn't think it was going to help Dana.

Already seeing the truth on my face, Dana murmured, "So it really has begun?"

"I'm not yet certain. We can still hope it was your upset body reacting to too much upheaval today. How are you feeling now?"

"Okay. A little weak. But nothing like when you first came downstairs."

"Good." With a last stroke of her cheek, I straightened. "Then we'll get back to our chores and—" I glanced at the TV that had been paused. I could tell by frozen scene that it was the classic film rendition of, *Jane Eyre*, starring Orson Welles and Joan Fontaine, an old favorite of mine. "You try to enjoy the rest of the movie."

I didn't have to say anything to Sybil and Maggie. They followed me to the kitchen, and as soon as I heard the dialogue resume on the TV, I penned the time in the steno pad. Urging the others farther into the kitchen, I shared my feelings.

"We're kidding ourselves if we try to believe the contractions haven't started." I glanced at the microwave, and saw that it was after two o'clock. "That means I should get the feeding and milking done so we can all be here when Dana needs us most. Can you hold the fort for the next half hour?"

My question had Sybil snorting. "It took you over a half hour in simple snow to just care for the horses—and that was with you rushing. Who are you kidding, Retta? You're getting on that tractor, too, aren't you? In *these* conditions?"

Knowing I was wasting precious time, I went to the mud room and started to change into my boots. It was enough of an answer for my friends who doggedly followed.

"For God's sake, Retta!" Maggie appeared close to panicking. "Charlie died on that thing on a clear day. Those big old critters will make it one night without their damned salad bar."

Maybe, but they'd already gone without pellets for a day, too. "If it wasn't for the generator and pounding ice, you'd be able to hear how desperate they're feeling. I did when I got the last load of wood. If that continues through the night, it will add to Dana's stress." Plus, I silently brooded as I slipped on my jacket and reached for my gloves and hat, there weren't only adult cattle.

"Listen, I lost one calf yesterday. I have another half dozen between a week and a month old. Without nutrition, the mothers' milk production slows radically. What's more, the calves group together at night and use the remaining hay as a nesting place to stay warm."

Ever the teacher, Sybil said, "It's the fact you'll be rushing that scares me most. I always tell my students during tests, you don't want to rush. That's when mistakes happen. Retta…at least take Carly. Maggie and I will be here with Dana."

I loved her for the thought, but recognized a flaw in her reasoning. "Carly is her coach, as well as her best friend, and let's not kid ourselves, there's going to be another contraction while I'm gone. Dana will have to deal with a difficult reality check. It's more important for her to have Carly here."

With a throaty growl, Maggie left, only to return with my cell phone that I'd placed on a counter. She stuffed it into my deepest pocket. "I'd shove it into your brassiere like the old country girls used to do their money, but you're already buttoned up to your chin. Just keep checking to be sure that thing is still there if you need it."

"Will do, but don't you call me unless it's a life-or-death emergency. Besides, there's a good chance the satellite towers may not be able to receive or relay signals in these conditions. The last thing I need is to worry you're wandering around outside looking for me."

"Smart ass. Then how are we supposed to get your attention if things get dire?"

I pointed to the propane lantern on top of the two-door cabinet where I kept all things Rosie, and dragged a wool scarf to help me try to escape the bruising ice. "Sybil, I know you remember how to work it. Swing it back and forth off the porch. Hopefully, I'll be able to see it. If not, surely Rosie will and alert me."

Maggie was only minimally convinced. "As bad as it's coming down, we can barely see the barn, and nightfall isn't supposed to be for another couple of hours. I think you should give me one of your shotguns. I won't aim it at where you'll be. I know to shoot toward the sky."

For what I was thinking, I would have to say a great number of prayers to be worthy of the next communion at church. "Oh, sure. The punishing ice isn't enough to have to duck? May I remind you what goes up comes down? I don't want to have to dig pellets out of my dog, my cattle, or for that matter, my own thick skull. Now, let me go because if labor has started, Dana is due another contraction in no more than twenty minutes. Rosie—come."

Twelve

*D*ESPITE MY crusty tone and attitude with Maggie, my insides were probably not much steadier than Dana's. I dreaded going back into the miserable weather. Yet, I couldn't let my friends' fear of abandonment, or concern for my safety, stop me from what had to be done.

I had a mini-inspiration, as Rosie and I descended the stairs to alter my routine. If I followed my usual schedule, I would be far more tired and cold by the time I got onto the tractor. Doing that first would give me more energy and I'd have all my faculties intact.

Diesel engines could be cranky in winter temperatures. Add to that, as comfortable as I was with farm work, the laws of physics and mechanics have taken their time to befriend me, which is one of the reasons why I sold our largest tractor a few years ago, and hired people to do the cutting and baling part of things. The 55 HP model tractor I'd kept was as familiar to me as my pickup truck, so once I had the old workhorse running, I decided to go into the barn and milk Elsa while waiting for the engine to warm up sufficiently to where the hydraulics functioned at their optimum.

The fierce pounding of ice had eased somewhat, but the new damage was already significant—more split trees, and some bowing so sharply, they would never stand erect again even if they didn't break. I planned to take photos with my cell phone once this was over, so the kids would have a record of the year that would undoubtedly go down in history, as it pertained to our land. It could well be that once I was gone, my loved ones would sell the place; but until then, I wanted them to know what we'd experienced—and survived.

Once the barn work was accomplished, I left Holly and Buzz lapping away at a pan of fresh, warm milk, Elsa munching her pellets, and closed the doors for the night. The tractor was rumbling away steadily, so I lifted the front forks, then backed out of the extra-large carport.

Due to the depth of the snow and strength of the ice, the smaller front tires fought me as I maneuvered to impale a bale of hay with the rear forks, and then do the same with the front pair. By the time I'd succeeded, my arm muscles were feeling the workout.

The cattle ruckus intensified as I aimed toward my herd. They remained in the northeast corner of the pasture taking what protection they could from the natural barrier of trees and brush. Rosie tried to stay ahead of me, her adrenaline in overdrive. Even as she was sliding on ice, she looked back to bark at me. She knew it was her job to let me know we were on course. Considering the weather, though, I hated she was such a good work dog that stayed almost too close. There is little tread on the small front tires, and that caused some sliding and slippage. Thank goodness most of the terrain here was flat. But the gullies were ahead of us.

Periodically, I had to take one hand off the wheel to balance both hydraulic levers in order to control the bales on either end of the tractor. We didn't need a snow-plow effect in front, or a ditch-digger in back. What a relief to see I was finally getting close to my destination. The cold was permeating my clothing, and the ice forced me to squint, which challenged my vision.

In taking a deep, relieved breath, I inadvertently over-compensated on the front lever. My error brought the bale too high, momentarily blinding my line of vision. Instincts kicked in, and I took my foot off the accelerator, expecting the tractor to slow. It didn't.

The machine started to slide downhill.

What hill?

I stomped on the brake pedal willing the large-treaded rear wheels to dig deep and grip ground. At that moment, I didn't give a fig if the whole thing buried itself in mud until August. I just wanted it to stop.

The momentum literally slid me off the slick leather seat, until my torso hit the steering wheel so hard it should have fractured my sternum. And yet the tractor continued sliding like the first deadly creeping of an avalanche.

Charlie.

His name and his presence were one in my mind, as I fought the urge to panic. Don't ask me how I thought of it, but I instinctively shoved both hydraulic levers down to regain balance with the help of the descending bales. A few seconds later, the four-wheeled escapee came to a stop as though hitting an invisible wall.

I was still lying over the steering wheel looking into a gray-white sea of dusk, snow, and ice, when I realized the horn was blaring away. Even with the harsh wind, it was a rude-enough sound to have me pushing myself upright.

Dear God.

Although logically, I understood what had just happened, it came to me that I wasn't quite getting the "it" of things yet. Yes, the accumulation of snow, along with the complications of icing had made me lose my bearings and, subsequently, my confidence, ultimately triggering my overreaction. Yet through it all, Charlie had been a definite presence around me making me understand I still needed to grasp something—the message behind it all.

Accidents do happen, and it's either your time, or it isn't.

I shivered—and not from the latest lashing of the wind. The instant I accepted the words, I knew they were locked in my mind forever, like a cattle brand on hide.

"Yes," I whispered.

This had suddenly become a sacred place and a part of me would have loved to sit here, to digest the nuances of it all. However, the same presence I felt had stopped me, now directed me to move on—for good reason. The cows had grown so excited by the sound of the approaching supply of food, they were coming this way. In no time, they would create another traffic hazard. I needed to back up as much as conditions allowed to gain traction, then start driving parallel to the gully, until I could find the shallowest part of the draw where I could ease out.

Rosie picked up on my strategy soon enough. She seemed to know what needed to be done, and challenged the herd repeatedly not to disobey her directives. In the meantime, I fought Mother Nature and geography until I championed my crisis. It wasn't pretty, and for the duration I doubted my right to still be breathing–evidenced by the salty tears stinging my cheeks. Nevertheless, I finally delivered at least part of dinner and the hope of a safer night to my herd. I determined to put out pellets now would cause too much waste. With luck, the storm would pull north tonight and I would be able to deliver the vitamin-rich supplements in the morning.

In comparison, the work in the stables was easy, as was the quick trip to the hen house to feed my ladies. They were so happy to see me, not one tried to poke me for raiding her nest.

As we headed back to the house, I saw the ice cover on the snow was now thick enough for Rosie to stay on its surface the whole way. She ran home with gusto, making me think of an adventure-junkie slalom skier on the wildest of courses.

She barked her arrival to the shadowy figure waiting on the back porch. It was Maggie, who leaned over to pat her with gusto. Once I got near enough, Mags offered her hand to help me up the ice-caked stairs.

"Thank God, you're safe," she said. "It seems like it took forever this time, and I hated having to scare the sparrows from the door, but I had to come out to check where you were. Then when Rosie came running and barking, my heart—Retta, my heart nearly stopped. I just knew she was telling me you were hurt, or worse."

What had happened in the pasture needed to stay between me and the other world—at least for the moment. Besides, time stands still for none of us, and wasn't doing so now. Tired and aching, I brushed my hand across her sleeve in appreciation for her concern. "Yeah, well, I got back as soon as I could," I said between breathless pants.

"It's not even four yet, and it looks like dusk," Maggie said peering at the ice that continued to come down from a slate-gray sky. Then she refocused on me. "You look like you belong out there with the other frozen sculptures. Get inside before I start to cry."

"Help me brush some of this off, so I don't create a lake," I entreated. "And fill me in on the latest."

Maggie stepped behind me working on what I couldn't reach, while I slapped my hat against the railing. Then I rubbed off what I could on my front side.

"She's had *two* contractions, and a third isn't far off."

"Bless her heart—and everyone else's, too. But thank goodness Sybil was there to get you all through it. Did you log everything?"

"I did. I'm not good for much else." Maggie tugged at my arm and opened the door for the three of us. "Come on."

Sybil joined us in the mud room. For once she was speechless. All she could do was frame my face with her hands and fight tears.

Still raw from the experience, I almost felt as though she'd seen what happened, her eyes radiated such a knowing, but then I gave myself a mental shake and found my voice. "How long do you think until the next contraction?"

Her tender gaze turned steely as she glared at Maggie. Such a look would have Sybil's students crawling under their desks. "You couldn't let her have thirty seconds to peel off those frozen-stiff clothes?"

"She asked me to fill her in."

Were things worse than Maggie grasped? As I handed my things to Maggie, I tried to mitigate my friend's agitation. "I'm sorry conditions made it impossible to get back faster. It sounds as though you all went through an ordeal, but while a third contraction at this stage isn't what we want, there's not much anyone can do about it."

"Retta, it's not that. Prepare yourself, darlin' because I don't think Dana's whole psyche is up for this."

Usually, Sybil would find something positive to say about anything, even a cake dropping flat in the oven. She would just cover it with icing and call the concoction fudge brownies. To hear her voice such doubt was grim news indeed. "Well, knowing what we know, I guess we shouldn't be surprised. Let me wash my hands and see where this goes."

When I approached the sofa bed, Dana was lying on her side facing the stairs. Carly was patiently massaging her back. It struck me that it would be a terrible waste if Carly didn't find someone with whom to share all of the nurturing and love still inside her.

When I made it to Dana's side, I sat down. She looked as pretty as ever, yet at the same time as fragile and fearful as I'd ever seen her. She grabbed for my hand with both of hers, and clung to it as though it was her tether.

"If I had a hundred dollars, I would have bet you were hitching a ride into town to escape all of this."

"The only reason I'd be out on that road," I assured her, "is if I spotted a plow that made a wrong turn in New York and had ended up here.

You know why? Because he would be able to get you to the nearest hospital. How are you holding up, dear?"

"Coward that I am, not too good, regardless of what Carly tells you."

Carly wasted no time in contradicting her. "She's being very brave."

"I glanced at the notebook on my way in here. Your contractions are staying at twenty minutes apart," I said to Dana. "That's good. You seem to be stabilized."

"Rah. More pain for a longer period of time."

"True, and I'm sorry for that. On the other hand, it increases the chances that we'll get you help when you need it most." I glanced at the tall plastic cup on the table. I see Carly has some ice chips for you to suck on. Is there anything else you'd like?"

"Yes. I'd like for this to be over."

"I understand." With my free hand, I stroked her clammy skin. "Unfortunately, it takes as long as it takes."

"I don't think I can last, Retta."

Ignoring the fear in Carly's eyes, I crooned to Dana. "We're all here to see that you do, sweetheart. And we're determined to make this as easy for you as we can."

"I'm so relieved you're back. You're in for good now?"

"Except to refuel the generator, yes. I'm going to see that it stays on now, so you have plenty of light." I looked at Carly. "Can I get you anything? It's been a long time since breakfast."

"Don't worry about me. You still look like you haven't thawed out yet. How is it out there?"

"About like what you've been hearing. I know one thing I can scratch off my non-existent bucket list—acupuncture by ice pellets."

Both women smiled.

"But the landscape is going to look like a beautiful snow globe in tomorrow morning's sunshine," I added.

Dana uttered a shallow sound of pleasure. "What a wonderful image. I'm going to focus on that."

Upon my return to the kitchen, Sybil asked, "See what I mean?"

"Yeah. I wish we knew more about her family tree and medical history. Is she prone to depression? Do her parents, or did her grandparents have any heart issues?"

Sybil shook her head. "We're stuck with flying blind. All I can think is that she's a performing artist and that often suggests a sensitive nature, and heaven knows she's been through a lot in the last year or so."

"Right. Well, at least we can provide the assurance that someone is close through this whole ordeal."

"Then you'd better recharge your own batteries, girlfriend," Sybil said. "What can I make for you, tea or coffee? I can put on a new pot. Maggie and I just finished the last one."

Unable to resist any longer, I had to massage my chest. Since the accident, the pain had built to a steady throb. "To be honest, I really would like a cognac." More than that, I yearned to curl up in the soft leather of my recliner and turn the TV to a music channel, particularly one featuring bluesy jazz and romance, so I could drift off to sleep and not feel my banged up body or listen to my worried mind.

"I can do that." Sybil pounced on the opportunity to stay busy.

All too aware of Maggie only yards away, her look keen and speculating, I added to Sybil, "Excuse me for not mentioning it sooner, but the house smells awesome, and you know how I complain about the overuse of the word. I caught the aroma of sautéed onions and garlic, as soon as I entered, and I see you have the crock pot going. You decided on making chili, didn't you?"

"This is the perfect weather for it," she replied, as she poured the amber liquid into the snifter she'd seen me drink from yesterday.

Across the room, Rosie kept lifting her nose to the tantalizing aromas, too. If we were soloing it, I would have taken a bit of meat before it was seasoned, cooked it, and mixed it with a bit of cheese, as a treat for her. But before I could think about getting at least the cheese for her, Maggie blocked my way.

"Stubborn mule," she said under her breath. "Just tell me you aren't having a heart attack?"

"If I was, I'd like to think I had the sense not to be drinking strong spirits. Stop playing detective. It's freaking cold out there. Brutal. The wind feels like glass shards are hitting your eyes and skin. In the morning, I may have as many black-and-blue spots as you do."

The only problem with my protest was I still had my hand against my chest, and Maggie saw that. Caught in the act. *Crap.*

"Nice feint," Maggie replied. "If it isn't that, then you're trying to be the last person on earth to admit to ever having a panic attack."

I could live with that reasonable, but incorrect assumption.

Sybil handed me the snifter. Covering my hands with hers, she whispered, "Forgive my eavesdropping. Did I hear 'panic attack?'"

Smiling, I kissed her cheek. "Even with the scarf over my mouth, my lungs feel bruised from breathing in the sharp air."

Maggie drawled to Sybil, "We'll inform the paramedics when they shoot that big, ugly needle into her heart."

Looking appalled, Sybil assured me, "I swear, she hasn't had a drink since you left."

"It's undoubtedly a caffeine high," I replied, before taking a grateful sip of the cognac.

With an arched eyebrow, Maggie backed off, however, not without a promise. "To be continued."

I didn't doubt it. No one and nothing stopped Maggie for long. She was the Jack Russell of willfulness. As the warmth of the alcohol spread through my torso, I felt the bolstering I needed.

"You're right," I said, "because I need to call Sam again. I promised I would keep him updated. Do me a favor and join the others in the living room. Put a DVD in the TV if necessary, and holler if Dana starts again before I get there."

"Retta wants privacy to..." Maggie made smooching sounds.

"Mags, *please*."

Sybil took hold of Maggie's arm. "Behave or I'll tell those two innocents out there that you slept with Elvis."

"Don't you dare! I would never take a lover who wears more bling than I do. Besides, he was too old for me!"

Shaking my head, I retreated to the back room where I dug my phone out of my coat pocket. As I brought up Sam's number, I quietly shut the connecting bathroom door for added privacy.

Almost immediately, Sam said, "You should know I was thirty seconds away from buzzing you."

"I'm sorry. I thought it would be smarter to do the outside work now."

"Retta, you didn't? I just checked the radar a minute ago and it looks like Texas is going Ice Age."

"You must have brought up the wrong screen. It's blindingly bright and 82 degrees here."

His lack of a response indicated he knew exactly what I was doing. Taking another quick sip of my drink, I grew serious.

"Sam, Dana's definitely in labor. She's due her fourth contraction at any minute."

His protracted silence reminded me of the time when Rachel fell off the monkey bars on the school playground. Jamie and I had sat an eternity in the hospital waiting room willing the doctor to come out and talk to us, while back here, Charlie was stuck feeding our livestock. It ended up that Rachel needed a cast for a broken arm, but until we got that news I'd imagined everything from paralysis to a fractured skull, while here at the ranch, Charlie prolonged his chores by racing back to the house several times to call the hospital for an update.

Poor Sam, where had his mind taken him in all the time between my calls? Back to years ago and his family's nightmare? No doubt there were moments when it still felt as though losing his son had happened only a short while ago.

"At least tell me you're all right," he finally demanded, his voice oddly thick. "Because even as I understand what you did and why you did it, I hate the whole idea of it all. The risks you took. Those you have been taking." He uttered a harsh sound. "I should have anticipated this better and been there to help you."

I'd never heard him this upset, but could only say what I thought was best. "No one knew it was going to get this bad. I promise after this is over, we'll talk. For now, though, Sam—please. I need to focus on Dana."

"Damn it, Retta."

I couldn't bear the anguish in his voice and leaned against the wall facing the dryer, closed my eyes, and soothingly rubbed the snifter against my bruised body. I wished I could tell him the truth: yes, my chest hurt. But my heart hurt, too, as well as the places in my mind that stored my tragic memories. Yet, there was no time.

"Sam, I can't afford to cry right now. You know too well what it's like to walk into a room and see how everyone is looking at you for reassurance that everything is going to be okay."

"Yes," he said quietly. "*Yes*. That doesn't mean you didn't just scare the crap out of me and make me mad as hell because of what you aren't saying. I lost a marriage from all of the negativity that comes from feeling helpless, Retta. The anger that consumes from experiencing one too many locked doors—the literal ones and the psychological kind. I won't make that mistake again."

Needing even greater privacy than I had, I could only strive for it with my muted voice. "I love you, okay?" I whispered raggedly. "*I love you*. And you're not going to lose me, or chase me away—unless you throw me away."

I expected him to repeat those precious words to me, or at least sigh or groan. There was nothing. I think it was the most horrible silence I'd endured, since hoping to hear Charlie breathe.

"Sam, are you there? Don't tell me after exposing my deepest feelings to you that it's too late? Have we lost our special connection?"

"I'm here," he said. "I'm just torn between aching to kiss you, wanting to carry you away to someplace safe–wherever the hell that is in this sick world—and rupturing a vocal cord by screaming bloody murder over the uselessness I'm feeling."

"Does that mean, I'll be the inspiration behind your next storm-on-the-Great Plains painting?" I asked softly. "Promise me you'll paint me in stunning sienna and fearsome charcoal and indigo? I always wanted to be someone's best and last something."

That earned me a sound that was as ardent as I suppose humans could get.

"Promise *me* you'll never again risk whatever it is you aren't telling me," replied. "Retta, if I lost you—I swear I would never be able to pick up a brush again."

I couldn't have responded to that if I'd wanted to. I didn't want to, let alone be the catalyst to put him in that position.

"Glad that got your attention," he said.

"I'm humbled, Sam. Truly. I don't take anything you've said lightly, either. But the time. I'm hearing voices rising in the living room."

"I understand." He did, however, take the time to sigh heavily. "As long as there are no complications, it sounds as though things are going as well as anyone could hope. This tactic you're attempting is going to drive you all crazy, because it prolongs the worst side of childbirth. It might help the time pass if you start collecting items you'll need should the baby come before you can get her out of there. Have you thought of that?"

"Frankly, no. I'll get on it..." I heard a telltale wail. "Sam here we go again."

"That's a helluva goodbye."

He disconnected. Had he done so in order not to hear me do it? Dear, dear man, I thought as I shoved the phone into my pocket, and hurried to the living room.

"That's right, breathe through it. You've practiced this a dozen times. You can do it."

Carly continued to go through the soft-voiced mantra, while letting Dana grip her hands. I was proud of her. She sounded so steady and assured.

When I stopped beside Sybil, she leaned into my shoulder. "This one came sooner. Only by about a half minute, but I wanted you to know."

"Thanks. Labor may be one of the few things not yet computer generated or controlled," I replied just as quietly. "You and I both know the pace of this can bounce all over the clock from here on."

We listened to Carly coach Dana through the rest of the episode, and then I patted Dana's leg in encouragement, only to detour to my office. It wasn't what Sybil and Maggie were expecting, and they followed, openly curious.

"What's up?" Maggie asked. "Did Sam say something you didn't want Dana to hear?"

"No. He agreed that so far, everything is going within the parameters of what's considered normal."

Maggie's eyes sparkled with some wicked thoughts. "So what did you two talk about?"

"Could you please stay with the subject at hand? Dana is *six weeks* away from her due date. That's no small thing. There's still a lot going on in a baby's body at this stage. The last month is vital to the development of the brain, lungs, heart, eyes, not to mention fine-tuning nerve endings."

Sybil offered, "Debra was two weeks early. I think she's been hot-wired to stay in overdrive her entire life. I'd like to know where to send the complaint letter."

"I'm sorry," Maggie muttered. "I know this is all my fault. I only wanted to lighten the mood a little."

"I know," I said. "Sam did remind me of something that will help us feel useful for a while. We need to start collecting the things we'll need in case the pace of Dana's labor keeps accelerating."

"Retta, what do we do if the baby can't get out?" Sybil asked.

Maggie gave her a startled look. "What are you talking about? All babies *come*," she said, thrusting her arms forward.

"No," Sybil replied. "Some have to be taken."

"Are you talking about a Caesarean?" Maggie gasped, backing away as though she was facing creatures that had stepped out of a TV horror series. "Neither one of you could slice her open like she's a watermelon. You wouldn't!"

She didn't want to know what I was willing to do in a crisis—and had done. Of immediate concern, though, was her growing anxiety. It was making her louder with each outburst, and I had to shush her. "Volume, Mags. We don't want to upset Dana more than she already is."

"Right. Okay, only you have to remember something." She gripped my wrist. "My first week as a candy striper in high school? I recognized right away I wasn't cut out for the work. There was that head nurse who had it in for me. She had me crying every day."

"Nurse Busfield," I said, nodding. "You called her Bitter Betty."

Maggie turned to Sybil. "She had such a sour personality, not even fat wanted to stick to that old bag of skin and bones. And everyone else got to do fun things like deliver flower arrangements, but I got the nasty chores—if you catch my drift."

"I've cared for my share of sick and dying folks. It can be unpleasant, but it beats being the one in their situation."

Taking the same approach, I reminded Maggie that things weren't quite the way she wanted to recall them. "Nurse B wouldn't have been so hard on you if you'd taken the hint and stopped flirting with the doctors. You refused to take them, or *her*, seriously."

Maggie waved away the technicality as though it was immaterial. "Just promise me no bedpans?"

"Right now what I need you to do is go upstairs and bring a plastic waste basket from one of the bathrooms."

"What for?" Maggie's suspicious stare suggested she expected the request to be followed by a chore as equally offensive as her candy striper experiences.

"Dana didn't get sick after the hot chocolate, but she could still get nauseous at any time, as the level of her pain increases."

"That's your idea of taking it easy on me?"

It was then I started to laugh. It might be seen as insensitive, but I couldn't help it. Only when Maggie smacked me with something—I think a computer mouse pad–did I recover.

"Sorry," I wheezed, wiping my eyes. "This is just so you. It's only been twenty-four hours since you had a life-threatening accident. You're in the middle of a health scare, and this is what you're fixated on?"

"Because it's every bit as real!" Maggie snapped, heading for the door. "You women are crazy talking about all this nasty stuff as though it was as simple as making a pitcher of peach tea. If the so-called fairer sex knew a fraction of what it takes to endure childbirth, the human race would be a third the size that it is—and should be!"

As soon as Maggie was out of earshot, Sybil asked, "You meant it? What Sam said...so far, so good?"

I shrugged. "Yeah, we take it contraction by contraction."

"Then I think I'm going to go churn some of your fine goat's cream and turn it into butter, until you give me something else to do. Some people do their best thinking in the bathtub, I do mine in the kitchen."

"Why not do that in the living room while sitting and chatting with Dana and Carly?" I asked. "You can entertain them with some of your stories. I'm sure Carly is running out by now, and the rhythmic sound and image of you stirring and whipping might soothe Dana."

"You know that's what I'll do," Sybil replied. "My Noah always said he loved to see me working in the kitchen. He said, 'If Mama is busy mixin' something, everything's gonna be all right.'"

As she, too, left, I thought of the pasteurized milk in the barn refrigerator. Although the power was out there, it was cold enough not to worry about anything going bad. And Sybil was going to run low on dairy products soon. I would need to bring over a new supply in the morning.

Several minutes later, as I worked on the list, I heard an odd sound and recognized it for what was. Our generator was about to run out of gas. As it began to sputter and the lights flickered, I hurried out of the office.

I called to Sybil and Carly, "Switch off as many lights as you can and start turning on the battery operated candles for a few minutes. I need to let things cool off out there before I refuel. I've done it while the generator was hot before, but we've had a lot going on and the can is still full enough to be heavy. I don't trust myself not to shake and spill gas."

"Got it." Sybil replied, rising.

Carly was already turning off the TV. "Be careful, Retta. And, you know—it's almost *that* time again."

"I hear you."

I dragged on my coat and boots, and managed to shut things off just before the generator ran out completely. Considering the machine would cool off quickly in these conditions, I hurried back onto the porch to retrieve more wood from our dry supply. Waste no trip, I reminded myself, especially when the more we opened the door, the more heat we lost inside the house.

After my second trip, I went back under the porch and felt the engine. It had, indeed, cooled enough to safely replenish the reservoir. It was a little after five o'clock, and it would be almost dusk in clear weather. Now, however, I needed the assistance of the flashlight that I tucked under my arm. This refill would buy us two more hours of light inside. I couldn't help but wonder about Dana's condition by then.

Just before I started back into the house, I looked at the sky. The icing continued, but it had slowed to a deceptive, soft mist. As subtle as it was, I knew it would wrap itself over and over every surface, like paper mâché creating art out of everything. That would make it all the more treacherous for those trying to clear roads and make repairs or address other emergencies.

"Stop soon," I entreated.

Back inside, I saw my friends had noticed the machine's steady rumble and were turning on lights again. Interestingly, Maggie was only now coming downstairs with the wastebasket I'd sent her to get, over fifteen minutes ago. I suspected she'd made a few phone calls while upstairs.

"How's Phil?" I asked, guessing on what had delayed her.

Unusually subdued, she said, "The oldest priest in their parish fell and broke his hip."

"Poor man." I'd heard men respond to that injury worse than women. "No doubt he never once thought of cutting back on his duties, even in these conditions."

"Well, he'll have to now." Maggie set the waste basket on Dana's side of the bed. "Here you go, sweetie."

"What's that for?" Dana asked.

Maggie looked over her shoulder at me. "Really? You had all this time to warn her, and you're leaving it to me? Uh-uh."

I brushed my hands together after loading a few new logs into the fire and said to Dana, "You might start to feel nauseous at some point. Better safe than sorry."

With a soft moan, she replied, "It's going to be one humiliation after another, isn't it?"

"Believe it or not," I told her, "before this is over you'll have a different perspective of what is and isn't embarrassing." However, Dana continued to look doubtful, so I changed the subject. "It might be comforting to know that it's only misting out there now."

"It's raining?" Carly asked hopefully. "That means it's getting warmer!"

"No, it's still ice, but it is easing up." I gestured toward the TV. "Would you like me to turn it on again? I'm about to go set the table. I know you aren't hungry, Dana, but the rest of us need to keep our up our strength. Carly, what about you?"

"I'm good, thanks. If that changes, I can easily make a peanut-butter-and-jelly sandwich."

"You've been doing a great job managing here. You have to be a little tired. If you'd like a glass of wine and to be alone to relax a few minutes, I'd be happy to stay with Dana."

Her expression turned shy. Or was I seeing embarrassment?

"The truth is I rarely drink. I only asked for some that first time because I was ultra-nervous about coming here. Even though Walter was diabetic, he liked a drink at the end of the day, but I couldn't stand the taste of scotch, so I would let him pour me a half glass of wine. Until now, it's the last time I indulged. You see, I'm terrified of ending up like my mother."

"Oh, sweetheart..." I both ached for her, and was proud, too. "Thank you for sharing that, and let me just say I think you're far too disciplined a young woman to ever succumb so easily to any kind of addiction."

I returned to the kitchen feeling buoyed by Carly's sharing. We'd been dealing with too many negatives. It was good to hear something uplifting for a change.

My good mood ended as soon as I saw Sybil. She had taken the lid off the pot and was checking the chili; however, when she tried to cover it again there was an uncharacteristic lack of control in her movements, causing glass and pottery to clang loudly. No one was more confident in the kitchen than Sybil, not even me. I immediately went to her side, and put my arm around the back of her waist. She looked positively aggrieved.

"What's happened?" I whispered.

She leaned into me. I could only think of one or two things to shake her so badly.

"Is the family all right?"

She nodded "Thomas called while you were outside," she began softly. "Naomi has taken a turn for the worse. He's giving the okay for hospice care." Finally, she met my gaze. "You know they can't get there. That means there's yet another crisis going on tonight, Retta."

What a heartbreaking moment for the couple, and for Sybil. Her devotion was torn more than ever. Aching with and for my friend, I hugged her. "I'm so sorry. I don't know why these things happen. But you mustn't brood for not being able to be there."

"I'm not. What's going on from this point is not my business. At the very least, Naomi would have hated being surrounded by people at the end. She gave most of her life to others on behalf of the Lord, and the church. She would want a little quiet time between her and Thomas." As convincingly as she spoke, Sybil's eyes filled with tears. "Retta...coming here was a gift to more than me. It was a gift to all three of us."

Hearing something I wasn't quite sure I grasped, I pushed myself to arms' length. "You think she'll pass, the way you and I believe Dana's baby is coming, whether we get help or not?"

Sybil paused, taking her time to choose her words carefully. "I know the hospice people are gifted, even remarkable, but that's not what Naomi needs. Thomas will talk to her, read to her....hopefully sing to her, whether she's conscious or not. You know that voice of his. I don't want the hospice people to get there, Retta. God forgive me for such a thought, but I want privacy for my pastor and his wife, more than I want anything."

What a risk she'd taken to speak so openly, and how moved I was to be the one with whom she'd shared such honesty. I embraced her again for her courage and generosity. "There's another mystery to life," I told her. "We don't know what we don't know, and we have to trust in God's wisdom."

In the background, I had been hearing fragments of Maggie's sales pitch to the girls. She had been trying to interest them into watching a DVD instead of listening to music, as they'd started to do. Carly had it on some station featuring soothing spa arrangements—a good choice, considering Dana's state of mind. Anyway, Maggie wasn't having any success. Still, I silently applauded her for trying to be involved and helpful.

Before I could tell Sybil I was going to intercede, I heard Dana keening. "Not now, Maggie,"

Then came Maggie's urgent, "Oh. Oh!"

Thirteen

THOSE SOUNDS of distress had Sybil and I exchanging worried glances. I gave her arm a squeeze, signaling my promise we'd talk more as soon as possible.

In the living room it was clear what was happening. Upon checking my watch, I confirmed the process had advanced by two minutes.

"Uh-huh," Sybil murmured from behind me. "Sure wish we could make that quit."

Once Dana's contraction waned, I said to her, "Well done, my brave girl. We'll be back in a minute. We have more things to collect."

In the kitchen, Maggie asked, "Did I cause that?"

She certainly hadn't helped; however, I knew her intentions had been good, so I edited my reply. "She's scared, Mags. Don't take anything she does or says to heart."

"What now?"

She was looking a little more overwhelmed, which was understandable. This was hardly what a woman with a head injury, and pending surgery needed to be experiencing.

"For one thing, the bed's not ready," I said.

Maggie's answering glance was doubtful. "You could have fooled me. She's laying there looking pretty comfortable–when she isn't trying to dig her fingernails through your six-hundred-thread-count sheets."

"It's not set up for when her water breaks," I explained.

"More information that I could live without hearing." Maggie's expression grew hopeful. "Maybe it won't happen until tomorrow, so there won't be a need. Surely, we'll be able to get help by then?"

She'd heard the same weather report I did when we last turned on the radio for a minute. Temperatures would hover just below freezing overnight, and wouldn't get much above that in the morning, despite the prediction of sunshine at some point.

"Even if they send help, the momentum of Dana's labor pains has increased. We need to put plastic under the sheets."

"If you're in a pinch, trash bags will work," Sybil suggested.

I started to nod then remembered something. "I think I still have a pair of plastic sheets upstairs in the linen closet from when Rachel was here and still potty-training the twins. I'll go get them."

Upon returning, I saw Dana was sitting upright on the edge of the bed. Although Carly had been trying to reason with her, she announced to us she wanted to go to the bathroom. She wasn't the first expectant mother to get a little headstrong between bouts of pain.

"Fine," I told her. "Girls," I called into the kitchen. "Let's carry her the way we did before."

"That's just so silly."

I knew Dana had forgotten the reason for all of our care. "Dear, we're trying to slow your contractions, not have you deliver in record time. Actually, this works out perfectly for us. While you're in there, it will give us a chance to get the bed water-proofed."

Fortunately, she hadn't thought of that and reluctantly acquiesced. It was Maggie who won a smile from her when midway across the living room, she complained about Dana feeling heavier than before.

"Exactly how many cups of ice chips have you devoured already?" Maggie demanded in mock annoyance.

"Enough to inconvenience you all," Dana replied. "I think I'm driving Carly nuts with my crunching, too."

"Oh, I don't mind, as long as you don't crack a tooth," Carly said. "If I was in your condition, I'd be chomping away just to burn nervous energy."

Once we had Dana settled comfortably, we left Carly to stand watch outside the doorway. It would be her job to keep Miss Independent from trying to sneak back in here on her own. In the meantime, the rest of us tore off the blankets and sheets and prepared things for the next round of excitement.

After we had our expectant mother resettled, I lingered, talking about little things to relax her. Only then did I take her temperature and blood pressure. They were staying close to the same as they had been. "That's good," I assured her. "I'll go get this posted."

I washed my hands, and tried to think of what I needed to do next. My mind didn't want to cooperate. *Fatigue,* I thought, unhappy with the realization.

"You might set the table," Sybil said. "We should eat while we have the chance."

Maggie helped, and before we were through, Carly quietly joined us. I raised my eyebrows in question.

"Would you believe she's dozed off?"

"It's about time," I said. "She's already gone through several hours of this."

"I figured I might have that peanut-butter-and-jelly sandwich and a cup of coffee now."

She insisted on fixing it herself. As she quietly worked, Sybil brought the chili and we sat down. Once Carly joined us, Sybil said grace, and bowls were filled.

Maggie savored her first spoonful of chili. "I can't remember the last time I had this."

"Filet mignon girl," I mused. I added to Sybil, "I'll bet she hasn't had enough in the last fifty years to remember if she likes it with beans or without."

Maggie pointed her spoon at me. "I'll have you know once in a while Hollis and I would run over to Pittsburg for some of their hot links."

"Which you did only out of love," I continued, a twinkle in my eye. "He was the one who was addicted to those gristly things. Bet you even ate them with saltine crackers, too, instead of on a bun."

Maggie barely suppressed a laugh as she nodded. "I would so want a beer chaser, but back then Camp County was still dry."

"Since we had beans the other day, I decided to leave them out of here," Sybil said. "Plus, it cooked faster."

Carly washed her first bite of her sandwich down with a sip of coffee. "To be honest, it does smell tempting."

"Then you *are* one disciplined lady," Sybil said with open admiration. "I think I love the smell of a house with good cooking going on more than I love perfume." She patted her belly. "It sure hasn't done me any favors, either. My attitude, yes. My waistline, no."

"For me, it's a toss-up between my herb garden and a clean barn or stable," I said.

Maggie looked revolted. "You are one sick puppy. Quit trying to ruin my appetite."

"I think I get that, Retta." Carly said with a smile. "I could get addicted to the smell of horses and leather."

She slid a cautious glance at Maggie, as though expecting criticism.

To everyone's surprise, her nemesis shrugged. "Why not? You look born for equestrian attire, just as Retta looks like she arrived in this world on the back of a horse. It's a given you already look disgustingly incredible in jeans."

As Carly stared in stunned disbelief, I murmured, "Now that's the Maggie I know and love. She's frank, even if she's giving a reluctant compliment. And in this case, she's right," I added to Carly.

"Well, thank you, ladies. I'd better start stuffing my face," she added, "before I start blubbering nonsense. I am so not used to this much flattery."

"Oh, I bet Walter complimented you plenty until the last day of his life," I told her.

She blushed and started to reach for her mug again, clearly wanting to avoid the subject, only to change her mind. "I did ask him why me?" she began softly. "I wasn't put off by the difference in our ages, Walter had a dignity, even majesty, that intimidated me more than his money. Yet at the same time, you knew you could trust him—you know what I mean?"

"I certainly do," I assured her.

"Don't keep us waiting," Maggie chided, "what did he say?"

"As simply as anyone else would respond to a question about the time, he said, 'You showed me your heart.' He was referring to the few times he saw me with Willow." Suddenly, a delightful smile spread all over her countenance. "Then he said, 'And the truth is—whether a man will admit it or not—most of us fantasize about being the knight in shining armor to a beautiful damsel in distress. The way I see it, you're my last chance.'"

I sat back in my chair and smiled back at her. "Walter was a dreamer and poet."

"He was a romantic, yes."

That last statement was so quietly spoken, I knew she had shared all she wanted to at this time, so I began telling her about an English saddle in the stables from when Rachel was in her, I-want-to-be-an-Olympic-equestrian-rider phase. Carly sat barely eating, thoroughly engrossed in what I had to say, her tone excited when she asked questions.

About to tell her how despite her name, Rachel's lovely bay, Pickles would be an excellent horse on which to start practicing, we heard an anguished cry. It launched all of us out of our seats.

"No! No! No!"

Carly practically knocked over her chair to head for the living room, while my impulse was to go through the kitchen to get to the bathroom. It was then I realized what had happened.

Despite our repeated warnings, Dana had awakened, noticed we weren't close, and committed the most reckless act. She went sneaking off to the bathroom on her own.

When we converged, we saw Dana straddling the rug in front of the vanity. Looking close to tears, she was holding up her gown at almost knee level. Amniotic fluid was still dripping down her legs.

"Retta, forgive me," she said tearfully. "All I wanted was for you all to have a little break from tending to me."

"Sweet thought," I told her. "But now you've probably bounced yourself ahead to contractions coming even faster. We have to get you cleaned up, out of that wet gown, and back into bed."

"But I don't have another," Dana said, looking even guiltier.

I turned to Maggie. "Do me a favor? Get my short terry robe hanging off the back of my bathroom door?"

"On my way!" she said, and made a bee line for the stairs.

"Don't run!" I called after her. "You can't afford another fall, and we can't handle two patients!"

Calm and steady, Sybil was already running hot water into the sink. I opened a drawer for her, indicating where the clean washcloths were kept. Then I helped Carly ease Dana to the commode.

"Another contraction is coming," Dana warned us.

That had me immediately changing my intent. I lowered the lid, and quickly dragged a towel off the rack. I put it under her, just in time to spare her the shock from cold, glazed wood and, if things had progressed way too fast, to keep the baby from dropping into the bowl.

Momentarily leaving Carly to manage the contraction, I rolled up the rug and carried it outside. By the time I returned, Maggie was back with the robe, and Dana was almost over her latest labor pain.

"Did anyone time that?" In my rush to get things done, it never crossed my mind to direct someone to check.

"Nine minutes," Carly told me.

Although she spoke quietly, her eyes reflected her shock. Yes, that was quite an advance, and I nodded subtly to let her know I felt the same way. There went my hopes of a broken, but otherwise controlled night of sleep for us. We might get to nap in rotation, but I already knew my nerves wouldn't allow me to accommodate my body's need.

"Sybil, could you go post that please?" Mentally, I was making adjustments, hoping I didn't expose I was as concerned as our mother-to-be looked frightened.

Sybil said, "Will do. And I'm going to give you some privacy by cleaning off the table. Maggie, why don't you help me, until they call us to get Dana back to bed?"

"Glad to," she said.

Of course, I stayed to help get Dana cleaned up, and changed. We alternately stroked her back, and offered assurance, but the way she abruptly pressed her fist to her lips to hold back sobs had me worried.

"What is it, sweetheart?" I asked. "Is the pain returning?" The only thing worse would be if she'd started to bleed.

She waved off my question. "I'm just being crazy. I can't help but see Jesse in this situation. When he was healthy, he could have carried this fat version of me in one arm—he was so strong. And he would have laughed doing it. It would have tickled him to no end. Instead, I'm never going to be able to look any of you in the eye again. I feel like such a mess and burden."

"Thanks a lot, friend," Carly quipped. "May I remind you my days of being a foster mother are about over. Willow is getting closer and closer to leaving the nest, and I'll have nothing but time on my hands. I was looking forward to becoming an honorary auntie."

As Dana turned her face away, her struggle transparent, I added,

"Me, too." It was an assurance that came easily and from the heart. I was already dealing with dread if she gave up this child. "Leave us with at least one of our daydreams, will you?"

After accepting the tissues I offered her from the box on the counter, Dana blew her nose and managed a weepy laugh. "I guess I have to if I want you to help me get off this hard seat."

By the time we had her back under the covers Dana looked more exhausted than ever. "I can't believe it's possible, but I think I could drift off to sleep again."

Of all people, it was Carly who eyed her with skepticism. It had a humbling effect on Dana.

"Oh, Carly, please don't look at me that way. I've learned my lesson, honestly, I have."

With gentle encouragement, I said, "She knows. Go ahead and doze if you can. They call them power naps for a reason."

While she slept, we quietly dispersed, each with something in mind to address. Only when we regrouped in the kitchen did Carly join us.

"Dana's still out cold, but I don't expect that to last much longer. Is there anything I can do?"

"9-1-1?" was the first question out of Maggie's mouth.

With a heavy sigh, I said, "Give me a minute. I need a few sips of the fresh pot of coffee, Sybil made." I would have liked to continue drinking my cognac, but it would only have made me drowsy.

"Carly baby, I poured yours out," Sybil said. "You get a fresh cup, too."

"Keep talking," Carly said. "Even as quiet as you're trying to be, I can hear you. I developed a good ear keeping track of a sneaky mother."

Bless her heart, I thought, reaching out so my fingers brushed against hers as she crossed the room. It was beyond my ability to grasp what it would be like to grow up having to be cautious and suspicious of a loved one's behavior.

"You're right," I said, finally answering Maggie's question. "Ready or not, it is about time. First, however, let's get the other things we're going to need. There's alcohol, cotton balls, and scissors in the downstairs bathroom. Put them in that container," I said, pointing across the room where I'd placed it earlier. "Before you do, though, wipe the inside with alcohol, too. It may be new, but sanitary? Who knows."

"Twine?"

It was Sybil, who reminded me. I had mentioned it earlier. "Mud room. Up where the lantern is. I'll get that."

"Seriously?" Maggie almost squeaked in her attempt to keep her voice down. "What for? Are you planning to hog tie Dana to all four corners of the bed? There aren't even any posts!"

"It's for the umbilical cord, you goose."

As soon as I returned with the string, Carly placed a mug of black coffee in front of me. After I thanked her, she nodded at the spool and confessed, "I wouldn't have thought of that, either."

"That's her farm experience showing," Sybil replied.

"And she's being modest." I said of Sybil, "She's had plenty of mid-wife experience with her own farm animals."

With a half shrug, Sybil said to Carly, "But who did I call when our pregnant goat was having complications on a Sunday afternoon with the vet out of town on another emergency call?"

I pressed a hand to my lips to keep from laughing out loud. "Do you know I'd forgotten? Poor mama goat—a ballooned placenta, the butt of one baby, and the hooves of another trying to squeeze out at the same time."

"She got it all straightened out, though," Sybil explained, "and we didn't lose one kid." She turned to me and intoned, "And you're going to do *fine* today, as well, Retta Cole."

Maggie returned with her arm full of supplies. "Retta, I was think-ing…maybe you should talk to Sam again to see what he thinks of what's happened?"

"Believe me, I would love to, but not before we do the obligatory emergency call. I'm not about to get him in the middle of a possible law suit, since his specialty had nothing to do with OB-GYN practices."

Carly nodded thoughtfully. "I see your point. Not that Dana would ever…" She left the idea hanging in the subsequent silence.

"No, she wouldn't," I said. "On the other hand, we've heard nothing but negatives about the rest of Dana's relations. Who knows if they're the type that smell money, whether they sincerely have feelings for Dana or not. Then there's the DA. He could open an investigation, heaven forbid. It's smarter to err on the side of an abundance of caution."

Actually, I had it all clear in my mind as to what we should do. "Sybil, would you make the initial call? I'll take notes to help me report to Sam afterward. That will leave Carly free to tend to Dana. It won't be long before she awakens again. Maggie you're looking a bit pale. It's making your bruises stand out more. Maybe you should sit down for a few minutes and put up your feet."

"I'm fine. Really," she insisted. "Don't make me sorry I ditched my vanity sunglasses and scarf."

I knew her scalp was itching and that she craved a shampoo. She was also self-conscious with her hair's matted state. "Sorry. Maybe in the morning, we can move a stool to the kitchen sink and you can lean back to where we can use the wand to get you fixed up without wetting your wound."

With a sigh, I nodded to Sybil to initiate the call. I really thought we should use my cell phone, since that was the back-up number to my land line with 9-1-1. However, given the fact we knew no one was coming, I didn't think it mattered for this instance.

Upon connecting, she said, "This is Sybil Sides. I'm at Loretta Cole's ranch." She recited the address to confirm the operator had the correct information. "We have a premature birth in progress." After a pause, she said, "Six weeks. And the subject is a forty-year-old, first-time mother." A moment later, she sent me a panicky look.

"No, don't transfer me anywhere. What? Tyler EMS? Sir, we can't make it to our local hospital. What on earth makes you think an ambulance can get up here, let alone make the return trip to Tyler?"

Maggie dropped the cotton ball that she was using to wipe the storage container, only to grab the phone from Sybil. "Oh, for pity's sake," she muttered. "All rural 9-1-1 calls go to the county sheriff's office, and I know exactly who's on duty. He's about as useless as a bull in a milking barn. Henry? It's Mrs. Lamar. Now, no stonewalling me, I'm at Retta Cole's ranch with several ladies, one of whom has gone into labor. We need you to send help."

After a longer pause that left her square-shouldered and rigid, she snapped, "I'm tired of hearing that, Henry. There must be something y'all can do locally. I repeat, childbirth is going on here!"

We watched Maggie listen and nod, and listen some more. Then she said to us, "A chopper is too dangerous, due to the icing, and they're otherwise shorthanded. One ambulance is stuck axle-deep in a ditch, another has been routed to a local call. The third is in transit to an emergency north of here. The two major interstates in our region are shut down from a series of wrecks that have blocked traffic in both directions for hours, and every other alternate route is getting logger-jammed by the minute."

Sybil looked at me with all innocence. "I am so glad she grabbed the phone. I wouldn't have realized conditions are so bad, even if I'd heard all of that."

"Just keep looking at her bruises," I said, patting her shoulder, "and consider she might actually believe it's sunny and mild a mile outside of the front gate."

Maggie covered the mouthpiece with her hand. "I heard that."

"Good, then give the phone back to Sybil," I replied, "before Henry disconnects on you. Let Sybil have him transfer us over to Tyler EMS, as he first suggested."

Looking much maligned, Maggie did so. "Wait until I get back into town. This isn't the end of the matter, let me tell you."

Sybil covered her free ear with one hand to block out Maggie's indignation, and said, "Henry, this is Sybil Sides again. On second thought, I think that's a good idea. Please go ahead and shoot this call to Tyler... and thank you very much."

While Sybil waited for the transfer to be completed, Maggie went around the counter and slid onto a barstool. "I was only trying to help," she grumbled.

"Understood," I replied.

"I used to be respected in this town. If Hollis was alive, they would have brought in snow mobiles from Colorado or Missouri to help us. It's just because I'm a woman they think they can get away with blubbering any old B.S. they feel like."

"Oh, please, hush." I indicated how Sybil was straining to hear. "The fact is you're the one not being reasonable. A sensible doctor would have already ordered you to bed. Now stop trying to play Dragon Lady, and enjoy the time off of your feet. You're probably going through wine withdrawal. Behave and I'll pour you a small glass."

That seemed to mollify her, and I returned to listening to the one-sided conversation between Sybil and the Tyler 9-1-1 operator. Despite her precision with details, and respectful approach, it didn't sound like things were going to go any better than they had with Henry.

"I get it," Sybil said, starting to sound weary. "I'm not asking for a chauffeur and limousine. I just want to get a hurting lady some relief and save her baby's life."

With commendable patience, Sybil reached for the notebook on the counter and repeated all of the data we had been recording since the contractions started. There followed such a long pause I found myself involuntarily holding my breath. Sybil quietly said, "That sounds like the reasonable thing, sir. Thank you so much. How do I do this again? Is there a special number to contact you directly, or do I have to repeat this process all over?"

Hating the sound of the latter half of her question, I couldn't wait for Sybil to disconnect. When she did, I immediately asked, "Is he telling you we have to start from scratch the next time we call?"

"Insofar as we'll again be routed through our county's 9-1-1 unit. But once they transfer us to Tyler, they can access the information we gave them during our initial conversation." Sybil pinched the bridge of her nose as she recollected the rest of the conversation. "They said it's time to see how far she's dilated."

Already knowing how Dana would feel about the request, I dealt with my own reservations. "I know about cattle birthing and horses. It's been too long since the other. What about you?"

"As a matter of fact, I witnessed my first grandchild's birth, even though it was in a hospital. The range is one to ten centimeters with the average width of a finger being close to a centimeter. The Tyler operator said when the contractions get closer, we're to call again."

Carly raised a finger to request silence. Then hooking her thumb in the direction of the living room, she retreated.

Apparently Dana was rousing. Only seconds later, I could hear the conversation starting. It was no one's fault, but there was less and less time between labor pains to figure out what else needed to be done preparation-wise.

"So, we better get in there and check her."

"Yes," Sybil agreed. "We have to have that information."

It turned out our timing was perfect. Dana had begun struggling with Carly, trying to get up. Tendrils of her damp hair were beginning to cling to her glistening forehead.

"I was about to call you," Carly said, looking more than a bit distressed. "Could she have come down with a fever? Why else would she act like this? It's like she doesn't even know me."

"The pains are growing stronger," I replied. "She's fixating on that, and it's making her panic. We have to redirect her focus onto something positive."

I sat down on the other side of Dana, and gripped her hands to demand her attention. "Talk to me."

"I can't do this."

"Yes, you can," I crooned, "because you have to help the baby. You want to do what's beneficial, don't you? You also have to work with us. And let me add, it's not safe to hold your breath. Both of you need oxygen, you know."

She apparently hadn't even realized what she was doing. When she did gasp for new air, and purged it, she naturally relaxed deeper into the pillows.

"Good girl," I said. "Now, Carly is going to keep reminding you, while we check under the covers to see how far you've dilated. Please don't be embarrassed. You're among friends, but we have to gauge where the baby is at this stage so we can report it to the 9-1-1 operator."

"You have to call now?" Dana asked. "Couldn't it wait a while, so I can get my mind around the idea?"

"We've already had the initial conversation. They know about you and they're helping us monitor things. They're waiting for us to call back with the information." I wasn't being quite accurate, but it seemed to be getting the right response out of Dana.

She covered her eyes with one hand. "Do what you have to do."

"You're not going to show us anything we haven't seen before," I told her, reaching for the latex gloves among the supplies we'd gathered. "Me, especially. I've witnessed every kind of birth imaginable around here, and the gratifying news to me is you don't weigh a half ton and want to kick me senseless."

My attempt at humor won me a wobbly smile from her. "Just know I'm going to get seriously nervous if I suddenly feel you trying to stuff clean hay under me."

I laughed softly. "That's the spirit, cutie."

We warmed our hands by the fireplace then worked as quickly and gently as we could. Sybil and I soon agreed she was dilated to about four centimeters. Thankfully, that told us we weren't in crisis mode yet. The mystery was whether the rest of the dilation would go at this pace, speed up, or even slow down? More than ever, time and weather meant everything.

Lifting her head to see beyond her belly, Dana asked, "Am I close?"

"Baby girl, I know it feels like your tonsils are coming out between your legs," Sybil said, "but there's more work to do."

"Please just tell me," Dana cried.

"You're not halfway yet," I said. She had a right to know, despite what she'd said earlier.

"Oh, dear God." She fell back against the pillows and stared up at the ceiling. "I already feel as though I'm being ripped apart."

"Believe it or not," I said truthfully, "there isn't one sign of bleeding. Your body is stretching, just as it was made to do."

"Like you would tell me the truth."

Removing the gloves, I let the others readjust the bedding and tuck the ends under the mattress. I sat down beside Dana again. "Sweetheart, bringing life into the world is one of the greatest blessings anyone who's participated in the experience talks about, whether it's a doctor, nurse, police officer, fireman…and it looks like today we get that honor. We're not anywhere nearly as qualified as they are, but we have as much appreciation and respect for what we're going to do. We're not here to torment you, we're here to help."

Dana's gaze searched my face for several seconds, before she sighed and nodded. "Regardless of what comes out of my mouth from here on, can I just tell you how grateful I am to have you here with me? Carly, if I get rude again, you have my permission to stuff an ice chip into my mouth."

"Are you kidding, I'm going to the freezer right now for a whole cube," she drawled.

Grinning, Sybil, Maggie, and I headed back to the kitchen. We were around the breakfast bar when Maggie caught my arm.

"So when should I start boiling water?" she asked.

Fourteen

"UNLESS YOU think we can find forceps and a scalpel around here that need sanitizing, I don't think boiling water will be necessary," I began, bemused. "Or are you telling me you're still hungry? Check the freezer. You'll find some lobster tails in there that might really hit the spot."

Maggie narrowed her eyes. "You quit making fun of me."

"Okay. The truth is, I'm not about to risk wasting those crustaceans on someone who could endanger instant coffee."

"What a relief," Sybil added, a smile playing around her lips, too. "I was about to tell you to give her the bedpan, and I'd deal with the high dollar seafood."

"Under the circumstances, I guess I deserve that," Maggie replied. "I just remember the line being said in several movies and thought there was something to it."

I'd teased her enough and let her off the hook. "Actually, the twine will need to be sanitized. Cut off about a foot or so. We'll use it to tie off the umbilical cord in two places. I'm going upstairs to check the fire."

By the time I returned, Dana started moaning again. Another contraction had begun.

Carly encouraged her, by directing, "Roll over onto your side toward me and I'll count you through it. One, two, three..."

The two women went through that series until Dana purged a final breath and groaned, "It's over."

"Good," Maggie said, turning to me. "Because something else struck me while you were upstairs. You and Sybil are kidding about the chamber pot. Right?"

"Not that again," Dana moaned. "I told you I'd be good."

We needed a moment of levity to keep our greatest fears at bay. "Did I ever tell any of you what my grandfather said to me when I saw my grandmother's chamber pot for the first time? I'd asked him what it was, and he answered with a question of his own. 'Do you know the difference between a rich girl and a poor girl? A rich girl has a canopy over her bed, and a poor girl has a can of pee under hers.'"

Sybil slapped at her thigh and shook her head. "My people used to tell it all the time."

Dana made a sound of utter frustration. "But it's an expression that drives me completely nuts. *'My people,'* that is so tribal, or sectarian, or...I don't know what."

Nodding in agreement, Carly added, "I can't tell you how often Walter would try to introduce me to someone, and I could tell immediately by a certain calculation in their eyes they were about to ask, 'And who are your people, dear?' when it was already clear they'd decided I wasn't socially acceptable." Arching one eyebrow, she continued, "And more than one of them had a relative serve time in prison for one reason or another."

Maggie had grown silent, but finally offered, "It's not always done with malevolent intent. I get what you're saying, and I'm guilty of it as anyone, but you'll have to remember we're *all* immigrants to Texas. I mean, what else do the six flags over Texas represent? And we're larger than many countries in Europe, plus, we've been through our share of trials. To me, it's natural curiosity to ask about each other's ancestry."

"Heaven help us," Sybil muttered. "That was practically diplomatic. If the blow she took last night puts the thought in her head that she should run for congress, I'm going to start to really worry."

Although I leaned toward her as though to speak conspiratorially, I made sure everyone could hear, "Don't worry. It would seriously compromise her wardrobe."

"You two in particular don't know a damn thing about my wardrobe," Maggie huffed. "If Sybil isn't at school, she's helping out with Naomi, and *you* can't come to *my* house. *I* always come to yours because some critter or chore needs your attention. My closet is a mystery to both of you."

"I know you're not a quitter," Carly replied. "But I didn't know you couldn't take a joke."

After pursing her lips, Maggie gave her a challenging look and replied, "Show me your birth certificate that states one of my exes was your daddy." She pointed to the floor, "Then I promise I will drop right here and die laughing."

Without missing a beat, Carly replied, "I wouldn't want you to do that. Think of all the fun we could have going around town with me introducing you as my step-mommy."

"Is it just me," Sybil ventured, "or are these two actually starting to get along?"

"Step-mommy. Don't make me laugh," Dana moaned, wincing as she stroked her belly. "It hurts and seems to be bringing on another contraction." Suddenly, an odd look came over her face. "You're not doing all this to hide some terrible news, are you?" She stared at each of us in turn. "I already know it's entirely possible I'm going to die."

That wiped the lingering smiles off of our faces. Yet, as shocking as the statement was to hear, it wasn't out of the realm of possibilities. Nevertheless, it was vital we made her believe no such thing would happen. We weren't going to lose either her or the baby—not under our watch. Before I could reply, a shocked Maggie protested our slow reaction.

"Retta, *tell* her. It's going to be okay."

Having survived far too many heartbreaks of her own, Maggie wanted instant reassurance for our mother-to-be. Instead, I thought of a more useful and inspirational idea.

"You know, my grandmother had my mother during a particularly wet and stormy summer," I began. "East Texas hadn't seen such a season in decades, and days of rain had produced flash flooding that had already carried away my grandparents' truck. They were afraid the house would be next. The conditions were indescribable. Dams were already failing, and stock ponds overflowing everywhere. Yet in the midst of everything, my grandmother—young as she was—ordered the midwife and her own older sister to *focus,* because she was a true believer in that saying 'God helps those who help themselves.' Just as my mother was born, my grandfather arrived with a horse and buggy to get them to another neighbor's place on higher ground. It just goes to show you, while there are no givens in life, if you keep trying and sustain your faith, things usually work out."

Maggie lowered herself to the foot of the bed, as though she'd suddenly grown weak-kneed. "I remember when they sent me to your house as Mama was dying, and not even you would give voice to what was happening, although I knew you knew."

"Maggie," I said, despite thinking this was not the time for one of the sad exceptions to my theory. "You never wanted to deal with reality, let alone pain. Believe me," I added, "I never blamed you for that."

She turned away to stare at the Christmas tree for a few moments. "I know. But it bothered me that I never got to say goodbye to my mother." She sighed. "I guess it's time to grow up."

Unable to resist, I came behind her for an impulsive hug. "You're going to get there."

"Retta..."

Dana drew my attention, only to be startled by her intense stare. "What's happening, dear?"

"Nothing. Everything. I...I have been listening to all of you talk. It all just reinforces my feelings. We have to be realistic. Sometimes hope and faith aren't enough, and so..." She took a stabilizing breath. "I think I need a will."

"Dana," I began, "I'm sure the one you already have will suffice."

"I don't see how you can say that, given the fact my husband is dead and it's common in wills for the deceased to leave everything to their surviving spouse. And that's if you have a will, but I don't. The joke is I almost don't need one, considering I'm about to lose everything anyway."

She was rambling so, I was beginning to worry something else was happening to her. "What are you saying, sweetheart? I think your focus is all wrong, but if it will ease your mind for the moment, tell me what you need us to do?"

"*You*, Retta." She struggled to sit up, and reached for my hand. Her grip was surprisingly strong, and disturbing in its desperation. "Raise my baby."

I gasped. Whatever I'd expected to hear, it certainly wasn't this. "Dana, I'm old enough to be *your* mother. I'm not sure I'll live long enough to witness a child born now graduating from high school, let alone college."

"Then, make sure he or she is given to the right people, people who would be equally gentle and loving as you, but most of all have your courage."

I felt the room spin around me; it seemed to be closing in on me, too. Most of all, beneath the sternum pain, my heart ached. So many feelings and thoughts assaulted my senses. One second I felt trapped, and the next I was almost sick with fear of what a cold and impartial court might decide for her if she didn't protect herself.

That was the insanity of the next hour. Two aging widows, an educator who was learning new, unanticipated lessons, and a gorgeous graduate of the school-of-hard-knocks, stumbling as we were through the rest of our lives, challenged to convince a bankrupt, middle-aged, first-time mother that all would be well. It was ludicrous.

I continued to try to give Dana a different perspective of her situation. Sometimes she came close to being reasonable, only to panic or get stubborn, and lock onto what she saw was the only bottom line for her. During all of that, she experienced several more contractions.

"Dear," I entreated, increasingly concerned with her flushed face and agitation. "You can't just give up on things you and Jesse worked so hard for."

"I don't give a damn about any of it. They can do with the restaurant and my house whatever they will, but I want *you* to control my child's future. My trust in you is absolute, Retta."

Reluctantly accepting that time was not on our side, I started scribbling down her directives. When she finished, I extended the notebook to Maggie.

"Would you go type this up in my office, so we can all witness it?" I knew full well the document might not be worth the paper it would be written on, since it could be alleged we were all co-conspirators to Dana's plan—or one of our own.

Although Maggie looked surprised at first, she recovered quickly. "Absolutely. I'm on my way."

"Wait!" I called after her. Some technicality struck me. "You're going to have to have a place for only the three of you to sign as witnesses under Dana's name because I no longer qualify, considering what she's asking of me."

As Maggie disappeared into the next room, Dana nodded with satisfaction. "Thank you, Retta."

I could see where she was in danger of psychologically shutting down, and I couldn't allow her to do that. "We're pacifying you about getting some legal documentation out of precaution, nothing more. Now there's other work to do, and you have to cooperate with us."

"I thought I was—that is since my water broke."

Her look of contrition was endearing, but I couldn't let her under-mine me again. "This baby is coming and he or she can't do it alone. What's more, the child will need a name."

She looked away.

"Dana."

"I don't want to."

With a sound of exasperation, and tears welling in her eyes, Carly leaned over and placed both hands on Dana's belly. "Enough. I get your disappointment with Jesse, and God knows I understand your emotional pain, but do not attempt to reject this child of yours. Don't transfer your agony to this innocent life. It's time to step up, Dana. Choose a name."

"But I have no right. I'm not keeping the baby."

"That's not acceptable. So the child will have less than nothing from you, except your DNA?"

Clearly uncomfortable, Dana looked everywhere to avoid our scruti-ny. "I'm trying to do the right thing, and not drag it down more."

"The only one acting dragged down is you. So you plan to start your child's life with two strikes against it?"

"No, of course not."

"Early on, when you and Jesse spoke of having a family, didn't you talk about names?"

That won a pained look from Dana. "I would tell him he needed a Jesse, Jr., even though he didn't always like his name. I explained we could call him J. J."

"And what if you had a girl?"

"Jesse needed a son."

Carly recoiled as though she'd been stung. "You didn't just say that?"

"Dana reached out to her. "Honey, you don't understand."

Carly slapped Dana's hands away and rose from the bed, only to pace around the room. Fiery-eyed, she pointed at Dana.

"Don't you dare suggest a female child has no value. I was held in the hospital an extra day because my mother couldn't be troubled with naming me. A nurse finally made a suggestion, and she said, 'Fine.' You want to know how I know? Because in one of her few sober moments, she thought I needed to have that precious piece of information. Now, do you need me to tell you who named Willow?"

"You," Dana whispered.

"Exactly. Do not do that to your child. You don't think it will come out? We *always* find out the ugliest truths, thanks to people who are all too willing to tell us how worthless we are."

I suppose there had been other resounding silences through time, but I swear I couldn't remember one. Then I looked up, and saw another jarring occurrence—Maggie standing in the doorway of my office wiping tears from her eyes.

Dana's cheeks were already wet when she reached out to Carly and sobbed. "Oh, come here."

As they hugged, I tried not to have my own breakdown. Then Sybil came around the bed, needing that human connection, too. As we embraced, over her shoulder I saw Maggie give me a weepy smile and thumbs up. For the first time since all this began, I had a wisp of hope. It was as if some spirit had joined us in the room offering the reassurance things wouldn't end up the total catastrophe I'd been fearing they might.

Sniffing, Dana asked, "How about Shea? That's my maiden name and I always liked it. Besides, it brought me luck in my profession. Maybe she'll like music."

Not yet able to speak, Carly nodded enthusiastically.

"Now that I've opened that door, I can't help but wonder whom the baby will look like," Dana said.

What a centuries-old concern. This went back to the Greeks, the Romans, and no doubt earlier. As far back as Biblical times to be sure, but Sybil was able to provide an answer better than I ever could.

"There have been studies," she began, "at least regarding the animal kingdom, concluding how offspring tend to look like the father in order to keep the male from killing his own."

Maggie held up her hand as though ready to claim the floor. "There has to be truth in that. There's no denying I look like you-know-who, and not my beautiful mother. Nevertheless, he always acted like I was chicken gizzards to be sold for fish bait."

"Honey, don't say such a thing about yourself," Sybil said. "I see a lot of your mother in you."

Maggie's smile didn't come close to reaching her eyes. "Only for the reason I did get her hair and I made a point to style it as close to hers as possible, just to torment him."

Carly shuddered and wrapped her arms around herself. "Oh, Maggie, what a dangerous game you played. Your comment about fish bait? There's another side of it that works the opposite way. My mother styled my hair like hers from the time I was seven. At first, I was thrilled. I thought it meant she really loved me. It only took me a few weeks, and a few too many close encounters with men, who would make your skin crawl, until I realized it had *nothing* to do with love. I was the fish bait—the dispensable worm squirming on a hook."

Maggie clamped a hand over her mouth and the other around her waist. In that instant, I knew she was in serious danger of losing what little she'd eaten at dinner.

"If you share one more truth," she managed to rasp, "I do believe what's left of my heart will pulverize."

Carly nodded without satisfaction. "The Bible speaks to the truth setting you free, so how does that feel, Maggie? I never thought it would mean losing my only parent and my home—even the lousiest version of her."

"Frankly, I am beyond grateful you two are connecting on this level." Sybil raised her hands. "This is a praise God moment if I ever experienced one."

"Baptists," Maggie muttered.

For my part, I pressed my clasped hands to my lips until I could manage a soft, "Thank you, Carly. I can't imagine what such a heartbreaking disclosure cost you."

Dana stared at Carly in wonder. "Here I was, feeling sorry for myself about my childhood. I didn't know how good I had it."

Maggie just shook her head and retreated back into my office. The room stayed uniquely quiet, as though we were all needing a few moments to come to terms with our own life-changing events. It was Dana who finally forced us to return to the crisis at hand.

"I hate to break up this party, but here I go again."

Carly glanced at her watch. "Eight minutes, Retta. Okay, Dana, remember your breathing."

Once the pain had subsided, I motioned to Sybil to stay close, and said to the other two, "This is the perfect opportunity to check how the dilation is progressing. Sorry, Dana, but we need you on your back for a minute."

Carly helped her friend shift to accommodate us, while Sybil and I warmed our hands again before lifting the bedding.

"I'd call that a six," I said to Sybil. "You?"

"Yeah. Unless things calm down, I think we'll be seeing the head in another few contractions."

As we rose and tucked everything back in place, I said to Dana, "Did you hear? You've progressed two numbers. The baby's head will be crowning soon."

"I need to push," she replied.

"No!" the three of us said simultaneously.

"Sweetheart," I added, "your body isn't ready. You could do real damage."

Carly asked, "What if you roll to your side again? I'll help you."

It took a few moments, but soon enough Dana's coloring improved. When she sighed with relief, we retreated to the kitchen.

As glad as I was for her improved state, I was shaking. All of the emotional and psychological upheaval had my bruised body reacting, and I leaned against the island to get a grip as much as to massage my chest.

Sybil noticed and demanded, "Talk to me."

"This is all so wrong," I moaned.

"What? Her will?" Sybil shrugged. "As far as I'm concerned, she's chosen the best person she could—and I'm not only referring to under this roof."

That was a heady compliment, but one that didn't provide any relief. "You don't understand. I've as good as made a commitment to Sam, yet now I've legally bound myself to something of huge importance without his input. I had no right to do it."

"It's a problem," Sybil agreed. "But this is a unique situation. It's not as though her decision can be put off for another day. On the other hand, I don't see this as something you can't get through. He's a doctor. Surely, he doesn't hate children?"

"He had a child." I dropped my voice to a whisper. "But he lost him due to an incurable heart condition."

At first stricken, Sybil's expression lit with understanding. "That's why he left the medical profession?"

"Yes, and it also cost him his marriage. We haven't talked about it much—I'm letting him choose when he's ready. There's no missing he continues to carry a great deal of anger and pain from those losses. Dumping the news of a newborn could dredge up a lot of trauma for him."

This time Sybil came to me offering deeper comfort. As she hugged me, she muttered, "And here I am acting like it's a cake walk for you. I'm so sorry. I was only trying to be encouraging. Just don't assume he wouldn't be as generous, and welcoming, as you are. And as you said yourself…trust the answers will come."

She was right, and I squared my shoulders. "It's both soothing and annoying to have such wise friends," I admitted.

"How about our Carly?" Sybil intoned. "Wasn't she impressive?"

Our Carly. I did like the sound of that, and I could see it was as true as if she'd said, "Our Dana."

"This has been as big a revelation to her as it's been to us," I replied.

"I have a feeling that child has needed to get a whole bunch out of her system for a long time." She went to the cabinet and motioned to the glasses, "What's your poison? I think it's time."

I shook my head. "It'll only make this doggone weepiness worse." I drew in and purged another deep breath as my thoughts returned to Carly. "I wish you could have seen her with the horses. I don't think there's going to be any holding her back now. And you know she's going to be a wonderful aunt to Dana's baby. Isn't it a shame how we allowed others' perceptions to taint our early opinion of her?"

"Those life lessons just keep on a comin'."

Knowing I'd delayed this long enough, I said. "Now, I have to call Sam."

"You want me to leave the room? Or, are you going to go to the of-fice?" she asked.

I gestured to indicate it was a moot point. "Dear friend, considering what we've been talking about, and what we've just gone through out there, is this a time to start keeping secrets?"

"Bless you. Nevertheless, I'll check on Maggie. Do you think it would be okay to take her a glass of wine?"

"I promised her one earlier. Go ahead. She's had enough shocks to her system to where she's undoubtedly yearning for some bolstering."

While Sybil poured a small glass of red wine, I jotted our latest data in the notebook. As Sybil left the room, she sent me a crossed fingers sign.

Mouthing, "Thank you," I reached for my phone and hit the number to speed-dial Sam.

He answered immediately. "I hope you know what you're doing to my nerves?"

"When you hear what's happened, you'll understand this latest delay. However, what I want you to know is I've been thinking about you just as much."

"Now, that's what I wanted to hear," he replied, his tone intimate. "How's your patient?"

"As usual with best laid plans, Dana did sneak around us and, in the process, her water broke. The contractions are down to about eight minutes apart, and she's dilated to a six. Unfortunately, the pressure and pain is getting so bad she wants to push. In fact, her whole state of mind is such, she's asked us to draft a will."

The way he whistled softly told me he was as taken aback with this news as we had been. Not an encouraging reaction at all.

"I'll bet that won her a few opinions she hadn't counted on."

"It did." My insides twisted into a harder knot. I knew the moment for the sharing of weighty news was upon us.

"How do you get to her age and not have something in writing?"

"If you're not impressed with that," I replied, "you're really not going to like the rest of what I have to say."

"What is she asking you to do? If the worst happens, does she want you to keep her ashes to give to her child when he or she is twenty-one?"

"No. Dana wants me to be the legal guardian of the baby."

I heard him utter something under his breath, but he must have moved the phone from his mouth because I couldn't quite make it out.

"Surely, I'm not hearing you correctly?" While he retained enough control to keep his voice low-key, his careful enunciation exposed an edge. "She can't ask such a thing."

"Well, she did."

"Only because you must have given her some indication you'd be receptive to the idea. Retta, I know you're generous to a fault, but—" He checked himself. "I thought you said she had family?"

I could feel our conversation racing toward a slippery slope, and knew I couldn't endure one more upheaval of this magnitude. Not in one night. Placing my hand against my heart, I tried to reason with him. "Sam—the important thing to keep in mind about this is we are *not* going to lose her."

"But you're not God."

I closed my eyes, thinking again of his tragedy. "I should never have told you, at least not yet and not this way. Only...you have the right to have input here because...you come first." I'd found it difficult to voice my feelings. Now that I had, I could only hope he believed me.

"Those words means the world to me, Retta—except they're hardly the truth, are they?"

Fifteen

*D*ear God. There was no rancor in his voice; however, there didn't need to be when the truth was spoken with such razor-sharp accuracy.

When the silence between us stretched to awkward, he groaned softly. "I was too blunt. Maybe it would be best to focus on your friend's condition."

Now he was starting to sound clinical—and distant. *Your friend.* He knew her name, only he didn't want to say it, any more than he wanted me to consider an idea that would create a human chasm between us.

"The call to 9-1-1 was interesting." It was a miracle how I managed to pluck even that much from my thoughts, since my conscience was rapidly shredding all brain matter into confetti. "They transferred us from the sheriff's office here in Franklin County to Tyler. Dana's contractions were ten minutes apart at the time. We're about to call again."

"How's her blood pressure?"

Flustered by his just-the-facts-ma'am tone, I mumbled, "Sorry. I was too anxious to hear your voice and forgot to take it. I will before we deal with 9-1-1."

"Good luck."

"I'm sorry…" I cringed at the repeated apology. "I should have waited to call you, until after I talked to them. But I felt this need to bring you in on Dana's request."

"Yeah." Sam cleared his throat. "At some point, I'll appreciate the gesture, but this is all a lot to take in."

And then some. I didn't only have to deal with his disappointment in me; I felt the chili I'd ingested threaten to come back up. Honesty had a terrible cost, and I felt uncontrollable sobs threatening.

"Retta, you can't expect me to be as welcoming or even supportive as you clearly are. I haven't had a chance to digest any of this. What's more, I've never even met the woman."

"Okay."

Upon hearing my weak agreement, he blurted out, "Don't cry. I'm not cutting and running."

Not yet anyway.

When I didn't reply, he asked, "Have you already drawn something up and had it witnessed?"

"Maggie is typing it in my office as we speak."

He snorted. "Well, then all of this tortured dialoguing is probably irrelevant, isn't it? Considering how she is in the kitchen, she's probably already fried your computer."

That was so close to the truth it might have been hilarious—if this had been someone else's issue to deal with. Now it just added to the pounding at my temples.

"You could be right. I'd better go check for smoke."

Exhaling, Sam asked, "You are going to call me again?"

"The delivery...I think we're getting close."

"Retta."

"Seriously. I might get tied up with 9-1-1."

After a pause, he said simply, "I'm here."

Yes, I thought, as I disconnected. He was there, and I was here. Geographically, it wasn't much over a hundred miles. Psychologically, we might as well be continents apart.

Lost in my brooding, it was a moment before a whispery voice had me looking over my shoulder. Sybil was peering around the washroom doorway. "Sorry—what?"

"Can you spare a moment? Maggie can't get your printer to cooperate."

I began to turn away and shook my head. *Not now,* I begged in a silent prayer.

"No, I mean it," Sybil continued, clearly misunderstanding. "I use the brand that isn't compatible with anything I see in your office."

I automatically followed her knowing I had only a few yards, a precious handful of seconds, to pull myself together, unless I wanted to be bombarded with questions for the pain I was experiencing and risk falling apart completely.

Sam was probably right about Maggie; her ability to get the will typed up in something close to legalese was undoubtedly a Hail Mary pass at best. Why I'd given her the chore in the first place, I have no idea, except that it was Sybil's experience and attention to detail I'd needed while examining Dana. At least Maggie could type—better with her thumbs than the rest of her digits—but, as always, beggars have few requirements and lower expectations. I only hoped what she'd produced in our moment of need was semi-useful, and we could get it signed before Dana descended into the final phase of her labor.

All of the making-lemonade-out-of-lemons thinking fell by the wayside when I entered my office and saw Maggie banging on the top of the printer. She'd replaced her scarf on her last trip upstairs and the turban had slipped to where she was starting to look like a tipsy fortuneteller. She was also growling epithets that would have peeled off my toenail polish if I'd been wearing any.

I lunged to grab her hand before she accomplished another blow. "Do you mind? This isn't an effigy of your Dickens or von Horn."

"Well, make it work then."

After giving my machinery a quick study, I realized the problem was readily apparent. She had punched so many buttons, she'd duplicated the print order to where the poor computer didn't know what command to follow first.

Cancelling the whole process, I said, "Why don't we read what you've drawn up, before we waste paper and ink? The cartridge is getting low. It will take precious minutes to align a new one, and I think we're running out of time."

Although she gestured for me to have a seat and read away, I could see I'd offended her. For the moment, that was the least of my concerns.

Two paragraphs in, I went back to reread what she had typed, certain that my eyes were fooling me. Surely, I was willing myself to see what I thought we needed. Yet, as the phrasing sunk into my mind, I realized the declaration was not only concise, it read in what I thought as legal form.

"This seems perfect," I said.

"You're welcome."

One thing about Maggie—when she was proud of an achievement, she couldn't help but show it; only not like a kid getting a gold star on a school drawing, or even someone being honored with the key to a city. No Maggie acted like she expected the combination to a bank vault. "How did you do this?" I asked, inevitably suspicious.

I could tell she badly wanted to claim the experience and skills to pull this off, yet managed to restrain herself. Shrugging, she admitted, "I called a lawyer friend. But I typed in the blank spots myself."

The best I could manage at the moment was a crooked smile. "Well, bless you, and your connections." Some of the pounding in my head eased, and once I finished reading, I hit the print button and made two copies.

When we rejoined the younger two in the living room, Carly rose. She looked a little anxious.

"I'm glad you're back. In all this excitement, I can see Wrigley is getting restless. I'm going to take him outside. Retta, do you want me to let Rosie out, too?"

Rosie always told me if she had a need, but I nodded anyway. "That's fine, if she wants to go."

I took Carly's place, and smiled with reassurance at Dana. "Okay, we've printed up what you asked for. Maggie has had a lawyer put it into correct terms. Do you want to take a look at it?"

"It's not about want, it's about necessity."

As I watched her read it, I could tell there was a lot going on in her mind. "Go ahead. You know you can ask anything, or even change your mind."

She shook her head immediately. "No, everything looks fine."

"Then, when Carly gets back, you all can sign it."

"I'd just as soon have it over with."

I didn't know for sure whether it mattered or not, but I thought in the event—Heaven forbid—we were put in a witness box and forced to testify,

I wanted everyone to be able to honestly attest they signed at the same time. "I think it's best we wait. It won't be more than another minute."

"Okay."

"What else?" I asked, sensing she had more to say.

"How long do you think I have?"

Even under the circumstances, the question disturbed me. "How about you rephrase that?"

"I'm not talking about dying now. How long until the baby is born?"

Placing the paperwork on the coffee table, I said, "There's no telling. Childbirth is different for everyone. The baby could come in the next five minutes, or you could have to endure this for another several hours."

"That's not helping me one bit. You've had children, Retta, and grand-children. Sybil, you have, too. Give me an experienced answer."

There was a little too much anxiety in her voice. I hoped what I was about to say would show her it wasn't about choices, but learning to adjust to the situation.

"It was a Thursday when my water broke with Jamie. I distinctly remember because that's the weekly sale day at the livestock auction in town, and Charlie seldom missed. Regardless of whether he was buying or selling, he wanted to know the latest cattle prices. It was mid-after-noon and I'd been canning. You remember, don't you, Maggie?"

Sitting at the foot of the bed, Maggie smiled, as though looking fond-ly into the past. "How could I forget? Since I loved peach preserves so much, I'd decided for once I'd learn to make them. As you well know, Retta, we never got to finish."

Nodding, I turned back to Dana. "Jamie was my first, and I had no idea what to expect. I'd had a little cramping that morning, but I didn't think anything of it. Maggie was peeling peaches when I felt a gush of water run down my legs." I looked at Maggie, "Thank God you were there. My parents were out of state for a distant relation's wedding—a real treat for Mom—and Charlie's had both died earlier in the year, only months apart. It was back before the days of cell phones so Maggie called from the house to the sale barn and asked that someone tell Charlie to meet us at the hospital. The woman who answered took the message to the auctioneer, and he announced it over the microphone. Later, when I learned what happened, I was mortified, especially when the hospital staff complained it looked like half the town showed up with him and were creating a racket honking in the parking lot. Charlie had bought a couple of boxes of Travis Club Senators, and proudly passed around the cigars to everyone like he'd fathered a future governor of Texas."

"I still have mine," Maggie said with a grin.

That won a double-take look from me. Until now, I had no idea. "Why am I not surprised?"

Sybil offered her own memory. "When I went into labor with Joseph, Elvin had been working as a mechanic down at the Chevrolet house for about a year. James Harris owned it then, and he expected a full day's work. Elvin was good at what he did and brought in a lot of business, but he had his trials. One was Frank Edmondson, a previous board member at First State Bank. He had just brought his car in for a tune up when I called the dealership and told Elvin it was my time. Maggie, Retta, do y'all remember what a crotchety old man Mr. Edmondson was?"

Maggie sniffed. "Hollis said plenty of times he was a slave driver and everyone was scared to death of him."

"As far as I'm concerned," I said, "he was an evil man. If anyone was even a few days late on a loan, he would hear about it and threaten a foreclosure, before the bank officer had a chance to say anything. He pulled that enough times to solidify his reputation as the Scrooge of Franklin County."

"Yes, ma'am, I'll tell you exactly how mean he was," Sybil said. "That afternoon he told Elvin he wasn't going anywhere, baby or no baby, until his car was serviced. It was Mr. James who intervened, and told Mr. Edmonson he would give him the pick of any new car on the lot to drive until Elvin was able to get back to finish the job. He agreed, but with reluctance. Elvin couldn't do enough for Mr. James from that day on."

Looking miserable, Dana said, "You all were just killing time to get me to my next contraction, knowing how I'm dreading it."

"We wouldn't think of such a thing," I said, stroking Dana's back as she began to curl up into a ball again. "But since it's coming, let's get you through this one and we'll check your progress."

"Retta, two minutes apart," Sybil said. "I'll mark it down in the book."

As she left, I said to Dana, "Wow! Did you hear that? You've really jumped. Now, breathe. The baby's getting ready. Don't push yet. Just breathe."

"Retta," Dana moaned. "Something is happening…"

"Maggie, quick! Come here and take my place, while I look under the blankets."

We shifted positions and I all but ripped the bedding free from under the mattress. In the soft glow of the firelight, I had my first peek. But what a sight! The baby's feet were out of the birth canal.

Oh, sweet Lord, the baby's breech.

We heard the back door open and close. First came a grinning Rosie, followed by a puffing Wrigley and, finally, Carly entered bearing an armful of firewood.

"Carly, go scrub your hands now. Fast!" I called. "Sybil, you, too, and then bring our container of supplies, the clean towels and blanket."

Maggie clapped her hands together. "We're fixin' to have a baby!"

"Not the way we want it," I warned. "This little one is coming feet first."

The next succession of pains had Dana arching off the bed and clutching at pillows, blankets and sheets in her frenzy. Her cries became screams until, suddenly, she blurted out, "Oh, God. *Oh, God!* Jesse, why did you leave me?"

I'd heard a number of cries and screams in my life—some of them my own—but Dana's torment threatened to break my heart anew. As soon as Carly took my place, I yanked off the remaining covers.

Carly couldn't stifle a gasp when she saw the position of the baby. "What do we do?"

"Try to keep Dana's legs still. That flailing is dangerous to the baby, too. Sybil where are you?" I yelled. "This is it!"

"I'm here." She placed everything within reach then sat down on the other side of me.

Dana begged, "Retta..."

"Next pressure, sweetheart, I promise. Push!" Then I said a silent prayer that she had widened enough to pass the child.

I didn't know if through her agony, Dana had heard me, but I understood the body probably would react regardless. Sure enough, we saw we had a little girl coming.

"You're having a daughter, Dana!" Carly gasped.

"It hurts. It hurts so much." The tearful admission came between moans of pain.

My tone coaxing, I said, "Yes, sweetheart, only we need another good effort. And the shoulders are the widest part."

"I can't. I can't."

"But then the rest will come quickly."

Despite her half-hysterical cries, this was no longer about Dana's choices or entreaties, it was about nature. Momentum had begun directing this show. As the next contraction came, she did push, and the baby's shoulders emerged. Only a few seconds later in the last watery gush, the head.

"Oh, my," Maggie laughed breathlessly. "Dana, she has your beautiful abundance of dark hair."

I wish I could have been as excited; however, my first reaction was dread. The newborn wasn't breathing, and her coloring was an ominous purplish-blue. As I lifted her, I urged Sybil, "Clean off her nose and mouth."

She did, while I gently massaged the baby's tiny chest to get her circulation going. I knew my hands were shaking—all of me was shaking as I struggled with panic.

Beginning to catch her breath, Dana asked, "Why don't I hear crying?"

"They're cleaning her," Carly said. "Just a minute." She'd seen what was happening, and grabbed a clean wash cloth to wet it in the melted cup of ice cubes, and dabbed the sweat from Dana's face and neck, in the process successfully compromising her view.

Despite our efforts, things were still not improving. When I caught Sybil's worried and questioning glance, I made my next decision.

"I'm turning her over."

Laying her belly down along my forearm, I continued my massaging by rubbing on her back. It must have had some effect, because Sybil suddenly gasped.

"Oh, look!"

Sure enough, a small amount of fluid dribbled from the baby's mouth. That was followed by a cough, a whimper, and a tired cry. Praise and murmurs of gratitude swept around our circle, followed by blooming smiles.

"She's okay?" Dana asked, struggling to rise from the pillows. "Let me see my baby!"

Sybil and I exchanged satisfied glances, as I gently eased the infant onto Dana's chest. Her robe had come open during her last contractions, and now child and mother could lay skin-to-skin for the first time feeling each other's heartbeats. If I didn't secretly suspect Dana was in the process of changing her mind about her plans, I think this would have been the rest of the impetus needed for her to do so. I don't know any mother, who doesn't speak of the "wave of love and peace" that comes over them at such a moment.

"Thank you, God." Dana's whisper was barely audible, as she gazed at the tiny creature. "And forgive me."

As the baby nestled comfortably against Dana, our relief turned to wonder. It looked as though everyone was blinking away tears, or hugging in celebration.

"We did it," Maggie whispered, pressing her shoulder to mine.

"*She* did it," I said, smiling anyway. Just seeing how Dana tenderly folded her arms around her child told me that was *not* the conduct of a mother about to give away her own flesh and blood. "Time, Carly?"

"8:10. November 23."

It was Sybil who rose. "I'll be happy to write that down."

"As soon as you do that, bring the sterilized twine, and wipe down the scissors again," I told her.

"Do you have a soft dressmaker's measuring tape?" she asked. "We'll need to tell them her height, too."

"Goodness, I forgot. It's in my sewing box in my bedroom closet. That's usually where I have a need to repair things. I'll be right back."

When I returned, the other three were still gazing upon the little miracle lying contentedly with her mother. I don't know if anyone else had quietly counted fingers and toes, but I did so as I measured her. "Eighteen inches," I reported, nodding in satisfaction.

"She's totally gorgeous, Dana," Carly said. She followed by giving her friend a challenging, but hopeful look. "Are you going to be the one to say her name for the first time?"

Sixteen

ANA LOOKED almost radiant, as she gazed in wonder at what forever would stand as the most positive symbol of her and Jesse's love. "Welcome, my angel. Welcome, Jessica Shea."

"Maggie." Tearing my gaze from the sweet scene, I forced myself to remember what else needed to be done. "The kitchen scale is on the counter by the pantry. Would you bring that—but first post the baby's height? Then we'll get her weighed."

"I'd love to." Head and chest high with pride, Maggie took off to complete her task, passing Sybil, who came in with her items.

Pausing, I glanced from Dana to Carly and back again. "Dana, would you like Carly to do this part?"

"Oh! I couldn't," Carly replied, all but scooting off the bed.

"The reason I ask," I said calmly, "is because you two have become so close during your pregnancy, and it's often said the person who cuts the cord sometimes finds a particular link with the infant. I know it's true because I was there to welcome Rachel's firstborn, Adam. He's thirteen now, and Rachel complains all he wants to talk about is Annapolis—well, and getting his license. But when he comes here, he's like Carly with the horses, and he shadows me around while I do other chores. Always offering a helping hand, and very often anticipating what needs to be done next. Most touching is every week he texts me some goofy or darling note, even if it's only a line or two. I love all of my grandchildren, but with Adam the connection is a little unique."

Dana reached for Carly's hand. "Then it's settled. Having you cut the umbilical cord would be the second perfect thing to happen today."

Although Carly looked doubtful at first, she was too tempted to resist. "Okay, what do I do?"

"Go wash your hands again. Twice."

When she returned, I instructed her as I cut the twine into smaller pieces. Then Carly tied off the cord in two spots and snipped the excess a few inches from the baby's navel as directed.

When she was done, she dropped everything and pantomimed a silent scream and foot stomping celebration, which had us chuckling in appreciation of her awe. Seconds later, she pressed her right hand to her chest.

"That was terrifying—and wonderful." Carlie started to reach for Dana and checked herself. "Thank you, dear friend. I'm going to wash again now."

She was barely at the bathroom door before Maggie came from the kitchen. "How is this supposed to work?" Maggie had returned with the scale, and placed it on the coffee table. She looked anything but convinced that balancing a baby on the rather small, flat center would be possible. "As tiny as she is, I still see a problem here. Those metal edges are sharp for such tender skin."

Of course, the food scale was the wrong style for what we had to do. However, my gaze fell on a two-foot-long, shallow basket of pine cones on the fireplace. "Empty that, and bring it here."

Once she handed it to me, I set it on the scale and added two plush hand towels then gauged the weight. "Okay, Miss Miracle, let's see if you weigh enough to move the needle any farther on this thing."

Easing the baby into the basket, we all waited for the red arrow to stop rocking back and forth. The scale finally stopped at five pounds, six ounces, which would be tiny enough for any newborn; but then, I mentally subtracted the weight of the basket and towels. I whispered, "Four pounds, fourteen ounces." Not about to rely on my own vision at this point, I shifted out of the way to give Sybil room. "Proof me. The weight without child, I read at one pound two ounces."

She did as I asked, all seriousness, too. "Yes, that's what I'm figuring."

Once I eased the baby out of the basket for the final time, I placed Jessica Shea into her mother's waiting arms. That was another promising sign. Maybe now was the moment to ask the all-important question. We were running out of time.

"Come to Mommy, precious. Girls," Dana continued, "what do you think? Am I imagining things, or does she have my eyes?"

"Hair, eyes, size," Sybil quipped. "That's almost a Dr. Seuss rhyme."

Trying to be discreet as I checked the time again, I said, "You may discover that she has her grandmother's toes, and Jesse's ears, too."

Dana pressed her lips together to keep back a giggle. "Oh, I hope it's the other way around."

Glad to see her memory of pain was taking a back seat to humor, I said, "We do need to take the baby in a minute. She needs to be cleaned. You do, as well, and we have to change you and the bedding before you realize how exhausted you are. First, however, I suppose we should notify 9-1-1."

"Why do we still have to do that?" Maggie's gaze held a militant look. "The baby's here and fine, no thanks to them."

"Exactly. There's a new human being among us. That's official data and important to get recorded. Any kind of delay can cause problems down the road. I know of someone whose parents were naturalized—and she was in the courthouse when it happened, a child of six. Nearly two decades later, when she tried to get a passport, she was told while she did seem to exist, there was no official documentation she belonged to her parents. It turned out because her family had shortened their name at the time of citizenship, they didn't know to ask for a legal attachment for her birth certificate."

"Dana's not doing anything of the kind—are you?" Maggie asked her, as an afterthought.

Looking confused, Dana quickly and emphatically shook her head. "I want to be sure she has paperwork, though. But...do we still need an ambulance? I feel fine, and though small, Jessica Shea seems perfectly healthy, too."

Here was my moment, I thought. "The baby *is* small. She needs to be in the hands of qualified care. They may even think she could do with incubation for a few days, to take the pressure off of her lungs. Then, they'll want to know."

Dana frowned. "Know what?"

"Is she still available for adoption?"

There are moments in life you remember with almost photographic precision. This was one of them, and Dana's expression upon hearing my question seared itself in my mind forever. She looked as though I was about to take off a mask, and betray everything she believed about me.

Despite thinking I knew how this would turn out, I could feel an invisible hand threaten to squeeze the blood from my heart, as I waited for her to reply. It reminded me while a picture may, indeed, be worth a thousand words, a single word can also change a life forever.

"You told them I was considering that?"

I didn't have the heart to prolong her dread. "No, dear. Not yet."

"Thank heavens." She closed her eyes for several seconds, before meeting my gaze with determination. "I know what I said before, but I...I was wrong. This is my child. Maybe the challenge of making all of this work still terrifies me, but I was a fool to think I could give her up."

That's what Carly heard upon her return, and she all but crumbled in relief beside Dana. "I knew you couldn't do it."

As satisfied as I was proud, I rose and gestured to indicate the work to be done. "Okay, we'll postpone the call for a few more minutes. Ladies, let's get this place cleaned up, and those two comfortable. In a gentler tone, I added, "Afterward, Carly, you may want to handle monitoring Dana's fluid intake. She needs to replenish. It will also help her with rebuilding her strength."

"I didn't realize that," Carly replied, and hurried to the kitchen with Dana's cup.

Smiling my thanks, I called after her, "Whenever you need a break or anything else, we'll be close. I doubt any of us will be going upstairs tonight. Am I right, ladies?" I asked, looking to the others for confirmation.

"That sounds like the best idea," Maggie said. "Besides, I'm so excited, I don't think I could sleep if I wanted to. Babies are like puppies...only with less hair. And they wear diapers."

Sybil saluted her agreement to my suggestion. "Everything is about keeping those two warm and ready for transfer."

Having read my share of fairytales to my kids and grandkids, I had never read one where an elf, fairy, or fairy godmother had worked with more tender adoration than we did to get our new princess and her mother clean and clothed. Testament to our care, only moments after Dana and baby were back under fresh linens and blankets, they looked as peaceful as anyone could hope after such a strenuous few hours.

While Maggie carried off the wet linens to the washroom, Sybil and I retreated to clean up at the kitchen sink. As much as I enjoyed her soft crooning of a lullaby, if it wasn't for the clocks around, I might have guessed that it was the middle of the night, rather than only minutes after nine o'clock.

"Adrenaline is still pumping away," I told my humming friend.

"Mine, too."

With a mixture of amusement and sympathy, Sybil asked me, "Who are you callin' first?"

I did like how after a few days away from school, she had gone back to Southern speak and had dropped her g's, as we all did now and then. "You know who I want to call. However, I'd better notify Tyler so they can put us on a list—whichever kind they have."

Carly tiptoed into the kitchen. "I just had to tell you," she whispered. "There wasn't time when I first came back in with the dogs because of all the excitement. The icing has stopped. I wanted you to know before you called." Scrunching her shoulders, she grinned like a kid certain she'd heard Santa's sleigh bells overhead.

"That's wonderful news," Sybil said. "I know they have the latest radars, but let's check again, so you can report as much to them. I agree with your hunch how the baby needs incubation, so the sooner they can be convinced it's possible to get here the better."

"You're right," I said. "But just because the precipitation has stopped, doesn't mean it's safe driving or flying weather."

"It's the best sign we've had yet."

Accepting she was right, the three of us went through the mud room exit and soon saw Carly's report was mostly accurate. The icing had stopped. What was happening was rather magical. There were a few large, widespread flakes drifting through the air in no hurry to reach the ground.

"They look like the souls of butterflies, who stayed too late and were caught by winter's early arrival," I said.

"What if they're angels come to welcome the baby?" Carly whispered, mesmerized.

No sooner did she say that than the flakes stopped coming. The others vanished into the darkness, as though, having been spotted, they were directed to hide—save one. And it didn't descend, either. It lifted upward, rising higher and higher into the starless sky, until all three of us lost sight of it.

"Tell me you saw that?" Sybil asked, continuing to gaze upward.

"Yes," I said, still watching. Since when did snow flow upward without the help of traffic or wind?

"Me, too." Carly's reply was barely audible.

It could have just been a quirk of nature, a storm's finale, only no one was going to convince us. We believed we were meant to come outside and witness this moment for a reason.

Raising her hand in tribute, Sybil urged us back inside. "Thank you for heeding the pull of the moment, Carly. You should go share what you saw with Dana."

"You don't think she'll accuse us of being silly, do you?"

"I think there's a great deal going on in this world tonight," Sybil told her, beginning to sound like she was drifting toward a place very deep inside herself. "And I believe we just experienced a moment of grace between this world and the other side."

"That's what it felt like to me, too."

After my hushed agreement, Carly led the way back inside. She detoured through the bathroom to get to the living room.

Sybil and I remained quiet as we came in. The air around us literally reverberated with the beauty and peace of what we'd experienced. We were reluctant to break that spell.

Rubbing my hands together to warm them, I finally succumbed to responsibility. I asked Sybil, "You are going to stay close, aren't you? I'm afraid I might forget to give them some fact, or otherwise mess up somehow."

"I've got your back, baby."

That was all the reassurance I needed. I began to dial.

Henry at the sheriff's office was happy to hear we'd had a safe conclusion to our crisis. As soon as he transferred me over to Tyler, we were given to a female operator, who identified herself as Meghan. She did as we'd been assured would happen: she brought up our previous call. Then she also voiced her delight upon learning our situation was going well. That's where the happy talk ended.

"Unfortunately, we've experienced a number of emergencies during this storm, Mrs. Cole," she said, her tone growing more serious. "A colleague is proceeding with the notification to ETMC Tyler that the baby is breathing on her own, but to prepare for all contingencies upon a medical crew's arrival there."

"Can you tell me when that will be?" I ventured. "I can confirm the precipitation has stopped here."

"Excellent. However, ma'am, you're over an hour north of us, and even with conditions improving here, we're dealing with temperatures below freezing, and a deluge of emergency calls. It sounds like you have things under control there, so we're counting on you to sustain that. I'm pretty sure tonight is out of the question, but we will do our best to get there tomorrow."

After thanking Meghan again, I disconnected, only to set the phone back on the cradle with a new feeling of dejection. Having stayed close, Sybil leaned her head on my shoulder. She had obviously heard enough to know the news wasn't what we'd hoped.

"So there's really no chance of a transfer anytime soon?" she asked.

With a rueful smile, I replied, "This is our reward for being competent."

"Blasted waiting lists," Sybil muttered. "All we need now is one of those solar calamities we're threatened with every time there's a big sun flare-up."

"Say what?" I asked, not following.

"You know—they're always talking about how communication satellites could be fried, sending us back to pounding on drums to signal each other."

"Bite your tongue." I nudged her hip with mine before growing serious. "Are you going to call Thomas and see if hospice has been able to make it over there?" I could think of nothing worse than Dana having to deal with childbirth the way she had, except for a man struggling by himself to keep his wife, his love, alive.

"Retta, the truth?" Her expression reflected a myriad of emotions; most of them degrees of mental torture. "I want to, but the situation? If it's their last moments together, I don't want to be the person who intrudes on that."

"Well," I said. "If I happen to see you tucked in a corner somewhere with a phone pressed to your ear, I'll give you wide berth and make sure everyone else does, too."

Sybil nodded her gratitude and asked, "On the other hand, what about Sam?"

"Yeah, it's time."

"Then I'm going to go have a word with Maggie," Sybil said. "But I suspect she might have ducked into your office to call Father Phil."

As I pressed Sam's contact number, I thought how sweet it would be if Maggie asked Phil to say a blessing for Jessica Shea at evening prayers. But my smile waned as the phone rang and rang in Fort Worth. It triggered a bad feeling about my timing. Of course, Sam could be out having dinner with a friend. On the other hand, he might only have been polite about wanting me to call back, or had since changed his mind about wanting to talk more.

I was so much my own worst enemy when he did answer, I blurted out, "Is this a good time? I can call back later?"

"No need. It's just you, me and a bottle of Glenlivet—whose seal, I guess I should add, remains unbroken."

I knew that was his favorite sipping whisky for special or rare occasions. "That's...interesting. Tell me more."

"First, let me say I'm glad you called."

Now, I began to relax. I could even feel a smile tugging at my lips. "You're going to be more pleased in a moment. Jessica Shea Bennett was born at 8:10. Mother and baby are doing fine."

He exhaled loudly. "You girls have been busy."

"So busy I never got to call 9-1-1 after talking to you. Well, until a minute ago when I reported Dana had delivered."

With a throaty sound, Sam said, "I can't imagine how scary that must have been for all of you, considering the prematurity. Were there any complications? You don't sound like you've been in a panic."

"Oh, believe me, we had our moments. It turned out to be a breech birth."

"Ach. Bless you—and them," he murmured. "But there was every chance of that being the case, considering the timing. Did you experience difficulty in getting the baby to breathe?"

"Only until I thought to turn her onto my forearm and massage her back. You know, of course, I was relying on my experiences with animals?"

"Good instincts."

"She spit out some fluids and everything has been good since. My one concern is that she is small—four pounds, fourteen ounces. But, oh, my, that baby has her mother's lovely mahogany hair and eyes. Sam, Dana went from six minute contractions to *nothing* in a heartbeat." I knew I was prattling; however, I couldn't share all of the news fast enough.

"I'm proud of you," he said, his voice reverberating with emotion. "I wouldn't have guessed it would happen this quickly for someone of Dana's age and condition. Yet, you sensed the way things were going and adapted. That's commendable."

"Thanks. But I'm worried for tonight. With a newborn under five pounds, she probably needs incubation, and there's no promise from 9-1-1 when they'll get here. They've all but said tonight is impossible. I already figured out we need to stay up all night. I'll keep the generator and fireplace going, and the others will help tend to Dana's and the baby's needs. Any other suggestions?"

"Can Dana nurse?"

"She hasn't tried yet, but I'm guessing the lactation process hasn't begun."

"Then my thought is to tell your goat, Elsa, she's been drafted."

That hadn't yet crossed my jam-packed mind. His suggestion filled me with hope. "Are you sure?"

"Goat milk is highly digestible."

"I had heard that, but we're talking about a newborn, Sam."

"Do you have canned formula on hand?"

"No."

"So, what's your other option? Just be sure you use your pasteurizer."

"Of course. Oh! And I still have Sienna and Bianca's baby bottles," I said, reminding him of my twin granddaughters. "In fact, I've already brought them down to sterilize just in case."

"Job well done, darling."

That last verbal caress nearly did me in. "Sam, I may need to hang up now."

"Why?"

"Because it's time to cry."

At first that gave him pause. "What haven't you told me?"

"Why does there have to be anything else? We've been at the brink of death, and we've welcomed life."

"Wait a minute—who was at the brink of death? Dana sounds like she had a trying, but pretty smooth birth."

"Yes," I began replaying my words in my mind. Had I insinuated my own experience outside? Oh, damn.

"And Maggie's not showing signs of a bad concussion?"

"Ignore a silly woman's drama, Sam," I entreated, hoping he would let the matter drop. "All we want is a helicopter or a truck, and to get this baby, and Dana to safety."

He hesitated for another moment, as though he was about to press me further, only to relent. "You're exhausted. I'll do what I can from this end. Try to get in a nap."

I gasped, remembering. "Sam, I forgot to tell you. The icing has stopped here, too."

"I know. I've been watching the radar."

Something about the way he spoke told me he was giving me a message. "Sam," I asked softly. "Are we okay?"

"I told you I'm not a quitter."

His response had me smiling as I disconnected. It hadn't been the phone call to dread at all, and my step was light as I returned to the living room. Everyone was there, still enraptured by the new little addition to our party. Dana continued to hold her daughter against her breast, and we all agreed—due to the way twitches of smiles played around the baby's mouth—that Jessica Shea was sleeping while being serenaded by angels. Perhaps the ones we thought we'd been visited by outside.

I'd come in midway in a conversation and finally asked, "Did I hear you mention a job offer, Dana? Is that the one you didn't want to talk about earlier?"

"Yes," she said. "But it's not one I think I can consider seriously. They want me to be the children's director at the church, and you know it's more than a full-time job, even without having a newborn."

"Oh, gosh, yes." Yet as I thought about the offer, I knew how good she would be in the position. When she'd been the church pianist, she'd spent time before and after services with the little kids teaching them one-handed ditties on the piano, and asking about progress from those taking music lessons. "But, it was a wonderful compliment, and a good choice on their part. Keep the faith something else will come up that will be perfect."

Dana smiled. "You're beginning to convince me that perspective has merit."

"You're too accredited for what they want anyway, aren't you?" Maggie asked.

"I don't know. However, my parents did insist I get my Master's degree in my field of choice."

"Then you're qualified to teach at the university level," Maggie told her, "and I happen to have contacts."

"Where don't you have contacts?" Carly drawled.

Maggie pointed at her and replied, "Use your money wisely, and you will, too."

"Well, I'm grateful for the thought," Dana said. "But please don't get into any strong-arming. I hope you understand how imperative it is for me at this stage to be a real asset in a position. I couldn't bear it if I knew an offer was extended because I was being forced upon someone."

"I'm just asking," Maggie said. "To my knowledge, there are no positions open yet, but one thing I pride myself on is that I know talent when I see it."

With a slow nod, Dana replied, "Fair enough. I do thank you, Maggie, because it would kill me to have to transfer so far away Jess and I wouldn't be close to our best friends and aunties now."

IN AT LEAST one of his appearances, Pope Francis said, "Grace is not part of consciousness, it is the amount of light in our souls, not knowledge nor reason." Our night passed with that light. There were sweet conversations, periods of hushed queries, reassurances, and much gratitude that no medical emergencies arose.

As agreed, we did spend the night downstairs. Some of us napped, some didn't—or couldn't. But we stayed together primarily because we were no longer willing to be apart. We were survivors, and each of us had gone through our own personal hell; yet, together we had achieved something miraculous. While no one voiced the thought, we wanted to savor the event for as long as possible.

Every two hours, I went outside to refill the generator. On my last trip—4:00 a.m. to be exact—I saw we were down to the next-to-last container of gas. That had me pausing to pray anew for conditions to improve so we could get Dana and Jessica Shea out of here.

When I returned inside, I found Maggie frowning at the coffee machine. She looked a sight with her turban off again, and her hair spiking in every direction. She was wearing her blanket like a shawl. Beneath her elegant caftan-style robe, she wore a pair of my insulated long johns that I'd lent her. It was obvious from the way she was squinting she was trying to gauge the ratio of coffee grounds to water.

"Sorry to disturb," she whispered, "but I need caffeine *now*."

"I'm ready for some myself, and enjoying this togetherness too much to miss any of it. We can sleep later."

After I dealt with the measuring for her, I leaned over to give Rosie an affectionate rub then hung up my jacket. Taking a seat on the second bar stool—I'd left the first for her—I watched her get two mugs, and the sugar and cream for herself. Still waiting on the coffee to finish dripping, she came closer and leaned her hip against the other side of the counter.

"How are you feeling otherwise?" I asked. "No more headache? Blurry vision? Any after effects?"

She sent me a droll look. "If you didn't keep reminding me of the humiliating experience, I might actually forget it happened—at least until I pass a mirror."

There was a reason for me to bring it up this time. Something was bugging me, and I had to ask. "Maggie, your other health issue...why didn't you tell me?"

"Because I have enough of my ancestors in me to be superstitious in believing if you give something voice, it's apt to become the truth."

I should have guessed it was something in that order, but I still wanted to shake her. Instead, I got up, circled the counter, and hugged her. She hugged me back so fiercely, I couldn't help but whimper.

As soon as she heard me, she backed away. "Now, what the hell is that?"

"Just a little soreness from handling machinery and whatnot," I said with a dismissive shrug, trying not to rub my sternum.

She looked anything but satisfied. "What the frost on Jack's butt does that mean?"

Her voice had grown a level louder and I tried to shush her. "Mags, let the others sleep."

"Then you damned well tell me what happened that got you hurt."

"I'm fine."

"Until someone tries to give you a simple hug."

"Well, in your enthusiasm, little old you has the hug of a polar bear."

"So help me, I will…" She snatched my phone off the counter. "I will call Sam and tell him what just happened if you don't come clean."

With no desire to have a wrestling match with a woman about to undergo surgery, I relented. This was, after all, my Maggie, my best friend, and I needed to remind her *I* was the good friend I wanted *her* to be.

"Mags, it got momentarily scary, and even strange yesterday."

Her eyes widened and grew more searching. "What are you talking about? You mean while you were feeding before the baby came?"

"Yeah. Conditions were worse than even I anticipated and, though careful, while I was balancing the hydraulics and those blasted hay bales, my mind was half back here with you all. I lost focus, and the next thing I knew I was sliding down into the ditch."

"Oh, Lord."

"Well, it was unnaturally dark for that time."

"Damn it, what happened?"

"I felt him. I felt him like I hadn't since I held him in my arms while fighting to keep him alive. And if you won't believe that, you won't believe the rest."

"Tell me."

"It was while I struggled to make the hydraulics work and keep the tractor going in the right direction so it wouldn't tip over. I could have sworn he was telling me exactly what to do."

As the coffee machine made its last gurgle and hiss announcing it was done, Maggie started. "Retta…that's downright spooky."

Nodding my agreement, I still added, "I'll swear on any Bible you want me to. He was there. He didn't want what ended his life to happen to me. It wasn't my skill or experience that got me out of that mess. He had been sent back, or had been allowed to help me survive. Only—I've been thinking about it a great deal—he also wanted me to understand he hadn't been careless. Neither had I, but I knew I had been thwarted by conditions out there."

"Then what *did* happen to Charlie?" she whispered.

"I don't know. That direction faces the west. Maybe the sun got in his eyes for few seconds? At any rate, I believe it took his mind off what he should have been focusing on. He saw something. Shoot, maybe it was your red fox, but in the end he wasn't careless. I'm certain of it now."

I didn't know how important that technicality was to me, until I realized tears were streaming down my cheeks. That's when I saw Maggie getting weepy, too. This time when she put her arms around me, she was gentle.

"It wasn't a fox," she said slowly. "I thought I saw and heard Hollis—on your driveway. I didn't know if he spoke to me or spoke in my mind or what, but it made me move. He said, 'Maggie, come here.'"

I gasped, understanding perfectly. "Maggie, do realize what you're saying? If you hadn't obeyed, there's no question the bulk of that limb would have smashed your skull wide open."

We stood there pondering our experiences anew, as well as the underlying messages we'd been slow to fully comprehend. What life-changing gifts.

"Well, this is humbling," Maggie said. "This weather had better clear up soon before I turn into a Catholic."

"And I can't wait for your next conversation with Phil." Even though I chuckled saying that, I had to reach for the tissue box. We were both sniffing.

We sat, drank coffee, and talked. Maggie admitted sleep would be a hit or miss proposition, until she got her procedure behind her. I shared I wouldn't do much better in the sleep department because I'd made it clear to Sam I was ready to take our relationship to the next level.

"If I didn't love you like a sister, I'd be eaten up with envy," Maggie groaned.

We kept on with our frank and sometimes irreverent conversation while I cleaned and re-bandaged her wound. As she re-tied her scarf, I told her it was good to see her twin black eyes weren't as pronounced this morning.

"That's sweet, but you never could tell a decent lie," Maggie replied. "I look like I've been kicked by an ambidextrous mule."

She sent me into a new peal of laughter and I had to hide my face in a kitchen towel to muffle the noise. "Maggie, you are one of a kind," I wheezed when I could speak again.

JUST AFTER FIVE o'clock, the baby stirred. Although Dana was still asleep, we lifted the child from her makeshift bassinette to her mother's breast. That roused Dana, and she gasped as the baby successfully latched on. Clearly, the rest and relaxation had helped Dana's milk to flow.

That bit of excitement woke Carly. An exhausted Sybil was the last to rouse, but she was quickly alert and broke into a wide grin. We all watched this first feeding knowing it was another moment we would talk about for years, God willing.

Once the baby was sated, we changed her diaper. Then little Jess drifted off into another contented sleep, and we put her back in her bed. Dana watched the whole time before falling back to sleep, too.

As the others headed for coffee, I knew it was time for me to make use of the caffeine I'd ingested. "I'm heading out to the stable," I said.

I don't know who perked up faster—Carly or Rosie. Rosie went straight to the door, and Carly started to gulp her coffee.

"I'm coming, too," she said between swallows. When she saw me glance over my shoulder, she amended, "If that's okay with you?"

"Very okay, but don't burn your throat in the process." She would help get my mind off the hope an ambulance would come this morning. "I'll take Wrigley out for you, while you finish."

We only did the initial basics with the horses, and then with Elsa in the barn. After taking care of the cats, we collected the fresh milk, eggs from the chicken house, and returned to our friends.

Sybil had showered and dressed in another sweat suit—this one brown with embroidered sunflowers and sparkling beads. "My going home clothes," she drawled. "It's time to think positive."

"I thought we had been," I said, hooking my thumb toward the living room and the new addition in the house.

"I asked her if I'd missed news about a hot date?" Maggie added, looking up from setting the table.

Out of the corner of my eye, I saw Sybil return her focus to the stove. I decided to let Maggie's comment lie, too. "I do love your optimism, though," I told Sybil. "But remember it's not expected to get above freezing today. If anything melts, it will be only if the sun burns off clouds. Then—if we're lucky—the ice and snow may slide off of roofs, but that's about it."

"I know," she sighed.

"What are you planning on cooking?"

"Oatmeal. I hope you don't mind the simplicity?"

"Perfect. Besides, you deserve a break."

"I hate oatmeal," Maggie muttered. "Didn't I hear something about omelets for today?"

Sybil took a step back from the stove. "Stop your grousing. You want to take over? I'll give you full rein in the kitchen, if Retta doesn't mind."

"I mind," I informed both of them.

Our light banter went on for another minute. Time enough for Carly to emerge from the bathroom in a dry pair of black jeans, black turtleneck sweater, and a short denim jacket.

"What is that sound?" she asked. "I hear the generator in the back, but this is in the front."

About to shake my head, I suddenly heard it, too. With an excited squeal, I ran to the living room, the nearest front window, and opened the shutters. In the growing daylight there was swirling snow, like an icy tornado in my front pasture. "Oh, my—come look!"

Maggie, Sybil and Carly joined me and opened other shutters just as a helicopter started to descend. Our view was momentarily obstructed as the chopper landed in the midst of the flying snow and ice particles. Overwhelmed with the sight, we came together, arms around waists and shoulders in awe and relief.

Behind us, Dana said in sheer contentment, "This is how I will always remember you. My flock of sparrows, taking care of Jess and me."

We glanced back and smiled at her. It was as sweet a memory as any we could have asked for. Then our attention was pulled forward again, as we heard the helicopter engine get tapped down.

"I don't know what you told them last night, Retta," Maggie said. "But you must have made an impression."

The passenger door opened, and a man stepped out. He took only two long strides toward the house before I thought my heart stopped beating.

"Sam!"

Even as the others started questioning me at what I knew and when I knew it, I ran for the door. I made it down the steps and skidded over a few yards of ice before I realized I wasn't wearing a coat and had on my good suede slippers. Then it didn't matter because Sam swept me into his arms.

"How on earth...?" was all I could manage, as he spun me around.

"I told you I'm not a quitter," he said, and kissed me.

What a kiss it was. Not only was it impossible to say another word, incredibly, I didn't even feel yesterday's injury. I was totally overwhelmed.

It turned out Sam had called in favors. God bless a man of such a good reputation others were willing to take untold risks on his behalf. After introductions were made, the crew checked mother and child, then gently wrapped Dana and Jessica Shea in blankets, and carried them to the helicopter. They took off with the same speed and skill with which they'd arrived.

"Where are they taking them?" Carly asked in wonder as we watched the storm of snow fly again. "I didn't think to ask."

"ETMC Tyler," Sam replied. "They're expected."

I was delighted, but surprised Sam stayed behind. "Well, now you're stuck here with us," I said to him.

"I wouldn't exactly call it that," he said, sliding his arm around me again.

"Maybe I'll freeze the oatmeal," Sybil announced. "This calls for a celebratory breakfast."

"A champagne breakfast," Maggie said, starting to clap her hands in renewed excitement.

Carly offered a mock groan. "Oh, jeez, here we go again."

Epilogue

APRIL: THE promise of spring meant more this year than it had in some time. It's been almost five months since that crazy and scary few days back in November, and in some ways recovery remains ongoing. Cleanup has been an especially challenging and tedious process. Initially, some areas in our region looked like war zones; the damage from our epic snowstorm had been heavy and widespread. Countless trees of all ages, sizes, and varieties had been decimated. In our vicinity at least two commercial peach orchards were brutalized, which accounted for the loss or severe trimming of thousands of specimens. We were still waiting to see what some of our relatively young vineyards would be reporting. Wineries were a small, but growing market in the region, yet a welcome one.

You couldn't attempt to see all of the damage in one day without being humbled. Neighbors lost roofs, others saw businesses ruined when flat roofs—overwhelmed by the weight of snow and ice—caved in. Although word-of-mouth about damage and loss proved fast, it was by no means thorough. We looked to the newspaper for the full listing of those who had suffered injuries or worse.

At least four perished in our county. Two died in a traffic accident, one was crushed by the century-old tree that fell onto her house, and the other from smoke inhalation when the fireplace he was using proved unsafe, causing the attic, then the entire house to burn to the ground. Only the smoking chimney was left. The photo in the paper made it look as though a specter was raising its hand in guilty admission of what the blaze had done. I knew the first two, poor souls, and attended their service, remembering their warm and generous spirits. They had been out trying to help others, when their vehicle slid in front of an eighteen wheeler.

It's written somewhere that a person dies twice: once when their spirits actually leave their bodies, and then when the last person who knows them on earth speaks their name for a final time. Having attended far too many funerals in the last few years, the levels of meaning in that saying becomes excruciatingly poignant at times. It's also why Maggie and Sybil joined me at that service. They had known Doug and Barb Deaver, too.

Technically, a fifth soul was lost but not due to the weather. Naomi left this world, the very night Jessica Shea entered it. Incredibly, the hospice worker made it to the Tidwell home, although she, too had slid off the road in the process, and had to walk the last mile to her destination. Sadly, Naomi suffered a final, mortal stroke only hours later. I think about that night often, and suspect she was breathing her last, as we sat in the kitchen drinking coffee. I know at least part of Sybil's mind was with her.

Naomi's service was beautiful and so well attended, people spilled out of the vestibule, and stood looking in windows to be a part of it. It was a fitting tribute for a woman who tirelessly supported her husband's vocation.

Sybil suffered tremendous guilt over her passing, and had been keeping her distance ever since. I knew because I was with her at the funeral, just as she'd been there for me at the service I'd attended.

Afterward, she threw herself into her teaching with a renewed fervor. But that was all she did. Come evenings and weekends, she kept to the house. She didn't even attend church services for a few weeks. When Maggie learned what was going on, she actually asked her if there was such a thing as "cloistered Baptist nuns?"

Finally, the day after Valentine's Day, Thomas knocked on Sybil's door, and bluntly asked her, "Sybil, how long is this going to go on?"

She admitted to me later she'd had no answer. She'd felt more inadequate and awkward than when dealing with her first crush. She could only step back and let him enter. Apparently, that was all he needed.

Thomas More is a wonder of a man—too great in mind, heart, and soul for his already big-bear body. I'm always a little in awe when I'm in his presence, too, but I've never seen Sybil happier—or prettier. What she might be stepping into is a busy and demanding life, a challenging one. Yet it seems like a role she's good at and one she wants. At the very least, I can see she's in love. I couldn't be more pleased for her.

Maggie had her procedure just a week later than scheduled. That's why she missed Naomi's funeral. Sybil and I raced from the service to the hospital to be present when she awakened in recovery. We were relieved to learn the tumors proved benign, but to be safe, the doctor took out both ovaries just to err on the side of safety. When he first warned her he might, she'd put up a classic Maggie fuss. She'd even nicknamed him, "Morris the Boorish," to his face.

In the end, he'd snapped, "You're a pain in my ass, Maggie. It's not as though you need them anymore. My suggestion is to enjoy the freedom. Consider this your final emancipation proclamation."

Obviously, he'd done his homework, and had a good fix on our Maggie. I just wish I'd been in the office when he'd finally succeeded in shutting her up.

No one will ever accuse Maggie of being slow when it comes to hints. Thereafter, she became the model patient As she tells it, she so dazzled Dr. Morris, "Mo," as friends and colleagues referred to him, that he claimed at the end of the surgery, he barely resisted writing his phone number just above her navel.

There must be an ounce or two of truth to the tale. They've now had dinner—several times.

Maggie's approach to gratitude is sweet to watch. In the midst of all of her personal excitement, she has played fairy godmother by paying off Dana's business debts, then bringing the house mortgage payments current. That has allowed Dana to put the house up for sale. Maggie staged the interior herself, by using many items from her own home. The place sold quickly, which could have created a new challenge for Dana, and her daughter, but that's where I stepped in.

You can't survive a life-changing adventure, as we did, and not be moved to continue improving yourself and the lives of others when you can afford to. That said, mother and child are currently living in my guest-house. I wanted her to take one of the rooms upstairs, so I could better hear her if she needed help with the baby during the night, but I could see how necessary some independence was for her, while she worried I would have enough privacy. There's another lesson: good friends are thoughtful friends, whether you need them to be, or not. To that point, Maggie astonished Dana one day with some contact information—specifically that of the theater director at Texas A&M University-Commerce. It appeared there was a need to expand the department and a position was available for which she was more than qualified. Dana confirmed it would break her heart if she had to relocate, but hoped she could commute for at least the next year.

Carly was wholly prepared to miss her neighbor, but soon admitted it all was working out for the best. She has also been generous, buying the baby many things, including an entire bedroom suite. In fact, when we held the baby showers, we had to specify all we needed were clothes, toys, and incidentals. That little girl is going to be a mini-fashionista before she can spell s-h-o-p-p-i-n-g.

We tease Carly that she's at my place so much, she should sell her house, too, and move in. When she isn't with her best friend and adopt-ed niece, she's working with me in the stables or honing her riding skills.

Interestingly, Carly turned down Maggie's offer to meet a "certain someone." However, it appears that "Trace" Parker Easton is turning out to be the good guy Maggie claimed, as well as a determined one. He owns a home construction business, and has just bought a small run-down farm north of town. He also rides. When he learned Carly was helping me out here, he found the excuse to drive over one afternoon to introduce himself, and his beautiful quarter horse, Cowboy. Trace claimed the place where he was currently stabling the animal while he worked nights to get his own barn and house habitable, wasn't working out for him. He asked if I had room to take Cowboy in as a temporary boarder. Carly witnessed the whole exchange, and I don't think it was possible for anyone not a virgin to blush so much. She might have been onto his strategy, but she wasn't disinterested. It's going to be wonderful fun to watch what happens next in that department.

As for me, my cup runneth over. After Sam and friends landed in my front pasture like something out of a movie, my disappointment at his reaction to Dana's will request was quickly replaced with yet more gratitude. It had actually been Sam—once he learned Dana's entire story—who suggested Dana move into the guesthouse.

"Of course, that will leave me out in the cold," he'd added, watching me with a smug smile.

"Well, not necessarily," I'd replied, being as demure as a woman can be at sixty-something. "You know I have plenty of bedrooms. You can experiment, until you find one that suits you."

It was then he'd pulled me into his arms and said with a gleam in his eyes, "You know damned well, there's only one bedroom that interests me, Retta Cole."

"I do," I'd admitted, and it had been the same for me. "But I have family, Sam. Children. Grandchildren. This is their ancestral home. Our family doesn't just attend church, we are living spiritual members. It's up to me to set an example."

As I explained myself, my heart had pounded as fiercely as when I survived that slide into the ditch the last night of the storm, and a part of me had wondered how I would survive it if he protested, or even criticized my feelings as archaic or silly. But that just showed how much more I'd needed to learn about Sam.

His gaze radiated adoration, and a little amusement, when he said, "I might enjoy sleeping under the same roof with you, while you pine away wishing I'd come warm your cold feet."

We're getting to the end of that transition period. He met my family, and while Jamie almost immediately gave us his blessings, Rachel was slower to come around. Voicing shock and concern at first and, admittedly, shedding a few tears, she now sees Sam's undeniable qualities, as well as the positive changes he's making in me. In fact, she's given us her blessing, too, and Sam and I will be marrying in July. He's sold his house, but will continue doing business through the gallery in Fort Worth. Most wondrous is he is insisting on taking me to New England for our honeymoon—especially Maine where the Wyeths painted those magical images that remain such a part of my spirit. We're planning on announcing all of that tomorrow.

Tomorrow...tomorrow is Easter, and I'm expecting a full house, and forty for lunch. My family—*our* family—has become like that never-to-be forgotten flock of sparrows huddling together in times of need. Sybil and I have been making preparations for days. We'll start by attending our individual churches' sunrise service, then an Easter egg hunt here for the little ones. The scheduling is crazy if we had stopped to dwell on it, so we haven't. Everyone knows they will be welcome whenever they can get here. It's all good.

What else is there to say, except, "Amen, amen, amen."